SPECI DERS

THE ULVERSCROFT FOUNDATION
(registered UK charity number 264873)
wa established in 1972 to provide funds for research,
mples of
Foundation
are:-

- The Children's Eye Unit at Moorfelds Eye Hospital, London
- The Ulverscroft Children's Eye Unit at Great Ormond Street Hospital for Sick Children
- Funding research into eye diseases and treatment at the Department of Ophthalmology, University of Leicester
- The Ulverscroft Vision Research Group, Institute of Child Health
- Twin operating theatres at the Western Ophthalmic Hospital, London
- The Chair of Ophthalmology at the Royal Australian College of Ophthalmologists

You can help further the work of the Foundation by making a donation or leaving a legacy. Every contribution is gratefully received. If you would like to help support the Foundation or require further information, please contact:

THE ULVERSCROFT FOUNDATION
The Green, Bradgate Road, Anstey
Leicester LE7 7FU, England
Tel: (0116) 236 4325

website: www.ulver g.uk

GIRLS WHO LIE

When single mother Maríanna disappears from her home, leaving an apologetic note on the kitchen table, everyone assumes that she's taken her own life ... until her body is found in the Grábrók lava fields seven months later, clearly the victim of murder. Her neglected fifteen-year-old daughter Hekla has been placed in foster care, but is her perfect new life hiding something sinister?

Fifteen years earlier, a desperate new mother lies in a maternity ward, unable to look at her own child, the start of an odd and broken relationship that leads to a shocking tragedy.

Police officer Elma and her colleagues take on the case, which becomes increasingly complex, as the number of suspects grows and new light is shed on Maríanna's past — and the childhood of a girl who never was like the others ...

EVA BJÖRG ÆGISDÓTTIR
Translated by VICTORIA CRIBB

GIRLS WHO LIE

Complete and Unabridged

ISIS
Leicester

First published in Great Britain in 2021 by
Orenda Books
London

First published in Iceland in 2019
as *Stelpur sem ljúga* by Veröld Publishing

First Isis Edition
published 2021
by arrangement with
Orenda Books
London

This is a work of fiction. Names, characters, places and incidents are either products of the author's imagination or are used fictitiously. Any resemblance to actual events, locales or persons, living or dead, is entirely coincidental.

A catalogue record for this book is available from the British Library.

ISBN 978–1–78541–985–0

Published by
Ulverscroft Limited
Anstey, Leicestershire

Printed and bound in Great Britain by
TJ Books Ltd., Padstow, Cornwall

This book is printed on acid-free paper

For Gunni

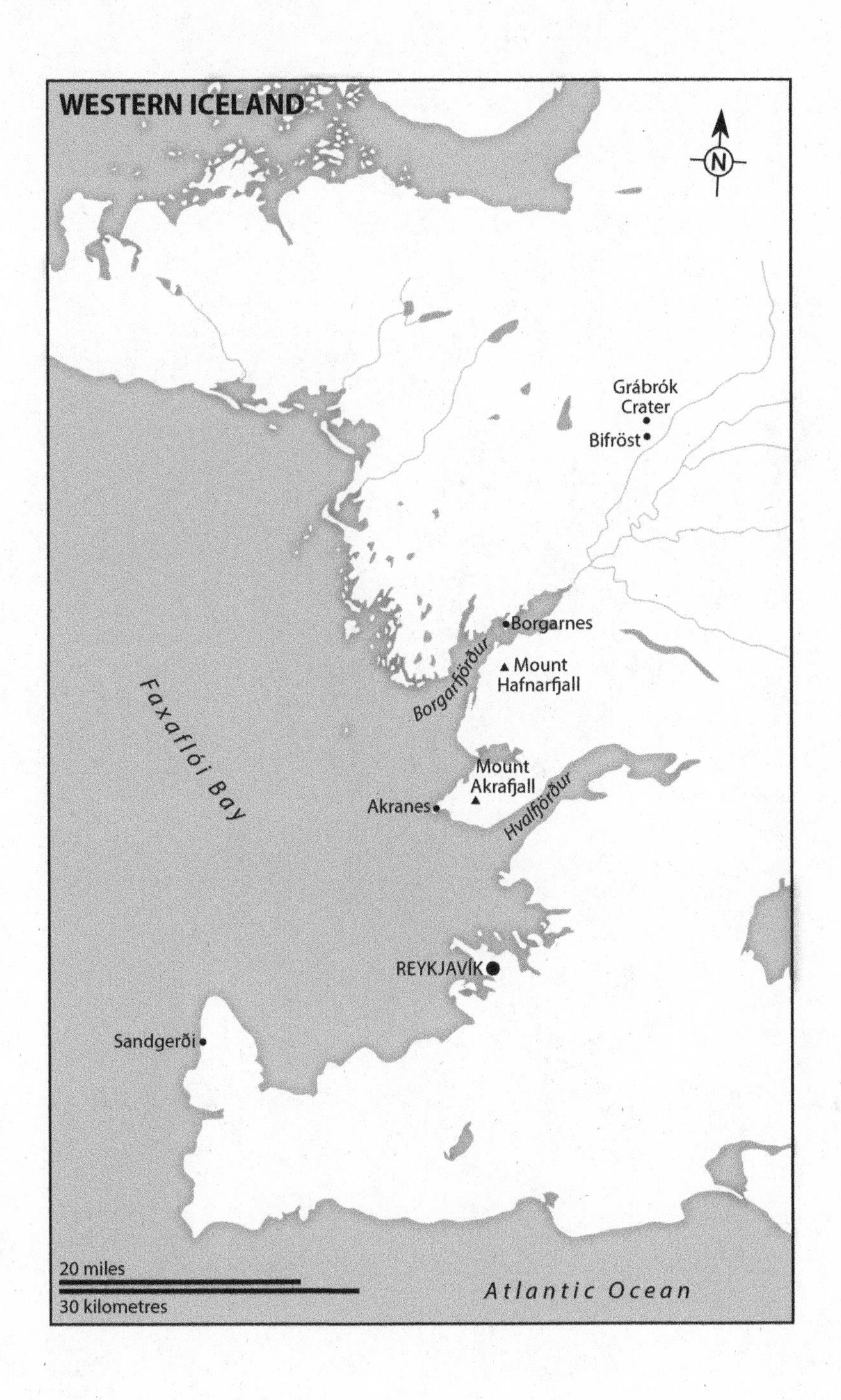
WESTERN ICELAND
N
Grábrók
Crater
Bifröst
Borgarnes
Mount
Hafnarfjall
Borgarfjörður
Faxaflói Bay
Mount
Akrafjall
Akranes
Hvalfjörður
REYKJAVÍK
Sandgerði
20 miles
30 kilometres
Atlantic Ocean

Pronunciation Guide

Icelandic has a couple of letters that don't exist in other European languages and which are not always easy to replicate. The letter *ð* is generally replaced with a *d* in English, but we have decided to use the Icelandic letter to remain closer to the original names. Its sound is closest to the voiced *th* in English, as found in *th*en and ba*th*e.

The Icelandic letter *þ* is reproduced as *th*, as in *Th*orgeir, and is equivalent to an unvoiced *th* in English, as in *th*ing or *th*ump.

The letter *r* is generally rolled hard with the tongue against the roof of the mouth.

In pronouncing Icelandic personal and place names, the emphasis is always placed on the first syllable.

Names like Anton, Begga and Elma, which are pronounced more or less as they would be in English, are not included on the list.

Aðalheiður — AATH-al-HAYTH-oor
Agnar Freyr Steinarsson — AK-narr FRAYR STAY-N-ars-son
Akranes — AA-kra-ness
Bergrún — BAIR-kroon
Bergur — BAIR-koor
Birna — BIRRD-na
Borgarnes — BORG-ar-ness
Bryndís — BRIN-deess
Dagný — DAAK-nee

Davíð Sigurðarson— DAA-veeth SIK-oorth-ar-son
Dísa — DEESS-a
Elín (Ella) — ELL-een
Fannar — FANN-arr
Gígja — GYEE-ya
Grábrók — GROW-brohk
Guðlaug (Gulla) — GVOOTH-loig (GOOL-la)
Guðrún — GVOOTH-roon
Hafliði Björnsson — HAV-lith-ee BYUHS-son
Hrafntinna (Tinna) — HRABN-tin-na
Hvalfjörður — KVAAL-fyurth-oor
Hörður Höskuldsson — HUR-thoor HUSK-oolds -son
Jón — YOEN
Jókull — YUR-kootl
Kári — COW-rree
Lára — LOW-rra
Leifur — LAY-voor
Lína — LEE-na
Margrét — MARR-gryet
Maríanna Þórsdóttir — MAR-ee-ann-a THOHRS-DOHT-teer
Sigurður — SIK-oorth-oor
Skagi — SKAA-yee
Stefán — STEFF-oen
Sævar — SYE-vaar
Sölvi — SERL-vee
Unnar — OON-narr
Viðar — VITH-aar
Þór—THOHRR
Þuríður — THOO-ree-thoor

The Birth

The white sheets remind me of paper. They rustle every time I move, and my whole body itches. I don't like white sheets and I don't like paper. There's something about the texture, about the way the stiff material sticks to my tender skin, that makes me shudder. It's why I've hardly slept since I got here.

My skin is almost the same colour as the sheets and also, ironically, paper-like. It is thin and white and stretches oddly when I move. I feel as if it might tear at any moment. The blue veins are clearly visible. I keep scratching, even though I know I shouldn't. My nails leave red tracks and I have to force myself to stop before they start bleeding. If they did, it would only attract more sideways glances from the doctors and midwives, and I get enough of those already.

They obviously think there's something wrong with me.

I wonder if they walk in without warning on the other women in my ward. I doubt it. I feel as if they're just waiting for me to do something wrong. They ask me intrusive questions and examine my body, inspecting the scars on my wrists and exchanging grave glances. They criticise my weight, and I'm too tired to explain that I've always been like this. I'm not starving myself; I've just always been thin and had a small appetite. I can forget to eat for days on end and don't even realise until my body is shaking from hunger. It's not like I do it deliberately. If there was a pill containing the recommended daily dose of nutrients and calories, I'd take it like a shot.

But I don't say anything, and I try to ignore the doctor's penetrating gaze and dilated nostrils as he looks at me. I don't think he likes me much. Not after I was caught smoking in my room. Everyone behaved as if I'd gone and set fire to their bloody hospital, when all I did was throw the window open and blow the smoke out into the night. I hadn't expected anyone to notice but they piled straight in, three or four of them, barking at me to put out the cigarette. Unlike me, they couldn't see the funny side. They didn't even smile when I flicked the cigarette out of the window and held up my hands like there was a gun pointing at me. I couldn't help laughing.

Since then I haven't been left alone with the baby. I'm relieved, really, because I wouldn't trust myself with it. They bring it in and put it on my breast, and when it latches on to my nipple and sucks, the feeling is like being stabbed by a thousand needles. I can't see anything of myself in the creature lying on my chest. Its nose is too big for its face and there are clumps of dried blood still matting its dark strands of hair. It's not a pretty sight. I flinch when, without warning, it stops sucking and looks up, straight into my eyes, as if it's inspecting me. So there she is, my mother, I imagine it thinking.

We stare at each other. Under the dark lashes, its eyes are a stony grey. The midwives say the colour will change with time, but I hope not. I've always found grey beautiful. My tears threaten to spill over and I turn my face away. When I look down again, the baby is still staring at me.

'Sorry,' I whisper. 'Sorry you've got me for a mother.'

Sunday

'Not so fast.' Elma quickened her pace but Alexander, ignoring his aunt, kept on running. His blond, slightly over-long hair gleamed in the December sun.

'Try and catch me, Elma.' He glanced back at her, his eyes shining, only to trip and fall flat on his face.

'Alexander!' Elma ran over and saw that he hadn't injured himself, apart from a few grazes on his palms. 'There, there, you're all right. You're not hurt. Not much, anyway.' She picked him up, dusted the grit off his hands and dried the tear that had trickled down one red cheek. 'Shall we see if we can find some interesting shells on the beach?'

Alexander sniffed and nodded. 'And crabs.'

'Yes, maybe we'll find some crabs too.'

Alexander soon forgot his accident. Refusing to hold Elma's hand, he went charging on ahead.

'Be careful,' she called after him.

When he reached the black sand, Elma saw him stop and crouch down. Something had caught his eye.

She followed him unhurriedly, breathing in the salt tang of the seashore. The sun was shining brightly in spite of the cold, and the thin sprinkling of snow that had covered everything when she woke up that morning had vanished. The waves rippled gently in the breeze. The scene was tranquil. Elma loosened her scarf and bent down beside Alexander.

'Can I see what you've got there?'

'A crab's leg.' He held up a small, red, jointed limb.

'Wow,' Elma said. 'Hadn't we better put it in the box?'

Alexander nodded and placed it carefully in the Tupperware container Elma held out to him, then raced off again in search of more treasures.

Alexander had just celebrated his sixth birthday and for him the world was packed with interest. Trips to the beach at Elínarhöfði came high on his list, as there were so many exciting things to find there. Elma had loved going to the seashore too as a child. She used to take along a box for shells and would become utterly absorbed in examining what the beach had to offer. There was something so soothing about the sounds and smells of the shore, as if all the world's troubles receded into the background.

She vaguely remembered hearing the legend of how Elínarhöfði had got its name. Something about Elín, whose brother was the medieval priest and sorcerer, Sæmundur the Wise. She had a sister too, named Halla, who lived on the other side of the fjord. When Elín wanted to talk to Halla, she would go to the headland and wave her handkerchief to her sister, who would sit on Höllubjarg, or Halla's Rock, on the other side. Elma was thinking of sharing this story with Alexander but just as she caught up with him, the phone rang in her pocket.

'Elma…' It was Aðalheiður, sounding out of breath.

'Is everything all right, Mum?' Elma perched on a large rock beside her nephew.

'Yes.' Sounds of rustling and heavy breathing. 'Yes, I'm just getting out the fairy lights. I'm finally going to put them up. I can't understand why I didn't get round to it sooner.'

Her parents always put up way too many Christmas decorations, usually in November. Or, rather, her mother did. It wasn't that her father didn't want to help, but Aðalheiður never gave him the chance. She tended to seize the opportunity while he was at work, which gave her a free hand to decorate every inch of the house.

'Want some help?'

'Oh, no, I can manage. I was just thinking ... your father will be seventy in two weeks. Couldn't you and your sister go into Reykjavík together and find a present for him? I know he'd like some new waders.'

'Just the two of us?' Elma pulled a face. She and her sister had never been close, though there were only three years between them. 'I don't know, Mum...'

'Dagný was really hoping the two of you could go.'

'Why don't you come as well?'

'I've got too much else on,' Aðalheiður said. 'I thought you could go next weekend and make a day of it. I've got a gift voucher for the spa that your dad and I will never get round to using, but you two could go while you're in town.'

'The gift voucher I gave you for Christmas?' Elma didn't bother to disguise her indignation.

'Yes, oh ... Was it from you? Anyway, I'd really like you two to use it. Have a sisters' outing.'

'But I bought the voucher for you and Dad. You could both do with a bit of pampering. You never go anywhere.'

'What nonsense. We're going to Prague in the spring. You must be able to go...'

'In other words, it's already been decided?'

'Don't be like that, Elma—'

Elma cut her off: 'I'm only joking. Of course I'll go.

No problem.'

She pocketed her phone and set off after Alexander, who was down by the water's edge now. It was a long time since the sisters had last spent any time alone together. Elma sometimes looked after Alexander, especially as he tended to ring up himself and ask her to come and fetch him. Apart from that, she and Dagný mainly communicated through their parents. Elma sometimes wondered if they'd have a relationship at all if their mum and dad weren't there.

'Elma, look how many I've got.' Alexander held out a fistful of multicoloured pebbles. He grew more like his father, Viðar, with every year that passed. The same delicate features and blue eyes; same easy temperament and soft heart.

'They're beautiful,' she said. 'I bet they're wishing stones.'

'Do you think so?'

'I know so.'

Alexander put the stones in the box that Elma held out to him.

'I think so too,' he said, and grinned, revealing the gap where he had lost his first tooth. Then he reached out and brushed a strand of hair from Elma's face.

She laughed. 'Oh, thanks, Alexander. Is my hair a mess?'

Alexander nodded. 'Yes, actually.'

'So, what are you going to wish for?' She straightened up, dusting the sand from her trousers.

'I'm giving them to you. So you can make a wish.'

'Are you sure?' Elma took his hand and they set off back towards the car. 'You could wish for anything you liked. A spaceship, a submarine, Lego…'

'Oh, I'll get everything I want anyway. I'll just write

a list for Father Christmas. You need the stones much more than me because Father Christmas only listens to children, not to grown-ups.'

'You know, you're right.' She unlocked the car and Alexander climbed into the back seat.

'I know what you're going to wish for.' He gazed at Elma seriously as she helped him do up his seat belt.

'Do you, now? Are you a mind reader?'

'Yes. Well, no. But I know anyway,' Alexander said. 'You want a boy just like me. Mummy says that's why you're sad sometimes. Because you haven't got a boy.'

'But I've got you, haven't I?' Elma said, dropping a kiss on his head. 'Why would I want anyone else?'

The phone vibrated in her pocket before Alexander could answer.

'Are you out and about?' It was Sævar. Hearing how hoarse he sounded, Elma felt grateful that she hadn't accepted his invitation to go to the dance last night. Akranes's nightlife wasn't exactly buzzing these days, with most people preferring to party in Reykjavík, but the town did host the odd social event, like the one the previous evening. Elma still hadn't got round to going along. She imagined it would involve meeting loads of people she hadn't spoken to for years and having to fend off questions that she had no wish to answer.

'I woke up early and came out for a walk with my nephew,' she said. 'How are you doing? Was it fun last night?'

Sævar replied with a groan, and Elma laughed. Despite his big build, Sævar was a complete lightweight when it came to drinking. It usually took him several days to recover from a hangover.

'That's not why I was calling, though I must tell

you about it later…' He cleared his throat and added in a graver tone: 'A body's been found.'

Elma glanced at Alexander, who was sitting in the car, examining his pebbles. 'What? Where?'

'Where are you?' Sævar asked, ignoring her question. There was a hiss of static on the phone.

'Elínarhöfði.'

'Can you come and pick me up? I don't think I'm fit to drive yet…'

'I'll be there.' Elma shoved the phone in her coat pocket and got into the driver's seat, smiling at Alexander in the mirror. Smiling at the boy who wanted to give her his wishing stones so she wouldn't be sad anymore.

After dropping Alexander at home, Elma drove over to the blue block of flats where Sævar lived. There were only three detectives working at West Iceland CID, which was based in Akranes, and Elma counted herself very lucky to have a colleague like him. They had clicked from day one and, although the cases they had to deal with could be grim at times, with him laughter was never far away. Hörður, the head of CID, was a rather more serious type, but Elma wasn't complaining. As a boss he was scrupulous and fair, and Elma was happy in her job.

She had moved back to Akranes from Reykjavík more than a year ago now and the smallness of her old hometown no longer got to her. She had grown used to how close everything was, which meant she could walk or cycle everywhere she needed to go. She'd even started to enjoy being greeted by the same faces every day at the shop or swimming pool. The only thing she couldn't get used to was going for walks in the town's flat surroundings, where it felt as if all eyes were on her. So instead, she tended to head for the forestry plantation or the beach at Langisandur, where she felt less exposed. She had even caught herself pausing to admire the view of the town, Mount Akrafjall, the beach and the blue expanse of Faxaflói Bay, as if nowhere in the world could equal it for beauty. God, she was turning into her mother.

Sævar was standing outside his building with his hands buried in his pockets and his shoulders hunched up to his ears against the cold. All he had on were light-grey tracksuit bottoms and a thin, black jacket. His dark hair was tousled and stuck up at the back of his head, and he was squinting as if the daylight was too much of a good thing.

'You look summery,' Elma commented as he got in the car.

'I'm never cold.' He put his freezing hands on Elma's.

'Ouch, Sævar!' Elma jerked her arm back, shooting him a dirty look. She turned up the heater, shaking her head.

'Thanks,' Sævar said. 'You know, it didn't look that cold when I checked out of the window. All I saw was sun and blue sky.'

'Classic 'window weather',' Elma retorted. 'I thought everyone in Iceland had learnt their lesson from that kind of mistake. You know perfectly well that the weather changes every fifteen minutes.' She pulled out of the car park, adding: 'Where are we going?'

'Out of town, heading north.'

'Do we know who it is?'

'Not yet, but there aren't many candidates, are there?'

'Meaning?'

'Remember the woman who went missing in the spring?'

'Yes, of course. Maríanna. Do you think it's her?'

Sævar shrugged. 'She lived in Borgarnes and the officer who was first on the scene was sure it was a woman. Apparently there's still enough hair left.'

Elma couldn't imagine what state the body would be in if it was Maríanna. It was more than seven months since she had disappeared — on Friday, 4 May. She had left behind a note in which she begged her teenage daughter to forgive her. Maríanna had a date that night, so her daughter hadn't been expecting her home. There was nothing strange about that as the girl was old enough to put herself to bed. But when Maríanna still hadn't come home by the Saturday afternoon and wasn't answering her phone, the girl had called her support family, a couple who looked after her every other weekend. They had rung the emergency number. It transpired that Maríanna hadn't turned up for her date. After several days' search, her car was discovered outside the hotel at Bifröst, an hour or so north of Akranes, but there was no sign of Maríanna herself. Her note gave them reason to believe she might have killed herself but, as no body had been found, the case remained open. There had been no new evidence until now.

'Who found the body?' Elma asked.

'Some people staying in a nearby summer house.'

'Where exactly was she?'

'In a cave in the lava-field by Grábrók.'

'Grábrók?' Elma repeated.

'You know, the volcanic crater. Near Bifröst.'

'I know what Grábrók is.' Elma took her eyes off the

road to roll them at him. 'But wasn't it supposed to have been suicide? That was our assumption, wasn't it?'

'It's still possible. I haven't heard any different, though presumably we'll need a pathologist to work out what happened. The body must be in a pretty bad state after all this time. It's not that far from where her car turned up, so perhaps she crawled into the cave, hoping she wouldn't be found.'

'Strange way to...'

'...kill yourself?' Sævar finished.

'Exactly.' Elma put her foot down, pretending not to see the way Sævar was looking at her. It wasn't that the subject was too sensitive for her to discuss. Not at all. Yet her thoughts couldn't help flying to Davíð whenever suicide was mentioned.

Elma had been in the second year of a psychology degree at the University of Iceland when she met Davíð, and had already decided that the course wasn't for her. He had been taking business studies and had been full of big dreams and grand ideas about how he was going to build something up. Nine years later and nothing had come of those dreams, but in spite of that Elma had assumed things were OK. They both had good jobs, owned a flat, a car and everything they needed. Davíð seemed a bit down sometimes, but she hadn't given it too much thought. She had just taken it for granted that he was asleep at night when she was, and that he would be there as usual when she came home that day in September. She had been wrong.

'Maybe it isn't her,' Elma said, firmly pushing these thoughts to the back of her mind.

'No, maybe not,' Sævar agreed.

They took the turning north to Borgarnes. Akrafjall,

the distinctive dish-shaped mountain that formed Akranes's main landmark, took on a completely different shape close up. The car in front of them slowed down and turned off onto a dirt track leading to the mountain. Probably someone planning to take advantage of the sun and clear skies to walk up to the summit at Háahnjúkur. Elma stole a look at Sævar. His eyes were bloodshot, and when he'd got in the car, even the smell of his aftershave and toothpaste couldn't mask the alcohol fumes.

'Anyone would think you were still a bit pissed from last night,' Elma said. 'Or that you'd fallen into a bathtub full of landi.' Landi was the name Icelanders gave to illegally distilled spirits. 'Have a good time, did you?'

Sævar stuck some chewing gum in his mouth. 'Better?' he asked, exhaling in her direction.

'Do you really want me to answer that?' She had every intention of rubbing his nose in the fact he'd overdone it. God knows, he did it to her every time she had a heavy night — most recently in the summer, when Begga, one of the uniformed officers, had invited her colleagues round for a party. Elma didn't usually drink too much, but that evening something had gone wrong and she had ended up with her head down the toilet like a wasted teenager. She blamed the whisky that someone had brought out; at the time it had seemed such a good idea to try it. The bottle of red wine might have been partly to blame as well. She had a hazy memory of taking over the music and her DJing being greeted with a distinct lack of enthusiasm by her colleagues — well, apart from Begga, who had cheerfully bellowed along to the Backstreet Boys.

Sævar opened the window a crack, with an apologetic glance at Elma. 'Bit dizzy. Just need a quick blast of fresh air.'

'Do you want me to stop?'

'No, no. I'll be fine.' He rolled the window up again. 'Elma, next time I get it into my head to go to a dance, will you please stop me?'

'I'll try but I'm not making any promises.'

'I'm too old for this.'

'Yes, you are.'

Sævar frowned. 'You were supposed to say: 'Come off it, Sævar. You're still so young."'

Elma grinned. 'Thirty-five's not so bad. You've got plenty of time left.'

'Thirty-six.' Sævar groaned. 'It's all downhill from now on.'

Elma laughed. 'Rubbish. If you're going to get all self-pitying every time you go out, I'll do my best to dissuade you next time. Or at least steer well clear of you the day after.'

Sævar's only answer was another groan.

It was an hour's drive up the west coast from Akranes to Grábrók. Sævar fell asleep on the way. His head rolled sideways and jerked to and fro for a while, before falling back onto the headrest again. Elma turned down the music and turned up the heating, still feeling chilled from her walk on the beach. She couldn't help smiling as she thought of Alexander and the sweet thing he had said. If only she could pause time so that she could enjoy his innocence and candour for a little while longer. The years were passing far too quickly. It felt like only yesterday when she had first held him in her arms in the maternity ward, all crumpled and red, with that pure-white hair on his head. Since moving back to Akranes just over a year ago, she had been able to spend much more time with him and his little brother Jökull, who had turned two in September. As a result, they didn't seem to be growing up quite so terrifyingly fast.

She drove along the ring road, open sea to the west, mountains to the east, passing close to the brown, scree-skirted slopes of Mount Hafnarfjall, a notorious black spot for wind, where the road often had to be closed to traffic. Ahead, the landscape opened out into the flat, grassy country around Borgarfjörður, with its big skies and the odd white farmhouse reflected in the waters of the fjord. Halfway along, the road turned north across a bridge that brought them right into Borgarnes, a small town of mostly white buildings that nestled into the landscape, perching on low cliffs above the sea. Since the ring road ran straight through the town, summer and winter the local shops and petrol-station cafés tended to be crowded with tourists, giving it a very different feel to Akranes, which suffered from being a little off the beaten track, out at the end of its peninsula.

After leaving Borgarnes, the road led them past red-roofed farmhouses and a few stands of trees, followed by endless fields of withered, tussocky grass. Directly ahead, a bump on the horizon marked the pyramidal form of Mount Baula, which rose out of the landscape just to the north of their destination, growing ever larger the closer they came. After twenty minutes, the grazing land gave way, first to rockier country clothed with pine plantations and native birch scrub, then to the lava fields with their piles of mossy stones, as they approached Grábrók. A collection of ultra-modern, geometric, black-and-white blocks and slightly older, red-roofed accommodation buildings marked the site of the university campus that had grown up here at Bifröst, its population swelling with students during the winter months. It was a popular area for summer houses too, and Elma could see cars parked outside most, suggesting that people were taking advantage of the good weather before the full weight of winter descended.

Just beyond the university buildings rose the distinctive brown form of Grábrók, a small volcano that had last erupted a thousand years ago. It wasn't high enough to be called a mountain but had a pleasingly conical shape and a large crater in the middle. In fact, there were three craters, but the two either side of the main cone were smaller and less conspicuous. Grábrók had smooth flanks of grey and rust-red cinders, with pale grass extending up the lower slopes here and there, in contrast to the surrounding jumble of moss-covered stones that made up the lava field. Elma caught sight of a police vehicle parked at the foot of the crater and turned off just before she reached the car park, which was usually full of tourists and buses. They bumped up the narrow gravel track and drew up beside the other police car.

She nudged Sævar, who blinked several times and yawned.

'Feeling better?' Elma asked as she opened the door.

Sævar answered with a nod, but his appearance suggested otherwise. If anything, he looked even more tired and drained than before.

A uniformed officer from the Borgarnes police force was standing by the other car, a middle-aged man who Elma didn't remember seeing before. He had arrived at the scene before them and spoken to the people who'd found the body. These turned out to be two young boys, who were staying at a nearby summer house. They had been playing hide-and-seek in the lava field when they came across the remains. The policeman was shielding his eyes against the sun. Although there was hardly any wind, the cold was biting enough to make Elma shiver. She wrapped her scarf more tightly around her neck, noticing out of the corner of her eye that Sævar was hugging his thin jacket to his body.

'It's not a pretty sight,' the policeman said. 'But I suppose you're used to anything in CID.'

Elma smiled. Most of the cases that landed on her desk were traffic offences or burglaries. She could count on the fingers of one hand the times she had laid eyes on a corpse. When she left Reykjavík to join West Iceland CID, she had been prepared for a quiet life, despite the size of the region, but no more than a week had passed before a body had turned up by the old lighthouse in Akranes. The ensuing murder case had gripped the nation.

'The terrain's tricky up there,' the officer continued. 'The cave itself is pretty deep and narrow. You have to bend down to get inside. It gave the poor boys a horrible shock — they thought they'd seen a black elf or a goblin or something.'

'A black elf?' Elma raised her eyebrows, puzzled.

'You'll understand when you see it.'

The scramble over the rough lava proved harder than it looked. It took all Elma's concentration not to trip on the jagged snags of rock. She kept her eyes fixed to the ground in front of her, searching for safe footholds, but twice the moss gave way beneath her and she came close to losing her balance. She paused to catch her breath and take in the magnificent landscape. They were to the south of the crater, higher ground hiding them from the ring road and the members of the public using the car park.

The officer from Borgarnes had marked the spot where the body had been found with a yellow hi-vis jacket, which was just as well, since it would have been impossible to locate it otherwise, given that every rock looked identical to the next. Even when they came to a halt, Elma couldn't work out where the body was. It wasn't until the officer pointed that she spotted the narrow opening concealed among the moss. In fact, she wasn't sure whether to call it a cave or a fissure. The opening slanted down and didn't look particularly large, but when she squatted in front of it, she saw that the cavity was much deeper and wider than she had initially thought. Once through the entrance, there would be room for a fully grown man to stand, if he ducked his head.

Sævar borrowed a torch from the policeman and directed it into the gloom. The beam lit up the dark rock walls and roof as Elma squeezed through the opening, picking her way carefully over the uneven floor. The moment she was inside, all sounds faded to a hum. Perhaps it was just the noise of her own breathing, echoing from the rocky walls. She glanced back at Sævar, feeling a moment of shrinking fear in the cramped space. Then she steeled herself and peered towards the back of the cave. When the torch beam lit up the space, she gasped.

No wonder the boys thought they'd seen a black elf. The body was dressed in dark clothes, its head lying a little higher than its torso. The skull wasn't black but pale grey and brown, with tufts of hair here and there. There was nothing left of the face; no skin, just gaping eye sockets and grinning teeth.

Sævar ran the torch beam down the body to reveal a black coat, blue top and jeans, all ragged looking and darkened by moisture from their long stay in the cave. Without warning, the circle of light vanished. Elma jerked her head round and saw Sævar's chalk-white face for an instant before everything went dark as he turned away, took a few steps to one side and doubled over. Next moment she heard retching, followed by the sound of him vomiting into the lava.

Two Months

They said it was normal; that the feeling would go away with time. The baby blues, *the curly-haired midwife said as I lay weeping in hospital for days after the birth. Most women get them, she added, looking at me sympathetically through her ugly chrome glasses. I felt an urge to rip them off her face, throw them on the floor and stamp on them. But I didn't do it. I just dried my tears and smiled whenever the midwives came in. Pretended everything was fine and that I was over the moon about the child that I had never meant to have.*

They were all taken in. They stroked my daughter's chubby cheeks and hugged me goodbye. They didn't see how the smile vanished from my lips the instant I turned my back. How the tears trickled unchecked down my cheeks as I got into the taxi.

Since I got home from hospital the darkness in my head has become ever blacker until I'm afraid it might swallow me up. There's none of the promised joy or contentment, only emptiness. I sleep and wake. The days pass in a monotonous blur, and all the while she lies there, this little, dark-haired girl, who appeared after so many hours of pain. Even her crying has receded into a distant buzzing that I hardly notice.

For the first few weeks I struggled with the desire to shake her when she cried. I just wanted her to stop so I could hear myself think. When her screaming was at its most ear-splitting I had to leave the room or I would prob-

ably have gone ahead and done it. I would have shaken her like a rag doll.

It sounds terrible, but that's how I felt. I was angry. Mostly with her for demanding so much from me, but also with the world for not caring. I pictured myself accidentally dropping her on the floor or putting a pillow over her face, and how it would all be over. I would be doing her a favour. The world is an ugly place, full of hateful people. These thoughts and visions came to me during the night when I hadn't slept for days and felt as if I was neither living nor dead, just existing in some limbo state in between. Like a different person. Like there was nothing left of me.

And to be completely honest — if such a thing is possible — I didn't find her beautiful. She just wasn't. Her face didn't belong on a baby. Her features were too strong, her nose too big and her eyes so watchful that I was sure that inside the baby lurked an adult; someone who watched me all the time, just waiting for me to make a mistake. This couldn't be my daughter, the child I had carried for nine months. During the pregnancy I had told myself it would all be worthwhile when she arrived, but I still don't feel that. I just don't.

That's why I avoid her eyes. I soon stopped breastfeeding and started giving her a bottle instead. I didn't like the feeling of her sucking her nourishment from my body. I found it uncomfortable having her too close to me, seeing those little grey eyes flick open and stare up at my face while she was drinking. When she cried, I put her in the pram and rocked her to and fro until she stopped. Sometimes it took minutes; sometimes hours. But she always shut up in the end.

Then I would get into bed and cry myself to sleep.

By the time forensics arrived at the scene, Sævar had more or less recovered and was sitting in the police car. After a few minutes the interior had begun to smell like a nightclub at five in the morning so Elma had got out. She leant against the door, gazing over the lava field to where forensics were at work. The day turned abruptly darker. The sky, which had been blue only a short time ago, was now grey and overcast. A great bank of cloud overshadowed the sun and a chilly gust of wind swept across the landscape.

Elma buried her nose in her scarf, trying not to dwell on how cold she was. Eventually, she spotted her boss Hörður's SUV approaching up the gravel track towards Grábrók. He and his family had been at their summer house by the lake in Skorradalur, some forty minutes' drive away, when the phone call had come in about the body. He greeted her briefly, donned his Russian fur hat, then set off to join forensics. To Elma's surprise, Hörður negotiated the lava field with the swift surefootedness of an experienced hiker. When he came back, he opened the boot of his SUV.

'Gígja insisted on sending this along for you two,' he said, taking out a thermos flask and some disposable paper cups.

'Darling Gígja. Do thank her from me,' Elma said, gratefully accepting a cup. Hörður's wife was the opposite of him. Where he was inclined to be stiffly formal, she was easy-going and friendly, treating Elma from the very first as if they'd known each other all their lives.

Hörður poured coffee into the cup she was holding out, then nodded at the car. 'What's up with him?'

'He's a bit under the weather.'

'Under the weather?'

'Yes...' Elma smiled ruefully. 'Apparently he had a good time last night.'

Hörður shook his head. 'Isn't he a bit old for that sort of nonsense?'

'That's what I said.' Elma took a wary sip of coffee. It was still scalding hot.

'It doesn't look good,' Hörður said after a short silence. He turned his gaze back to the lava field, where the forensic technicians were moving around in their blue overalls. Although it was still daylight, they had set up lights to illuminate the interior of the cave.

'No, the body looks as if ... well, as if it's been lying there for months.'

'Could the person have fallen?'

'No, I don't think so,' Elma said. 'Not given the angle of the cave. It wouldn't be a long enough drop, would it? It's more like she crawled in there, not wanting to be found. And perhaps she never would have been if the boys hadn't thought the cave would make a good hiding place.'

'So she might have gone in there to die?'

'Exactly. Maybe she didn't want anyone to have to stumble on her body.'

'Are we sure it's a woman?'

'Yes, fairly sure,' Elma said. The remaining tufts of hair on the skull had been long and the coat had looked like a woman's. The trainers had been small too, probably no more than a size thirty-six. Elma wouldn't have been able to squeeze into them herself. 'But I don't know if it's Maríanna. It seems likely, though. I mean, it's not like many women have gone missing in recent months or years.'

'No, Maríanna's the only one who hasn't turned up.' Hörður threw his cup in a litter bin that had been installed next to a bench. He adjusted his hat and rubbed his hands together.

It felt like ages before they heard a distant cry and raised their eyes. A member of the forensics team was beckoning to them. Hörður hurried over while Elma rapped on the passenger window of the car. She nearly winced when she saw how awful Sævar looked. His face, which had been white as a corpse, now appeared positively grey. His eyes were red and puffy, and he was shaking. Nevertheless, he got out, making a pathetic effort to smile.

'Do you want my scarf?' she offered, though she was freezing herself.

'No, I—'

'Sure you do.' She took it off and wrapped it round Sævar's neck, trying to hide the shiver that assailed her as the wind clutched at her bare neck with icy fingers. 'It suits you.'

'Thanks.' Again, he tried and failed to smile.

'Come on. Not long now and you'll be able to crawl back into bed,' she said, giving him a nudge as they set off side by side.

'You think so?'

'No, actually.' Elma laughed. 'We'll probably need to go back to the office afterwards. But I'll stop off at a petrol station on the way home so you can buy yourself something deep fried.'

'Oh, God. Don't even talk about it.'

'That bad, is it?'

Sævar never normally turned down the offer of junk food. Elma had seen him put away two deep-fried hot dogs with cheese and chips, followed by crisps for pudding, and still have room for more.

'I'm never going to drink again,' Sævar announced with a groan.

'They've found an ID,' Hörður told them when they reached the cave. The man from forensics handed over a clear plastic bag containing an ID card that had obviously got wet in the damp cave. Although the black print had faded, the name was still visible: Maríanna Þórsdóttir.

'How long is it since she went missing?' he asked.

'She vanished at the beginning of May,' Hörður replied. 'That makes it more than seven months.'

'Well, it looks to me as if the body's pretty well preserved, all things considered,' the man said. 'Especially where it's protected by the clothes. Everything, that's to say, except the head and hands. Though there are still some patches of soft tissue on the skull — on the back of the head and neck, for example. We've had a look at them and we're fairly sure there's a fracture in the skull, so it's probably best to call out the pathologist. There'll be a post-mortem, I assume?'

'Yes, of course,' Hörður said. 'Could the fractured skull have been caused by a fall?'

The man grimaced a little. 'Unlikely. You've seen the way the cave is angled. You have to crawl to get to where the body's lying. If you ask me, the blow was caused by something else.'

Hörður thought for a moment. 'Yes, right,' he said.

'We'll call out the pathologist.'

Elma saw that Sævar was having difficulty swallowing his disappointment. Waiting for the pathologist to drive up from Reykjavík would mean hanging around for at least another two hours in this bitter cold.

Darkness arrived from the east, reaching out with terrifying swiftness across the sky towards the setting sun. They had watched the forensics team at work all day. By the time the pathologist arrived, dusk was already falling. But, in the event, he required less than an hour to assess the situation and take a few samples before the body could be transported to Reykjavík, where the post-mortem would take place the following day.

Both pathologist and forensics team were in agreement that the injuries to Maríanna's skull could not have resulted from a fall. Moreover, there was a large, dark patch on the front of her shirt, which might well have been blood. The body was so badly decomposed that it was hard to be certain, but there were various indications that her death was suspicious. Nevertheless, it struck them as odd that Maríanna's remains hadn't been put in a bin bag or covered with a blanket. Or at least hidden with a pile of rocks. The person who had dumped her there had simply trusted that no one would find her.

After what felt like an interminable day, Hörður, Elma and Sævar had headed back to the police station in Akranes to decide their next steps. Elma was now sitting in the meeting room cradling her fourth mug of coffee. She'd almost finished the packet of biscuits that had been lying unopened on the table when they arrived. Sævar sat opposite her and yawned as he pushed away his laptop. The colour had returned to his cheeks, though he had subsisted on nothing but fizzy drinks all day. He glanced at his watch and then at Elma. Feeling his gaze on her, she looked up.

'What?' In the yellow glow of the ceiling lights she suddenly felt sleepy too and had to smother a yawn with her hand.

'Shouldn't we talk to Maríanna's daughter?'

'I'll take care of that,' Elma said. The girl's name was Hekla. She had been taken in after her mother's disappearance by a couple called Bergrún and Fannar, who had fostered her when she was younger and later looked after her every other weekend. Elma didn't know exactly how the girl had come to be fostered by them in the first place, though she was aware that Maríanna had had a few problems. Bergrún and Fannar had been very helpful during the search for her back in the spring and more than willing to provide Hekla with a permanent home.

'Is there anyone else we should be in touch with?' Sævar asked.

'Well, Maríanna's father lives in Reykjavík,' Elma said, remembering. 'But, as far as I can recall, her brother and mother are dead. She didn't have any other close family.'

Elma reached down to pat Birta, who was sitting at her feet. Sævar's dog usually made a beeline for her when he brought her into the office, which had been pretty much every day since he'd split up with his girlfriend of seven years. He didn't have the heart to leave the dog alone at home, so she had become almost part of the furniture at the police station. The ex-girlfriend had already got together with another man, and they were expecting a baby. Sævar claimed he was happy for them, but Elma doubted this was entirely genuine. He didn't seem that pleased about Birta's preference for Elma either, however much he joked about it. Elma had seen him staring fixedly at the dog lying at her feet, as if silently commanding her to come to him. But Birta ignored his summons, as she did any other orders he gave her in Elma's presence. Instead, the dog would turn an enquiring gaze on Elma and wait for a command from her.

'I'll speak to her father,' Sævar said, his eyes on Birta.

'Whatever you think,' Elma replied, and got up. Birta instantly sprang up too and followed Elma obediently into the office where she settled down again at her feet.

Bergrún and Fannar certainly looked good on paper. She was a dentist, he an engineer, and they lived in a house in one of the newer suburbs of Akranes — a dark-grey, boxlike building with a concrete patio. In addition to Hekla, they had a son called Bergur, who they had originally fostered then subsequently adopted. He had just started school. The first time Elma met Bergrún, the woman had told her straight out that the decision to adopt had been taken as a result of repeated miscarriages. Not everyone could bring themselves to take in children who weren't their own flesh and blood, but there was no sign that Bergrún and Fannar were any less fond of Bergur and Hekla than parents would be of their biological offspring. The couple both came out to greet Elma and Sævar, who'd decided to come along too, and led them into their home, which was covered in photos and artworks, the latter consisting of abstract splashes of paint and the names 'Hekla' or 'Bergur' spelled out in uneven letters in the corners.

Hekla herself was sitting at the kitchen table with her school books spread out in front of her. The black hoodie she was wearing was several sizes too big, and her dark hair was caught up in a high pony-tail. She raised her head when they came in and removed the wireless earbud from one ear.

Elma smiled at her and received a tentative answering smile.

'Shall we take a seat through here?' Bergrún suggested, gesturing to her right. She let the two detectives go into the living room ahead of her while she waited for Hekla, placing a reassuring hand on the girl's shoulder as they followed. Bergrún was several centimetres taller than her husband and towered over Hekla, who was quite small for her age. She only came up to Elma's shoulder, although Elma herself wasn't particularly tall at a very average 168 centimetres.

'Earlier today...' Elma began, once they were all sitting down. She watched their expressions change as she reported the discovery of the body near Grábrók, avoiding going into details, just keeping it short and to the point. As she spoke, she tried not to think about the grisly remains that had long ago ceased to resemble the person they had once been.

'Who found the body?' Fannar asked, shifting to the edge of the sofa. He was a short, fairly nondescript man, with light-brown hair, grey eyes and glasses. From somewhere in the house came the sound of a television; the squeaky voices of cartoon characters.

'Two boys who were playing in the lava field,' Elma said. 'Maríanna's remains will be sent to the pathologist, who will carry out a more detailed analysis tomorrow. After that we'll hopefully have a better idea of the cause of death.'

'The cause of death? You said she'd...' Bergrún glanced quickly at Hekla who was sitting beside her, then lowered her voice '...that she'd probably vanished of her own accord?'

There was no sign that her words were having any effect on Hekla, but then the girl had probably heard all kinds of theories about her mother's disappearance and had had a lot of time to think about them. It was impossible to tell what thoughts were passing through her head at the news. She stared at them impassively, her eyes wide, the corners of her mouth turned slightly down.

'That's what we guessed at the time,' Sævar said. 'But as we couldn't find her body, it was impossible to confirm. It was just one theory.'

Bergrún put an arm round Hekla's shoulders, and the girl leant her head against her. Her gaze shifted away to fix on a glass bowl on the coffee table.

'We'll be in touch the moment we know any more,' Elma said.

'We're reopening the investigation, of course,' Sævar added. 'So we wanted to ask you if there was anything you'd remembered — anything that didn't come up in the spring — that might be important? Anything at all.'

'I just ... I don't know.' Bergrún looked at her husband. 'Can you think of anything, Fannar?'

Fannar shook his head slowly.

'Hekla,' Elma said gently. 'You last saw your mother on the evening of Thursday, the third of May, am I right? Do you remember if anything was different from usual?'

Hekla shook her head. 'She was just like normal.'

'What about in the days before that? Did your mother seem different at all?'

'I don't know.' Hekla dropped her eyes to her black-painted nails and began to pick at the polish. 'I mean, she was just, like, happy. I think she was excited about … that man. She was always on the phone.'

This was exactly what Hekla had told them in the spring. When they examined Maríanna's laptop, they had found countless messages between her and the man she had been planning to meet. Most had been sent via her social-media accounts, to which the police had been granted access.

Elma studied Hekla. The girl was hard to read. She didn't really respond much and didn't speak unless asked a direct question. Elma had had the same impression of her during the original inquiry. It was hard to engage with the girl; hard to get her to reply to questions with anything more than the bare minimum. She had neither wept nor shown any other signs of distress. Of course, every child was different, and there was no one correct way to react in a traumatic situation. Clearly, Hekla wasn't someone who showed her feelings. Besides, the circumstances around Maríanna's disappearance had been a little unusual. They hadn't been sure whether she was coming back or not. In some respects, a missing-person case was tougher on a family than the death of a loved one. The element of uncertainty complicated the grieving process, leaving friends and relatives in limbo, unsure if they would ever get closure.

'What now?' Bergrún asked.

'As Sævar said, we're reopening the investigation,'

Elma replied. 'We'll be in touch the moment anything new turns up or we need any further information from you.'

They said goodbye and Bergrún accompanied them to the door.

'I think Hekla would benefit from trauma counselling,' she said, glancing round to check that the girl wasn't within earshot. 'It's hit her hard.'

'Of course,' Elma said. 'I'll make sure someone gets in touch with you. That goes without saying.'

Bergrún nodded.

'How do you feel Hekla's been getting on otherwise?' Elma asked.

'Getting on?'

'In the last few months, I mean. Has she adjusted well to her new circumstances?'

'Yes, very well, considering,' Bergrún said. 'But she doesn't know how to deal with the whole thing, and I get the sense she's a bit confused. That's why I feel it wouldn't hurt to seek professional help. Her relationship with Maríanna wasn't like a normal parent-child relationship. Hekla often didn't want to go home after her weekends with us, and we'd have to persuade her.'

'I see.'

'Yes,' Bergrún continued. 'So in a way this has been good for Hekla. I'm not saying it's good that Maríanna died — absolutely not. But Hekla's circumstances have changed for the better, and I know she's happy to be able to live with us permanently at last.'

Elma smiled politely, though she found the comment a bit odd and inappropriate, to say the least. It was obvious that Bergrún and Fannar were more comfortably off than Maríanna: they had a bigger house and a nicer car. But, as far as Elma was aware,

Maríanna hadn't had a damaging effect on Hekla, although she'd needed a bit of support from social services.

'When did you first foster her?'

Bergrún smiled. 'When she was three, just a tiny little thing. She was such an adorable child that all I wanted to do was cuddle her and never let her go.'

Five Months

I wasn't always this empty. As a child I was full of emotions — anger, hate, love, sadness. Perhaps I had too many emotions and that's why there are none left now. It's the numbness in my body and soul that makes me do all kinds of things that other people might find horrible. But I don't care. It's like there's no emotion left inside me except a boiling, churning, red rage that I can't control. Just like when I was a child and my fingers would tremble and my face grow hot. I always felt like a balloon that would go on expanding and expanding until it burst with a loud bang. Sometimes I took my anger out on my parents, sometimes on a doll called Matthildur. She had no hair, and her eyelids closed when she was tipped up. I wasn't interested in pushing her around in a doll's pram like my friends, let alone in dressing her up and giving her a bottle full of white liquid that looked like milk.

Once I flew into a terrible rage. I don't know why. I expect it was connected to something my parents did or didn't do. But that's irrelevant. All I remember is slamming my bedroom door and trying in vain to fight back the tears of rage. As I stood in the middle of the room, my gaze fell on Matthildur, sitting on my bed in her smart dress. Her eyes were staring vacantly into space and she wore that stupid smile, as if she was always happy. I picked her up and, without stopping to think, smashed her head against the wall, over and over again until my hands hurt and I was out of breath with the effort. In the end I let go and she dropped to the floor. Then I stood there, feeling the numbness spreading through my body. I didn't know if it felt good or bad. My anger had gone, but when I looked at the doll lying on the floor with a streak of pink paint on her forehead, I felt as if I had done something wrong. I stooped and picked her up and held her tightly, rocking her against me and chanting over and over: Sorry, sorry.

It's strange to be six years old and feel as if you're a black stain on a white sheet. As if the world is in headlong flight and all you can do is grab hold and try not to fall off. My wickedness was something I tried to hide but I knew it was there — a little black creature with horns and a tail, perching on my shoulder, whispering orders and jabbing me with its sharp prongs. Although I couldn't understand exactly why, it gave me pleasure. More pleasure than anything else. This isn't something I came to realise as a teenager or an adult; no, I've known it ever since I was a child at nursery school and used to amuse myself by pinching Villa. Villa was an ugly, boring little girl who always smelt of wee. She was a year younger than me and used to talk in a whiny voice, regardless of what she was saying — even when she was happy. Whenever I think of her I picture her runny nose, her little tongue darting up to lick her top lip as if her snot was a sweetie. Every time the teacher left the room I would sneak over and pinch her on the back of the arm, making her flinch and cry. It was one of the few things that made me happy in those days. I think I must have been five years old.

Of course, that was before my actions started having consequences. You see, children aren't responsible for what they do, but adolescents are. Even though they don't really know what they're doing either and are still just children, however much their bodies are changing and their world is expanding. I discovered this when I was thirteen and took a photo in the changing rooms of this grotesquely fat girl, whose name I've forgotten. We just called her Lardy, which I have a feeling rhymed with her name. I showed the picture to the boys in my class during break. They laughed and made gagging noises, while the girl watched us from a distance, her plump cheeks as red as the jumper she wore every day of the week, every day of the year. When the whole thing came out, I was forced to apologise to her and attend a meeting with my parents and her parents, who looked at me as if I was something you'd find blocking a drain, while the school principal droned on about bullying and its consequences.

After that I was clever enough not to get caught. Mostly, anyway. Of course, I grew up and realised the importance of making a good impression if you want to get on in the world. Don't let anyone see what you're really thinking, even when you know everyone else is thinking the same ugly thoughts that no one dares say aloud. I learnt pretty fast to keep quiet and smile. Be nice. Say yes.

To most people, I appear perfectly ordinary. Perhaps a little hot-tempered, as my grandmother would have said. But recently I've had the feeling that I can't control myself anymore. I've been imagining my soul changing colour; sometimes it's yellow, at other times blue and occasionally a bright, screaming red.

'Just try to be nice to your sister, Elma. It doesn't cost anything to be polite.'

'What do you mean? I'm always nice.' Elma gaped at her mother, who was engaged in trying to untangle the Christmas lights, prior to draping them over the hedge in front of the house, although it was already past nine in the evening. Elma had missed supper because of being kept late at work. When she got to her parents' house, she found a plate of roast lamb and potato gratin waiting to be heated up in the microwave for her. She wolfed the food down in record time while her mother interrogated her about the discovery of the body. Aðalheiður's curiosity knew no bounds; she kept bombarding her with questions, no matter how often Elma assured her that there wasn't much to tell.

'Right.' Her mother gave the impression of taking her claim with a pinch of salt.

Elma wrapped her arms around herself. She couldn't get warm after all the hours spent hanging around outside and kept fantasising about her nice, cosy bed. Then she noticed that her mother was struggling with the lights. 'Let me help,' she said, taking hold of one end. Once they had strung the wire and bulbs from the branches, she looked back at her mother and repeated: 'I'm always nice to her; it's her who ...'

She was brought up short by her mother's sigh. 'Oh, Elma, why do you two have to be like this? Ever since you were small, always this endless bickering.'

'But Mum …' Elma was almost speechless. 'You know what it was like for me. She was the one who didn't want anything to do with me. If she'd only, even once, shown any interest in me…' Realising she'd raised her voice, Elma bit her lip before she could come out with something she would regret. 'You've just forgotten what it was like.'

'Is that so?' her mother exclaimed, then smiled. 'The way I remember it, you cut a hole in her favourite dress.'

'But that—'

'And I also seem to remember you putting soap in her fish tank so all her fish died.'

'That was just—'

'And I could go on, Elma. You were no angel yourself. You always talk as if you were the victim, but it takes two to start a fight.'

Elma felt her cheeks growing hot. 'You said yourself that she never wanted me to be born. She hated me from day one.'

'Oh, Elma!'

'What?' It came out louder than she'd intended.

Aðalheiður straightened up. 'You can't hold that against a toddler. She was only three when you were born and it was tough for her, no longer being the baby of the family. For the first few months after you arrived she behaved as if she was a year younger. She started using a dummy again and sleeping with her teddy bear and even her voice changed.' Aðalheiður laughed as she reminisced. 'It turned into … well, a baby voice. All of a sudden she couldn't say her r's anymore. But your sister was always good to you, Elma. She would lie with you for hours, stroking your chubby cheeks. Always with one finger, as if she was afraid of hurting you.' Aðalheiður smiled. 'All I ask is that you be nice to each other. That's all. You know, love, you can be a bit sharp at times.'

Elma was silenced. How could she make her mother understand what her life had been like with Dagný as a big sister? Living in the shadow of someone who everyone thought was so perfect. Never being anything but Dagný's baby sister?

'Hello!' Dagný's voice suddenly rang out from inside the house, and Elma groaned under her breath. 'Is anybody home?'

Aðalheiður's expression was stern when she looked at Elma. 'Right, shall we have a cup of tea?'

'There you are,' Dagný said, opening the door to the patio. She looked like a ballet dancer with her hair pulled back in a perfect bun, not a single strand out of place. Elma would have loved to be more like her, but people tended to react with astonishment on hearing they were sisters, and Elma knew why: Dagný was beautiful while Elma was … well, what she was. Not ugly, but not particularly pretty either. Perfectly ordinary. With light-brown hair, pale skin and freckles. Nothing special or memorable about her. When Elma was a teenager she had tried to attract attention with her clothes and haircut but all she had earned were sideways glances for being odd — a bit weird. And since she didn't agree with the idea that any attention was better than none, she had chosen instead to be self-effacing and eventually became reconciled to merging effortlessly into the background, where few people even noticed her.

'I baked *kleinur* today,' Dagný announced, beaming, and held up two plastic bags full of the cinnamon doughnut twists.

'Now you're talking,' Elma said, discovering that she did actually have a small hole left for an after-supper treat. She picked up the box containing the rest of the fairy lights, which wouldn't be used this year, and they went into the kitchen.

'What did you get up to today?' Aðalheiður asked as she switched on the kettle.

'Well, I baked *kleinur*, as you can see.' Dagný put the bags on the table. 'And Viðar took the boys swimming.'

'That's nice. The pool's looking so smart after all the improvements.' Aðalheiður put plates and cups on the table along with a box containing a selection of teabags. 'Right, what do you two say to this? Your father's got a landmark birthday coming up, and I want to throw him a surprise party. Just for family and a few friends, but I think it could be fun. I've always wanted to give a surprise party, but I don't know how to deal with ... oh, you know, all the preparations for that sort of thing, so I was wondering if you two could take care of organising it?'

'Me and Elma will do it,' Dagný volunteered instantly. 'Won't we, Elma?'

'Yes, of course,' Elma replied. 'We could find you a venue too.'

The kettle came to the boil, and Aðalheiður filled three cups with hot water, then joined her daughters at the table. Elma selected a teabag and dipped it into the steaming cup.

'Good idea,' Dagný said. 'What do you say we go into town on Saturday? We could buy the decorations and find him a present as well, and he probably needs a new shirt while we're at it, and...' She broke off and burst out laughing. 'All right, I admit it: I love throwing parties.'

'Sounds good,' said Elma, dunking a doughnut in her tea. Dagný didn't seem to have any issue with spending time with her. She wondered if it was only she herself who still bore the scars of their past relationship. Surely Dagný must be aware that she had barely said a word of condolence to Elma after Davíð died? And Elma could count on the fingers of one hand the number of times her sister had visited her and Davíð in Reykjavík. Sometimes Elma got the feeling that Dagný had forgotten she even had a sister.

Their father came into the kitchen, bringing Elma back to the present. When she bit into her doughnut, she discovered that a large chunk of it had broken off in her tea as she had completely forgotten to take it out of the cup.

* * *

The window in Hekla's bedroom was a brilliant design. It could be closed so tightly that you couldn't hear a thing, even when there was a storm raging outside. In the flat where she had lived with Maríanna, the screaming of the wind through the gaps round the window frame used to keep her awake at night. Another, even better, advantage here was that the window could be opened wide, almost like a door, allowing her to climb out whenever she wanted to, without anyone noticing. The only problem was closing it again in such a way that she could open it from outside. It was tricky, but she'd worked out a solution some time ago. By looping an elastic hair tie round the catch and then the outside frame, she could hold the window shut. Later, when she wanted to crawl back inside, all she had to do was free the tie.

That evening, however, she was afraid it might blow open, snapping the elastic. The wind was so strong that the band stretched alarmingly. Hekla added two more hair ties to be on the safe side, then, hoping for the best, she tiptoed along the wall of the one-storey house, ducking down as she passed Bergrún and Fannar's bedroom window. The car was waiting for her at the end of the street.

She got into the passenger seat and smiled at Agnar. He smiled back awkwardly, then stamped on the accelerator so hard that the engine emitted a roar loud enough to piss off the neighbours. Hekla felt her body being pressed back against her seat as the car leapt forwards.

'It was Maríanna,' she said after a while. 'Who they found. You know, the body.'

Agnar took his eyes off the road to look at her. Reaching out, he laid a hand on her thigh. 'Are you all right, or ...?'

Hekla nodded. She didn't want to talk about Maríanna but felt she had to tell him. Agnar seemed to be having difficulty finding the right words too. Almost stammering, he said: 'Should I, er ... Is there something you'd like me to do?'

She stared at him, wondering what he meant. There was nothing he could do now. He'd already done more than enough. 'Have you got any money?' she asked, determined not to think about Maríanna anymore for now. 'I'm dying for an ice-cream.'

Agnar smiled. He headed for the drive-through kiosk and stopped by the window, making it just as it was closing. The girl looked sulky as she served them.

Shortly afterwards Hekla had the ice-cream in her lap and was shovelling it down, gorging on the Daim chocolate and liquorice topping until she felt sick.

They cruised around town for a while, then stopped by the harbour, where Agnar stuck a wad of tobacco under his lip. Hekla hated the way it made him look like a hamster. She lingered over her ice-cream, aware that the moment she finished it, Agnar would want to start kissing her.

'Shall I get rid of it for you?' he asked.

'Yeah.' Hekla gave up stirring the dregs in the bottom and handed him the carton.

He put it in the plastic bag he kept on the floor behind his seat. Then he took her hand, running his long, thin fingers over the back. Strange how childishly short and stubby her own fingers looked against his. She felt like a little girl who shouldn't be sitting in a car with a boy who was nearly twenty. He leant over and started kissing her. She tried to think about something else.

When Hekla got into bed later that evening, her conscience was troubling her. She'd done all sorts of things with Agnar and promised him a load of stuff that she wasn't sure she could deliver. It wasn't like he'd done anything wrong. It was just that Hekla could feel her interest waning with every message he sent her and every look he gave her. The more clingy he became, the less she wanted to see him.

Hekla didn't even think he was hot anymore. To be honest, she'd never actually found Agnar hot, except right at the beginning. Maybe that had been because he was the first boy who had shown any interest in her, and at the time she'd needed that interest.

They'd met one evening when Hekla was out in

Akranes with her friends, Tinna and Dísa. The girls, excited at the thought of driving around town with the older boys, had gone down to the end of the street so their parents wouldn't see. When a small blue car had screeched to a halt by the kerb, they'd jumped in, all three of them squashing into the back seat.

She'd found herself sitting next to Agnar; tall and skinny, with too much gel in his hair. Their arms had touched every time the driver made a sharp turn and when he put his foot down once they'd left town. Someone had lit a cigarette and the car had filled with smoke, then with icy air as they rolled down the windows. Afterwards, when the boys drove them home, Agnar had asked what she was called on Snapchat, ignoring his friends' banter and laughter. The following day she'd found a message waiting for her, and over the next couple of weeks their conversations had become increasingly intense. She'd told him a lot of stuff she'd never said out loud before, about her mum and school and the bullying and her anger. Agnar had said all the right things in reply. He'd understood her and been willing to listen. At last, here was someone who had understood who she really was and wanted more.

It wasn't a feeling she was used to. Tinna and Dísa were the first friends she'd ever had, and she still didn't really understand how that had happened. At school back in Borgarnes no one took any notice of her and even Maríanna didn't seem that interested. She'd occasionally ask how Hekla was doing, but Hekla could see her eyes flickering away as soon as she started to answer. When Hekla wanted to change schools, Maríanna hadn't taken it seriously, and when she'd asked if she could move in with Fannar and Bergrún, Maríanna had gone ballistic. Like Hekla owed her something.

Once, in a fit of rage, Maríanna had hit her over the head with a wooden spoon, snarling: *Have you any idea how much I've sacrificed for you*? Hekla remembered it vividly because that's when she'd started to hate her. Since then she had never thought of her as Mum — only as Maríanna.

Hekla had met Agnar again the next time she had gone to stay the weekend with Bergrún and Fannar in Akranes. He'd come round with a friend to pick her up because that was before he'd passed his driving test. The first time they'd met it had been dark and she hadn't been able to get a good look at him. By daylight Agnar turned out to have acne and a pasty face; she had a bit of a shock when she realised. He'd looked quite different in her imagination. The pictures he'd sent her on Snapchat hadn't shown his skin or those long spindly arms that reminded her of an octopus. He moved strangely too; his arms and legs sort of flapping back and forth, his shoulders a knot of tension. This wasn't the boy she'd been obsessing over for the last couple of weeks.

It was odd how quickly she'd forgotten her reservations. All he'd had to do was say something nice and treat her like she was this amazing person. She'd never felt like that before. So she'd overlooked the rest; just concentrated on the nice things he said and not on his physical appearance. Only now did it dawn on her that she'd never fancied him, just liked the way he made her feel. Well, she didn't need that sort of validation anymore. The only question now was how to get rid of him.

Seven Months

Reykjavík's just like I remember, a small town pretending to be a city. For most of the year the skies are grey and the cars compete to be the dirtiest. Those who venture out of doors walk briskly, dressed in identical thick anoraks, their hoods pulled down over their eyes. After all, there's nothing to see but greyness, wind and drizzle.

I wish I'd never had to come here.

I got the keys to the flat today. For the last few months I've been living in a rented place on the outskirts of Reykjavík. It's a strange feeling to be a property owner all of a sudden. I feel like I'm too young to own something this big. Not that it is that big; it's only a small, cheap flat in an ugly square block that could do with a lick of paint. Behind the building there's a large communal garden enclosed by a broken fence, with a grassy sandpit in the middle.

The flat is on the second floor. When I finally make it up the stairs my heart is pounding from having to cart the baby, who's no lightweight; a ten-kilo lump, perched on my hip.

I put her down on the floor while I find the keys. She doesn't move, just sits there quite still in her red snowsuit, staring into space. Her arms hang lifeless at her sides and her face wears that perpetually solemn expression; her mouth turned down, almost in a scowl.

'Right, our new home,' I say, opening the door. I often do that these days — talk aloud, to myself and her, but there's

no one there to answer anymore; nothing but an oppressive silence.

I'm not prepared for the stench of mildew that hits me. My shoes leave wet marks on the worn parquet as I carry the girl inside. It's actually not that bad. Kitchen, living room and two bedrooms. A battered, black-leather sofa in the living room and a small dining table in the kitchen. Apart from that the flat is empty. It's nothing like the house I grew up in: there's no grand piano in the sitting room or fireplace to fill the evenings with a cosy crackling. The only sounds in this flat are those that carry through the badly insulated walls from the neighbours, and the heavy roar of traffic from the street outside the kitchen window.

My shoulders and back are aching, so I put the girl down on the floor again. Her grey eyes take in her surroundings as she examines our new home. She's still too big, as she has been from birth. Much bigger than other children her age. A few days after she was born, her face started to break out in small pimples. The midwives said it was perfectly normal, but I couldn't touch them without feeling sick. Luckily, her skin is nice and smooth now, but she still doesn't look like other babies. There's something adult about her expression. She doesn't babble or drool or smile. But she knows how to cry and scream when she's not happy, though she doesn't shed any tears and there's no way to pacify her. All you can do is wait until she stops of her own accord. The rest of the time, she just stares into space, making me feel like a failure. Of course, she's only a baby, as I'm always reminding myself, but I can't shake off the feeling that she's watching me, judging me.

I sit on the sofa and light a cigarette. It's not as if the smell could get any worse in here. As the grey smoke curls up to the ceiling, I decide it will be my last. There's no one to smoke with any longer. My friends have all melted away.

My parents too. No one's been in touch since I moved. Like I care. They were nothing but a bunch of losers with no future, only a past. I'm not like them.

When the cigarette's burnt down, I open the window and flick it out. I watch as it makes a little mark in the snow below. I don't know these streets or buildings; they're completely new to me. I've never visited this neighbourhood before except to view the flat, but the unfamiliarity is good because it means no one will recognise me, and for as long as that lasts, I'll be safe.

As long as that lasts, I'll have nothing to fear.

Monday

Bergrún couldn't stand people who took it for granted that they could have children. Perhaps that's why she had never liked Maríanna. She stood up, scraped the rest of the porridge into the bin and put her bowl in the dishwasher.

The coffee machine ground the beans with the usual racket. Then the black liquid trickled into the cup, and after that there was complete silence. Bergrún's hair was still damp from her shower and her body felt pleasantly lethargic after her morning's exercise. But her thoughts kept returning to Maríanna, which prevented her from enjoying this time of day as much as she usually did. She saw again the casual, offhand manner, the constant attempts to get people to feel sorry for her. Sometimes Bergrún had wanted to yell at Maríanna that the world didn't revolve around her. Yet she had pitied the girl the day they first met. Bergrún sat down again with the newspaper, but instead of opening it, she stared out of the window.

The day she had met Maríanna had been defined by two fateful phone calls. The first had been from the hospital to tell her that her third attempt at IVF had failed. Unable to believe it, she had laughed hysterically, saying there must be some mistake. They'd better double-check the results. Could they have got them muddled up with somebody else's? Because she could feel it, feel the strange movements in her womb, as if tiny soap bubbles were floating around inside her. 'Hello, little person,' she had whispered as she stroked her belly the night before. 'Hello, you.' She could have sworn that someone inside her had returned her greeting with a little kick or wave or whatever it was that babies did in the womb.

In the end Fannar had taken the phone out of her hand and put his arms around her. Hugged her before she even realised she was crying. Had she really screamed at the friendly doctor? She, who never lost her temper with anyone. Her father used to say she was completely bloodless. Was she even alive? She didn't feel like it. Not when she wept in Fannar's arms and felt the soap bubbles bursting, one by one. Pop, pop, pop. 'Goodbye, little person. Goodbye, little soul who never existed.'

That had been the first phone call. The second had been a great improvement. It had been the Child Protection Agency ringing to say they had a young child who needed fostering. Would they be willing? While she hadn't exactly been over the moon, a small spark of hope had kindled inside her. Fannar had been doubtful, and she herself had seriously wondered if she would be able to cope, but as she scrolled through online forums full of pregnant women complaining about aches, tiredness, reflux and insomnia, she knew she was stronger than them. So she said yes, and then the child arrived and she had never regretted it for a second.

Hekla. With her dark, unruly hair and her shy smile and her odd questions. Bergrún knew she was special — a bit different from other children. A little backward and withdrawn. Which might be the effect of an upbringing that Bergrún didn't even want to think about. She believed that Hekla's arrival was no coincidence but, rather, some sort of compensation from God for the child she couldn't have. So it had been a devastating shock six months later when she got a phone call to tell her that Hekla's mother was ready to take her back again. Bergrún had wept even more than she had when she received the three fateful phone calls from the hospital. Because this time the child wasn't merely a figment of her imagination: she had held Hekla in her arms, lain beside her while she slept, held her hand in countless playgrounds, kissed a hundred grazes better and wiped away even more tears.

Fortunately, Maríanna had agreed that Hekla should spend every other weekend with them, which was better than nothing. Bergrún had invited Hekla on holiday with them and to the summer house they rented at Easter, but handing her back had become ever more of a wrench. Bergrún had done her best to maintain a good relationship with Maríanna, in the hope that one day the other woman would recognise that Hekla would be better off with them. But Maríanna didn't seem to care. Bergrún had tried repeatedly to persuade her, in a friendly way, of course, only too aware that she could lose Hekla for good if Maríanna chose to end the arrangement. But nothing she said and no amount of pleading on Hekla's part, made any difference: Maríanna wouldn't listen.

Hearing footsteps in the hallway, Bergrún finished her coffee. She had a long day ahead at the dental practice and needed to get on with preparing packed lunches, sorting out clothes and making breakfast for two. She couldn't help smiling. Bergur was seven; he'd come to them for fostering at six months old. Several months later it had become clear that the arrangement would be permanent. At last. It had taken Bergrún a long time to accept the fact, and she hadn't been able to relax properly until she had the adoption papers in her hands. Unlike Maríanna, Bergur's mother had done what was best for her child and given him up. Whereas Maríanna stubbornly insisted on holding on to her daughter, regardless of Hekla's own wishes and what was obviously in her best interests. Maríanna didn't even seem to like Hekla that much. Her own daughter! If there was one thing Bergrún was sure of it was that Maríanna had never deserved Hekla.

* * *

The post-mortem was due to begin at nine. Elma, Sævar and Hörður trooped into the house on the corner, which was part of Reykjavík's National Hospital, although from the outside it looked like a residential property. There were no signs on the front and few people would have suspected that the basement contained rows of corpses in specially designed cold chambers; that it was a place where bodies were opened and their internal organs removed and placed on steel trays.

Elma, who had attended post-mortems before, had a pretty good idea of what the procedure entailed. However, as soon as the examination began she realised that she had never been present at the post-mortem of a corpse in this state. While the pathologist was searching methodically through the clothes, she found herself staring at the skull. It looked different under the lights of the pathology lab. Much more real, yet, simultaneously, more unreal. Elma always found it hard to get her head around the fact that everyone was like this under the skin, regardless of their external appearance. Regardless of their thoughts, feelings or character. When it came down to it, everyone was just flesh and bone that would ultimately decompose, break down and disappear.

As the pathologist carefully snipped off the clothes to reveal the flesh underneath, Elma's stomach began to churn. The skin was mottled pale brown and grey. The pathologist explained that he would have to be especially careful because the skin had decayed to the point where it wouldn't take much for it to disintegrate. It yielded to his touch like soft cheese or porridge.

'It's lucky conditions in the cave were so favourable,' he said. 'It was a wet summer, hardly any sunlight penetrated inside and the temperature remained suitably low and constant.' As he spoke, he placed the clothes in a plastic bag and laid them to one side.

'Shouldn't moisture speed up decomposition?' Sævar asked.

'Good question.' The pathologist became positively animated. 'Yes, usually moisture would cause the tissues to break down faster, but certain conditions result in the formation of a greyish, waxy substance in the tissues called adipocere. The chemical reaction involved prevents bacteria and insects from consuming the tissue. It's common in lakes and bogs, for example.'

'But the body was found in a cave,' Sævar pointed out.

'Quite.' The pathologist smiled. 'The reaction can also take place in narrow, damp caves where the air is static. The floor was covered in a layer of wet clay and moss, and the body had sunk into this, the skin underneath fusing with the clay.'

The remaining tissues no longer resembled skin. Where the red blood had once flowed through veins and arteries, there were now only rusty brown flecks. Elma made an effort to control her breathing as she watched. She didn't want to disgrace herself by throwing up like Sævar yesterday.

'This doesn't apply to the whole body, though,' the pathologist continued. 'The parts that were less protected, like the hands and face, have mostly been reduced to the bare bones, though there are remnants of tendons and ligaments, since these are generally slower to decompose. The brain and eyes have completely vanished, of course, but the abdomen has retained considerably more flesh, as you can see. Soft tissue has also been preserved on the skull, tendons and so on. Mainly on the back of the head, though, and in other areas where the body was in contact with the ground.'

'Is there any chance of spotting injuries?' Elma asked, averting her gaze.

'Yes, we'll try,' the pathologist said. 'If you look here, for example, you can immediately see dark patches on the skin of the stomach and breasts that could be evidence of kicks or blows.' He pointed a gloved finger at the chest, then picked up a camera and snapped some shots. 'The skull fracture is so negligible that I doubt it would have been fatal. Death is more likely to have resulted from the haemorrhaging caused by the blows. The fracture is on the forehead, here, indicating that the person who inflicted it must either have been standing over Maríanna at the time or else have been shorter than her.'

'Why do you say that?' asked Hörður, who up to now had been silent.

'Well, because if the assailant had been taller than Maríanna, the fracture would have been higher up on the skull. That's assuming that a blunt instrument was used to beat her over the head. But if Maríanna was on the ground at the time, there's no way of working out the height of the person who hit her, and that would also be consistent with the other injuries. That's to say, that she was lying down when she was struck.'

'But why would she have bled so heavily if she was beaten?' Hörður asked. 'Wouldn't the haemorrhaging have been mainly internal, if no edged weapon was used?'

'Well, she was hit on the head with some kind of blunt instrument, though I can't tell precisely what it was,' the pathologist replied. 'I can't quite work out where most of the blood would have come from. There's evidence of some internal haemorrhaging but also of considerable blood loss.' He frowned at the body, then pulled over a steel trolley and contemplated the array of scalpels lying on it.

'Do you think she was dead when she entered the cave?' Elma asked.

'Yes, I believe so. I gather they found very little blood at the scene, so it would be the logical conclusion.'

'Was she beaten to death?' Hörður asked.

The pathologist put down the camera and looked at them. 'Yes, that would be my guess,' he said. 'Of course, with decomposition this far advanced, it's hard to say with any certainty whether death was a result of the beating, but judging by the bruising on her body and the fracture to her skull, I'd say it's highly likely. However, I'm still not sure of the precise cause of death. We'll have a better idea of that after we've examined her internal organs. They often preserve evidence of injuries.' He picked up a scalpel and gave them an encouraging smile before getting down to work.

'I'll compare the teeth to Maríanna Þórsdóttir's dental records for confirmation, but I think it's safe to assume it's her,' the pathologist told them two hours later. They were standing outside the pathology lab, and although the smell was better out there and there was no dissected corpse before her eyes, Elma was still feeling faint.

Traces of blood had been found in Maríanna's throat, and although the skin of her face had not been preserved, the pathologist was fairly confident that she had received a full-frontal blow that had broken her nose, which would have accounted for most of the blood loss. The blood would have run down her throat, filling her airways and making it hard for her to breathe. But he couldn't say for sure whether the cause of death had been blood loss, internal haemorrhaging or suffocation. Still, it was quite clear that Maríanna had been beaten to a pulp and that the injuries would have brought about her death in a relatively short space of time.

'Right, we'll be in touch.' Hörður was already halfway up the stairs.

'One more thing,' Elma said. 'Do you have any idea why the killer didn't try to conceal her body, by putting her in a bin bag, for example?'

The pathologist shrugged. 'That kind of speculation isn't really my job,' he reminded her. 'But I can tell you that when a body is put in a thick refuse sack, everything is preserved far better — hair, bodily fluids and DNA. Perhaps the person who deposited her in the cave was hoping that nature would take its course and destroy all that sort of evidence. And in normal circumstances that wouldn't have been such a bad idea. But I doubt the killer could have predicted the chemical reaction that would take place thanks to conditions in the cave.'

'Could she have been transported there in a plastic bag?'

'It's possible, of course, but unfortunately I can't prove it.'

Elma nodded. She had been wondering how it would be possible to cart a dead body over the rough terrain at that time of year without being spotted. At the beginning of May, sunset didn't occur until just before midnight, and it would have remained light for some time after that. In addition, it seemed unlikely that anyone could have lugged the body around the lava field while searching for a good hiding place. All she could think was that the person who hid the body must have been very familiar with the area and probably knew about the cave beforehand. Something else she was fairly confident about was that it would have taken two people to carry Maríanna.

'I'll send you the photos and the preliminary report later today,' the pathologist said in parting.

Once they were outside, Elma gratefully filled her lungs with cold, fresh air and immediately felt better. She couldn't get used to watching post-mortems. It was beyond her how anyone could do them for a living. Presumably you became accustomed to them, like anything else. The pathologist went about his work with an air of calm deliberation and showed no sign of being affected by the body, whereas Sævar and Hörður's ashen faces betrayed the fact that they were in the same boat as her. After they got into the car, no one spoke for a while.

'Maybe we should get a bite to eat,' Sævar suggested eventually.

'I couldn't face food right now, to be honest,' Hörður said, but he agreed to stop at a petrol station that sold sandwiches.

Elma felt more herself after half a can of fizzy drink and a piece of chocolate, but that was all she could stomach.

'We'll have to review the whole thing from the beginning,' she said. 'The case is quite different now from how it looked in the spring.'

'There was nothing suspicious about it at the time. That's why it seems so unbelievable.' Sævar scrunched up the wrapper of his prawn sandwich. 'I mean, she left a note for her daughter — a message that looked like a goodbye note — and we just took it for granted that Maríanna had driven herself up to Bifröst. The whole thing looked like a premeditated suicide.'

'I know,' Elma said. 'What made the search so difficult was that her car was found near the bus stop at Bifröst, which meant she could theoretically have gone anywhere in the country, though none of the bus drivers could remember her. And since the dogs didn't pick up any trail near the car, that made it a reasonable conjecture.'

'Then there was her phone, of course,' Sævar said.

'Her phone?' Elma turned to look at him.

'We tracked the movements of her phone and the last signal came from Akranes, remember? That was why we focused our search there to begin with. Then, after her car turned up at Bifröst, the focus changed. It was all a bit of a mess.'

'Yes, you're right,' Elma said. 'So presumably she went to Akranes before heading up to Bifröst.'

'Exactly. But her phone stopped sending a signal in the early afternoon in Akranes. The battery could have run out or...'

'Or someone could have got rid of it,' Elma finished for him. 'Nowadays most people are aware of the big role phones play in investigations. Anyone who reads or listens to the crime news couldn't fail to have heard that they can be traced.'

'The press will have a field day when this gets out,' Hörður said glumly, and sighed.

Although Maríanna Þórsdóttir's case was still fresh in Elma's memory, she called up the files to make sure she hadn't forgotten any important details. It was rare for young women to disappear in Iceland, and the case had attracted a great deal of attention at the time, so Hörður was probably right: now that it was clear Maríanna had been murdered, the media frenzy would be off the scale.

Elma looked at the photo of Maríanna on her desk. It was the picture they had circulated to the media back when she was reported missing. A selfie from her Facebook page, probably taken for some special occasion. At least, she was all dolled up in it, wearing a black top, with her hair set in waves and an enigmatic smile on her red-painted lips. It seemed impossible to believe that this was the same person as the gruesome remains they had seen on the pathologist's slab that morning.

The original investigation had quickly revealed

that Maríanna had a long history of mental illness. She had been on medication for depression and had gone through several episodes of drug and alcohol addiction. The message that had been waiting for her daughter when she got home from school had been scribbled on the back of an envelope and left on the kitchen table of their flat in Borgarnes, along with a crumpled five-thousand krónur note.

Sorry. I love you, Mum.

Although it was out of character for Maríanna to leave a note like that, Hekla hadn't given it much thought. She had used the money to order a pizza, then gone to bed before midnight. It hadn't occurred to her to wonder why her mother hadn't come home since she knew Maríanna had a date that evening. It wasn't until the following afternoon that Hekla had begun to grow anxious. She had tried to ring her mother, only to find that her phone was switched off. When Maríanna still hadn't come home by that evening, Hekla had rung Bergrún, who had driven up to Borgarnes to fetch her and had alerted the police.

As soon as the police started making enquiries, they discovered that Maríanna had failed to turn up for her date. Only then did things begin to look serious, by which time she had been missing for more than twenty-four hours. The man she had been planning to meet was called Sölvi and worked shifts at the ferro-silicon plant at Grundartangi in Hvalfjörður, like so many people who lived in the area. There was nothing to connect him to Maríanna's disappearance since they had only recently started seeing each other. He had seemed quite hurt and annoyed that she had stood him up and had rung her repeatedly before eventually giving up, as his phone records confirmed.

Maríanna had an ex-boyfriend — more than one in fact — but all her past relationships had been short-lived. The police hadn't dug very deep into her dating history, though, as she hadn't been in contact with any of her exes. Her only living family member had been her father, who lived in Reykjavík. Hekla hadn't seen him since before her grandmother died, which had happened when the girl was ten. Maríanna also had a brother, who had apparently killed himself at the age of twenty-five, when she was pregnant with Hekla.

After the police had combed Akranes and the surrounding area in search of Maríanna, her car, a rusty old Golf, had turned up seventy kilometres north of the town, by the university campus at Bifröst. This had been a cause of some consternation, since they had traced her phone to Akranes and based their search on this information. The records showed that the phone battery hadn't in fact run out; it had been switched off manually. Had Maríanna done this herself or had somebody else done it for her? At the time, they had guessed the former.

There had been nothing of interest in her car; no phone or handbag, no blood or other signs of a struggle. The car had been filthy — in a disgusting state — with leftover food and drinks cans on the floor and a bag containing a mouldy swimming costume and towel. All the indications were that Maríanna had simply abandoned the car in the car park by the hotel at Bifröst and either continued on foot or got on a bus. For days, searchers had scoured the area around the car, walking the surrounding landscape and dragging the lakes, but they had found no trace of Maríanna. Even the tracker dogs had failed to pick up her trail.

There was nothing particularly suspicious about the fact she hadn't been found. The volcanic landscape around Bifröst was riven with dangerous cracks and fissures that a person could easily fall down. Every now and then people vanished without trace there. In the end, the search was called off. Although the case remained open, the general belief was that the missing woman had taken her own life. Now that this assumption had been proved wrong, however, Elma could think of several details that should have roused their suspicion.

For example, on the morning of her disappearance Maríanna had put on a wash. Not that remarkable, perhaps, yet Elma had had an uneasy feeling when she noticed the wet laundry during their examination of Maríanna's flat. She would hardly have bothered to do a wash if she had been planning to kill herself. The flat was a total mess, the beds were unmade, and the fridge contained both mince and raw chicken. Why go to the trouble of buying food if the intention had been to commit suicide? Surely she wouldn't have expected Hekla to cook it.

The police had watched the CCTV recordings from the supermarket the day before Maríanna's disappearance and seen her wandering around the shop with her trolley. Elma remembered thinking that wasn't someone who had decided to end it all. But then her thoughts had strayed to Davíð. She would never have believed he was capable of killing himself either, so perhaps her judgement wasn't to be trusted. This was why she had kept quiet at the time, just watched the woman, who was several years younger than her, putting fizzy drinks and sweets in her trolley, then carrying two bulging shopping bags out of the supermarket. All the same, the thought of the clothes in the washing machine and the mess in the flat had continued to niggle at Elma, which might explain why she had periodically opened and flicked through the file since May. When Davíð left, he had made the bed, neatly folded his clothes and put them away in the wardrobe. Davíð never used to make the bed and usually left a pile of dirty clothes on his side of it. This was what had immediately led Elma to suspect that something was wrong.

On the other hand, the mental-health issues, the note for Hekla and the abandoned car all supported the theory that there had been nothing suspicious about Maríanna's disappearance. No one had a grudge against her; there had been no stormy relationships or dubious business deals, nothing to link her to anything remotely shady, and therefore no reason to prolong the investigation once several weeks had passed and no new information had emerged. The police had turned their attention to other, more pressing concerns.

Elma was dreading the media coverage, picturing headlines about the incompetence of West Iceland CID. Minor details they had missed or interpreted wrongly would be blown out of all proportion. She leafed back through printouts of Maríanna's phone and computer records. They had gone through them all systematically at the time. Her phone had never been found and the records from the phone company, which covered the previous six months, hadn't shown anything of interest. Maríanna had used Facebook on her laptop to communicate with her female friends. She had also used the site to message Sölvi, her date for the evening of 4 May. He had been planning to pick her up and take her out to dinner. When she didn't answer his calls, he had kept trying, as the records showing his phone usage confirmed.

Bergrún, Hekla's foster mother, had rung Maríanna a number of times during the week before she went missing: they had spoken almost every day. Elma couldn't remember exactly what Bergrún had said about these phone calls, so she made a note to ask her again.

The records also showed that Maríanna had tried repeatedly to reach Hekla during and after lunchtime on Friday, 4 May. Hekla hadn't answered, presumably because she had been at school until 14.00. The last call had been made at 14.27, but since Hekla's last class had been a swimming lesson, perhaps she had still been in the changing rooms and had forgotten to unmute her phone.

Elma sighed and leant back in her chair. She couldn't see anything new in the files or any obvious suspects. If it weren't for the badly decomposed remains on the pathologist's slab in Reykjavík, she would have come to the same conclusion as they had in the spring: that Maríanna Þórsdóttir had disappeared of her own free will.

* * *

Hörður's desk was covered in crumbs from the bread roll he had just eaten. He swept them together to form a line. His to-do list was already far too long and now this case had been added to it; a case they would be criticised for not having solved earlier. Hörður toyed with the idea of giving up work next year. He had almost reached retirement age and just didn't have the energy anymore. Actually, that wasn't quite true: he had the energy, he just didn't have the heart for his job. His interest dwindled with every month that passed, and he had begun looking forward to doing something else. He wanted to use his time to enjoy himself and travel, as he and Gígja had always dreamt of doing. It had come home to him that the time he had left wasn't infinite, all the more so since Gígja had been diagnosed with breast cancer. The tumour was still small, according to the doctors; it hadn't spread. But that didn't make it any less frightening. He moved the line of crumbs back and forth before finally collecting it in the palm of his hand and chucking it in the bin under his desk.

It seemed that every other person his age was being diagnosed with some illness or other, and he was terrified that things would end badly. The cancer, even though it had turned out not to be as serious as they had originally feared, had put everything in a new light. Time was precious, and he meant to use his remaining years well. Death had a way of sneaking up on people when they least expected it. Even in old age there was a tendency to believe that there would be another day tomorrow. Another year after this one. It scared him to think that it might not be true.

There was a knock at the door, and Hörður dusted the last crumbs off his hands.

'Come in.'

Elma opened the door. 'Wasn't the meeting supposed to be at four?'

Hörður glanced at the clock. 'What, yes, is it that late? Give me a couple of minutes. I've just got to make one phone call.'

Elma nodded and pulled the door to behind her.

She had changed since she joined CID just over a year ago. On first acquaintance she had come across as rather serious, but then she'd had a good reason for that. Hörður hadn't heard about the death of Elma's partner until Gígja, who knew everything about everyone, had asked him about it much later. He could hardly begin to imagine the pain she must have felt at losing someone so close to her. He himself had only lost his elderly parents, but of course that was something he'd had many years to prepare for mentally. It was quite different to lose a partner or other close family member who should have had years left to live. Hörður could see now that Elma hadn't been herself at all when she first joined CID. These days she generally came into work with a cheery smile on her face and, if anything, talked rather more than necessary.

Hörður picked up his phone and selected Gígja's number. She was in Reykjavík for her radiotherapy. He hadn't been able to accompany her as he'd intended, but their daughter had gone instead. Gígja had been in a good mood that morning, so good that he'd wondered if she was glad he couldn't go with her this time. Mother and daughter were planning to combine the trip with a bit of shopping, a meal out and maybe even a film. They'd probably be back late, Gígja had said. He just hoped his daughter wouldn't exhaust her mother with a shopping marathon.

One Year Old

I don't sing on her birthday but I do buy a cake and put it on the table in front of her with a single candle stuck in it. We watch it burn down, the noise of the bin lorry outside filling the silence between us. Then I blow out the flame and hand her the cake.

It wasn't supposed to turn out like this. I had a plan. I did everything I could to follow it through, but things didn't go quite as I'd intended — because the world can fall apart in an instant and one small lie can change how people see you. Although I don't believe in God, I do wonder if he's punishing me — whether this child was sent here as revenge for what I did. Because when I look at her I see nothing, feel nothing; she might as well be a stranger, someone else's child. She doesn't look a bit like me with that thick, black hair, and she's far too big for her age. The folds of fat on her thighs make it hard to find trousers to fit her. During my pregnancy, I bought loads of expensive clothes for her that I couldn't really afford, but I might as well not have bothered. She's nothing like the children in the advertisements and looks ridiculous in dresses from Ralph Lauren or Calvin Klein. They don't suit her at all as she's not one of those pretty little girls the clothes were designed for.

At first I thought of giving her up for adoption. I pictured the couple who would take her in and care for her as if she were their own. If I had done that, perhaps my parents would have stayed in Iceland. The last I had heard from them was a few days after my daughter's birth when they sent me a letter in the post. I instantly recognised my mother's writing on the envelope and ripped it open like a hungry child. The envelope contained nothing but a card with a conventional message, underneath which my mother had written their names. Not Mum and Dad, just their Christian names, as if I were a distant relative rather than their own daughter.

So I try to moderate my expectations the day after her birthday when I see an envelope with her name on it in my mother's decorative hand. The envelope is crumpled and dirty, as if the postman had dropped it in a puddle. When I get inside the flat, I put it on the kitchen table, make myself a coffee and try to control my breathing. I don't open it until I am sitting down with my mug.

The envelope is thin but there's something loose inside it. When I open it, a delicate silver chain falls out onto the table. It's designed for a child's neck and attached to the chain is a small silver pendant bearing the letter H: the first letter of my daughter's name.

Bergrún heard the laughter as soon as she opened the door. The sort of laughter that makes your stomach ache and stops you from breathing. When had she herself last laughed like that? Probably not since she was a teenager. Fannar was a good man, clever, safe and dependable, but he wasn't funny. They sometimes laughed together, but it seldom lasted long and it wasn't the kind of breathless hilarity she could hear now, coming from Hekla's room.

She went to the door and listened for a moment or two before knocking. Just so she could experience it again — those days which, in memory at least, had been so full of tantalising possibilities. When she was a teenager she had felt as if things would always be like that. As if adulthood was a long way off and she would always be this young girl who didn't have to make decisions about who she was or what she wanted to do with her life. Time had seemed to stretch out to eternity, but now that Bergrún thought back, it was incredible how few years that stage had in fact lasted. Adulthood had crept up on her and, before she knew it, everything had changed. She still had the same friends, but these days when they met up they no longer lay on the bed, listening to music on a cassette player and giggling about boys. No, they talked about mortgages, politics and pay rises. About their husbands, children, colleagues and other people they knew. They never laughed like the girls were laughing now.

'Hekla?' She opened the door cautiously, and the girls finally caught their breath. All three were lying on the bed, the inevitable phones in their hands, their socks in a heap on the floor.

'Yes?' Hekla said, sitting up a little, still breathless from giggling.

'Would you like to stay for supper, girls? I was thinking of ordering pizza.'

'Uh, yeah,' Dísa said, then caught herself up: 'I mean, yes, please.'

'I just need to ask my mum,' Tinna said.

'Me too,' Dísa added.

'I'll call your mothers,' Bergrún said, thinking what sweet girls they were. Always so polite and well spoken, yet so different from each other. Tinna was tall, with a mane of what looked like dyed-blonde hair, big-boned without being overweight. She was quieter than Dísa and didn't say much, but when she did speak, she chose her words carefully. She wasn't exactly shy but came across as reserved. Withdrawn. Quite unlike Dísa, who didn't have a shy bone in her body and spoke to Bergrún almost like an adult. Bergrún sometimes forgot she was only fifteen; she would often come and sit in the kitchen for a chat while Tinna and Hekla were absorbed in their phones.

Bergrún knew both girls' parents quite well, their mothers especially. They had become good friends through their daughters, or as good friends as women can be at their time of life. That was another thing that had changed as Bergrún grew older: she didn't have intimate friendships like before. She no longer had confidantes she trusted and who knew her inside out. Nowadays, she and her friends chatted over coffee and shared the odd secret or a little gossip; enough to bring them closer to one another, but never too close. Never enough to risk showing anything other than their best side.

It wasn't long after Bergrún had closed the bedroom door that the giggling started up again. She wondered if Hekla had been this happy at Maríanna's. She was pretty sure she hadn't. There had been endless problems with friends, or rather with the lack of them, at her school in Borgarnes. Hekla had confided in her one Sunday evening before Maríanna's disappearance. Bergrún had noticed her growing increasingly apprehensive as the day went on. Hekla had become ever more silent, her eyes more distant, until Bergrún had eventually taken her aside and asked what was wrong. Not if something was wrong but what it was.

Hekla had burst into tears and said that she was always alone at school. That being alone among a group of people was so much worse than being alone when no one else was around. 'Please, please, don't make me go back,' Hekla had implored her, and of course Bergrún had phoned Maríanna and explained the situation. Couldn't she let Hekla stay a little longer in Akranes until she was feeling less miserable? But, no, of course it wasn't possible: Hekla had to go to school. Always the same indifference from the woman who called herself a mother. Not that this was a problem anymore, Bergrún thought to herself, as she selected the number for Tinna's house.

* * *

Gígja was sitting at the kitchen table when Hörður got home. In the high chair beside her was the latest addition to their horde of grandchildren; number five, a dear little thing with a fine head of hair who had just celebrated her first birthday.

'Should you be babysitting?' Hörður asked as he opened the fridge. He knew Gígja was often tired after her radiotherapy, and his attention had been caught by all the shopping bags in the hall when he came in. His wife and daughter clearly hadn't been idle while they were in town, and now here Gígja was, looking after her granddaughter instead of resting. He didn't mention the shopping, though, as he didn't want to sound critical.

'Oof, don't be like that,' Gígja said without taking her eyes off the grandchild she was feeding. 'I find this far more relaxing than lying on the sofa with my feet up.'

'Yes, but don't the doctors recommend —?'

Gígja interrupted: 'If I die tomorrow, I'd rather spend my last day with my family than alone in bed.'

Hörður grunted, unable to understand how she could refer so casually to her own death. It made him uneasy. Gígja smiled at him, the wrinkles deepening around her eyes. She complained about them, but Hörður found them beautiful. They gave her a warm, merry look, reminding him of what a good life they'd had together and how much laughter they had shared, and when she smiled like that of course he couldn't help smiling back. Laying his hands on her shoulders, he kissed the top of her head.

Gígja had cut down her hours at work while the treatment lasted — officially, at least. She thought Hörður didn't know that she sneaked in every day and brought work home with her, as well as babysitting her five grandchildren, completely ignoring the doctor's orders to take it easy. Of course he should talk to their kids and ask them to spare their mother during the weeks that she was undergoing treatment. He would have to take care that Gígja didn't find out, though, or he'd never hear the end of it.

Hörður sat down opposite her and made a face at the little girl. She put her head on one side and stared back at him with her big eyes. He had never been particularly good with small children. He never knew what to say to them or how to behave, and felt stupid if he put on a baby voice, like so many people did.

'Shall we just order a takeaway this evening?' Gígja suggested. 'I didn't have time to go to the supermarket and there's hardly anything in the fridge.'

'I'll do it,' Hörður said, getting up and going into the sitting room.

Gígja popped a piece of bread and pâté into the little girl's mouth, only for her to spit it straight out again, the saliva dribbling down her chin.

'Are you full, sweetheart?' Gígja said, wiping her mouth with the bib. 'Shall we see if Sibbi and the others want to stay to supper?' she called to Hörður. 'They're meant to be coming round in a few minutes.'

'Yes, we could do that,' he replied. He rang his son's number, resisting the urge to flop on the sofa and close his eyes. He loved Gígja and often reflected that he couldn't have chosen a better companion in life, but he couldn't help wishing they were a little more alike. Gígja was never happier than when she had a house full of people and children, and all the accompanying commotion. Of course, he wanted that too, but it was possible to overdo it. Sometimes he would have given anything just to enjoy a quiet evening alone with her.

* * *

The floor of the showers in the Jaðarsbakki pool was awash with soap suds. A group of girls who had just finished a swimming lesson had been vying with each other to pump soap out of the dispenser on the wall in order to blow bubbles. Elma picked her way carefully over the slippery floor to the only free shower for the obligatory pre-swim wash. Then she hurriedly pulled on her costume and went outside, relieved to leave behind the deafening shrieks of laughter in the changing rooms.

The darkness and the underwater lights that billowed when Elma lowered herself into the pool combined to give the scene a slightly eerie atmosphere. The chilly air made the water seem pleasantly hot, and she immediately launched herself into swimming lengths. It was good to feel the water caressing her body. She always felt as if she were entering another world the moment her head went under, blocking out almost all sound. She had quickly given up on the gym, which was heaving as usual at this time of day. People were queuing for the few machines on the terrace above the sports hall.

Swimming allowed her to mull over the case in a relaxed way. She, Hörður and Sævar had met that afternoon to go over the details again, but had drawn no new conclusions. Maríanna had left her job on reception at an earth-moving contractor's at twelve on the day she vanished. A signal from her phone had been picked up in Akranes at 15.07. Had she been alone or had she had company? And what had brought her to Akranes? According to the data from her computer and phone, no one called or messaged her. Could she have thought Hekla was here?

And what about Sölvi? His alibi was slim. He lived

alone, and when Maríanna didn't show up for their date and didn't answer his calls, he had just hung around at home then gone out for a drink somewhere. Then there was the question of Hekla's father. There was no record of his identity. Elma had tried without success to discover who he was back in the spring. No one had known anything about him, least of all Hekla herself, who took her second name, Maríönnudóttir, from her mother. Elma would have to dig deeper to find out more.

So was there any chance it could have been a stranger — someone with no link to Maríanna? These were the toughest cases to crack. When there was no overt motive, just a random killing. The wrong person in the wrong place. But in Iceland, murders were hardly ever random. There was generally a motive, however trivial it might appear. A quarrel in a bar or friction between neighbours. Hörður's hunch was that the killer was someone Maríanna knew well.

In the end, Hörður had told them to start the next day in Borgarnes, with the police officers who originally handled the case, then to talk to Maríanna's colleagues and friends, and Sölvi, of course.

After forty lengths, Elma heaved herself out of the pool and got into the hot tub. She was out of breath from powering up and down, but the tiredness soon melted away in the delicious heat. It was peaceful outside and there were only a few other people in the hot tub. Small droplets glittered in the glow of the outdoor lighting and she closed her eyes, letting them land on her face.

Suddenly two hands grabbed her shoulders from behind, making her gasp.

She whirled round. 'Sævar! Are you trying to kill

me?'

Sævar laughed and lowered himself into the hot water beside her. 'I knew you'd be here.'

'So you decided to scare the living daylights out of me?' Elma was suddenly aware that her face must be all red and blotchy from her swim. After a physical effort, her complexion sometimes looked like a map, with its irregular patches of red and white.

'Guilty.' Sævar grinned.

'You should have come for a swim with me. The exercise would do you good.'

'Are you saying I'm fat?'

'No, that's not what I meant.'

'I feel as if you're saying I'm fat.' Sævar glowered at her.

Elma rolled her eyes. It didn't pay to take Sævar seriously. He enjoyed winding her up and was always catching her out. She fell for it every time, only cottoning on when she spotted that teasing glint in his eye.

'Anyway,' she said. 'I went over the times of the phone calls again. There were very short intervals between Maríanna's calls to her daughter. It looks as if something must have come up. She kept ringing Hekla every few minutes, so it must have been urgent, whatever it was.'

'Mmm,' Sævar said, tipping his head back to wet his hair. 'Like what?'

'Search me. Then there are all those calls Bergrún made to Maríanna in the days before her disappearance.' The water was getting too hot: Elma raised herself up a little, letting the chilly air play over her shoulders. 'They must have been about Hekla. Perhaps Maríanna went to Akranes because she thought

Hekla was there.'

'It's possible,' Sævar said. 'But that doesn't explain why she was found dead in the lava field by Grábrók. Unless you're implying that Bergrún killed her.'

A man in his sixties got into the hot tub with them and reached out to switch on the massage system, then reclined in the spot with the strongest jets, closing his eyes.

Elma had to raise her voice a little so Sævar could hear her over the noise of the water. 'No, I'm not implying that at all, just wondering what happened on the way there. And also whether Hekla could have something to hide; whether she could have gone over to Akranes. Then again, of course, it could have had something to do with Maríanna's family. Or with the man she was going to meet. Sölvi could have come round early, and Maríanna could have been in some sort of trouble or even danger. But why ring Hekla in that case? Why not ring the emergency number or—?'

'Elma, I only caught about half of that,' Sævar interrupted, his eyes still closed.

Elma gave him a nudge, then shook her head, resigned. Even to her, it sounded as if she was blurting out a stream of incoherent thoughts, so perhaps it was just as well Sævar couldn't hear her. She had a tendency to become so obsessed with work that she couldn't focus on anything else. Sævar obviously didn't suffer from the same problem. He looked perfectly relaxed at her side. Perhaps she should follow his example and turn her thoughts to something other than work. But that was hard with cases of this magnitude. She leant back and closed her eyes too. Shortly afterwards the massage jets stopped and the hot tub grew quiet again.

'Anyway, what were you saying?' Sævar sat up.

Elma shot a glance at the man who was sitting nearby, then murmured: 'I just said we ought to interview Hekla more thoroughly. She's the main person who might know something.'

'I agree. Let's do it tomorrow,' Sævar replied.

'Though we'd also need to check...' Elma began but her words were drowned out by gurgling sounds as the old man switched on the jets again. Sævar leant forwards to hear but Elma shook her head. She lay back with her head on the side of the tub and watched the billows of steam dancing in the air above them.

Eighteen Months

The midwives said it would get easier with time, and I suppose they were right. Some things are easier now that I've started work. We wake up, I get her dressed and drive her to the childminder's. Then, for a whole eight hours, I don't have to think about anything except myself and my job, and I love my job.

I work on reception at a legal practice in the centre of town. I get to dress smartly, answer the phone and greet people who come to the office. I make a note of meetings, send letters and finally feel like myself again. Most of the lawyers are men, but there's one woman working there. She's tall and dignified, always wears a trouser suit; her hair is immaculate and so are her long, beautifully manicured nails. She's a few years older than me and we sometimes chat in the coffee room. I want to be her friend but most of all I want to be her. When no one's looking, I check out the information about law degrees on the university website and day-dream that one day that could be me. I immerse myself in this world that seems so remote from the life I've been living for the last couple of years, but, after work, reality takes over. I'm a single mother again, living in an ugly high-rise flat, with neither the time nor the money to do a degree.

The traffic is heavy, but I'm in no hurry, though I'm already late. When I finally arrive, it's obvious from a mile off that the childminder isn't happy. The door opens the instant I knock, and she's standing in the hall with the girl in her arms.

'You're late,' she says tersely, pushing the untidy, mousy hair back from her face. She's got a large, purple birthmark covering half her right cheek that I can never stop myself staring at. It looks like a map.

'Sorry, I got held up. It won't happen again.' I smile and try not to think about the fact that my daughter is only a few centimetres away from that revolting blemish.

'You'd better pull your socks up,' the childminder says. 'There are plenty of other kids waiting for a place, and I can't be doing with people who make me overrun. I finish at five.'

'I understand. Of course I understand,' I say, taking my daughter from her. I refrain from pointing out that it's only ten past five. What could she possibly have been intending to do in those ten minutes that was so important?

'Next time I'll have to charge you.'

'It won't happen again.' I keep smiling, though I have a strong desire to punch her in her unmade-up face. The childminder literally pushes me out of the door before I can dress my daughter in her outdoor clothes. Of course she starts screaming the moment I take her in my arms, and I hurry to the car, child perched on one hip, her things clutched in my other hand.

'Damn,' I mutter as I drop a mitten in the freshly fallen snow. With difficulty I manage to open the car door and manoeuvre the little girl into the child seat. She screams, and snot leaks out of her nose, smearing across her cheek. Why do children have to be so dirty? She hits me in the face and pulls my hair while I'm strapping her in. I want to scream back at her but bite my lip and count to ten. When I turn to retrieve the mitten, I get a shock.

'Did you drop this?' A man is standing behind me, holding out the brown glove.

'Yes, thanks,' I say, taking in his straight nose and dark eyebrows.

'Tough day?' he asks with a grin.

'Er, yes, actually.' I laugh. I brush my hair back from my face and hope I still look OK. I always make an effort for work: straighten my hair or put it up, wear black eyeliner and regularly touch up my lip gloss during the day.

'She got you there,' he says.

'Sorry?'

'Your cheek's bleeding.'

'Oh,' I say, wiping my face and feeling it sting. 'Poor thing, she's tired and ... I suppose we've both had a bit of a rough day.' I try to laugh again but am suddenly conscious of how ridiculous I must look. The bun that was so smart a few minutes ago is now leaking strands of hair, and I'm probably scarlet in the face from the struggle. I'm wearing nylon tights and high heels too, despite the wind and snow. I don't exactly look like the mother of the year, but then I already knew that.

'Don't apologise, I can imagine what it's like.'

I doubt it but I don't say so. Just nod and give an embarrassed smile, then get ready to go, suddenly eager to escape the situation.

'Going to pick up her daddy now?' he asks before I can get in the car.

I stop, smiling inside. That question can only mean one thing.

'There is no daddy, just us two.'

'Oh, right,' the man says, and now it's his turn to look embarrassed.

I decide to make life easy for him. Before he can utter another word, I say: 'I'll give you my number.'

He rings the following day and we arrange to meet up. As I'm pretty much alone in the world and don't exactly have babysitters coming out of my ears, the only option is to invite him round to my place. I can hear him hesitating. He'd probably rather have met me at a restaurant or bar, well away from the baby and the flat, which just shouts out that a single mother lives there. Then he says yes. Yes, he's prepared to come round. Why not this evening? That sounds good. Better than good, I want to say. I don't want to think about how long it is since I last spent an evening with someone other than her.

That evening she seems to sense that something's up. She cries while I'm bathing her. Cries while I'm putting on her night things and refuses to eat. As usual when she's in this mood, it's not enough for her simply to cry. No, she attacks me as well. Tries to scratch and bite, then flings herself on the floor, at the risk of doing herself a serious injury. I grab her head to protect it, but then she gets hold of my cheek. She squeezes and I scream, and before I know it my hand has swung at her face. An involuntary reaction. I hear the slap echoing around the flat and for a few split seconds there is complete silence. But only for a few seconds, because then the screams begin, more ear-splitting than ever before.

Looking at the clock, I see that it's far too late, and before I know it I'm crying too. The tears stream down my cheeks, stinging as they enter the grazes left there by my little girl. I happen to glance in the mirror and flinch at the sight of myself with swollen eyes and scarlet cheeks, scored with scratches. How am I supposed to meet the guy now? How am I supposed to meet any man? The girl is still lying on the floor, and I straighten up and look at her, feeling a twitching in my fingers. I'm so angry. It's all her fault. I want to pick her up and hurl her into her bedroom. The longer I stare at her, the more violently angry I feel until in the end I can't bear it anymore.

'Shut up, you little brat!' I scream, and, grabbing hold of one of her arms, I drag her into the bedroom.

The moment I've shut her in, there's a knock on the front door. I freeze and stand there, paralysed. There's another knock. I lean back against the wall, then slide down it, hiding my face in my hands.

He doesn't knock again, just turns round and leaves, and I never hear from him again. I picture him running away from the building, getting into his car and wiping the cold sweat from his brow. Thinking, that was a narrow escape. Of course, he must have heard the screams, the crying and all the rest. How long had he been standing out there? What must he think of me?

I heave a sigh, rub my eyes and look towards the bedroom door. The girl is still crying but the sound is quieter now, more like a monotonous mumbling. At that moment I feel no desire to comfort her. No desire to see or hear her. At that moment I wish she was somebody else's problem. I'm ashamed of my thoughts; I'd never voice them aloud, but that's how I feel. I can't go in to her. I have no love to give her. Instead, I lie down on the sofa, pull a blanket over myself and fall asleep.

Tuesday

Hekla gave up trying to drag the brush through the tangled clump of hair at the back of her neck. She tried to smooth it down with her hands, hoping no one would notice the bulge it created. Then she pulled on a hoodie and slung her school bag over her shoulder.

'I'm off,' she called as she passed the kitchen, where they were sitting eating breakfast. She could hardly believe this was her family now. Of course, Hekla had been part of it for as long as she could remember, but she no longer had to drag herself away on Sunday evenings.

'Don't you want anything to eat?' Bergrún called after her.

'I'm not hungry,' Hekla replied, putting on the big, thick down jacket they'd given her for her birthday.

'I can give you a lift,' Fannar said, looking up from the paper. 'And you know you don't have to go in. Everyone will understand if you'd rather take it easy at home today after the news you've just had.'

'No, I want to go in.' She'd been at home all day yesterday and actually couldn't wait to get out of the house for a bit. 'I'll walk. It'll wake me up.'

Fannar studied her for a moment or two, as if to reassure himself that she was OK, then dropped his eyes to the paper again and carried on reading.

Over the last few months, Hekla had grown used to living full time in Akranes. She didn't particularly miss her mother and enjoyed having a normal family at last. A family that went on trips and ate supper together. They even had a curfew and were angry if she broke it. This struck her as funny, but in an odd way she appreciated their scolding, as it showed that they cared.

She glanced back over her shoulder at the house as she set off towards school. This was where she lived now, a large detached house with two cars outside and a Jacuzzi on the terrace. Oh, how she used to envy Bergur those times when she had to go back to Borgarnes. Back to Maríanna. The name alone was enough to stir up memories that she preferred to keep locked away in the deepest recesses of her mind.

The first time Maríanna went missing, she had been alone for three days. She was so young at the time that all she could remember was her hunger and her terror during the nights. Perhaps they weren't even real memories, just something she had invented in her own mind because she knew that's what it had been like. But she couldn't forget the fear that had filled her every time she was left alone after that. She did have a clear memory of the second time. Then she had been on her own for more than a week without anyone noticing. At ten years old she had at least been able to look after herself; take herself to school and eat what she found in the freezer or in tins in the cupboard. No one had found out until Bergrún and Fannar came to collect her for the weekend. Hekla had wished then that Maríanna would never come back and that she would be allowed to stay with Bergrún and Fannar forever.

She paused for a moment to adjust the music on her phone. Then she put in her wireless headphones and carried on walking with Radiohead blasting in her ears. She had reached the footpath connecting two streets when someone grabbed her from behind.

'You jumped,' Dísa laughed. 'God, how you jumped. Seriously, you should have seen your face.'

'Oh, shut up.' Hekla jabbed an elbow at Dísa and grinned at Tinna.

The friends all walked the same way to school, along a gravel path that ran through a residential area. They usually went together, but this morning Hekla hadn't opened any of the others' messages as she'd wanted to be alone. Obviously there was no chance of that now.

Dísa talked nonstop. She was outgoing and cheeky, the polar opposite of Hekla, who was terribly shy and reserved. Dísa had curly hair that she described as chestnut but was really just ginger. Tinna made merciless fun of the fact, though she herself dyed her hair blonde, so it wasn't as if she was happy with her original colour either. Tinna's mother read the news on TV, and her father sometimes invited them for a drive in his convertible. Tinna thought it was horribly cringy. What kind of loser would think of buying a convertible in Iceland?

Tinna and Dísa helped Hekla forget that they were surrounded by a hundred other kids who she used to find so intimidating. These were friends she could laugh with, and the anxiety that used to dog her steps the whole time at school was a thing of the past. For as long as they were together, at least.

Before this, no one had ever taken any notice of Hekla, whether it was the other kids at her school in Borgarnes or Maríanna. She might as well have been invisible. Maríanna used to want Hekla to stay in her room and not get underfoot, saying she had enough trouble coping with her own problems. She used to have visitors round and go out on the town, while Hekla had felt unwanted. She'd been made to feel as if her birth had destroyed something important in Maríanna's life, though she didn't know exactly what. But she could see it in her eyes; there was never a moment when she wasn't aware of it. Recently, though, it had dawned on Hekla that Maríanna hadn't been much older than she was now when she got pregnant, and this had helped her to understand a number of things. Then again, Hekla had never asked to be born, so why should she have been made to suffer for not fitting into Maríanna's vision of her future?

It was quite different with Bergrún. She actively wanted Hekla near her. She wanted to do all kinds of stuff with her, wanted to talk to her and would ask her several times a day how she was feeling. Not in a superficial way that invited the standard 'I'm fine' — no, her interest was genuine, and she even used to ask if Hekla was quite sure — was she quite sure she was OK?

Before, Hekla had always envied her friends, but now she no longer needed to. She had a mum and a dad, a younger brother, a new coat and a smart phone — how could she fail to be happy? There was only a very small part of her that missed Maríanna, that remembered the hugs and the odd kind word. A tiny part, like an insect gnawing at her insides, that refused to go away.

* * *

Dagný's messages ran into the dozens. Links to pages offering catering; suggestions for decorations and alcohol, and who should make the speeches and which music they should play. Elma knew her sister loved organising parties, but it had never occurred to her that she herself would be expected to pore over every tiny detail. Who cared whether the napkins were white or royal blue? But Elma should have known better after going to the birthday parties Dagný had given for her sons, Alexander and Jökull. Going by the fancy cakes, the giant bunches of balloons, and all the cake pops, anyone would have been forgiven for thinking they were to mark landmark occasions, like the boys' confirmation. Whatever happened to just baking a sponge cake and letting the kids decorate it themselves with smarties? Elma suspected it would have made her nephews just as happy, or even happier, judging by the way they unceremoniously picked the icing off their beautifully decorated birthday cakes. And she was quite sure that her father wouldn't notice, still less care, whether the napkins were blue or white.

Elma started to write a reply, asking if it really mattered, but had second thoughts and deleted the message. Recalling what their mother had said at the weekend, she wondered if she was perhaps too sharp with Dagný. Not polite enough? Taking a deep breath, she opened the websites again and tried to form an opinion. Dark-blue napkins rather than white, lamb rather than beef, and meringue rather than French chocolate cake.

She was just pressing 'send' when Sævar knocked on the door. 'Ready?'

As they set off for Borgarnes it started to rain. Leaden-grey clouds piled up overhead, the sky turned dark, and Elma felt as if she had been enveloped in a blue-grey cocoon. Large raindrops exploded on the windscreen, forcing the wipers to work overtime.

'They're quite soporific,' Elma remarked. 'Those raindrops.'

'You know you mustn't fall asleep, Elma,' Sævar said. 'Not while you're in charge of a valuable cargo.'

'Which is what? You?'

'Of course. A priceless cargo.'

'I'll do my best,' she promised.

Sævar was used to her nodding off when he was driving and she was in the passenger seat. There was something about the noise of the engine that meant she slept better in the car than anywhere else.

'She was very young when she had Hekla,' he remarked, after a short silence. 'Only sixteen.'

'And we never did find out who the father was.'

There wasn't much background information on Maríanna in the files, only a list of places where she had lived and worked, and the names of close members of her family.

'I suppose it isn't that strange that his name wasn't registered,' Sævar said, 'considering that Maríanna was only fifteen when she got pregnant. Perhaps the father was a kid of the same age.' He turned up the heater as he gazed out over Borgarfjörður, or what he could see of it through the dense, grey rain. He added, after a pause: 'Why would someone move to Borgarnes, of all places?'

'Why did you move to Akranes, of all places?' Elma shot back.

Sævar was from Akureyri, the capital of north Iceland, but had moved south to Akranes as a teenager with his parents and younger brother. Several years later, his parents had been killed in a car accident, leaving the two brothers alone in the world. Sævar never spoke about the accident but he did talk a lot about his brother, who was called Magnús, nicknamed Maggi, and lived in a community home. Elma had never seen him without a smile on his face, and whenever they met he gave her a long, affectionate hug. The thought made her smile too.

'Dad got a job in Reykjavík, but Mum wouldn't hear of living there, so I think Akranes was a compromise. I'd happily have carried on living in Akureyri.'

'Why didn't you move back?' Elma guessed the answer as soon as the question was out of her mouth.

'Because of Maggi,' Sævar said. 'He was happy in the home here, and I was too young to look after him on my own.'

'I hope you don't have any regrets.'

'Never.' Sævar grinned.

Elma slowed down as they drove over the bridge into Borgarnes. The town was small and pretty, sitting on its isthmus, almost surrounded by the waters of the fjord. On a good day, it had a spectacular view of the mountains that rose in ranks along the west coast, right out to the Snæfellsnes Peninsula. Elma had always loved the white church with the pointed spire, black roof and long, narrow, arched windows that dominated the town from the top of its little mound. It was all the rocky hillocks and fir trees that made Borgarnes so different from the bleak, flat landscape around Akranes.

The two towns enjoyed a certain rivalry. Elma remembered that a group of children from Borgarnes used to be bussed in to her school in Akranes when she was young, but they had been regarded as outsiders, and fights had frequently broken out between them and the local kids. Since Akranes was closer to Reykjavík, it was easier for the inhabitants to go shopping in the city or even to commute there. They tended to look down on Borgarnes as a country town, which was ironic since its popularity with tourists these days meant that it could boast far more shops and restaurants than Akranes.

When Elma was younger, her family used to go on outings to the swimming pool in Borgarnes, especially when the three water slides were put in. Afterwards, they would go to Skallagrímsgarður and eat the big iced buns called snúðar, or to the Hyrnan service station for hot dogs. In her memory the town was always bathed in sunshine, but that seemed improbable, given how rarely the sun broke through the clouds in Iceland. But then the world seemed a much brighter place through a child's eyes.

Maríanna's former co-worker couldn't tell them anything of interest, and their conversation didn't last long. The son of the owner, he was a young man in his early twenties, with long hair and a ring in one ear. He said Maríanna had gone home at midday as she always did on Fridays. He hadn't noticed anything unusual in her behaviour, but then they hadn't talked much or been particularly good friends. It was the same as he had said back in the spring.

After that, Elma and Sævar had dropped into the Borgarnes police station and talked to the officer who had been the first to visit Maríanna's home after the phone call from Bergrún. It was the same story there: the officer couldn't add anything to what had been written in the report. He had looked around Maríanna's flat without noticing anything of interest. As Hekla was a minor, he had got in touch with the Child Protection Agency, after which it had been decided that she should stay with Bergrún and Fannar until Maríanna turned up.

Neither visit produced any new information or brought them any closer to finding out what had happened. Elma was hoping that their next visit might prove more profitable, however, as they were going round to see Maríanna's closest friend, a woman called Ingunn. Elma drummed impatiently on the steering wheel, leaning forwards as she tried to spot the house numbers.

'Are you sure it's the right address?' She had driven back and forth along the same street several times without seeing the number they were looking for. 'I just don't understand it. This part of the street ends at twenty and the next part begins at thirty-eight. Where the hell are the numbers in between?'

'Do not despair,' Sævar said with mock formality. 'I'll activate the satnav on my phone.'

A few minutes later they had found the address, which turned out to be numbered completely out of order with all the other houses in the street.

'This just doesn't make sense,' Elma growled, as they pulled up to the kerb, exasperated by the illogical arrangement. 'Who on earth would think up—?'

Sævar put a hand on her arm. 'Shhh, breathe in … and out,' he said, in the soothing tones of a yoga teacher.

'Hey, I am calm!' Elma protested, grinning in spite of herself. His hand was warm and surprisingly soft. Sævar winked at her, let go of her arm and undid his seat belt.

It was still raining. Elma put up her hood as she got out of the car and scurried over to the house, which had a covered porch.

Ingunn turned out to be a heavily built woman whose loose blonde hair reached right down to her waist. She came to the door with her baby son in her arms and another boy, a toddler of about two, clinging to her thigh.

'Come in.' She moved, causing the little boy to fall over and start howling. 'Sorry, Davíð, love,' she said, trying to bend down, which was easier said than done.

Elma's heart gave a slight lurch when she heard the boy's name. This little Davíð could easily have been her Davíð as a child. There was something about his features and those brown eyes. She bent down and stroked the boy's head. He was so surprised, he instantly stopped crying.

'What have you got there?' she asked, pointing at the teddy bear he was clutching.

The boy eyed her doubtfully.

'Is it a grizzly bear?' she ventured.

'Polar bear,' the little boy said, loud and clear, after a moment's hesitation.

'A polar bear, of course. Silly me.' Elma smiled and straightened up.

Ingunn took the toddler by the hand and led him inside. 'We can sit in the kitchen.'

Elma and Sævar sat down at a large table. Elma trod on something that crumbled under her foot. She lifted it to see a Cheerio ring. Looking around, she noticed that the floor was covered in them. Ingunn put the younger boy in a high-chair, then poured Cheerios onto the table in front of him. He immediately swept most of them onto the floor, before carefully placing one ring in his mouth. From elsewhere in the house they could hear more children's voices.

'You've got enough to keep you busy,' Elma remarked to Ingunn, who was fetching mugs and a carton of milk.

'Five boys,' Ingunn said.

'Wow, that's almost a football team,' Sævar exclaimed.

'Getting on for it,' Ingunn said, looking unenthusiastic at the idea. Davíð followed his mother around the room, clinging to her trouser leg, with no apparent intention of letting go.

'There,' Ingunn said, putting a pot of coffee and some mugs on the table. 'Do you take milk? I've got sugar too, somewhere. And I swear there were biscuits as well.' She started opening cupboards and drawers.

'This is absolutely fine, we don't need any biscuits,' Elma hastened to assure her.

'Here they are,' Ingunn announced, triumphantly holding up a packet. She took out a small tray and arranged them on it. 'I have to hide them, or they're gone before you can blink. The trouble is, I'm always forgetting where I've put them, so I keep finding ancient packets at the back of the cupboard.'

Elma smiled as she studied her. Ingunn was wearing a baggy T-shirt with Relax written on the front, which seemed ironic in the circumstances. She probably hadn't noticed that the baby had puked up on her, leaving a crusty white streak on her shoulder. Elma's eyes were drawn to Ingunn's incongruously long fake nails, painted with dark-pink polish, which seemed totally out of keeping with the rest of her appearance. They could hardly be practical when she had to take care of all these children. Not that Elma had any experience of long nails. Or babies, for that matter. Dagný hadn't trusted her to babysit Alexander until he was out of nappies and could talk. She still hadn't been allowed to look after Jökull, who was only two.

Ingunn hoisted Davíð onto the chair beside her and clipped him into a harness before handing him a biscuit. Only then did she finally take a seat herself, pour the coffee and draw a deep breath.

'Right,' she said. 'You wanted to ask about Maríanna, didn't you?'

'Yes. You've probably heard that her remains turned up at the weekend.' As he said it, Sævar glanced at the little boy.

'He doesn't understand,' Ingunn said, and she was probably right. Little Davíð was murmuring something to his polar bear, and feeding it and himself in turn.

'It now appears to be a criminal matter,' Elma said, realising how formal she sounded. 'I mean ... Maríanna was murdered, so we're investigating the whole thing again and trying to discover what happened.'

Ingunn nodded. 'I knew she'd never kill herself.'

Elma regarded her in surprise, then leafed back through her notebook. 'But ... I understand Maríanna sometimes talked about wanting to die. You said that last spring when we were investigating her disappearance.'

'Yes, sure, but that was a long time ago. She could be a bit up and down — she had good days and bad days, you know? But the week before she vanished she was in a really good mood. She was so excited about Sölvi.'

'How did you two get to know each other?'

'By coincidence. Maríanna moved here five years

ago, and we met at the swimming pool. I was there with my brats and when one of my older boys fell over, I had to get out and go and get it seen to. She offered to keep an eye on the other boys for me and after that we became friends.'

'Do you know why she moved to Borgarnes?' Maríanna hadn't had any family in the town or any other links to it that the police had been able to discover.

'Er ... no, not exactly. She'd lived in Sandgerði before that, then moved to Reykjavík the year Hekla was born. But I don't think she ever liked living in the big city.'

'I see,' Elma said. 'Then why didn't she just move back to Sandgerði?'

Ingunn shrugged. 'No idea. All I know is that when her mother died — what ... five years ago? — she came to live here. She didn't have any contact with her dad, so I'm guessing she just wanted a fresh start, but I didn't interrogate her about it. I got the feeling that something happened to make her family leave Sandgerði. Something to do with her pregnancy, maybe. I mean, she was only fifteen. But that's only a guess. Anyway, it felt like it was a long time since she'd last been depressed, so there were no problems like that. Well ... of course she had problems, but nothing she couldn't handle, you know?'

Elma nodded. 'Did Maríanna never say anything about Hekla's father?'

'No ... only that the boy hadn't been ready for fatherhood. I got the impression he was some kid her own age. But then, you know, boys always get away with it, but girls are left holding the baby — their lives changed forever, while you can't see the fathers for dust.' Ingunn shook her head. 'Look, maybe I didn't make it clear enough back in the spring, but the more I thought about it, the more convinced I was that Maríanna couldn't have disappeared deliberately.' The younger boy began to wail. There were no more Cheerios left on the table and he was stretching out his arms towards the biscuits.

'What makes you so sure?' Ingunn hadn't said a word about these suspicions when Elma spoke to her on the phone during the original inquiry.

'Oh, because of Hekla. Maríanna would never have abandoned her like that.'

Elma took a sip of coffee and tried not to wrinkle her nose. It was like dishwater. 'How was their relationship?'

Ingunn shot a glance at the little boy, who was still straining towards the biscuits, in spite of the harness. 'Well, there had been some problems with Hekla, but nothing serious. Just typical teenage stuff. She wanted to go out in the evenings and to school parties in Akranes. Apparently she had friends in the town because of the family she used to visit there. Maríanna also suspected she had a boyfriend.'

'Right. Her support family.' Elma had to raise her voice to be heard over the baby's screams.

Ingunn gave in and handed him a biscuit. The screams stopped immediately and he beamed from ear to ear. 'Yeah, the support family.'

'Didn't Maríanna get on with them?'

Ingunn sipped her coffee, narrowing her eyes at Elma. 'Why? You don't think they had anything to do with it?'

'Is that something you find likely?'

Ingunn shrugged. 'It did cross my mind but it

seemed so … well, far-fetched. I know Maríanna wasn't too keen on them, but the few times I met them they both seemed really nice. At least the woman did — Bergrún.'

'Why wasn't Maríanna keen on them?'

'I suppose it must have been because of Hekla. I know Bergrún made no secret of the fact that she wanted Hekla to spend more time with them. All her time, preferably. And I think Hekla would have preferred to live with them, which can't have been much fun for Maríanna.'

Elma nodded. That fitted with what she'd heard before.

'So you didn't believe she could have deliberately done a disappearing act — because of Hekla,' Sævar recapped. 'Do you have any theories about what did happen, then? Could there have been someone who had it in for her, for example? Was she in some kind of trouble?'

'Um, I don't know…' Ingunn seemed to hesitate before going on: 'I just … I thought she seemed in a specially good mood the week she vanished and I assumed it was because of Sölvi.'

'Do you know Sölvi?'

'Yes, very well,' Ingunn said. 'He's my husband's best mate. We set them up. Or, you know, if the relationship hadn't ended before it began…'

Elma put down her coffee mug. 'To be honest, we have very little to go on in our investigation into what happened to Maríanna, so we'd be grateful for any information. Even minor details could be important, so if there's anything you know…'

'I don't. I can't think of anyone who would have wanted to harm Maríanna. I mean, she wasn't the type to get into quarrels with people. She always avoided any sort of conflict.'

Elma nodded again. 'So you can't think of anyone?'

'No, but...' Ingunn looked down at her mug, then up again. 'But Bergrún had been ringing her non-stop all week and it was driving Maríanna mad. It was something to do with her wanting to have Hekla to stay, although it wasn't their weekend. I'm not saying she had anything to do with it, but it's the only thing I can think of. I mean, she was the only person Maríanna quarrelled with, apart from Hekla.'

* * *

Sölvi, who had obviously just woken up, received them in a vest and checked pyjama bottoms. All the curtains were drawn and his flat smelt of stale air and sleep.

'I work up at Tangi,' he said, and Elma knew he was referring to Grundartangi, the big ferro-silicon plant in Hvalfjörður. 'I was on night shift.'

They were shown into a tidy living room, to which Sölvi had obviously tried to add some homely touches. Elma took a seat on a dark-grey chaise-end sofa and studied the paintings on the walls. They were all abstracts, which looked as if the paint had been spattered randomly onto the canvas.

They explained why they were there, and Sölvi repeated what Elma had already read in the files. He had got to know Maríanna through Ingunn and chatted to her online for a while before they decided to go on a date. He'd only actually met her once before the fateful day. A few days earlier, they had gone to Kaffi Kyrrð in Borgarnes and, after chatting there, had agreed to meet up again later in the week.

'I didn't really know her, though,' Sölvi said. 'I mean, we didn't chat about anything very personal; it was just small talk. I told her stories about my travels, because I've been all over the world. When you're single and don't have any kids, there's nothing else to do.' He smiled, then continued. 'I got the impression Maríanna wanted to travel but couldn't because of the girl. What was her name again?'

'Hekla,' Sævar said.

'That's it. I asked her about Hekla's dad, but all she said was that he wasn't part of their lives. Maybe she didn't even know herself who he was.'

To Elma's ears, this sounded a little judgemental. If Maríanna had got pregnant at fifteen, she was unlikely to have slept with that many people. Elma thought it more likely that Hekla's father had been unwilling to acknowledge the child. Perhaps he had only been a kid too, as Ingunn had suspected, or else had been someone older who had a family — a wife and children. If so, that would have made Maríanna the victim of abuse too.

'What happened the day you were supposed to meet?' Sævar asked. 'When were you last in contact?'

Sölvi scratched his head. 'Haven't I already answered all these questions?' He searched their faces, then, receiving no answer, went on: 'Like I said, we decided to meet up that Friday because I was due to finish a stint of shift work. I finished on a night shift and slept until midday. We were planning to go out to dinner at a fancy restaurant, so I sent her a text at lunchtime. She replied, saying she was looking forward to the evening and asking what time I was going to pick her up. I asked if six was OK but she didn't answer.

Then, yes, as the day went on, I did ring her, just to check what time she was expecting me.' He took a deep breath then let it out. 'Her phone was switched off.'

Elma dropped her eyes to her notebook. 'You rang just after three?'

'What? Yeah, right. Something like that.'

'Why so early?' Sævar asked. 'You weren't meeting until that evening.'

'I just found it strange that she hadn't answered my text, so I decided to try calling her.'

'You drove past her flat too, didn't you?'

'Er, yes.'

'And knocked on her door?'

'No, I just drove past. I couldn't see any movement. All the lights were off and there was nobody home.' He smiled bitterly. 'Anyway, I just thought, *Fuck it. She's obviously gone out*. I drove past again that evening anyway and all the lights were still off.'

'But this was in May, when it wouldn't have got dark until late,' Elma said. 'So how could you see if the lights were off?'

'I don't know — maybe it was a bit later. Maybe it was night by then. I'm not sure.' He laughed, only to break off abruptly when they didn't join in. 'I wasn't going to let some girl make a fool of me again. I was pissed off, to be honest. I'd reserved a table and everything. Bought a new shirt the day before that cost an arm and a leg. It was a bit shitty of her not to let me know, don't you think?' He directed his question to Elma, as if it was her job to explain why women were so inconsiderate.

Elma met his eye. 'Well, there was a good reason for that.'

Elma couldn't contain herself once she was back in the car. 'What a prick! What the hell did she see in him?' Apart from his biceps, Sölvi didn't seem to have much to offer.

'Bit pushy,' Sævar agreed. He had got in the driver's side this time and started the car.

'A bit?' Elma snorted. 'When she doesn't reply to his text, he rings her, and when she doesn't answer the phone, he turns up outside her house. I don't know about you, but I find that more than a bit pushy.'

Sævar shrugged. 'The passionate type, maybe? Won't give up straight away but is determined to chase after love?'

'No, Sævar, that's not passionate; it's bordering on stalkerish.' She knew Sævar was teasing but she couldn't help taking offence.

'Well, maybe,' Sævar conceded. 'But the evidence suggests Marianna was in Akranes sometime between two and three, and he rang a number of times after that. Would he have done that if she was with him?'

'Maybe,' Elma said. 'Maybe it was deliberate, to cover his tracks.'

'We could check whether Sölvi's phone was picked up by a mast near Akranes at the time in question.'

'Men like him really piss me off. It's like they think they're entitled. Entitled to receive attention from girls. If they don't respond, they're bitches or worse.' Elma would have like to clap Sölvi in irons purely for being obnoxious.

'But isn't it a basic courtesy to tell someone if you don't want anything to do with them?' Sævar countered. 'I can understand why he was pissed off. But you're right — of course he should have just shrugged it off, not turned up outside her flat and kept phoning her like an idiot.'

'Mmm,' said Elma. Another aspect of the conversation was troubling her. 'Sævar, Hekla was home all evening the day Maríanna vanished, wasn't she?'

'Yes.'

'Then why were all the lights off?'

'Good question... But, like you said, the sun sets late in May, so he wouldn't necessarily have been able to see if anyone was home or not. And if it was late when he drove past the second time, she might have gone to bed.'

'I suppose so,' Elma said, then added, after a pause: 'But it doesn't fit with the descriptions we've had of Hekla. Wasn't she supposed to be the rebellious teenager who ran off to Akranes whenever she got a chance? Surely Hekla wouldn't have meekly stayed at home on a Friday evening when there was no one there to keep an eye on her? It would have been the perfect chance for her to slip out. Especially if she had a boyfriend in Akranes.'

Sævar abruptly pulled over, and Elma glanced at him, her eyebrows raised.

'We'll have another chat with Hekla when we get back to Akranes,' he said. 'But shouldn't we look in on Maríanna's old neighbours again before we leave Borgarnes? They might have noticed if Hekla was home or not that evening.'

Twenty Months

'She should be saying a few words by now.' The nurse wears a horribly insinuating expression as she says this. 'Are you sure she hasn't said a single word? Not even 'mama' or 'dada'?'

I shake my head slowly, wondering if I should lie, just to be spared all these questions and that penetrating gaze. 'Perhaps I just didn't understand,' I say, smiling. 'I mean, she's tried to imitate animals and that sort of thing. Or, at least, that's what the childminder says.'

'But not at home?'

I shake my head, biting my lower lip. It's a long time since I last tried to look at a book with her. The moment I sat down on the floor and took her in my arms, she started flinging herself around, grabbing at my hair and trying to bite me. It was all I could do to stop her banging her head on the floor, and in the end I gave up and turned on the television. She seemed contented with that.

The nurse makes a note, and I crane my neck but can't read her writing upside down.

'Has she started walking?'

'No, but she crawls all over the place.' That's not actually true. Mostly she just sits there, focusing intently on the TV or on the only toys that seem to interest her — the green plastic soldiers given to us by the woman next door. An old woman, who said her grandchildren were too big to play with them now. I don't suppose they're intended for toddlers, but at least she's quiet as long as she's chewing

them, so I leave her to it when we're at home.

'Can she stand up with support?'

'Not as far as I know...' It's starting to feel like an interrogation.

The nurse looks at the girl. 'Right, shall we see how big you are and how much you weigh?' she says, smiling at her. Of course she doesn't receive so much as a flicker of a response. My daughter stares at her watchfully with her grey eyes, and I just hope the nurse doesn't get too close because, if she does, the girl will probably hit her. She doesn't like it when strangers come too near.

The nurse tells me to undress her and lay her on the changing mat. I sigh under my breath, anticipating a struggle. She starts screaming as soon as I unzip her anorak.

'There, there, darling,' I say soothingly, as she grabs hold of my hair and yanks hard.

'Is someone in a bad mood?' the nurse says, as if she's seen it all before. But I'm pretty sure she's not used to children like this.

Once the weighing and measuring are over, all I want to do is cry. Not because she's way above average height and weight but because she behaved like a wild thing. Her screams have subsided into sobs, and she's sitting on my lap, her eyes red and swollen. It's no good trying to cuddle her because she'd be sure to sink her teeth into my cheek or pull my hair again. So I sit her on my knee, careful to keep a little distance between us. The nurse doesn't say anything. If she finds our relationship abnormal, she doesn't betray the fact.

Somehow I've got my daughter dressed again, but she's not wearing a jumper under her anorak and I'm fairly sure her trousers are on back to front. I want to run out of the room before the nurse can tell me what an unfit mother

I am. Perhaps she'll suggest that the child should be taken away from me and put in a home. The thought isn't that bad, and for a moment I have a vision of my life before she arrived, when I didn't have to be responsible for anyone but myself.

'Right,' the nurse begins, forcing out a smile. 'I'd like to take another look at her. There could be some obstacle that's preventing her from achieving her normal developmental curve, so there are a few things we need to rule out. And of course there are exercises you can do at home to help her.'

'I see,' I say. I listen to her talk, smiling and nodding, trying to act like a mother who actually gives a shit about what she's saying.

The girl is still shaking when I put her in her car seat but she's so exhausted that she sits unmoving while I do up the harness. I get into the front, pick up the jumper that's lying on the passenger seat and put it over my mouth before screaming as loud as I can. I want to hit something, preferably that interfering nurse who looked at me with those judgemental eyes. I think about my parents and so-called friends, all those people who are not here to catch me. Because I feel as if I'm falling. As if I'm in freefall, about to hit the ground hard.

Hot tears are trickling down my cheeks, and I let them. I catch sight of her in the rear-view mirror. She's staring at me, her red eyes now dry and grave. Then something happens to her face. The corners of her mouth twitch and slowly stretch upwards. Is that a smile? I wipe away my tears and gape at my daughter in astonishment. It is a smile. Small, crooked and freakish, but a smile nonetheless. I've never seen her smile before. Not at me anyway. She sometimes smiles when she's playing or looking at books, but never at me. Does she think it's funny that I lost control of myself like that? I dry my face, turn round and gaze at her. She doesn't take her eyes off me, still wearing what I believe is a smile on her face, despite the hiccupping sobs that break through at regular intervals. I turn back again and start the engine. I've come off worst in so many battles in my life recently, but this is one I have no intention of losing.

It was so boring. Totally pointless. She was never going to get a job that had anything to do with maths, that was for sure. So why on earth did she have to sit there and learn all those equations that the teacher wrote up on the board? Honestly, she couldn't care less what X stood for. Beside her, Tinna was focusing intently on the teacher, while Dísa sat at the desk behind them, regularly throwing them notes containing dirty messages.

Hekla stole a glance at Tinna. She had one hand under her chin and was sucking her lower lip, as she often did while she watched the teacher. Hekla was always envious of her skin. She was one of those girls with a seriously good complexion, smooth, without a single blemish. Tinna didn't even bother with foundation; she didn't need to, though she used black eyeliner, creating a perfect little flick at the outer corners of her eyes.

'Stop staring at me, you perv,' Tinna whispered suddenly, without taking her eyes off the teacher.

Hekla hastily looked away but was relieved when she saw that Tinna was grinning. That was the trouble with friends: she never knew how she was supposed to behave around them and she was terrified of losing them. Things could change so fast. One day, for example, her friends might want to build a snowman in the garden or watch *Mean Girls* in bed; the next, they'd rather go for a drive with much older boys. Sometimes they'd get pissed off when Hekla wanted to go home early and started behaving as if everything she said was terribly childish and lame. Hekla would feel utterly depressed and sure they'd never talk to her again, only to wake up next day to messages full of hearts and smiley faces as if nothing had happened.

'Guess what: Alfreð's been staring at you the whole lesson,' Tinna suddenly whispered in her ear. Hekla could smell her strawberry lip salve. Her stomach rumbled. She hadn't eaten any breakfast and had only nibbled a rye flatcake at lunchtime.

'Really?' she asked, automatically glancing round. Alfreð dropped his eyes to his desk, embarrassed, and tucked his mousy hair behind his ears. Hekla quickly returned her gaze to the front, her thoughts wandering guiltily to Agnar.

Tinna pinched her arm. 'Don't look round, you idiot.'

Hekla rubbed her arm, making a face.

Tinna smiled. 'Hey ... leave it to me. We'll go for a drive with him this evening. I'll sort it.'

'What about Agnar?' The thought of dumping him made Hekla a little nervous.

'I'll take care of that too,' Tinna whispered back.

'Girls!' The teacher was looking at them. His voice was sharp and a little weary. 'Are you paying attention?'

'Yes, of course.' Tinna smiled innocently.

'In that case, what was I saying?'

Tinna narrowed her eyes and considered the question on the board. The teacher sighed and was about to turn back to it when Tinna said: 'The lowest common denominator of one thousand and fifty is forty-three.'

The teacher glanced at the board, then back at Tinna.

'I'm right,' Tinna said. 'Just check it.'

The teacher cleared his throat. 'That's correct, Tinna. Maybe you'd like to come up to the board and show the other pupils how you arrived at that solution?'

Tinna gave Hekla an inconspicuous wink, pushed back her chair with a screech, and went up to the front. She solved the problem, quickly and confidently, before returning to her seat. Behind her, Hekla could hear Dísa smothering her giggles.

* * *

As they got out of the car, a cat sprang to its feet in front of the house and came over to rub against their legs, mewing pathetically. Elma bent down to scratch it behind the ears, only to whip back her hand when she noticed the state of its eye. It was so septic that the cat could hardly open it and yellow pus was seeping from a deep wound in the corner.

'It's a stray,' Sævar said, with a low whistle. As if sensing their suspicion, the cat suddenly darted off towards a dilapidated warehouse that stood nearby. They watched it vanish into a bed of withered nettles.

Elma shuddered. She looked up at the house, which consisted of a basement, ground floor and attic, with curved, decorative wooden roof and window boards, and a balcony with a wrought-iron rail. Maríanna and Hekla used to live in the basement flat, but it appeared that new tenants had since moved in. Elma glimpsed movement behind the Venetian blinds and heard music coming from an open window. At the end of the garden was a sheer drop, from below which they could hear the crash of waves. The rain had eased up while they were driving to the house, as abruptly as if someone had turned off the taps hidden in the clouds, and now warm rays of sunlight were breaking through. Two ravens had perched on a nearby street-light and were calling to one another, their harsh croaking echoing down the street, sounding preternaturally loud in the hush following the rain.

'I'd never send my kids out to play in that garden,' Elma said, looking towards the cliff.

Before Sævar could answer, the front door opened and a woman in a stripy jumper appeared.

She shook their hands, introducing herself as Elín. 'Unnar should have been home by now — I don't understand what's keeping him. Come into the kitchen. Mum's looking after my youngest boy, which should give us a bit of peace.'

They followed her inside. The house was old by Icelandic standards, with deeply scored floorboards and narrow doorways. Elma glanced into the sitting room as they passed and saw an older woman sitting in there with a child on her lap, reading a book together.

'Mum comes and babysits during the day while we're at work,' Elín explained, after offering them both a soda water. 'She's retired, which helps us bridge the gap until they're old enough to go to nursery school.'

'Are there new tenants in the flat downstairs?' Sævar asked.

'Yes, unfortunately. Teenage girls who were full of promises about good behaviour when they moved in. Now, though, it looks as if we'll have to throw them out. We can't get any sleep at the weekends.' Elín sighed as she put glasses on the table in front of them. 'Is there any news about Maríanna? Was it really her they found?'

'Yes, it was,' Elma confirmed. 'That's why we're re-examining everything and checking in case we missed something the first time round.'

'Ah, right, I understand. I can't believe anyone would have wanted to harm her. She was very nice.'

'Did you know each other well?'

'Yes and no. I mean, Maríanna had been living in the basement since before we bought the house. She'd rented it from the previous owner, then from us for the last two years. She used to knock on the door if she needed to borrow eggs or milk, and we'd take it in turns to mow the lawn in summer and that kind of thing, but our relationship never became any more personal than that. I don't really know why — perhaps it was just the age gap. She was ten years younger than me. Unnar used to lend her a hand if something needed fixing in her flat. Drilling holes for screws, putting up shelves, that sort of thing. They got on quite well together, though she and I never really became close. But then Unnar gets on with everyone.'

'What about Hekla? Did you have any contact with her?'

'Maríanna's daughter? No, she wasn't the outgoing type at all, I don't think. She hardly even said hello when you met her outside.' Elín gave a wry smile. 'But they were good tenants and never gave any trouble, not like those girls who are living there now.'

'Do you remember what time you got home on the Friday Maríanna vanished?' Sævar asked.

'Yes, I'd just gone back to work,' Elín said, 'so I'd have been home at around five.'

'Did you notice any comings or goings after that?'

'I don't really remember.' Elín wrinkled her brow. 'It's so long ago. But, yes … I told the police when they asked back in the spring that the basement door slammed just before suppertime. It sticks a bit and you have to slam it to make sure it closes properly. It's enough to shake the whole house. You can just imagine what it's like now that those girls are in and out at all hours.'

Sævar caught Elma's eye, no doubt thinking the same as her. The long time gap since Maríanna's disappearance made everything so much more difficult. People had started to forget, or to create new memories without realising it, since memories could be unreliable and hazy and had a tendency to change over time. Often what resulted was a mixture of truth and imagination.

'Did you happen to see any cars outside?'

Elín sighed and shook her head. 'No, I don't think so.'

'What about before that?' Elma wasn't prepared to give up yet. 'Did you notice if Maríanna and Hekla often had visitors?'

'Yes, sure. Maríanna sometimes had friends round, and from time to time I saw Hekla's foster parents pick her up. I chatted to them briefly once — an extremely nice couple. I also saw Hekla getting into a car late in the evening several times. I couldn't understand what her mother was thinking of to let her go out with a much older boy like that. But, having said that, I don't actually know if Maríanna saw him, because he parked further up the street and Hekla always left the house in a hurry. To be honest, I did wonder if I should mention it to Maríanna, but I didn't like to interfere.'

'Did you get a good look at the boy?'

'No, unfortunately. But he had a driving licence, so

he must have been quite a bit older than her.'

'Did you notice the make of car?'

'A dark-green Volvo S80,' Elín answered straight off. 'Probably a 1999 or 2000 model. A complete wreck.'

Sævar frowned. 'You don't happen to remember the licence number too?'

Elín laughed. 'No, I'm afraid not.'

Elma smiled and wrote down the make of car.

'Ella, love, you don't have a banana, do you?' The grandmother came into the kitchen. 'Sorry, I didn't mean to interrupt. The poor little thing's just so hungry. He's asking for a 'nana'.'

'There should be one somewhere.' Elín got up to look.

'Hello, I'm Bryndís,' the older woman said, holding out her hand. 'Ella's mother. The babysitter. And grandmother. Are you from Reykjavík? Or from Akranes, maybe? Is this about Maríanna? That was so awful. Don't tell me someone did something to her?'

Elma decided to answer only the last question. 'We're trying to find out,' she said. 'Had you started babysitting by the fourth of May, when she went missing?'

'Yes, actually,' Bryndís said, taking the banana Elín handed her. 'Thanks, dear. Yes, it was in March that I started babysitting, wasn't it?'

Elín nodded.

'Were you here on that Friday?' Elma asked.

'Yes, I expect so,' Bryndís said. 'Though I may have gone out for a walk with the pram. I can't quite remember.'

Yet again Elma cursed the long interval of time that had elapsed. 'Did you happen to see Maríanna or Hekla that day? Or anyone else, for that matter?'

Bryndís smiled apologetically. 'Oh, I'll have to think. Let's see, it was Friday, the fourth of May … No, you know, I can't possibly remember that far back.'

'Well, if you do remember something…'

'But Maríanna used to have Wednesday mornings off, and I'd always knock on her door and invite her up for a coffee. Silly for the two of us to be sitting here alone in our separate flats, not talking to each other. And I clearly remember the last time she came round, which must have been on, what, the second of May?'

'I didn't know that, Mum.'

'I don't have to tell you everything I do, dear.' Bryndís gave her daughter's shoulder a light squeeze.

'Did anything strike you as unusual about her that day?' Elma asked. 'Anything she was worried about or…?'

'No, nothing like that.' Bryndís seemed surprised. 'I'd have come to see you if I'd thought there was any reason to. Maríanna and I used to talk about this and that. I don't think she'd have been interested in sharing stories about her love life with an old woman like me, but we talked a lot about the past. I told her about my years in Copenhagen and my time at boarding school, and Maríanna told me about her youth. Though the subject always seemed to stir up … what shall I say? … sad memories for her. But then of course she'd lost both her brother and her mother.'

Elma nodded, a little disappointed. 'So nothing emerged that struck you as odd?'

'Well … there was that phone call,' Bryndís said at last. 'Her phone rang and she looked at the screen, then switched it off. She didn't want to answer.'

'Did she tell you why?'

'No, she just glanced at the phone and switched it

off. I've no idea why.'

It would be a simple matter to find out who had called by going over her phone records again. Elma suspected that the caller had been Bergrún, as they had checked out everyone who rang Maríanna in the months before her disappearance. 'Anyway, if you remember anything else, this is my number.'

Bryndís took the scrap of paper with Elma's number and studied it thoughtfully. 'I once asked Maríanna why she moved here. I always got the feeling she was a bit lonely. She didn't have any family here, any relatives. She didn't really answer, but I got the feeling that something bad had happened. At least, it was obvious she didn't want to discuss it.' She looked up. 'Anyway, what am I rabbiting on about? I'd better go and give that young man his banana.'

Bergrún had indeed tried to ring Maríanna on the Wednesday morning before her disappearance. They had obviously fallen out, and tomorrow Elma would ask her what it had been about. When she got back to the office, she went through Maríanna's social-media activity again but couldn't find any messages from Bergrún. In fact, Bergrún didn't have a Facebook account and there was very little information about her online. She seemed to be one of the few Icelanders who didn't use social media.

But there were two things that attracted Elma's attention when she examined Maríanna's interactions. First, there were the messages from Sölvi. He had sent Maríanna daily messages, which usually began with questions about where she was and what she was doing. It may all have been perfectly innocent, yet it seemed unnecessarily intrusive to Elma.

Why hadn't he just asked how she was?

Second, all Maríanna's interactions with Hekla consisted of reprimands or expressions of irritation. For example, Maríanna had frequently sent Hekla messages telling her to come straight home, to which she hadn't received any reply. Some of the messages listed the chores awaiting Hekla at home: hoovering, stacking the dishwasher, cleaning the bath. Others were criticisms of things she'd done: left her clothes on the floor, finished the milk or forgotten to turn off the lights. Elma searched a long way back in time without finding a single positive comment from Maríanna, however trivial. It was as if the messages to Sölvi and to Hekla had been written by two completely different people.

As Elma lounged on her parents' sofa, she tried to come up with reasons why Maríanna should have kept trying to get hold of Hekla the day she went missing. Hekla had had a swimming lesson, and her mother must have known that. What had Maríanna wanted and why had she gone over to Akranes?

She was distracted by the theme tune to the news, which suddenly resounded around the sitting room, after which a blonde woman appeared on screen and bid the nation good evening, in the firm, straight-talking manner that characterised newsreaders.

'She lives in Akranes,' Elma's father remarked, without looking up from his book of sudoku.

Elma made a noncommittal noise in reply and at that moment her phone, which was lying on the sofa beside her, vibrated with yet another text message from Dagný. Feeling she didn't have the energy to read it just then, Elma locked her phone, hoping Dagný wouldn't be pissed off with her. The plan was to go into Reykjavík together on Saturday to buy their father's present. Elma was dreading it, envisaging that the whole thing would be a disaster. There was so much she wanted to get off her chest, but she knew it wouldn't be a good idea. When visiting Maríanna's old home earlier that day, she had noticed a playground beside the house that had brought back an incident from her childhood. Or rather, it was a particular piece of playground equipment: the climbing frame. The dome-shaped kind that you could hang from, exactly like the one at the recreation ground near her parents' house before it had all been torn down and replaced with new equipment.

'Dad?' she said.

Her father grunted, which meant he was listening. He was sitting in an armchair, his attention switching back and forth between his sudoku puzzles and the television. From the kitchen they could hear the sound of water boiling.

'Do you remember when Dagný and her friends abandoned me at the playground and you had to come and rescue me?'

Her father grunted again, without raising his eyes from his puzzle.

'Why…?' Elma hesitated. 'How old do you think I was then?'

'I expect you were about six or seven.'

'They told me they were going to run and fetch me a lollipop,' Elma remembered. 'I waited there for hours while it chucked it down with snow until some woman who'd been watching me from her window got worried and came over.'

Her father took off his glasses and looked at her. 'It wasn't hours …' He appeared much younger all of a sudden, without his glasses, in the dimly lit room, illuminated only by the glow of the TV screen. Elma had always been a bit of a mother's girl, perhaps because her father was often a little distant. He worked as a carpenter and used to come home late, tired, dirty and smelling of sawdust and furniture oil. As a child, Elma had mostly taken her troubles to her mother, as Aðalheiður loved nothing better than solving problems and was happiest when she was needed by as many people as possible. Elma had been able to tell her mother more or less everything, whereas her father was more reserved and took little interest in everyday affairs. 'The way I remember it, and I have a good memory,' he said, 'is that Dagný was jealous about what had happened the evening before.' There was a slight smile playing over his lips.

Elma frowned. 'What happened the evening before?'

'Of course you wouldn't remember. After all, it wasn't anything you did or would have been particularly aware of.'

Elma sat up and turned down the volume a little.

Her father went on: 'The evening before, Dagný was revising for a test. She was supposed to learn all her times tables, but it wasn't working, as she never was any good with numbers. We were going over them with her when you came in — only six years old and just started school, and you knew them all. You effortlessly recited the tables Dagný was supposed to be learning. Since she was three years older, I don't think it exactly boosted her self-confidence.' He chuckled.

'I don't remember that at all,' Elma said. Though she did recall that she had always found her schoolwork quite easy, at least in the junior classes. She had been quick to learn to read and do sums, but that was mainly because she was always competing with Dagný or sitting like a little dog at her side while she did her homework.

'No, but I'm sure Dagný will never forget it. You should have seen her face.'

Elma laughed and lay back on the sofa. 'Even so, it was a bit drastic to abandon me out there just to … to punish me for being better at maths than her.'

'Oh, I'd have done the same,' her father said, and turned up the volume again.

⋆ ⋆ ⋆

It looked like moss, only browner and denser, as if it had been kneaded into a lump. Hekla watched the boy arrange the grass in a careful line on the white Rizla, then roll it up, deftly twisting one end.

'Who'd like to do the honours?' he asked formally, holding out the joint.

'Well, if no one else is volunteering,' Dísa piped up, before any of the others had a chance to say a word, and reached for the joint.

The boy held out the lighter, and Dísa leant forwards and sucked in the smoke. Then she blew it out at Hekla and laughed, before passing the joint to Tinna, who did the same.

The four of them were sitting on the back seat, Hekla on the right-hand side, Tinna in the middle and Dísa on the left, on the lap of a boy called Binni. He was a year older than them and his parents were very rich, according to Dísa. Apparently they owned a massive yacht in the Med and a house in Spain. He was also quite hot, with straight teeth and a strong jaw. Always dressed in clothes with prominent logos.

The car cruised along the streets of Akranes, past the docks and through the area where the cement factory had once stood but was now nothing but a ruin.

'Weird to think 'the Stub' will soon be gone,' said Alfreð, who was sitting in the passenger seat. He leant forwards to peer up at the factory chimney that did indeed resemble a giant cigarette butt, though it was a long time since any smoke had risen from it.

'It's quite sad, actually,' Binni said. He inhaled the joint Tinna had passed him and held the smoke in his lungs for a few seconds, before blowing it out, filling the car with grey clouds.

'Shit, man, I can't see a thing with you pot-heads in the car,' complained Gísli, who was sitting behind the wheel. He was a bit of a minger, but they put up with him because he'd agreed to drive them around town whenever they liked. He tried to make up for his appearance by being funny but didn't realise that his lame jokes only made things worse.

Binni grinned at the girls, then rolled down the window on his side and said, 'I mean, isn't it, like… the symbol of Akranes or something?'

'Are you seriously saying that the symbol of Akranes is a chimney that looks like a cigarette?' Tinna said mockingly. 'Isn't that kind of sad?'

The boys laughed.

'Maybe someone should paint it white. Then the symbol of Akranes could be, like, a massive joint. Wouldn't that be something?' Binni laughed at his own joke, then held out the joint to Alfreð.

'No, thanks,' he said, waving it away.

Hekla gave him a secret smile. Alfreð was a real sport nut. He was never seen in anything other than a hoodie and tracksuit, and always had his football boots ready in his bag. Hekla played football herself, and her trainer said she was in with a chance of being selected for the under-sixteen girls' national team. Hekla had never been good at anything, least of all games, but then Maríanna had never encouraged her to take up any sport. In fact, until Bergrún had persuaded her to go along to train with the Akranes Football Association, she had never even tried playing the game, except during PE lessons at her old school in Borgarnes, when she'd been too shy to move. The other kids had said she looked like a monkey when she ran, so she had tried to be as inconspicuous as possible on the pitch. As a result, she had been more surprised than anyone else when she turned out to be good at football. A natural talent, the coach had said, winking at her and making her cheeks burn.

Binni shrugged. 'What about you, Hekla?'

Dísa cuddled up to Binni, her eyes on Hekla. 'It's your choice,' she said, adding in English: '*Up to you.*'

Hekla hesitated and Dísa laughed. 'Oh, you're such a cupcake. Come on, give it here; she doesn't want any.'

'No, I *do* want some,' Hekla said quickly. Ignoring Alfreð's look, she took the joint. Her face grew hot as they all watched her inhale. Managing by some miracle to suppress her cough, she handed the joint on.

Dísa burst out laughing again and turned to Binni.

Hekla tried to shut her ears to the moans and sucking noises they were making. Tinna elbowed her unobtrusively and rolled her eyes. Although Dísa thought nothing of kissing boys in front of them, Hekla just couldn't get used to it.

'Everything OK?' Alfreð was watching her, but Hekla couldn't interpret his expression.

'Yes, sure.' Suddenly she was ashamed of herself. What on earth was she doing? Not that she felt any different from usual. The world didn't seem especially funny or weird. She was just so tired all of a sudden, so wiped out that she could have fallen asleep right there in the car, in spite of the smoke, the booming music and the sucking sounds emanating from Dísa and Binni. It was a relief when her phone rang and it was Bergrún, telling her to come home.

Two Years Old

We said goodbye as if we'd see each other again next week. 'Bye,' then the door was slammed. No 'it was nice knowing you' or 'thanks for letting me look after your daughter for eight hours a day, five days a week'. No, she literally slammed the door in my face as I stood on the steps with my little girl. Though, to be fair, the childminder did give my daughter a quick hug before handing her over. As usual, I had to tear her away, kicking and screaming, and straining her arms towards the woman. I'll never understand why my daughter preferred her to me.

Anyway, the nursery school is much better. It's a few minutes past five as I dash in through the gate. All the other children have gone home and so have most of the staff. I open the red-and-yellow door with the handle at the top. Breathe in the fug of nappies and damp outdoor clothes.

'Sorry I'm so late,' I pant when I see the only remaining member of staff. She's sitting on the floor with my daughter on her lap and a book open in front of them. I feel a sharp pang in my chest and can't work out why. Perhaps it's guilt because we never sit companionably together like that. Usually when she's at home she just watches TV or plays with the green toy soldiers. In my opinion, children shouldn't be too dependent on their parents, so I've done my best to bring up an independent individual. Sometimes I watch other kids clinging to their mothers and fathers, and wonder if my method is wrong. But I never had the

kind of relationship with my parents where we hugged or expressed our feelings, and for a long time I resented the fact. Then at some point it occurred to me that while the other kids couldn't make decisions for themselves and cried on school trips because they were missing their parents, I was always self-sufficient. I was decisive, independent and confident, and that's how I want my daughter to be. Not reliant on anyone.

'It's all right,' says the woman, who's at least three times my age, with grey hair and a kindly smile.

'I was held up at work,' I lie, taking my daughter's anorak off the peg. 'And then the traffic was absolutely terrible. An accident on Miklabraut,' I add, further embroidering the truth.

The woman just smiles. 'Do you know, she's getting so good at saying what's in the pictures. Have you got a book like this at home?'

It's a large, hardback book containing pictures of all kinds of objects and animals. We don't have one like that at home. In fact, we don't have any books at all. I've never read much myself, apart from the books we had to read at school. And even then I just used to skim through them and get my friends to tell me what happened. I've bought nice toys for her, but those are mostly left untouched in her room. A china tea set with pink roses and a white table with two chairs. A Madame Alexander doll, which cost a bomb. But the only toys she'll play with are the little green toy soldiers that she clutches in her clumsy fingers, stubbornly refusing to let go. She grips them so tightly her knuckles whiten. Even when she's asleep, it's like she's afraid I'll try and steal them. Now she's older, she likes to line them up. It's not an easy job, and I can't understand how she has the patience for it. Her fine motor skills aren't up to the task yet and it takes her forever to get each soldier to stand upright. But she obstinately keeps at it until she's lined them all up in front of her, then just sits and gazes at them for a while, before picking them up and starting to line them up again somewhere else. Meanwhile, the expensive Madame Alexander doll sits ignored on her chest of drawers.

'Er, no. We don't have exactly that book.' I crouch down, my eyes on my daughter, and tell her to come to me. She doesn't so much as glance at me or move until the teacher gets up and leads her over. The woman still has the book in her other hand and now she holds it out to me.

'Take it,' she says.

I laugh. 'No, I couldn't...'

'There's nobody here but us. Just take it. She's been enjoying it so much.'

'But...'

'She needs to learn the words.' A serious note has crept in, under the teacher's friendly manner.

'OK.' I take the book, then turn my attention to my daughter. I bend down and put on her anorak. She does nothing to help, just passively allows me to dress her. That morning I'd put her in a white top but of course she's smeared ketchup all over it.

I can't stop thinking about the pretty blonde girl I saw when I dropped her off at the nursery school this morning. She should have been my daughter — I could almost see myself in her. Which no one could say about the dark-haired child standing in front of me. She has food stains on her face, has pulled out the plaits I put in her hair this morning, and she's far too fleshy. Most people would say it's puppy fat, which will disappear in due course, but the blonde girl I saw this morning didn't have any puppy fat. I've tried to be careful of what my daughter eats, but she's always hungry. She gobbles down her food, chewing it loudly with her mouth open so I can hardly bear to watch.

'There, sweetie,' I say, putting on her hat. When I try to zip her anorak up to the neck, she starts screaming. 'What's the matter? Did I hurt you?'

Moving fast, the nursery-school teacher swoops and unzips the anorak. There's a cut on my little girl's neck, just above the chain with her initial on it.

'Oh, ouch,' I say, filled with remorse, and try to put my arms round her, but she shoves me away and reaches out to the teacher instead.

'It was just an accident,' the teacher says, giving my daughter a quick cuddle before directing her back to me.

The atmosphere is awkward because we both know that this is not normal. Little children are supposed to want their mothers to comfort them, not nursery-school teachers they've only known for quarter of an hour. Feeling myself blushing, I say a hasty goodbye and we make for the exit. The woman calls after me:

'Don't forget this.' She's holding out the large, brightly coloured book.

I take it and feel the woman's eyes boring into my back until the door has closed behind us.

Wednesday

Elma's mobile rang in her office as she was pouring herself some freshly made coffee. She hurried back in with the brimming cup, grimacing when some hot drops spilt onto her fingers.

'Elma, how are you? Did I disturb you?' The warm, reassuring tones belonged to Davíð's father, Sigurður.

'No, not at all. I was out of the room for a moment and I'm fine, thanks. Plenty to do here.' She sat down and took a sip of coffee.

Sigurður had rung her regularly over the past year. When Elma hadn't heard from Davíð's parents for several weeks after the funeral, she had interpreted their silence as meaning that they blamed her for his suicide. In her state of mind at the time, their reaction had seemed perfectly justified.

'I hope I'm not interrupting,' Sigurður added.

'No, not at all.'

'Oh, good. I hope everything's going well.' He paused, then continued: 'It's Davíð's birthday on Saturday, and we'd love to have you over. That's assuming you'd like to come. I'll understand if you've got too much on and—'

'No, no,' Elma interrupted. 'I mean, yes. Of course I'd like to come. Sure, we're busy here but I can always make time.'

'Right then, it would be good to see you. We're just going to meet up at our house at five or sixish, depending on when you can get here. You know the way, of course.'

'Of course. I'll be there.'

Elma picked up her coffee cup and rotated her chair to face the window. A knot of fear had begun to form in the pit of her stomach at the thought of meeting Davíð's family again. She had been in touch with his sister, Lára, but had hardly talked at all to Davíð's mother, Þuríður, over the last year. The situation was both odd and unsettling, since they had got on well while Davíð was alive. Þuríður couldn't have been more different from Elma's own mother, who might have been cut out of a textbook used at Iceland's old School for Professional Homemakers — small, plump and bustling, always in an apron, with something bubbling away on the stove or in the oven. Þuríður, in contrast, had a svelte figure and wouldn't be seen dead in sensible shoes or trackie bottoms. In fact, her clothes were trendier than Elma's, and she had her roots touched up every six weeks, so no one would see a single grey hair on her head.

Elma's office door opened and she turned. As usual, her colleague marched straight in without knocking and plumped down in the chair opposite her. Begga was a uniformed officer, a couple of years younger than Elma and so blunt that she sometimes left people gasping.

'Hot tub and a bottle of red at my place this evening. Are you up for it?'

Elma's eyes travelled to the window, then back to Begga. 'Seriously? Have you seen the weather?' A gale was blowing outside, sweeping great sheets of rain across the car park, and the road to Reykjavík was closed at Kjalarnes until the worst of it had passed over.

'Uff, that's nothing.' Begga waved a hand dismissively.

'But you haven't got a hot … aha!' Belatedly, Elma caught on. 'Have you got the keys?'

Begga grinned, her dimples deepening. 'You're looking at a proud new house owner, thank you very much.'

'Wow, congratulations.'

Begga had hardly talked about anything for weeks but the small detached house she had bought after saving up conscientiously for ten years while living in her parents' basement. The money had only just stretched to cover the deposit on the little place, which she'd shown Elma countless pictures of. House prices in the area had shot up in recent years, perhaps as a knock-on effect of the soaring cost of property in Reykjavík. Some people chose to live in Akranes and commute to the city, simply to be able to afford a reasonably sized house.

'Thanks. And now you can't say no to my invitation to try out the hot tub, so I'll expect you on the dot of nine.' Begga got up, then paused in the doorway and turned round. 'And bring some red. No cheap rubbish either. I want a proper bottle.'

Elma was left with no choice, but then that was typical of Begga. Once she had made up her mind, there was little point in trying to resist. As if to remind Elma of what a bad idea it was, the window pane in her office rattled with the force of the wind. She sighed and hugged her jumper around her. It was nearly 9.00 a.m., just time to top up her coffee before this morning's meeting.

No one had seen Maríanna since twelve noon on Friday, 4 May. The last confirmation that she was alive was her phone call to her daughter at 14.27. After that, her phone had sent out a signal at 15.07, which confirmed that the phone was alive then — but not necessarily that Maríanna was.

Sölvi had rung her for the last time at just past five. After that he had called a mate, dropped by the Ríki to stock up on booze, then gone round and proceeded to get drunk at his friend's place. The CCTV in the state off-licence showed Sölvi just before closing time, with a half-litre bottle of vodka and a ten-pack of beer. No one could confirm his whereabouts between two and five o'clock, however. According to his friend, Sölvi had come round at suppertime, which meant there was also a period between six and seven that he couldn't account for. But this would barely have given him the time to make the half-hour journey from Borgarnes to Grábrók and back again, let alone dispose of a body in a lava field.

Elma blew on the scalding coffee before taking a sip. The previous day's crop of interviews had hardly produced anything new, though her thoughts lingered on Bryndís, the old woman who had drunk coffee with Maríanna on the Wednesday morning before she vanished. Could Maríanna's murder have been linked to her past? Why had Maríanna decided to move away from her father, her only living relative? She'd had no obvious reason to settle in Borgarnes. There were few job opportunities in the town and it wasn't as if Maríanna had been studying at the nearby University of Bifröst.

So far, Sævar had taken care of communicating with Maríanna's father, but perhaps they should pay him a visit together. When Sævar talked to him back in the spring, the father had explained that he had little contact with his daughter. He'd been sure that Maríanna had simply relapsed and gone on a bender, and would turn up again in a matter of days or weeks.

'What kind of trouble was Hekla in?' Hörður asked, after listening to the report of their trip to Borgarnes.

'Typical teenage stuff, I gather,' Elma said. 'Apparently she was always sneaking off to Akranes and wanted to spend more time with her foster parents than at home.'

'Or with her boyfriend,' Sævar chipped in.

'Her boyfriend?' Hörður frowned. 'Did she have one?'

'We suspect so,' Sævar said. 'Maríanna's neighbour told us she'd seen a boy hanging around in a car outside the house on several occasions.'

'And you think he was a boyfriend?'

'He must have been,' Sævar said. 'Presumably a bit older than Hekla too — if he had a driver's licence.'

'Do you think the boyfriend could have picked Hekla up on the Friday Maríanna vanished? And that maybe Maríanna was trying to get hold of Hekla because she wasn't at school?'

'But Hekla *was* at school,' Sævar said. 'I mean, her teacher confirmed the fact.'

'The form teacher only had classes until midday. Hekla was supposed to be at a swimming lesson between one and two.' Elma shrugged. 'Do you really think teachers notice if the odd pupil doesn't turn up?'

'Well, we can see if the swimming instructor remembers Hekla being in the lesson,' Sævar said. 'Wasn't that something we checked back in the spring?'

'No,' Elma said. It was becoming increasingly obvious how sloppy their original inquiry had been. She saw now that they had failed to investigate a number of things that would have been followed up if it had been a murder inquiry. But everyone had been so sure that Maríanna had killed herself.

'It would certainly explain why Maríanna drove over to Akranes,' Hörður said. 'Remind me, why did Hekla have those 'weekend' parents?'

Elma looked down at the files and sighed. All the pages of text did nothing but get in the way of her thoughts. 'We only looked into it in a cursory way in the spring,' she said. 'It came up when we contacted the Child Protection Agency to get a better idea of Maríanna's mental state. Hekla was originally placed with Bergrún and Fannar when she was three years old. A neighbour had heard the little girl crying for three nights in a row. In the end he knocked on the door and found Hekla alone in the flat, starving and in a bad way. The police were notified, and the girl was sent to be fostered. It turned out that Maríanna had gone out on the town and got carried away. What was supposed to be one evening had ended up being a week-long bender.'

'What, and she got the child back afterwards?' Hörður asked, astonished.

'Yes. I don't think Hekla was away from her for very long — perhaps six months or so. After that Maríanna agreed to have a support family — a family who cared for Hekla every other weekend — though I gather from Bergrún that Hekla often spent more time with them. She used to stay longer over the summer months and sometimes went on holiday with them.'

'Right, then,' Hörður said. 'We'd better interview Hekla and her support family again.'

'Yes, and another thing,' Elma said. 'Bergrún rang Maríanna almost every day during the week leading up to her disappearance ... I mean, murder.'

'Except on the day she was killed,' Sævar pointed out.

Elma pored over the list of phone calls and saw that he was right: Bergrún had rung every single day except that Friday.

'Ask her about it,' Hörður said. 'But don't forget that Maríanna was beaten to death. It was a brutal attack, to put it mildly. We mustn't forget that. Can you imagine Bergrún doing it?'

Elma pictured Bergrún. She was tall, delicately made and didn't look capable of beating anyone to death. But appearances could be deceptive, and Maríanna had been small. It wouldn't have required much strength to get the better of her.

'The only man in Maríanna's life was Sölvi,' Sævar said. 'We're going to take a closer look at his movements; check whether his phone left Borgarnes at any point.'

'You do that,' Hörður said. 'But could there have been other men in the picture that we don't know about?'

'Fannar,' Elma replied. 'We haven't checked what he was doing that weekend.'

'No. Just as well to have everything straight this time round,' Hörður agreed.

'What about Unnar?' Sævar suggested. 'The neighbour who lived in the flat above Maríanna's and apparently used to help her with DIY, putting up shelves and that sort of thing. Could he have been out when we called round because he was trying to avoid us?'

* * *

The last patient of the day had cancelled, which allowed Bergrún to finish work unusually early. On the way home she stopped off at the Kallabakarí and bought a length of Danish pastry. She had a craving for something sweet, and the fact the police were coming round gave her an excuse to buy a sugary treat to serve with coffee. She had arranged for Bergur to visit a friend after school, and told both Fannar and Hekla to be home by four. As it happened, Hekla had football practice then, but she would just have to miss it for once.

Bergrún opened the garage door and drove the car inside. In the hall, she was met by the fragrance of lavender and vanilla. Lovely — but perhaps a little overwhelming? She removed the scent balls from the radiator. Her footsteps had a hollow ring as she walked across the tiles in her shoes. There was nobody home but her. Where were Hekla and Fannar? It was already half past three.

She put the paper bag from the bakery on the kitchen table and got out her phone, but Hekla didn't answer. Bergrún hoped she hadn't gone to football, forgetting that she was supposed to come home. If she had, it would be impossible to get hold of her for the next hour. Perhaps, Bergrún thought, she should ring Fannar and ask him to drop by the sports hall. On the other hand, maybe Hekla had gone home with her friends.

Bergrún considered giving Tinna a call. The two girls had met when Hekla started football training a couple of years back. Bergrún had found it absurd that Hekla didn't play any sports, so one summer, when the girl was staying with them, Bergrún had signed her up for football, even though she would only be able to go to training sessions at the weekends she was in Akranes. What kind of parent wouldn't sign her child up for any leisure activities? Children ought to do sport or play an instrument; preferably both. Bergur took swimming lessons and was learning the trumpet. Bergrún had mentioned this repeatedly to Maríanna but never got more than a vague reply.

It was fortunate that Bergrún had had the sense to sign Hekla up for football, since that was how she had met Tinna and later Dísa. Through them, Bergrún had got to know their mothers, particularly Tinna's mother, Margrét. It had begun with an invitation to coffee one day when Margrét was picking up Tinna, and after that Margrét had invited Bergrún in when she came to collect Hekla. From then on they had started meeting earlier and sat chatting for longer, until in the end they didn't need the girls as an excuse anymore.

Tinna wasn't answering her phone, so Bergrún selected Margrét's number.

'They've been in Tinna's room ever since they got back from school,' Margrét said. 'They claim they're studying but, judging by the loud music, I find that hard to believe. Do you want me to send Hekla home? I can give her a lift as I'm on my way out myself.'

Bergrún gave a sigh of relief. 'That would be great. You're an absolute life-saver.'

'We'll be with you in ten minutes.'

'Thanks, Margrét. And we must meet up soon. Why don't you and Leifur come round for a meal at the weekend?'

Once they had finished their call, Bergrún glanced

at the clock and saw that it was a quarter to four. She opened the kitchen cupboard, got out some plates and arranged the Danish pastry on a wooden board, which she placed on the table. Then she went into the bathroom, put more deodorant under her arms and sprayed herself with perfume. Her light-brown hair hung dead straight to her shoulders. From habit, she tried to fluff it up a little but that only ever lasted a few minutes. No matter what products she tried, her hair remained stubbornly flat and lifeless. She blinked a few times, feeling how dry and uncomfortable her contact lenses had become. They had been irritating her since that morning. Unable to bear them another minute, she took them out and put on her glasses instead, then looked in the mirror at the forty-five-year-old woman, who stared back at her and smiled.

* * *

There were two rings in Hekla's left ear that Elma hadn't noticed before. The girl was wearing a hoodie again, but this one was white with a large American flag on the front. When Elma and Sævar entered the room, she was sitting at the kitchen table with her arms folded. Her expression was one Elma had often seen on kids her age, a combination of indifference and insecurity, as if what was happening had nothing to do with them, yet they were ready to go on the defensive at a moment's notice.

'I've already told you that I went home after swimming,' Hekla said in answer to their question. 'At three, I think, and she wasn't there.'

'Your mother tried repeatedly to call you. Do you know what she wanted?'

Hekla shook her head.

'Didn't she know you were at school?'

'Yes, but…' Hekla hesitated. 'I don't know. We had a fight and then … then she left a note, and I just didn't think any more about it.'

'What did you two fight about?'

Hekla opened and closed her mouth, then shot a glance at Bergrún, who said: 'It was about a football tournament that Hekla wanted to take part in. I tried to persuade Maríanna to let her come but…' Bergrún shook her head. 'Maríanna could be very difficult to talk to.'

'Was that why you kept ringing her during the week?'

'Yes. I tried to get her to change her mind. I said I could give Hekla a lift but … anyway, the disagreement escalated. Maybe I shouldn't have kept on at her like that, but I just found her attitude impossible to understand. That she couldn't even …' Bergrún broke off mid-sentence and drew a deep breath.

Elma turned back to Hekla, asking: 'Do you know if she was intending to go to Akranes?'

'No, I … I don't think so.'

Elma noticed that Bergrún was watching the girl anxiously as she replied. Feeling a movement under the table, she wondered if it was Bergrún's leg that was fidgeting.

'What did you do when you got home?' Elma asked.

'Nothing.' Hekla picked at the black varnish on her fingernail.

'Nothing?' Sævar smiled. 'You didn't watch a film, or use your computer or phone?'

'Yeah, maybe. Something like that.'

'All right,' Elma said. 'What then?'

'Just...' The girl glanced at Bergrún again, then back at Elma. 'I ordered a pizza.'

'And you were alone at home all evening?' Elma tried not to let her impatience seep into her voice. It felt as if every single word had to be prised out of the girl.

'Yes,' Hekla answered, without meeting her eye.

'When did you go to bed?'

'Around twelve, I think.'

'OK,' Sævar said easily. 'And what about the next day? Didn't you find it strange that your mother hadn't come home?'

'I don't know,' Hekla said. 'No, not really.'

Elma groaned under her breath. It was going to be an uphill struggle to get anything out of the poor kid. 'All right, what about later that day?' she persisted. 'When did you start to get worried about your mother?'

Hekla bit her upper lip before answering. 'That afternoon. When I rang her phone and it was switched off.'

'Had you tried to get hold of your mother before that?'

Hekla shook her head. 'It was after lunch maybe when I first tried to call her.'

'Why didn't you ring back the day before when you saw that she'd been trying to get hold of you?'

Hekla didn't answer, just shrugged and began picking the black varnish off her nail again.

'OK,' Elma said, looking at Sævar. He didn't seem as exasperated by Hekla's brief answers as she was. If anything, he seemed amused. But she wasn't about to give up. 'Do you remember when you last spoke to your mother?'

'Er ... in the morning. Before school.'

Hekla's interview continued in the same vein, with every single detail having to be dragged out of the girl and every question eliciting the shortest possible answer. She had never met Sölvi, the man her mother had a date with; she knew little about her mother's family and had hardly ever met her grandfather.

'You were ten years old when you moved to Borgarnes,' Elma said. 'Don't you have any idea why your mother wanted to live there?'

'Maybe it would be better if I answered that,' Bergrún interrupted. She ran a hand through her mousy-brown hair and adjusted her glasses. 'When Hekla was ten, Maríanna did another of her little disappearing acts. Well, not that little, actually: she was away for more than a week. Luckily, Hekla was pretty capable of looking after herself by then and could get her own meals and so on. No one knew Maríanna had gone off until we turned up to collect Hekla for the weekend. Needless to say, we alerted the Child Protection Agency, and after that she spent the summer with us while Maríanna was sorting herself out.'

'I see,' Elma said, reflecting that after an episode like this it was no wonder there had been problems in Maríanna and Hekla's relationship. Yet children could forgive their parents the most unbelievable behaviour.

'Yes,' Bergrún said. 'After that, Maríanna wanted a change of scene. She moved to Borgarnes because ... well, it was a completely new start and suitably far away from all the ghosts of her past. Of course, she should have moved to Akranes, which would have made life a lot easier for everyone, but I don't suppose she would have wanted that.' The contempt in Bergrún's voice didn't escape Elma or Sævar.

'Right, Hekla, just one more thing to finish up,' Elma said, looking back at the girl. 'Have you got a boyfriend or a friend with a driver's licence?'

Hekla appeared startled by the question and her eyes darted to Bergrún.

Bergrún exclaimed: 'Of course she hasn't got a boyfriend. She's only fifteen.'

'We're just wondering how Hekla used to travel to Akranes.' Elma addressed this remark to the girl. 'We know you sometimes used to sneak over here. Believe me, I understand. When I was your age, I couldn't see why anyone would want to live in Borgarnes. But we were just wondering how exactly you got here. Because, obviously, you don't have a driver's licence yourself.'

Hekla bit her upper lip so hard it turned white. Her frantic picking at her nail varnish sent small black flakes scattering over the kitchen table. 'I just used to catch a bus or something. But I didn't do it often. Maybe only, like, once.'

'So there's no boyfriend or anything like that?'

Hekla shook her head. Seeing that she was lying, Elma thanked her for the chat, then asked to speak to Bergrún and Fannar in private.

'She's not much of a talker,' Fannar explained, once Hekla had left the room. 'Like most fifteen-year-olds.'

'But she's been happy since coming to live with you, hasn't she?' Elma asked.

'It's gone extraordinarily well,' Bergrún assured her. She smiled and clasped the small gold heart on her necklace as she spoke. 'She'd always wanted to stay with us. She didn't want to live with her mother.'

'Hekla first came to you after she'd been left alone at home, didn't she?' Elma asked.

'Maríanna left her all alone for three whole days.' Bergrún narrowed her eyes. 'She was three years old. One evening, when Hekla was asleep, Maríanna just walked out. I don't know what she was up to but she just abandoned her child.'

'And Hekla was placed with you after that?'

'Yes, not long afterwards. There had been other incidents; warning signs that social services had been noticing since Hekla had first gone to a childminder and later to nursery school. Things like nappy rash and her clothes being unwashed or too small, or Maríanna frequently turning up very late to collect her. Incidents that were reported to the Child Protection Agency. When she first came to us it was touch and go whether she'd ever go back to her mother, but Maríanna got her act together. Six months later, Hekla was sent back to her.' Bergrún's smile was full of bitterness.

'But you carried on having her to stay?'

Fannar, who was still on his feet, gripped the back of Bergrún's chair. 'Yes. We couldn't bear the idea of Hekla vanishing completely from our lives, so when it was proposed that we might like to be her support family, we leapt at the chance. We had her to stay every other weekend and sometimes more often.'

'It must have been extremely tough having to return her to her mother,' Elma said. 'You must have formed a bond with Hekla.'

'Oh, it was tough all right,' Bergrún said. 'We had no idea what sort of state Maríanna was in. I had my doubts and was afraid of what might happen when they were alone together — when I wasn't there to look after Hekla. The problem with these cases is that the authorities always give the parents the benefit of the doubt, not the children.'

'But the arrangement was better than losing her altogether,' Fannar added.

Elma sympathised. She couldn't begin to imagine how hard it must be to send a child back into a situation, knowing it might be unsafe. Or even downright dangerous.

Sævar had his notebook in his hands and his eyes trained on Bergrún. 'As we've already mentioned, you rang Maríanna repeatedly in the days leading up to her disappearance. In fact…' he held out a printout of Maríanna's phone records on which Bergrún's number had been underlined '…you rang every day that week except on the Friday.'

Bergrún quickly skimmed the printout, then put it down on the table. 'As I explained, we had a … disagreement about Hekla's football tournament that weekend. Did I mention that she's a very promising player? Anyway, Maríanna wouldn't let her go. Strictly speaking, it wasn't our weekend, but I just couldn't understand how Maríanna could deprive her of the chance. She didn't seem to care. She wasn't prepared to make a single sacrifice for Hekla.'

'Why didn't you call her on the Friday?'

There was silence in the kitchen, apart from the humming of the fridge, which seemed to grow louder with every second that passed.

'I …' Bergrún glanced at Fannar. 'I can't remember. I'd probably just given up.' She clutched at her gold heart pendant again.

'Where were you on the Friday Maríanna vanished?' Sævar asked. 'I don't think we asked you at the time.'

'I was here. At home. Actually, I was at work until three o'clock.'

Elma shifted her gaze to Fannar. 'What about you? Were you at home too?'

'That was the weekend I had to go to Egilsstaðir, wasn't it?' Fannar asked, adding, before Bergrún had a chance to answer: 'Yes, of course, I remember receiving the phone call about Maríanna and feeling awful that I couldn't be there with you and Hekla.'

Sævar turned his attention back to Bergrún: 'So you were alone when you drove over to Borgarnes to fetch Hekla on the Saturday?'

'Yes. She rang and I got straight in the car, but...' Bergrún was still fiddling with the pendant. 'I feel as if you're...' She broke off, let go of the pendant, then looked from Sævar to Elma, her expression firm: 'Maríanna and I didn't always see eye to eye, but I didn't wish her any harm. I just wanted her to ... to recognise what was best for Hekla. Maríanna wasn't a good mother. She was ungrateful and selfish, and never stopped to think about Hekla's wishes or needs. We were the ones who bought her clothes, who gave her a phone and a computer, and all the things other kids have. Do you know what Maríanna gave her for her birthday?'

They shook their heads.

Bergrún leant back in her chair and folded her arms. The pressure of her necklace had left a red line on her chest. She smiled scornfully. 'A towel. She gave her a towel for her fifteenth birthday.'

'Getting a towel's not so bad,' Sævar remarked as they were driving away from Bergrún and Fannar's house. 'I mean, it's something everyone uses. Something that lasts. I'd be very happy to get a towel for my birthday.'

'Even when you were fifteen?'

'Especially when I was fifteen. I was forever forgetting my towels in the changing rooms at the swimming pool or gym. I was always needing a new one.'

'Well, it certainly wasn't top of my wish list when I was that age.'

'Do you reckon we should take a closer look at her … at Bergrún, I mean?'

'Yes,' said Elma. 'Yes, I do.'

Bergrún had good reason to want to murder Maríanna, she reflected. They'd been quarrelling all week, and no doubt for years before that, about everything relating to Hekla. Elma wasn't in any doubt that Bergrún loved Hekla. Perhaps she'd reached the end of her tether. The business of the football tournament could have tipped her over the edge, reminding her of all the ways Maríanna had failed Hekla over the years and driving her to violence. Elma could feel herself growing angry when she thought about the bewildered three-year-old, left all alone at home for days.

'We could talk to the Child Protection Agency,' Sævar said. 'Find out more about Maríanna's relationship with Bergrún and Fannar. And about how Hekla and Maríanna got on. Personally, I can't see Bergrún attacking Maríanna, but that Hekla's a dark horse. She's hiding something. What was your impression of her?'

Elma emitted a loud groan. 'I wanted to scream. Talk about having to drag everything out of her — literally every single word.'

Sævar laughed. 'Teenagers … I was never one of them.'

'Oh no?'

'Or maybe I never stopped being one. At least, not

a lot has changed ... Anyway, I don't buy that she was at home all evening.'

'We examined Hekla's phone records without finding anything,' Elma recalled. 'But the thing is, kids hardly make any calls nowadays. They mainly use social media, and it's much harder to access that. Take Snapchat, for example: the messages vanish after a certain length of time, which makes life difficult for us. So, although there was no sign that Hekla had rung anyone on the Friday evening, that doesn't necessarily mean anything.'

'Did we check whether her phone had moved around at all?'

'No,' Elma said. 'No, I don't think we did. She was never a suspect, so there was no reason to check her movements.'

'Was she already fifteen when Maríanna went missing?'

'Yes, she'd recently had a birthday.'

'Meaning that ...'

'That she is — and was — old enough to be held criminally responsible,' Elma finished.

'Exactly.'

'I agree,' Elma said. 'We need to take a closer look at Hekla. It's like she's hiding something. Maybe we should pay a visit to her old school while we're about it.'

'Wouldn't that mean another trip to Borgarnes?'

'Yes, I'm afraid so,' Elma said. 'Do you think Hekla was telling us the truth about the boyfriend?'

Sævar snorted. 'Not a chance. And I'm not convinced by the story that she caught a bus. We need to find out who her boyfriend is and establish whether he gave her a lift that day.'

Sævar parked in front of the police station.

'OK, so that's yet another thing we need to look into.' Elma unfastened her seat belt, but instead of getting out of the car straight away, she leant her head back and said: 'It all adds up to so little, though. We've got no proper leads. Far too much time has passed since Maríanna's murder.'

'Maybe that's a good thing.'

'In what way?'

Sævar shrugged. 'Maybe we'll have a better chance of working out who's lying. It's hard enough to remember things that really happened seven months after the event, let alone to remember lies after all that time.'

'Yes, I suppose there's that.' Elma took hold of the door handle.

'By the way, what was on your wish list?'

'What?' She let go of the handle and turned to Sævar, puzzled.

'When you were fifteen. What did you want for your birthday?'

Elma laughed. 'God, I can't remember. Probably a Walkman or whatever was popular at the time.'

'Walkmans were popular when I was fifteen.'

'Oh, well, in that case, maybe an mp3 player. Weren't they popular once?'

It was Sævar's turn to laugh. 'I expect so. Oof, we're getting old, Elma. The kids today don't even know what an mp3 is, let alone a Walkman.'

'Speak for yourself,' Elma said, getting out of the car. 'I'm still young.'

Three Years Old

As I'm leaving to go to work I notice that there's a letter in the post box. The envelope is dark pink and my name is written on the front in black pen. Not my full name, just my Christian name. It's not from my parents — there's no stamp on it and no sender's details written on the back. The moment I'm sitting in the car, I tear open the envelope and pull out a pink card with an old-fashioned doll's pram on the front. A christening card.

I stare at it in disbelief. That can't be right. My daughter's three years old and although I had her christened, there was no party. No fuss. All I did was scrawl her name on the relevant forms. I open the card and my heart misses a beat when I see what's written inside:

Congratulations on your little girl. Now I know where you live, I might pay you a visit.

It sounds like a threat.

I put the card on the passenger seat and start the car. I find myself scanning my surroundings as I drive off, half expecting the sender to jump out of the bushes by our block of flats. There are quite a few possible candidates. When I left, a lot of people were angry. I sometimes picture their faces and wonder if they remember me or ever think about me. I bet they do. Those small-town types do little else but wallow in other people's business. They live off it. Feed on gossip and sleaze. They're no better than the chickens who peck at the head of the weakest hen in the flock until she is lying dead in the grass in a mass of bloodied feathers.

I don't care if they find me. In fact, I'd love the chance to laugh in their faces. It's my daughter I'm worried about. Unlike me, she's sensitive and fragile. But I've come to care for her, in spite of that. I don't know quite when it happened, but now, whenever she smiles, something happens inside me that I can't explain. The feeling makes me want to smile and cry at the same time. I don't want to share her with anyone. It's not like I need to worry about her father, since he's long dead, but his family are still alive. They don't know she exists but they would only have to look at her — she's the spitting image of him.

The thought of the card preys on my mind all day until I'm sitting with a glass of red wine after work, nibbling at a piece of bread and butter. It's the first time I've been out since my daughter was born. For three years I've made do with drinking a bottle of wine alone at home in front of a film. Then, several days ago, the only woman among the lawyers at our practice suggested we go out to supper the following Friday to celebrate her birthday. As usual, I assumed I wouldn't be able to go along, but that day I spotted a notice from a teenage girl pinned to the cork board in the supermarket. I tore off a strip with her phone number on it and rang her, and now she's sitting in my flat, stuffing her face with snacks, guzzling down Coke and no doubt rooting around in my wardrobe too, but I don't care. At long last, I'm having an evening out.

Later, we move on to a crowded bar with pounding music. The city hasn't changed. Only the music is different from four years ago, when I last had a social life. I've limited myself to two glasses of wine and done my best to keep up with the conversation, but as soon as it touches on anything work-related, my mind wanders. I only work on reception, so don't really have a clue what goes on in the office. They keep bandying about legal terms and quoting clauses, as if they're terribly clever and important.

When the waiter comes over they order another round, and this time I ask for a gin and tonic. We're at a place frequented by an older crowd — the over-thirties. Yet there's the odd teenage girl among them who doesn't look old enough to be allowed in. They attach themselves to men twice their age, who paw at them and buy them drinks. Was I ever one of those girls? All of a sudden a memory surfaces of panting breath and a sweating face. I push it away at once and take a big slug of my gin.

For the last three years I've done my best not to think about the past. I no longer feel like the girl I was then. She's just a distant memory now. My life is so different from how it used to be. No one knows me here, but the letter is an unsettling reminder that I'm not invisible. Someone has found me. Someone knows where I live. I knock back another mouthful of the G&T and grimace. It's very strong.

In this new life of mine I've recreated myself from scratch. If anyone asks, I tell them that my parents live abroad, but I don't explain why they went. Instead, I say they're both doctors who work in war zones. I've even listed exactly which countries they've visited, writing it all down in a file on my computer so I won't forget anything. The most common questions I get are about my daughter's father, and they're easy enough to answer. I tell them he was killed in a motorbike accident when I was eight months pregnant. I see this imaginary baby-father clearly. His name was Snorri and he was tall and dark (just like our daughter). With chocolate-brown eyes and a cleft chin. We'd just got engaged when the accident happened. The story has come to seem so real to me that I even wonder if I should tell it to my daughter later on. But of course she would want to see pictures and get to know his family, and all sorts of other things that wouldn't be possible, so it's probably best to stay silent. Tell her the truth: that she hasn't got a father. That her father never knew she existed and never will.

Since moving, I haven't met a single person who's recognised me, and so, with every year that has gone by, I've relaxed and let down my guard a little. I no longer scan places for familiar faces the moment I walk in. Anyway, I'm sure they wouldn't recognise me these days. My hair's dyed dark brown and I've changed; not just my hair and clothes, but I've put on a bit of weight too, and my skin's not as tanned as it used to be. Mainly because I no longer go on beach holidays twice a year but am stuck here in this wretched climate all year round. But now the letter is weighing on me like a nightmare, and I find myself constantly glancing around, scanning the faces of the other customers.

'Want another?'

'Sorry?' I look up to see the waiter standing over us again. Dropping my eyes to my glass, I realise it's empty. Did I really down it that fast? How much time has passed since I got it?

'Want another drink?' my colleague repeats.

'Yes, please,' I say. 'Perhaps the same again.'

The waiter nods, collects the empty glasses and returns almost immediately with more drinks. I down mine fast. Without meaning to, I can sense myself getting drunk and suddenly feel an overwhelming urge to pee. I stand up and gesture towards the toilets, but no one takes any notice. They're all too busy talking about something that's way over my head.

The toilets are upstairs, and a queue has formed outside the ladies. The floor is moving up and down, and the music is so deafening that I can hardly hear myself think. As I'm waiting in the queue, a man comes over and starts talking to me, but I can't hear a word. He's even drunker than me, his hair's all over the place and the top buttons of his black shirt are undone. On a whim, I pull him towards me and start kissing him. When it's my turn, I drag him into the cubicle with me, in spite of the other girls' protests. I lean over the toilet and pull down my trousers. Prop my hands against the wall as I feel him entering me. The sex is brief and rough. He tears at my hair and rams against my hips, almost knocking me off balance and I narrowly avoid banging my head against the wall. I moan loudly, but the music drowns out most of the noise. Afterwards, I shove him out of the cubicle and sit down on the toilet to pee. My fingers are shaking and the floor seems to be moving even more sickeningly than before.

When I emerge, girls are standing in front of the mirrors, putting on lipstick. They're slim, with tiny breasts and far too much make-up, and skirts so short that their knickers are almost visible. One of them gives me a look of such contempt that it's as if I've offended her personally, but that's impossible because I've never seen her before. Perhaps she heard us in the cubicle. I smile at her, but she drops her eyes and walks out.

I get a shock when I see myself in the mirror and burst out laughing because it's so absurd to think this is me. I didn't have a chance to go home and change, as we went out straight after work. I'm wearing my see-through black blouse. My hair is loose, and I haven't been to a hairdresser in so long that it reaches below my shoulder blades. After my little adventure in the toilet, it's messed up at the back, my eyes are red and watering, and my cheeks are covered in scarlet blotches. I stop laughing and try to comb my hair with my fingers, but really I couldn't give a shit. It feels almost like being in disguise. As if I've ended up in someone else's body and can do whatever I like without anyone recognising me.

I start down the stairs just as a group of people are coming up. Not one of them looks at me twice. People always used to look at me twice. I still remember what it was like to walk into places and see people looking up, even half turning to stare at me. I never needed to buy my own drinks; a constant supply used to keep coming as long as I wanted them, and when I was on the dance floor there was always someone eager to partner me. Always someone I could pull towards me or push away.

As I start to descend, lost in memory and already picturing my next drink, I suddenly feel someone push me so hard that I lose my footing and go flying down the steep staircase. My head bangs into the wall and I land on my shoulder, experiencing an agonising pain and tasting blood.

There are people all around me. Someone sits me up and another fetches a towel to press against the wound on my head. My heart is racing. Not because I fell or because I'm bleeding, but because I was pushed. I clearly felt hands on my back, giving me a violent shove. All of a sudden my colleague is there: the woman whose birthday we're celebrating.

'What on earth happened?' she asks, bending over me.

'Shome … someone pushed me,' I hear myself slur.

'What? Did someone push you?' she asks. 'Are you sure you didn't just trip?'

'No. No, I was pushed.'

I can see from the expressions on the faces around me that no one believes this. Probably because I can hardly get the words out and I'm feeling so faint that I have to lean against the wall. People start wandering off, and in the end there's only my colleague and me left.

'I was pushed,' I repeat, louder than intended. 'I want to

press charges. They'll have to check the CCTV. I need to go to hospital. I think I've broken something.' Now I'm crying and I can see that the woman can't be bothered with this. She takes out her phone, makes a call, then escorts me outside.

'They'll come and get you,' she says and goes back inside.

I'm left standing alone on the street corner, clutching my shoulder. All around me there are groups of people, laughing and shouting. Stupid little girls and boys, their heads full of nothing but sex. Someone drops a bottle and it smashes on the pavement. Then the heavens open and it starts to rain. I feel as if everyone's staring and laughing at me. The eyes resting on me are cold and hard, and with every second that passes I can feel myself shrinking and becoming more and more insignificant.

When I finally get home later that evening, there's another card waiting for me in my post box. This time the envelope contains a photo of my daughter's nursery school. Cute little girl you've got, is written on the back.

The next day I open the paper and start searching for a new flat.

Hekla could taste the Indian chicken curry she'd eaten earlier that evening repeating on her. She clamped a hand over her mouth and tried to blow the smell away.

'Ugh!' Tinna shouted, wrinkling her nose. 'Seriously, Hekla? That's gross.' She gave her a shove, and Hekla laughed. It was always a bit easier without Dísa, though things were undeniably more exciting when she was around. It was always her who wanted to go out and do something. She was never satisfied when it was just the three of them hanging out together.

'Sorry,' Hekla said. 'My stomach's killing me after the curry Fannar made for supper. There must have been something wrong with it.' This wasn't true, but it was better than admitting that she suffered from reflux, which sounded so disgusting.

Tinna didn't appear to be listening; all her attention was focused on the TV. Hekla lay back on the bed. She wasn't really interested in the series Tinna liked watching, which featured a rich American family with scarily little between their ears. But Tinna loved reality shows and, since they were at her house, she got to decide. The wall-mounted flatscreen was far too large for her bedroom. It had been passed down to Tinna when her older brother bought himself a new, even bigger flatscreen.

Beside the bed was a white desk with a big black lamp on it. On the shelf above was a photo of Tinna with her mother, who had her arms round Tinna's shoulders and was laughing down at her. The picture had always made Hekla feel envious. She had memorised every last detail: the way the sunlight gleamed on Tinna's mother's gilded hair, the pale sand behind them and the red top Tinna was wearing. Their olive-coloured arms and sparkling eyes. It looked so spontaneous, as if the picture had been snapped with only a fraction of a second's notice, and they'd had no time to pose. Beside the photo were a silver globe and a stone; not an ordinary stone of the kind you'd find lying around outside your house, but a lump of rock, jet black and shiny.

Hekla closed her eyes and relished the sensation of sinking into the mattress. Tinna's bed always reminded Hekla of a big, soft cloud, though the bedclothes were dark blue, not white. She felt as if she could be swallowed up by the big duvet, the fluffy blanket and all those pillows that smelt of the Body Shop strawberry-butter skin cream Tinna used.

Hekla's phone lit up beside her with a message from Agnar. He'd sent a picture of himself lying in bed at home, with the caption: *Meet up this evening*? Hekla darted a glance at Tinna, then wrote: *Maybe. What were you thinking*? The reply came almost instantly: *Pick you up*? She answered: *OK*.

Hekla wasn't looking forward to this but she couldn't put it off forever. Agnar had been bombarding her with messages for the last few days, and although they were mostly intended to be funny, Hekla had begun to find it uncomfortable. His desperation was so powerful she felt as if she could touch it.

'Who are you talking to?' The programme was over and Tinna turned over on her side, her cheek propped on her hand, and looked at Hekla. She was wearing pyjama bottoms and a vest, her blonde hair pulled back in a slide.

'Oh, just Agnar,' Hekla said. 'He's coming to pick me up.'

'Weren't you going to dump him?'

Hekla nodded.

'Do you think he'll cry?'

'Tinna!' Hekla felt a knot in her stomach.

'I reckon he'll cry.' Tinna yawned and reached for the remote.

Hekla's phone lit up again. *Outside*, Agnar had written. Hekla got off the bed, inspected herself in Tinna's big bedroom mirror, tidied her hair and applied some lip salve.

'Have fun,' Tinna called after her.

Hekla sighed. She wasn't in the mood for jokes right now.

On the way out, Tinna's mum stopped her. 'Leaving already?'

Hekla nodded.

'All right,' she said. 'But be careful, dear.'

Hekla smiled and said goodbye. She ran out to Agnar's car, with a thudding heart and a bad taste in her mouth.

* * *

'It's freezing.' Elma wrapped her towel more tightly around herself and dashed over the stone floor of the terrace on tiptoe.

'It doesn't get much better than this,' said Begga, who had already made herself comfortable in the hot tub. It was bitterly cold outside, though the wind had dropped. The stars shone down from a cloudless sky, lighting up the winter night.

'You're right, it doesn't get much better,' Elma agreed, once she was up to her neck in the blissfully hot water. She took a sip of the toffee liqueur that Begga had handed her, then reclined her head and closed her eyes. The heat gave her goose pimples at first, but after a few moments she felt her whole body relaxing.

But her mind wouldn't be distracted so easily. After she and Sævar had got back to the police station earlier, Elma had gone through Hekla's Instagram page. It was unbelievable how much you could learn about people via their social-media accounts, especially teenagers, who rarely locked their pages and always posted too much information; things so personal they would never have said them aloud. Hekla was no exception. Her Instagram page was open to all, but unfortunately she didn't seem to be particularly diligent at keeping it up to date. A lot of Hekla's photos were accompanied by sentiments in English, which Elma found a bit depressing. They seemed designed to give the impression that Hekla was simultaneously deep, mysterious and sad. Was that how she wanted other people to perceive her?

There were a few pictures of Hekla herself, sporting very different, much scantier outfits than her usual hoodies. These pictures were all recent, dating from after she had moved to Akranes, and seemed to have been taken for some special occasion. Hekla and a blonde girl were posing in one of their bedrooms, judging by the heaps of clothes on the floor. They were wearing high-waisted trousers and tight tops, showing bare midriffs. Elma hadn't realised that crop tops were back in fashion, but apparently they were trendy with teenagers these days. Elma imagined her mother's jaw dropping to the floor if she were to roll up in a crop top.

Elma scrolled through the comments on the photos. Most were from girls and featured more hearts than words. But there were several comments of a sexual nature in English, some of them so crude that she was shocked. Others were from Icelandic boys. Having checked out each of them in turn, she discovered that only one was over seventeen and lived in Akranes. He wrote that he was lucky, followed by the inevitable string of hearts. Agnar Freyr Steinarsson was nineteen and his Instagram page was locked. Typical, Elma thought to herself. Still, she reckoned he was probably the boyfriend: Agnar. She would do a background check on him tomorrow.

Elma sank deeper into the tub, wetting her hair and ears.

'This is the only reason I bought the house,' Begga said. 'I mean it, the only reason. I didn't even need to go inside: I just took one look at the terrace and the tub, and that was it.' She emitted a neigh of laughter, and Elma couldn't help smiling.

'Don't you find it uncomfortable living here alone?' Elma asked. 'I really like being in a block of flats, hearing the neighbours when I go to sleep, and that sort of thing.'

'I'm not alone, I've got—'

'Yes, yes, I know — you've got your cat,' Elma interrupted. 'But you know what I mean.'

Begga smiled, her dimples deepening. Elma always thought it made her look years younger, though Begga was already several years younger than herself. 'No, it doesn't bother me. I sleep like a lamb. Or, you know, like some animal that sleeps well.'

'Like a baby.'

'Yes, or that.' Begga emptied her glass, then fixed Elma with a look, the inevitable provocative glint in her eye. 'And the reason you like living in a block has nothing to do with any noises, Elma dear, and everything to do with you-know-who, who knocks on your door in the evenings and does you-know-what.'

Elma's only answer was a grin. Recently, her visits from 'you-know-who' had become more frequent. It wasn't serious, though, and they kept it strictly between themselves, but often she didn't realise until too late just how much she had blurted out to Begga. There was something about her that invited confidences and encouraged Elma to talk without stopping to think. For instance, Begga was the only person she mentioned Davíð to, and she had to admit that it was good to be able to talk about him at last. The anger and guilt that had tormented her for the first few months after she moved back to Akranes had almost entirely disappeared, and she now accepted the fact that he had been ill. That depression was an illness and she couldn't have foreseen his decision. Or, at least, this was the mantra she repeated to herself every day.

She stared up at the vault of the sky, so intensely black, so awe-inspiringly vast. Thousands of stars stared back at her, and she was suddenly conscious of how small and insignificant she was. Was he up there somewhere, looking down on her? Feeling dizzy, she sat upright again. She'd better not have any more to drink.

'It's a bit hot in here,' she said, heaving herself up higher to get her shoulders out of the water. Then, after a moment's reflection: 'But it's nice.'

'What's nice?' Begga had ducked her head under

the water, and her mascara was running down her cheeks.

'Having him there — you-know-who — in the flat next door.' She felt guilty as soon as she had said it, but pushed the feeling away.

'I always thought you and Sævar...'

Elma shrugged. She had thought so too. Hoped, even. But when nothing had happened between them, the tension had dissipated, and now she felt almost as if they knew each other too well.

'It would be far too complicated,' she said, after a little silence. 'We work together and we're friends, and I don't want to risk ... oh, you know.'

'I know,' Begga replied, and Elma smiled. Because that was the thing about Begga: she *knew*.

Six Years Old

Her first day at school and I'm a bag of nerves, whereas she seems perfectly unfazed. Of course she's only a child and doesn't realise what's happening or what a big turning point this is. But that's not why I'm nervous; I'm nervous because I know what goes on in schools. I know how vulnerable some children are, while others are as savage as hyenas. I'm afraid they'll tear her apart, like any other defenceless creature. Because that's what schools are like, and children are the cruellest predators in the world.

I reach for her hand as we approach the entrance.

'Are you excited?'

She doesn't answer. Sometimes it's like she just can't be bothered. Once I was so tired that I seized her by her shoulders and almost screamed at her: 'Answer me!' She just stared back at me, her grey eyes as cold as steel, her face blank. I immediately regretted it and let her go, and she carried on lining up the green toy soldiers on the dining table as if nothing had happened, the same soldiers she's been playing with ever since she was a baby. Nowadays she lines them up in two armies facing each other, as if at the beginning of a battle. Sometimes I can tell that something has happened, that one of the sides has won. Half the soldiers are lying on the floor, some with mangled arms or legs.

She's an odd child, and that fact is glaringly obvious, despite all the time I've spent trying to get her ready. I scoured the shops for a suitable dress for her big day and eventually found a pretty blue one with a shirt collar and long sleeves. It goes well with her dark hair, which is now braided in two plaits that hang down to her chest. Occasionally I catch a look of me when she tilts her head at a certain angle or laughs — which happens very rarely — but apart from that she's nothing like me, in character or appearance. I often feel guilty when I look at her because I know it's my fault she's like she is. All those years when I couldn't give her the care she needed are bound to have had an effect.

Sometimes I wonder what my life would be like if I hadn't got pregnant. Perhaps I would have met a man and had children who weren't so odd. I lose myself in daydreams, picturing the house we'd live in, the money I'd have to spend and the meals I'd cook. I imagine evenings sitting on the sofa and how we'd sleep with our limbs tangled together until the children crawled into bed with us in the morning. Two children. I always meant to have two. A boy who took after my husband and a girl who took after me. I have to be careful not to think like that because then I tend to blame her for the way my life has turned out. And of course this is unfair, because she didn't ask to be born.

The bell rings. She halts and watches the other children flocking to the door. Her dark eyebrows draw down, overshadowing her observant eyes. Her mouth is almost round, her lips compressed. She tightens her hold on my hand.

'Shall we go in?' I ask, and to my great relief she nods. She can be as stubborn as the devil and once she's got her mind set on something there's no way of reasoning with her. I've had to carry her screaming out of supermarkets before now, scratching and kicking at anything within reach. But mainly at me.

We start walking, again, slowly, and I sense that she's wary. She's staring at the ground, her shoulders hunched, as if trying to make herself smaller. I want to tell her to straighten her back and raise her head, but I know there's no point. I remember girls when I was at school who went around with hunched backs and eyes that never strayed from the floor. I remember how they used to sidle along the walls as if wishing they could melt into the background.

We stand outside the classroom. The bell rings, and the children are supposed to form an orderly line outside the door. They take up position, one after another, in a squirming row. The teacher surveys them, then notices that my daughter hasn't budged. She's clutching my leg, tugging at my trousers and suddenly I can feel all eyes on us. I smile apologetically to the teacher and parents who, from their expressions, seem to find my daughter's behaviour adorable, whereas I'm deeply ashamed.

'Mummy.' Her voice is almost too low to hear, and I bend my head to her. 'I don't want to be here,' she whispers. She stares at me imploringly. 'Can we go home? Please, please.'

At that moment the teacher comes over, a thin woman with a boyish haircut, wearing a knitted jumper. She bends down and puts a hand on my daughter's arm. 'Hi, what's your name?' she asks in a super-friendly, gentle voice. 'Would you like to come with me for a little while? We won't be long, I promise.'

She hesitates, then holds out her hand and goes with the teacher. The last I see of her before she vanishes among the pack of wolves is her dark head, staring down at the green lino. I heave a deep breath, put on a smile and walk away, pretending that it's all perfectly normal; that she's perfectly normal.

Though I know that both things are a lie.

Thursday

His name was Jakob, though Begga referred to him as you-know-who. It made Elma think of Voldemort in the Harry Potter books, but that was about all Jakob had in common with Voldemort. He had sea-blue eyes, dirty-blond hair, and his suntanned skin smelt of citrus. Elma sometimes missed the lemony scent he left on her sheets when it was a long time between their encounters. It was stupid, of course, but after nine years with Davíð, she still hadn't got used to sleeping alone and enjoyed having someone beside her again.

She and Jakob had met shortly after she moved into the flat. He lived opposite, so it wasn't far to go. Not far enough, in fact. He was two years younger than her, in his final year of an IT degree, and never tired of complimenting her. Sometimes he went so far that Elma wanted to beg him to stop. It wasn't true that her hair looked beautiful in the mornings or that her crooked front tooth had a charm of its own. Ditto the freckles on her fair skin. Regardless of what Jakob said, they weren't pretty, and she refused to believe that he thought they were. But most of all he waxed lyrical about her eyes, saying that the grey of her irises, flecked with brown and green, reminded him of a lava field. 'Are you sure that's a compliment?' she had asked. 'Absolutely', Jakob had assured her. 'You know all those tourists come to Iceland to see the lava. Well, really they should come all this way to see your eyes. Perhaps we should set up a website to advertise them.' Elma had groaned inwardly and shut him up with a kiss.

When she woke up on Thursday morning, his arm was lying across her chest and she moved it carefully aside as she twisted to turn off the alarm clock. He didn't even stir when she got out of bed. Hurriedly retrieving her clothes from the floor, she pulled them on, then stood there for a moment, studying him. She wondered if she should wake him or let him sleep. In the end she tiptoed out, pulling the bedroom door to behind her.

The first person Elma met when she arrived at the police station that morning was Gígja, or rather the lower half of her, as the upper half was hidden inside an SUV.

'Do you need a hand?' Elma called over the noise of the wind.

Gígja looked round. 'Hi, Elma,' she said. 'Yes, it might be good to have some help. I dropped in at the bakery on the way, but they packed it all in boxes, which are hopeless for carrying.'

'Here, let me take that.'

They went inside, loaded down with bags and boxes of pastries.

'Isn't this way too much, Gígja?' Elma asked, surveying the little table in the coffee room. Gígja had bought enough to feed an army.

Gígja looked at all the food and burst out laughing. 'You know, she said, 'you may be right. In that case you'll all just have to take the leftovers home with you.'

Elma shook her head. She was pouring yesterday's coffee down the sink when Sævar came in.

'The road's imp — ... Whose birthday is it?' he asked, distracted, glancing from Gígja to Elma.

'It must be somebody's somewhere,' Elma said.

'Yes, it's always somebody's birthday,' Gígja agreed. She put down the knife she'd been using to cut the length of Danish pastry into slices. 'Anyway, I'll be off.'

'Won't you stay and have some with us?' Elma asked.

'No, it's not good for me.' Gígja slung her bag over her shoulder. 'I need to get to work.'

'Aren't you...?' Elma hesitated. She hadn't discussed Gígja's cancer with her and didn't know if she preferred to keep it private. Hörður was reluctant to discuss it, and Elma had learnt the news from her mother rather than him. 'How are you feeling?'

'There's nothing wrong with me,' Gígja said. 'Hörður's behaving as if I should be lying with my feet up all day.' She glanced at the door, as if to make sure he couldn't hear, before adding in a whisper: 'Don't tell him about work. The poor man just needs to take it a bit easier.' She winked at them both, then headed off.

'What were you saying, Sævar?' Elma asked through a mouthful of caramel-iced doughnut.

'The road's impassable by Hafnarfjall,' Sævar said, referring to the infamous black spot, where the road wound round the foot of the mountain on the coast north of Akranes and the wind speed had been known to reach more than 250 kilometres per hour. 'We'll have to wait until the gale dies down before we can do our Borgarnes trip.'

Raindrops were rattling on the glass and there was a screaming from the window frame, even though it was closed. It didn't look as if they'd be going to Borgarnes any time in the next few hours. The storm wasn't expected to slacken off until after lunch at the earliest. Elma's thoughts flew to Jakob, and she wondered if he was still lying, snuggled up under her warm duvet. He always slept so deeply and so late, whereas she was normally wide awake on the dot of seven, even at weekends.

It was five days since Maríanna's body had been found and they had made little appreciable progress. The case was constantly in the news, with endless reports rehashing details of the original inquiry, accompanied by pictures of Maríanna. The police had published a phone number with a request for the public to get in touch if they had any information about her movements on Friday, 4 May. But, again, the seven-month interval was a big disadvantage — people simply couldn't remember that far back. So far, none of the messages currently inundating CID had stood up to scrutiny.

Elma got out the case files again. Top of the pile was the envelope Maríanna had left behind for Hekla. The note had been the main reason for thinking that she had taken her own life. Elma wondered why Maríanna had written it that day. What exactly had happened to make her feel she owed Hekla an apology? Could it have been about the football tournament? Elma had to admit that she found it strange of Maríanna not to let Hekla take part. After all, the girl wouldn't necessarily have had to stay with Bergrún: Maríanna could have accompanied her daughter herself, if she'd wanted to. If the note did refer to the tournament, it must mean that Maríanna had been expecting Hekla to come home, in which case she would hardly have gone chasing after her to Akranes. Unless the message had been left that morning, before Maríanna went to work, and something had come up in the meantime.

The envelope, which was unopened, looked like an ordinary bill. Elma stared at it for a moment, then tore it open. It turned out to contain a standard warning notice that if the bill wasn't paid within the next few days, interest would be charged. It wasn't for a particularly large sum — thirty thousand krónur for TV and internet usage. What drew Elma's attention, though, was the fact that the letter was dated more than a year before Maríanna had vanished. Why on earth would she have pulled out such an old piece of post to write a note to Hekla on? Elma closed her eyes and tried to picture the flat. She couldn't remember any piles of bills lying around. Was it possible that Hekla had put an old note from her mother on the kitchen table? They had got an expert to confirm that the handwriting was Maríanna's, but, all the same, there was definitely something odd about this. Elma leant forward and switched on her monitor. It was time to take a closer look at Hekla.

Eight Years Old

When I enter the flat after work, the air is so heavy and close that it's like walking into a wall. There was a storm last night and I made sure all the windows were tightly closed, forgetting to open them again before we went out this morning. I walk around the flat, drawing the curtains and opening all the windows. She should be on her way home by now. I scan the street for her, squinting against the sun that has momentarily broken through the oppressive layer of cloud. Children stream past on their way home from school, and I recognise several girls from her class. They are walking in such a tight knot that their arms are touching, all of them laughing and whispering together. Then I see her.

My daughter might as well not exist, although she's only a few steps behind them. She doesn't say a word, just follows them like a shadow. Her desperation to be part of the group, to belong, is almost palpable. It drips from every ingratiating smile she puts on that none of them notice. They totally ignore her. Aren't even aware of her. Yet she continues to trail after them, eavesdropping on their conversation, smiling when they laugh, staring mesmerised at their pink school bags. I hide behind the curtains, watching, though the sight makes me want to cry. Why is she like this?

Without warning, one of them turns, and I see my daughter's smile when they finally deign to notice her. Even from my post up here by the window I can see the hope quicken-

ing in her face. But then the girl leans towards the others and whispers something. They laugh and quickly walk on. My daughter stands still, staring after them. For a while she appears to be considering whether to follow them. Oh God, I hope she doesn't. How tragic would that be? She doesn't seem to have a clue about social interaction. Doesn't realise when she's being rejected; doesn't understand why they snap at her and make spiteful remarks. Doesn't understand boundaries or when she's being annoying or weird. Perhaps that's a mercy, because at least she doesn't understand what the other children think of her. But I dread the day when she does realise and what that will do to her.

As I'm thinking this, I notice the girls abruptly stop and turn round. It's a coordinated movement. Premeditated. My daughter halts because she can't do anything else. They are blocking the pavement, standing arm in arm. Although I can't hear what is said, I get a sick feeling in my stomach. I doubt they're inviting her to come home with them or complimenting her on her hat. A moment passes, and I pray to God that nothing bad will happen; that they'll just turn round again and carry on walking. But then one of them steps forward and something is said and done, and then it's impossible to see what's going on because they've formed a circle around her. There's a scuffle, and I try to see if she's OK, but my view is blocked by a wall of backs, until a moment later something red is flung into the road. Her hat.

I don't waste time pulling on a coat. I don't even wait for the lift but run down the stairs, all eight storeys. My heart is in my throat and the booming in my head drowns out all other sounds. I don't know what I'll do when I reach them. I want to scream at them and shake them until their heads jerk back and forth like ragdolls.

But they see me long before I can reach them. They prob-

ably hear my voice; the yelling that doesn't sound like me at all but like some mad woman. Their heads whip round, they exchange glances, then take to their heels, their school bags bouncing on their backs. I feel an urge to chase after them, to catch them and hold them down while I tear off their limbs one by one, but I don't do it. Instead, I bend down and pick her up. Some of the other kids are dawdling on their way home, watching us. I ignore them. Then a boy who can hardly be more than six years old taps my arm and holds out the red hat. It's wet from lying in the road, but I take it, studying the boy. He's small and fair with big, fat cheeks, and I could hug him. Instead, I put the school bag on her back and pick her up in my arms, something I haven't done since she was a baby. She buries her face in my hair, and all the way home I can feel her hot breath on my neck.

Her heart beating against mine.

Sævar and Hörður conceded that the date of the bill was a bit odd, but pointed out that there could be a natural explanation for that. Maríanna could simply have had the old envelope lying around in a drawer or among some other papers. But, envelope or not, they agreed on the need to take a closer look at Hekla, part of which would entail checking if she had a boy-friend or other friend with a driving licence. Elma did a background check on Agnar, the boy who had commented on Hekla's photo. After a brief search she discovered that he lived in Akranes and worked at a restaurant, so there was a good chance he would be at home in the mornings. That was convenient, since it meant she could use the time while the storm was blowing itself out to interview him.

Elma had never been particularly good at talking to teenage boys. They were as alien to her now as they had been when she was a teenager herself. She knocked on Sævar's door. He was staring with great concentration at his computer screen but looked up when she appeared.

'Bad news,' he said, before she could say a word.

'Oh?'

'Sölvi's phone didn't leave Borgarnes the day Maríanna vanished. Which means he can't have taken her to Akranes unless he left his phone behind, and there aren't many people who go anywhere without their phones these days, are there?'

'Not unless it was a cunning ploy to hide his movements,' Elma said.

'Yes, that's a possibility, of course. But we've got nothing else on him.'

Elma sighed. It was high time the investigation started throwing up some proper leads.

'Have you got any news?'

'Well, actually, there is one thing,' Elma began, then told him that she'd almost certainly found Hekla's boyfriend. 'But talking to teenage boys isn't my forte, so...'

'So you want me to come along as a true master of the art?'

Elma smiled. 'Well, I wouldn't put it quite like that but ... yes.'

Sævar stood up and took his coat off the peg. As he did so, a violent gust of wind shook the window glass and howled through the gaps. 'The things I do for you,' Sævar said, shaking his head.

Vesturgata was the longest street in Akranes and ran along the northern shore, with a view across the stormy grey sea to the Snæfellsnes Peninsula and the dome of the glacier rising at its tip. Many of the houses were noticeably rundown. Some lined the street, others were set back, and from their gardens it was only a few steps down to the black-sand beach.

'Bingo,' Sævar said as they parked in front of the address where Agnar was registered as living. 'A green Volvo S80,' he explained when Elma looked at him enquiringly. 'Does he live with his parents?'

'I don't know,' Elma said. 'But I doubt he lives alone in a house this size.'

It was a two-storey building, clad in red corrugated iron. They walked up the steps and rang the doorbell, then waited a while without being aware of any sound or movement.

'These houses often have basement flats,' Sævar observed, walking down the steps.

Elma followed him into the garden and round to a door on the left-hand side of the house. They knocked and after a brief interval the door opened. Elma hadn't known what to expect as she hadn't found any photos of Agnar online, but it certainly wasn't this. The boy standing in the doorway was so tall he was in danger of bumping his head on the lintel. His arms were unusually long and thin, the bones uncomfortably visible through the white skin. His face was similarly pale and thin, with a prominent jaw, high cheekbones and startlingly large, staring eyes. Elma felt as if his face needed correcting somehow. As if it was a rough sculpture that still needed to be tidied and polished.

'Agnar?' Sævar asked.

The boy responded with a 'hmm' that was presumably a yes. Sævar introduced them, then asked if they could come in a moment, and Agnar stepped aside. Elma gave an involuntary gasp as she entered the flat and was hit by a pungent stench. No doubt it came from the tray of cat litter in the hall that urgently needed cleaning out.

'We can sit here,' Agnar said, waving a hand towards a kitchen table with some folding chairs. On the table was a takeaway box, some empty glasses and the remains of a pizza crust. When Elma was younger she and her sister had never been allowed to leave the crusts: their mother had insisted they eat them all up before taking another slice.

'Do you live here alone?' Sævar asked, once they were seated.

'No, with my brother.'

'Right, well, we won't bother you long,' Sævar said. 'We just wanted to check if you knew Hekla?'

'Hekla? She's … or rather she *was* my girlfriend. We broke up yesterday.' Agnar yawned, and a gust of foul breath carried across the table to them. He gave no appearance of being distressed by the end of his relationship.

'Had you been together long?'

'Yes, nearly a whole year. Since way back in, like, January or something.' Agnar made it sound as if a year was forever, and Elma smiled inwardly. When she was a teenager a year-long relationship would have seemed like an eternity. Normally they hadn't lasted for more than a few weeks at that age; rarely for several months.

'So you were seeing her when her mother disappeared in the spring?'

'Yep.'

'Do you know if Hekla came to Akranes the day her mother went missing?'

'Er … yes.' Looking suddenly as if he'd said too much, he added hastily: 'Or, I don't remember. Maybe it was the next day.'

'You didn't see her at all on the Friday? It's very important that you tell the truth. You know it's a criminal offence to lie to the police. People go to prison for less.' Sævar smiled as if he were joking, but Agnar seemed to sense that he was serious.

He didn't answer for a moment, then sighed and said: 'Oh, fuck it, I don't owe that bitch anything after yesterday. She just dumped me after we'd been going out a year, like I was … like I was nobody.'

'So you did see her that Friday?'

'No. Or, you know, she asked me to pick her up from Borgarnes.'

'And did you?'

'Nope, I was on my way to the gym, and then I had work at four. I said I could pick her up in the evening, but she couldn't wait. She was going to find another way.'

'And did she?'

'What?' Agnar stared at Sævar as if he had no idea what he was talking about.

'Did she find another way?'

'Oh, yes. We were going to meet up in the evening.'

'And did you meet her in the evening?' Sævar asked patiently.

'No, all of a sudden she couldn't make it. She'd gone back home.'

'Back home? So she did come to Akranes?'

'Yes, she did.'

'Do you know how she got here?'

'No, I don't.' Agnar shrugged. 'Took a bus or something.'

'And do you know where she was while she was in Akranes?'

'Just with her family or mates. I don't know, man. I wasn't sure what was going on. Then she rang the next day and said that, like … her mum was missing or something.'

Sævar nodded. 'And when did you next see her?'

'On the Sunday.'

'So if we contact the restaurant, your boss will be able to confirm that you were at work all evening?' Sævar leant forwards, locking eyes with Agnar.

'Yeah, man.' He gave them a look as if indignant at the question. 'I worked till eleven, but my shift was only supposed to last till ten. I remember because I wanted to leave earlier to meet Hekla, but the bastard I work for wouldn't let us go. Not that we got paid any more. Isn't that, like, illegal or …?'

* * *

'Did you do it?'

'What?' Hekla asked, though she knew perfectly well what Dísa was talking about. They were sitting in the classroom, waiting for the next lesson. The teacher still hadn't arrived and there was a babble of noise all round them.

'Did you break up with him?'

Hekla nodded. She and Tinna shared a desk, but they had turned their chairs round to face Dísa, who had the desk behind them all to herself.

'Did he cry?' There was a gloating note in Dísa's voice.

'Oh, Dísa,' Tinna said, sending her a sharp glare.

But Hekla couldn't help smiling, and when the girls saw this, they started laughing. It was such a relief to have broken up with Agnar at last. Now she was free to do as she liked. Well, not quite what she would have liked to do, she reminded herself.

'Great,' Tinna said. She leant towards them, lowering her voice. 'Then we can really have a good time tomorrow. No hassle. Just the three of us. Or, you know, us and all the other girls in the class.'

'We'll ditch them later,' Dísa said. Tinna hushed her, glancing around, but there was no need, as none of the others were paying them any attention.

'Why?' Hekla asked.

Dísa and Tinna exchanged secretive glances. 'You'll

see.'

Tinna nudged Hekla before she could ask any more questions. Looking up, she saw Alfreð come in and take a seat. He noticed her and smiled. At that moment the teacher entered the room, and Hekla turned her chair round to face the front. She got butterflies in her stomach when she thought about what the next day would bring. The three of them were going to the birthday party of one of the girls in their class. Hekla tried not to dwell on the fact she hadn't been invited: Dísa and Tinna had insisted on taking her along. She didn't know the girl whose birthday it was, but the three friends weren't planning to stay at the party long anyway. Dísa and Tinna obviously had something else up their sleeve, which they were keeping back from Hekla. She was so excited that she found it hard to concentrate on anything in the Icelandic lesson apart from the strawberry fragrance of Tinna's lip salve and the prospect of Saturday night.

* * *

If Agnar was to be believed, Hekla had been lying. She *had* gone to Akranes after all, and it was possible that Maríanna had followed her there. Yet Elma found it hard to believe that Hekla could have played any role in her mother's disappearance. Of course, there were numerous examples of teenagers murdering their parents; not in Iceland, admittedly, but it happened from time to time in other parts of the world. Teenagers pissed off because their parents wouldn't let them do something, or wouldn't accept their boyfriend, or had committed some other crime that seemed of paramount importance to the teenage mind. In places like America, where guns were more accessible, it was easier for kids to get hold of them and fire them in a fit of rage. In Iceland, on the other hand, although gun ownership was relatively common, few people carried firearms as a matter of course, and they were much less accessible, since they were required by law to be kept in locked cabinets. Besides, Maríanna hadn't been shot with a gun; she'd been beaten to death, which would have required strength. Hekla wasn't that big, and Elma doubted she would have been capable of overpowering her mother without help. She didn't have a driving licence either. All this made it doubtful she could have murdered Maríanna on her own, driven to Grábrók and disposed of her body in the lava field. Someone would have had to help her, and there weren't many candidates. Perhaps only Agnar. Another possibility, though Elma found the idea far-fetched, was that Bergrún could have been involved as well.

Elma sighed and thought how preposterous the whole scenario seemed. However bad Hekla's upbringing had been, Elma couldn't believe the girl would be capable of such a crime.

Her thoughts were interrupted by Sævar, who put his head round the door of her office and nodded towards the window. 'Guess what?'

'What?'

'The wind's dropping. It's Borgarnes time.'

The social worker from the local branch of the Child Protection Agency was a woman in her forties with short hair and a broad bosom encased in a red blouse. She introduced herself as Hildur, with a firm handshake and a friendly expression.

'You're here to ask about Maríanna Þórsdóttir, aren't you?' she said once they had taken a seat in her office. 'I'm so sorry to hear what happened to her. The poor girl.'

She leant forwards, clasping her fingers on the desk. Elma couldn't help noticing how tidy it was. No papers, pens or collection of dirty coffee mugs. Perhaps this was because, unlike Elma, she had to receive visitors in her office. Or, at least, so Elma tried to convince herself.

'I know we were in touch with children's services in the spring,' Sævar said, 'but now we've reopened the case, it would be good if you could, well ... fill us in a bit more on Maríanna's history.'

'Yes.' Hildur straightened up and turned to her computer screen, clicking on something with the mouse. 'I see you got a court order at the time, so it shouldn't be a problem.' She looked back at them and smiled. 'Maríanna and Hekla moved to Borgarnes five years ago. Before that they'd lived in Reykjavík, so obviously I wasn't in charge of her case then. The agency just sent over her files, so all I can tell you is what it says in them. Apparently, there were a number of reasons for keeping a close eye on mother and daughter. Maríanna suffered from serious post-natal depression after giving birth to Hekla. She was very young when she had her — only sixteen — and had problems bonding with her. Of course, it was a shock when her brother killed himself during her pregnancy, but her problems went beyond normal grief.

'After that a close eye was kept on Maríanna and Hekla, as I said. Both nursery-school staff and nurses expressed concern over the fact that Hekla was very late in learning to talk. At the time, they thought there might be a developmental issue, but it became clear later that this wasn't the case. The staff at Hekla's nursery school contacted children's services on several occasions, mostly because Maríanna didn't seem to be changing her often enough. She had nappy rash, still wasn't toilet trained by the time she was four, and her clothes were too small for her. Maríanna also failed to let the school know when Hekla wasn't coming in. In other words, it was clear from early on that she needed extra support, so ever since Hekla was small, they had been receiving regular visits from social workers, who provided Maríanna with all possible assistance.'

'She went AWOL for several days when Hekla was three, didn't she?' Elma asked.

'Yes, that's right. That was when Hekla was placed with a foster family for six months — Bergrún and Fannar.' Hildur added, smiling: 'A lovely couple.'

'What exactly happened?'

'Well ... I suspect Maríanna had started taking drugs and just shut herself off somewhere. She probably lost track of time and didn't realise how long she'd been away.'

'Was it really safe to send Hekla back to her?' Elma found it hard not to sound scandalised. In many ways she agreed with Bergrún: children's interests should be placed before those of their parents. Judging by what she'd heard, Maríanna hadn't been fit to take care of a three-year-old child, particularly one who wasn't able to communicate properly.

Hildur drew a deep breath. 'Our aim is always to keep children with their parents,' she said. 'It's the most desirable arrangement and by far the best for all involved. Well, in most cases. And, as I said, we kept a close eye on the situation. We paid surprise visits and so on.'

'So we're talking about neglect rather than something more serious?'

Hildur frowned. 'More serious? If you mean do we think Maríanna was violent towards Hekla, then no, we don't believe that was the case. Maríanna was ... well, in a difficult situation. Her brother died while she was pregnant and her parents weren't able to give her the help she desperately needed at her age. Then Maríanna's mother died when Hekla was only ten. On balance, given the lack of support from her family, I think she coped pretty well.'

'Didn't she do another disappearing act when Hekla was ten?'

'Yes, that's right,' Hildur said. 'That was around the time her mother died and she got in a very bad state. She was doing a lot of drugs and used to vanish for days at a time.'

'Have I understood correctly that Hekla repeatedly asked to be allowed to live with her support family?' Sævar asked.

'She did, yes,' Hildur said. 'Which is understandable, considering all the things she got from them that she didn't get from her mother. Material wealth often assumes an exaggerated importance for children. Bergrún and Fannar are well off and were able to give Hekla all sorts of things that Maríanna couldn't afford.'

'Are you sure that was the only reason?'

'As far as I know, it was,' Hildur said. 'But our aim is always to keep children with their parents if we possibly can. It's the preferred option.'

'Were Bergrún and Fannar unhappy with that

arrangement?'

'I'm not sure. You'd have to talk to the Reykjavík branch of the Child Protection Agency. But I do know that Bergrún and Fannar had requested a child to foster permanently, and for a while there was a good chance that they would be able to keep Hekla because we didn't know if Maríanna would manage to turn her life around. But she did get back on her feet eventually, so I imagine they may well have been unhappy — disappointed, anyway. But in the end they agreed to become Hekla's support family and several years later they fostered a little boy who they went on to adopt, so I presume they're happy now.'

'Had things been going well for Hekla and Maríanna in the last few years?' Elma asked.

'Er, so-so,' Hildur said. 'Hekla had been a bit difficult in the last year. She kept trying to sneak out at night, and went over to Akranes without permission, that sort of thing.'

'When did you last speak to Maríanna?'

'As a matter of fact, it was shortly before she went missing,' Hildur said. 'Hekla had been discovered out on the Ring Road, trying to hitch a lift to Akranes. The police picked her up and notified us, so we paid them a visit.'

'Why was she going to Akranes? To visit her support family?'

'Er, no,' Hildur said. 'I think she wanted to go to a party or had a boyfriend there, or something like that. It's typical behaviour for that age group; they're always looking for trouble. Maríanna seemed at a loss, unsure how to handle Hekla.'

'I see,' Elma said. 'Did Maríanna seem her usual self the last time you met her?'

'She…' Hildur hesitated. 'Actually, she seemed unusually down, now that you mention it. Naturally, I assumed it was because of Hekla, as it can be a strain coping with a teenager. But perhaps there was more to it — given what happened.'

Elma wasn't sure how she felt after their conversation with the social worker. As she walked away from the grey building that housed the Borgarfjörður branch of the Child Protection Agency, the sick feeling in her stomach wasn't solely due to hunger. In the line of duty she had often seen broken homes, in which parents with addiction or mental problems were given endless chances that they rarely put to good use, while their children stood helplessly by, in situations that no child should have to endure. Often they couldn't express themselves or communicate their own wishes, and even when they did, the authorities turned a deaf ear. In Elma's opinion, the system was fundamentally flawed, designed to serve, not the best interests of the children, but some other purpose altogether.

She got into the car and stared silently out of the window.

'Are you OK?' Sævar asked.

'Yes,' Elma replied, without looking at him. She was picturing Hekla, three years old, alone in the flat, waiting for a mother who never came home. What impact might a traumatic experience like that have on a child?

'The system stinks,' Sævar said after a moment. Elma turned to him in surprise. 'I've seen it over and over again,' he went on, 'and I know you have too.'

Elma nodded. 'I just feel like … like it should be possible to do more. Do you know what I mean?'

'Yes,' Sævar said, and started the car. 'Still, at least we're trying.' He gave her an encouraging smile, then changed the subject. 'Hungry?'

It was well past midday and the energy provided by that morning's pastry had long been exhausted. They parked in front of Hyrnan. The service station had changed a bit since Elma was a little girl. Like many people, her family used to stop here on car journeys. In summer, the shop and café were generally busy with locals and foreign tourists, but at this time of year the place looked a bit empty, with only a few souls sitting in the café section, which resembled a school canteen. They chose a small, round table in a kind of conservatory attached to the shop. Sævar ordered two hot dogs and a Coke; Elma, a roast-beef sandwich and a carton of chocolate milk.

'What do you reckon?' she asked, after taking two bites of her sandwich and swallowing them so fast that she needed a large swig of chocolate milk to stop them getting stuck in her throat. 'Would Hekla have been capable of murdering her mother?'

Sævar shrugged, his mouth full. He swallowed his hot dog and drank some Coke before answering. 'Maybe if she had help. She had a pretty strong motive. Well, not that there's ever a good reason for murdering someone, but you know what I mean. Sometimes people do actually have a pretty understandable motive.'

'What about Agnar — could he have helped her?'

'Possibly,' Sævar said. 'We'd better check his alibi.'

'But if Hekla wasn't home that day, we have no way of knowing what time Maríanna vanished.'

'What about her phone? Weren't we also going by the time her phone was switched off?'

'Yes, but there may have been a natural explanation for that. Maríanna could just as well have come back home later that day and gone missing after that, which would put Sölvi back in the frame. Supposing he got drunk, paid Maríanna a visit and wanted to punish her for standing him up? For rejecting him?'

Sævar nodded. 'It's possible. We need to find out when Hekla really got home. It's time that girl was straight with us.'

'Do you think there's any point visiting her old school?'

'No idea.' Sævar ate the last bite of his hot dog.

Elma scrunched up the plastic wrapper from her sandwich and sucked up the dregs of her chocolate milk. 'Well, we'll soon find out.'

Nine Years Old

The voices in her room sound as if they're coming from a crowd of people, but she's alone in there. She's still playing with the toy soldiers, those little green figures, but now the game has changed and instead of lining them up, she makes them talk to each other. She has invented voices for every single one, and they quarrel and make up and have long conversations. She closes her door, which means I can't make out what they're saying unless they raise their voices and shout things like 'you idiot' or 'go away'. Otherwise the voices are usually so quiet that even if I press my ear to her door I can't make out a word, just incomprehensible mutterings. The doll I bought when she was a baby is still sitting on the chest of drawers, her dress as smooth and pristine as when she came out of the box.

I knock on her door at half past five. There's a class event at her school, which means I'm going to have to stand there for two hours, watching forty nine-year-old kids running around the hall. The parents are supposed to provide refreshments. Some make scones and prawn salad, others bake sugar-free cinnamon buns or chop up carrots. I didn't have time to make anything myself, so I bought some outrageously expensive iced buns from the bakery on the way home from work. If I put them in a basket, maybe I can pretend they're homemade.

She opens the door and smiles at me. It's new, this smile. She puts it on when you least expect it, like a vet-

eran TV newsreader. Her dark hair is pulled back in a pony-tail with an orange scrunchy that she must have picked up somewhere, perhaps at school, and she's wearing a short-sleeved red dress. They're not the clothes she was wearing earlier, so clearly she's made the effort to get changed and do her hair. A few weeks ago she asked for a mirror in her room, and I gave her a full-length one to prop up by her chest of drawers. I sometimes catch her out of the corner of my eye, posing in front of it and admiring her reflection, smiling or turning to contemplate her side view.

'I see you're ready.' The dress is old and too small. I haven't bought many clothes for her recently, but when I do, she grows out of them with record speed. I open her wardrobe and run my eyes over the contents, before finally taking out a loose-fitting, dark-blue dress with long sleeves.

'Try this one instead,' I say, taking the orange scrunchy out of her hair. Her dark mane is so thick and coarse that it's hopeless trying to tie it back in a pony-tail. The small hairs on her scalp stubbornly stick up in the air, however firmly I brush them flat. Once she's put on the dress, I braid her hair into a single thick, tight plait like the one I used to have in old photos at home. Always smiling and sweet, like a little princess. That's what Mum and Dad wanted me to be. As a child, I never wore the type of clothes you could get from discount stores. Instead, every time Dad travelled abroad for work, he would buy me tons of stuff from expensive shops, of the kind that none of the other kids wore. 'It's where the royal family shops,' he told us proudly. When I got older, I refused to wear these clothes, but for years I was just as they wanted me, like a little member of the British royal family.

Once the plait is finished, I inspect her in the mirror. 'There, much better,' I say, smiling at her.

When we arrive at the school, there's already a crowd of people there, and the fun and games have started. I put the iced buns on the table, smiling at the group of mothers who are standing off to one side. They are all older than me, with short hair and sticks up their arses, but I've made an effort to get to know them. I chat to them during school events and volunteer for all kinds of committees and associations. But just like with the kids, there's a certain pecking order among the parents. The mothers of the popular children stick together and organise the class socials. Their kids do sports together and meet up every day, but as my daughter still hasn't got to know anyone, I find myself dropping further and further in their estimation. Now they greet me with perfunctory nods and smiles, before carrying on talking among themselves, paying me no further attention.

'Shall we go into the hall?' I ask, trying to push my daughter away from my thigh. She nods. The movement is so slight that only I can see it. Really it's extraordinary how little she talks in company, given the torrent of words I hear coming from her bedroom every day. With me, she usually makes do with monosyllables. But she's obedient, and I can see that she's making more of an effort to please me these days.

We go into the hall and stand there like a couple of idiots, watching the other kids racing around. They slide along the floor and jump around like baboons. Then one of the fathers stops the music and the kids all slither to a standstill. 'We're going to play a game,' he says loudly, after shushing some of the boys. He explains the rules, not that most of the kids listen, but then they seem to know the game already.

'Go and join in,' I say, giving her back a push. She looks at me and for a moment I think I see fear in her eyes, as if

I'm asking her to do something bad. Then she obeys and walks out onto the floor. When the music begins she moves in time to it, and when it stops she runs into a corner like the other kids. When her corner isn't drawn out of the pack of cards, she looks over and smiles. Waves to me like she's an actor on stage, and I'm a member of the audience, come to see her. I feel a pang and blush when I notice some of the other girls looking at her and giggling.

'Which one of these brats is yours?' asks a voice behind me, and I glance round. I recognise him immediately, though I've only seen him from the seventh floor. He's recently moved into the flat on the ground floor of our block. I watched him carrying in furniture several days ago. And what I thought then is right: he is tall and strong, with light-brown hair. But what I hadn't been able to see until now were those friendly eyes.

'The girl in the blue dress,' I say. 'The one with the plait.'

'She looks like you.'

'Do you think so?'

'Yes, very like.' He smiles as if this is a compliment. To be fair, she has changed since she was a baby with that big nose and those overly strong features. She's grown into her nose, her features have softened, and her eyes have become quite arresting, with their piercing gaze and naturally dark surrounds. Maybe she'll grow up to be beautiful, but at the moment her looks are striking rather than pretty.

'Mine's the boy dancing as if nobody's watching.' He points to a boy who has fallen to his knees and is playing air guitar with flamboyant gestures.

I laugh. 'I wish I could be like that.'

'You could always take a turn on the dancefloor,' the man says. 'Like certain other people.'

Our eyes are drawn towards the father who, not content with controlling the music, has joined the children on the floor and is wiggling his hips embarrassingly, jerking them from side to side and waving his arms in a peculiar manner.

'Oh, no. I'm fine here,' I say.

We both grin as if we can read each other's minds, and without warning I feel my stomach turning a somersault. He smells good, and he's standing so close that I can tell he's just drunk a coffee.

'I feel like I've seen you somewhere before,' he says, studying me.

'Yes, I believe you've just moved into my building.'

'Ah, right,' he says. 'So we're neighbours.'

'Apparently so.'

'Hafliði,' he says, holding out his hand. I take it, and am conscious that our handshake lasts longer than strictly necessary.

'We should let our kids play together some time.'

'That would be fun,' I say, though I can't picture it. My daughter still hasn't had any friends round, and I don't suppose that's about to change. She doesn't seem to know anyone. No one goes over to talk to her or pays her any attention. Somehow she's more solitary among all these children than when she's alone in her room with her toy soldiers.

'I mean, my son and I are new to the area. Stefán doesn't really know anyone yet.'

'He seems confident, though,' I say, turning my gaze back to the dancefloor, where the boy is now bouncing all over the place like a kangaroo.

Hafliði sighs ruefully. 'A bit too confident.'

'Well, maybe he could help bring my daughter out of her shell.'

'Is she shy?'

I shrug. Shyness isn't the word I'd use to describe her.

'She's happy in her own company,' I say, after a little thought.

'That's a good quality.'

The music goes quiet, and one of the mothers calls across the hall that people can eat now. The children flock towards her. Hafliði says something I can't hear over the screeching around us. He shakes his head in defeat and next moment his son is there beside him. He tugs at Hafliði's sleeve, and then I feel a small, cold hand slip into mine and look down to see my daughter.

I watch him for the rest of the evening. He talks to some of the other parents, plays a bit with his son, and laughs at a comment made by another father. He's one of those men people are drawn to. I see the mothers smiling at him, and the fathers nodding every time he opens his mouth. When he shoots a sudden glance in my direction and grins, I drop my eyes in embarrassment.

It's a horrible evening really; the music's too loud, the kids are unbearable and keep crashing into me, and I step in a blob of mayonnaise on the floor. Yet I can't stop smiling all the way home.

Borgarnes School wasn't particularly large or impressive. Paint was flaking off the walls, though the scaffolding outside suggested that this was in the process of being remedied, and the football pitch was big and looked new. The grounds were overlooked by the picturesque church on the hill above.

'I was her teacher from when she was ten,' explained Lína, the young woman who was waiting to meet them. She had shoulder-length hair and bandy legs, her boyish appearance exaggerated by her outfit of jeans and T-shirt. 'I took over the class in year five and I'll stay with them right through to the bitter end — much to their horror.' Her voice was a little husky and her smile crooked. Elma guessed she was good at getting through to the kids. She certainly didn't seem to take herself too seriously.

'It must be nice staying with them for such a long time,' Elma remarked.

'Yes, it is. You get to watch them develop, you know. Grow up. Though they still seem terribly young when they leave us. But it's great meeting them later and seeing how they've turned out, you know? That's the best part. Especially when they take you by surprise.'

'What kind of pupil was Hekla?' Sævar asked, shifting in his seat. They were sitting in one of the classrooms, on chairs that were far too small for his big frame.

'She was...' Lína drummed her fingers on the desk and tightened her lips. She drew a long breath while she was turning the question over in her mind. 'Ye-es, what was Hekla like? That's not actually very easy to answer. She was pretty shy and quiet, you know? One of those kids who tend to get overlooked because you're always having to manage the rowdy ones. But she was hard-working. Maybe not the best pupil, but she did her homework and handed it in. Did what she was told — most of the time.'

'Most of the time?'

'Yes, well ... She started slacking a bit during her last year with us. She'd begun skiving off and that kind of thing, which wasn't like her. I asked if anything was wrong. She didn't answer, just sat there picking her nose.' Lína laughed, then her face grew more serious. 'Joking apart, I could see there was something bothering the poor kid.'

'Do you think it could have had anything to do with her situation at home?'

'I really couldn't say ... I mean, naturally she wanted to be in Akranes. She really liked her, you know, er ... her family there. She said she had good mates there too.'

'Didn't she have any friends here?'

'No. No, she didn't. She probably didn't try that hard to make them either. In fact, she did stuff that meant the other kids didn't want to hang around with her.'

'Like what?'

'Well, she could be ... what shall I say? She could lose it without warning. Lash out.'

Elma frowned. 'What do you mean? Did it happen often?'

'Errr...' Lína moved her jaw to one side consideringly, then said: 'There was, like, one time that springs to mind. The girls were doing games, and one of them obviously said something to Hekla, because she totally freaked out. She bit and scratched the girl so badly you could see the wounds a mile off.'

'When was this?'

'They were eleven, so it was a while back — four years ago.'

'Do you know what was behind it?'

'No, but it was a major drama … they were all crying and howling when I came in. Claimed all they'd done was ask Hekla if she didn't like taking showers. Of course, anyone could see what was behind that, and that they were being a lot nastier than they made out.' Lína sighed. 'But, like I said … Anyway, after that there was always a teacher present while they were changing. We made a big effort to help Hekla, but sadly you just can't force people to be friends. It would solve a whole lot of problems if you could, wouldn't it?'

'Did the bullying stop after that?' Elma realised they had strayed from the purpose of the interview. Hekla's problems at school didn't necessarily have any bearing on her mother's disappearance.

'We-e-ell … there may have been stuff that was hard to spot. Spiteful comments and so on. I wasn't aware of anything, but I tried to keep my eyes open. The team here are good at cracking down on that kind of thing. The kids get a lot of teaching about bullying from year one, and I'm happy to say there were no reports of incidents of that type at our school last year.' Lína smiled. 'Anyway, Hekla was obviously much happier in Akranes, and I couldn't understand why her mother didn't just move there. It wasn't like she had an important job here or … But what am I on about? I just think it would have been best for Hekla — if you ask me.'

'You had some communication with Maríanna, then?'

'Yeah, sure … Parent-teacher evenings and so on. We always have some contact with the parents. Some would say way more than necessary!' Her laughter ended in a coughing fit; a loose, phlegmy cough that made Elma suspect that she smoked.

'I assume you're aware that we found Maríanna's body a few days ago,' Sævar said, and the young woman immediately turned serious and nodded. 'That's why we're exploring all possible angles, trying to work out what happened. Is there anything you can think of?'

'Me?' She looked at them in astonishment. 'No. I mean…' She paused to think. 'When I heard where she was found, it occurred to me that maybe she'd run out of petrol and someone had given her a lift and … but what am I on about? Maybe it was someone she knew. Is that what you're thinking? I don't know anything. All I know was that Maríanna was a bit like Hekla and kept a pretty low profile here in town. But maybe she'd started seeing someone?'

Elma didn't know quite how to answer this stream of questions, and again it struck her that Lína must get on well with the kids, not least because she didn't seem so different from them. Not that she was immature, just that she was still in touch with her inner child. She'd adopted the kids' manner of speaking instead of being stiff and formal.

'We don't have much to go on yet,' Elma said after a pause. 'We're just examining…' She hesitated. How could she put it, without stating bluntly that they suspected Hekla of being involved?

Sævar stepped in. 'We're examining whether anything unusual happened before Maríanna went missing. We know Hekla had a boyfriend in Akranes and wanted to move there. But can you imagine that there might have been something else upsetting Hekla, something connected to school? Do you know if she had any more fights with the other kids or possibly with her mother? You know — was there anything you remember that we're forgetting to ask you about?'

'Errrr...' Lína raised her eyebrows and twisted her face in a peculiar scowl. 'Look, maybe it's not for me to say, but I got the impression Hekla was...' She stopped herself. 'No, it has nothing to do with this. I simply don't know what happened. I can't imagine that anyone would have ... have had it in for Maríanna.'

'You got the impression Hekla was what?' Sævar asked.

Lína sighed. 'Of course it's got nothing to do with it, but let's just say I'm surprised she had a boyfriend.'

'Oh?'

'I always got the feeling she wasn't into boys. That girls were more her thing.'

The day's interviews had left Elma with a lot to digest, but at least they were finally making progress. The conversation with the teacher stayed with her. She felt sorry for Hekla, sympathising with her desire to live near her friends in Akranes, with a family she was happy with. She pitied her, but even so there were various indications that Hekla knew more than she was letting on. Perhaps she was just a difficult teenager who lied and sneaked out without permission, couldn't stand her mother and wanted to get her own way. It needn't mean any more than that. But if Hekla had been forced to endure terrible things in her childhood, you never knew; it might have triggered a hatred that had slowly grown and festered inside her. Maybe until something had happened to push her over the edge.

Elma took out her phone as she sat in the car outside her block of flats and wrote herself a note to ask Agnar's employer if he had turned up to work that evening. It would have required physical strength to carry Maríanna over the lava field; strength that a fifteen-year-old girl wouldn't possess. Not Hekla, anyway. Elma pictured Agnar's long, thin limbs. He could hardly be that strong either, but he was tall.

It was a quarter to seven before Elma finally walked through her front door. She was absolutely shattered. She sent her mother a text to say she wouldn't make it to supper, only to regret the decision the moment she looked in her fridge. In the end she found a Thai ready-meal of chicken and noodles, frozen into a block of ice at the back of the freezer. While she was waiting for it to thaw in the microwave, she took off her jeans and got into her pyjama bottoms. Loosening her hair from its elastic band, she massaged her scalp.

Her phone started ringing the very instant the microwave pinged. Stomach rumbling, she sighed as she picked it up. Since she didn't recognise the number, she answered formally: 'Elma.'

'Good evening,' said an older woman's voice. 'I'm sorry to call so late. My name's Bryndís. We spoke on Tuesday, and you told me to ring you if I thought of anything else.'

Elma clicked at once. It was the mother of Maríanna's neighbour, who had been babysitting for her daughter when they went round. The one who used to drink coffee with Maríanna every Wednesday.

'Oh, yes, of course, I remember you,' Elma said.

'Good.' The woman was silent, then said: 'Well, I don't know if this will be of any use, but I've been racking my brains to think whether Maríanna said anything that could be important. It's been weighing on me, to be honest. That's why I've been going back over our conversations. I feel as if … as if she must have said something that…' Bryndís sighed, then went on: 'Anyway, I did remember one thing, connected to her brother.'

'Her brother?' Elma echoed.

'Yes, he died when Maríanna was pregnant with Hekla,' Bryndís said. 'She said her brother had been wrongly accused of something. She suddenly got terribly worked up and angry when she was talking about it. I don't know exactly why, but it just came back to me.'

'OK, thanks for letting me know.'

'You're welcome. I wish I could do more. Goodbye—'

'Just a minute,' Elma interrupted, before Bryndís could hang up. She had just remembered Sævar's suggestion about Elín's husband. 'Your son-in-law, Unnar…'

'Yes, what about him?'

'Your daughter mentioned that he and Maríanna got on well together…' Elma hesitated. She didn't know quite how to phrase the question without sounding too tactless. 'Do you know if they developed a close relationship or…?'

'A close relationship? I really don't know. But…' Bryndís paused. 'It wouldn't be the first time that…'

'That what?'

'That Unnar has — how shall I put it? — misbehaved.'

'I see.'

'Don't tell anyone I said that. It was years ago and I don't want … my daughter would…' Bryndís sighed again. 'Maríanna never said anything to suggest it, and I don't believe there was anything going on. I was much more struck by all the anger she seemed to be carrying around inside her because of what had happened to her brother. It was as if … as if she was on fire.'

After they'd said goodbye, Elma tried to call to mind what she knew about Maríanna's brother. It was very little: only that he had been quite a bit older than her and his name was Anton. He had killed himself fifteen years previously, and Maríanna's family had moved to Reykjavík in the aftermath. A sad story that showed how badly families could be affected by a blow like that. Maríanna's parents had apparently been incapable of helping their extremely young, pregnant daughter to cope with her grief, as the woman from the Child Protection Agency had told them. But it was the first time Elma could remember hearing about there having been accusations against Anton that had angered Maríanna. Neither her friends nor her daughter had mentioned this, which meant that the information Bryndís had provided was probably worthless, though she had meant well.

Elma took the meal out of the microwave and put it on a plate, regarding the five small chunks of chicken with disappointment. She sat down in front of the TV but didn't take anything in. Instead, she was picturing Hekla in her mind's eye, the picked-at black nail varnish and heavily pencilled eyebrows. Could she have suffered more at the hands of her mother than she was willing to admit?

Elma ate the last chunk of chicken, then put the plate down on the table. No way was that remotely filling: her stomach still felt half empty. Then she remembered the bar of chocolate in the cupboard. She had just settled down with it in front of the television when there was a knock at the door. A quick tap, so she knew immediately who it was.

An hour later she and Jakob were lying on the sofa. He propped himself up on his elbow and studied her face.

'We should go out on a date.'

'A date?' Elma giggled. 'You make it sound so formal.'

Jakob's mouth twitched into a smile, but Elma could tell that he was embarrassed. 'I mean it. What do you say we drive into Reykjavík at the weekend? Go for a meal somewhere classy, then to a gig? There's a brilliant stand-up at the Old Cinema on Saturday. My mate went and laughed so much it hurt.'

He made it sound as if he'd just thought of it, but Elma didn't believe it for a minute. She was still in her pyjama bottoms, but was now wearing a baggy T-shirt that Jakob had left at her place and she had appropriated for herself. He was lying behind her, with one arm around her, and she could feel his warm breath on the back of her neck.

Biting her lower lip, she turned to him. 'I'll have to see if I can get the time off work,' she said. 'There's quite a lot on at the moment.'

This sounded like an excuse but it was true: they had worked late every day that week, and she was envisaging having to tell Dagný that she wouldn't be able to accompany her to Reykjavík at the weekend.

But maybe it was an excuse too. Elma still wasn't sure what kind of relationship she and Jakob had. Up to now, it had been limited to their flats, to the sofa and bed, and when it started that had been the only kind of relationship she wanted. But now something had changed.

Jakob answered by kissing the top of her head. Elma turned away and tried to concentrate on the film again, but the atmosphere had changed. Something unsaid hung in the air between them, and she realised that she would have to come to a decision soon. The only problem was that she had no idea what her decision would be.

Nine Years Old

I watch him from my window on the seventh floor. He's wearing a black denim military jacket with shoulder straps. He doesn't appear to use anything to style his light-brown hair and when he walks it bounces in time to his strides. Although it's not far to the school and the weather isn't that bad — there's no wind, but heavy grey clouds threaten a downpour any minute — Hafliði and his son both get into the car. What was the son's name again? Stefán, that's it. Stefán's like his father: unusually tall for his age, with an innate self-confidence that's visible a mile off. Hafliði suggested at the class social that we should get our kids together for a play date — Stefán and my daughter. Hah! The idea is almost laughable.

I've been sitting at my post by the window on and off all weekend, and every time I notice a movement I lean towards the glass, hoping it's him. I've lingered longer than necessary in the entrance hall too, taking my time about opening my post box and collecting the junk mail and advertisements that I usually allow to pile up, but it hasn't led to anything. I haven't run into him or caught sight of him all weekend until now.

They drive away just as my daughter walks out of our building with both hands on the straps of her school bag and her eyes on the pavement. She's like an animal, curling up its body in self-defence. Really, it's extraordinary she doesn't bump into people or end up under a car. Her eyes never seem to leave the grey concrete pavement, and she moves fast, overtaking the other kids.

It works. Up to now she has done a good job of making herself invisible. She has no friends. One of the girls in her class lives on the next-door staircase, and I often see a group of kids outside her place. Every day the doorbell rings for this girl and children troop past our staircase without giving it so much as a glance. Are they even aware that she lives here? Do they even know she exists?

Still, I'm not too concerned, because it's not as if people really need friends. I've managed fine without them for years. All friends do is remind you of what you're not. I know — I used to have loads of them. They were nothing but hard work. Commitment. People who made demands on me, who needed to be taken into consideration. It drove me mad the way they would get offended by one harmless little comment, or make me feel like I had to go to places I had no interest in, just to be a good friend. Because friends do things for each other. God, I don't miss them one bit.

After work I stop off at the supermarket. Then I linger in the foyer of our building, checking the post box, but it's empty. Hafliði's car's not outside, and I'm hoping he might pull into the drive any minute. But nothing happens and in the end I take the lift upstairs.

'Hi, hun,' I say to my daughter, who is sitting on the sofa, watching TV. She has no interest in brainless cartoons. No, she watches documentaries about everything under the sun, then comes out with all kinds of bizarre remarks and references to them, like: 'Mum, did you know that prawns have hearts in their heads?' I just hope she doesn't talk like that at school, since the other kids must find her weird enough already. The programme she's watching now with such awestruck fascination is yet another of those natural-history documentaries. I start putting the shopping away in the fridge, then switch on the oven and stick in a

readymade lasagne. It's then that there's a knock at the door. Knock, knock. Two polite raps, and I know at once that it's him.

'Have you got any eggs?' He's wearing an ugly, thin T-shirt that can't disguise his little pot belly. There's a picture of some band on the front that he probably doesn't listen to, but which looks good on a T-shirt. An all-male band from the seventies, with long hair and cigarettes hanging from their lips.

'As it happens I've just bought some.' I gesture to him to come in, open the fridge and ask how many he needs. Then I take out two and hand them to him. 'Careful not to break them.'

'I'll do my best.' He smiles and is about to leave when my daughter suddenly blocks his way. 'Oh, hi. Nice to see you again.'

'Thanks,' she says, smiling that practised, newsreader smile. The one that lights up her face for a split second, then is gone again. 'Hey, that's my initial.' She stares at Hafliði, who wrinkles his brow for a moment before he grasps what she's talking about.

'Oh, you mean the necklace,' he says. 'Yes, it seems we share an initial. My mother gave me this when I was thirty, and I haven't taken it off since. I'd show it to you but my hands are full.' He holds up the eggs and laughs.

Only now do I notice that he's wearing a gold chain around his neck with the letter H on a round pendant. The chain must have been hidden under his shirt collar the last time we met, but now it's revealed by the neck of his ugly T-shirt, which gapes as if it's been stretched.

She doesn't laugh, just regards him thoughtfully, then puts a hand up to her own necklace which has the same letter on it.

'You've got one too,' Hafliði says. 'We match.'

She's still staring at him, and I can see that Hafliði is growing uncomfortable. He stands in the hall, shifting his feet as if he doesn't know if he's coming or going.

'Why don't you go back in and watch TV, darling?' I say, putting a hand on her shoulder. At that she turns away and settles down on the sofa again. I smile at him apologetically. 'She's a bit—' I begin, but he interrupts.

'Listen,' he says, suddenly appearing a little uncertain, as if he doesn't know quite what he's going to say. Yet he does know, precisely. It's a game, the embarrassed smile and the way he lowers his eyes to the carpeted floor of the hall before raising them to mine. 'Sorry to ask, but I've been trying to get the washing machine in the basement to work ever since we moved in, with no luck. You don't know the trick of starting it, do you? Stefán's running out of clothes for school. He'll be fed up if he has to resort to his stripy jumper, but there'll be no alternative if I don't manage to do a wash soon — there's nothing else left.'

I smile. 'Of course. I'll come down as soon as we've had supper. Shall we say at eight?'

The washing machine in the basement is enormous and available to everyone in the building but in practice few people use it. Like me, most of the residents have installed their own machines in the bathroom or kitchen. After all, it's such a bore having to lug your laundry downstairs, and the machine is pretty battered and leaves a bad smell in your clothes. I don't tell Hafliði this, though. Instead, I go and wait for him in the basement, which has one tiny window high in the wall.

The clock strikes eight. No one comes, and I can't hear a sound, apart from the constant humming from the heating pipes that run along the walls, as if someone's in the shower or running a bath. I don't often come down here, and there's a reason for that. The room's old and dirty, with peeling pale-green paint on the walls. You can store bikes and children's buggies down here, but I'd never be seen dead on a bicycle. Or with a buggy, for that matter. Please God, don't let me have another child.

I was forced to use the washing machine down here when we first moved in but only for a few weeks. It's simple to use, so I can't think why he needs help. Perhaps it's just a pretext to meet me. The thought sends a current of electricity zinging into the pit of my stomach. I listen for footsteps, but the minutes crawl by, and I begin to feel stupid standing there. Five minutes pass, then ten, and I'm just about to leave when I hear a sound: footsteps approaching along the corridor, and then he's there.

'Sorry, sorry,' he says, running a hand through his hair. 'I got a call from work, something about unrecorded measurements and ... Anyway, it doesn't matter. I'm just glad you're still here.' He's carrying a washing basket full of dirty laundry and smiles in a way that makes it hard not to smile back.

'No problem, I've only just got here myself,' I lie.

'Oh, right, I'm glad I didn't keep you waiting.'

'I was afraid I was keeping you waiting.'

'No harm done, then.'

'No harm done,' I repeat.

'Right. This washing machine. How on earth do I get it to work?'

He puts down the laundry basket and stuffs the clothes into the machine. I choose a setting and shortly afterwards the drum starts turning and the machine fills with water. I show him the best program and how to adjust the temperature and spin speed. As he leans closer, I can smell him; feel the warmth radiating from him.

'So, it was as simple as that.' He laughs, shamefaced,

and straightens up again. 'Now I look like a complete idiot.'

'Not at all. The machine's so ancient, it's no wonder you didn't know how to use it,' I say, while underneath I'm thinking that if he really couldn't get it to work, he must be stupider than I thought.

'I suppose I wasn't good enough about taking care of this kind of thing before.' He scratches his head.

'Before?'

'Before it was just the two of us. Dagbjört used to do all the washing. I know, a terribly old-fashioned arrangement. But I'm learning. I've even started ironing my own shirts.' He grins triumphantly.

'That's a step in the right direction.'

'What about you?'

'Me?'

'Yes, I mean, is it just the two of you? You and your daughter?'

'Yes,' I say. 'It's always been just us two.'

'I see.' There's a brief silence during which his gaze locks with mine. I don't look away. I can feel my heart beating in my throat, the heat in my body.

Then, without warning, he leans towards me. It's a pretty bold move, but typical of a man like him. I bet he's never been rejected. Never been pushed away or asked to stop. And I'm not going to be the first woman to do it. He places a hand behind my head and his lips touch mine. The room starts to dance around me, and the sound of the washing machine fades to a pleasant hum. The heat has become a raging inferno by now, and suddenly I feel ten years younger.

It's a long time since I've been with a man. So long that I thought when the time came I wouldn't know how to behave or what to do. But now that it's finally happening, it's easy, and all my movements are instinctive. I haven't forgotten a thing.

There's nothing embarrassing about his touch, and I don't even stop to think that someone could walk in any minute. Or that my little girl is sitting upstairs in her pyjamas, waiting for me. The only thing occupying my thoughts is the weight on top of me, the frantic breathing and the rhythmic sloshing of the washing machine.

Friday

Elma began the morning by ringing the owner of the restaurant where Agnar used to work. He reacted gruffly, telling her to talk to the woman who took care of the shift rota, and leaving her in no doubt that she had woken him up. The woman, on the other hand, was much more civil and willing to help, although she was obviously very busy, as Elma could hear from the children's voices in the background.

'I'm just dropping my son off at nursery and I'll need to look at a computer to check the shift rota.' She sounded out of breath. 'Can I call you back shortly?'

'Of course.' Elma hung up and reached down to scratch Birta behind the ears. 'Why aren't you with your dad?' she whispered.

Birta shook herself, then lay down again with her head between her paws.

Elma leant so far back in her chair, it creaked. The morning meeting was due to start in half an hour. She wandered out into the kitchen, filled her mug with coffee, then sat back down at her computer.

It was Friday, and while many of her colleagues looked forward to the weekend, Elma was glad that she would be on duty. She'd sent Dagný a message that morning to ask if they could postpone their Reykjavík trip. She was expecting to have to work both days, and even if she had a little free time, she was too preoccupied with the case to be able to switch off enough to enjoy a massage. Dagný had agreed, but asked if she could pop round after work so they could order some stuff, as it was only a week until their father's birthday. Now all that remained was for Elma to decide what to do about Jakob and his suggestion of a date. She sighed and was grateful when her thoughts were interrupted by the phone.

'Right, I've got the file in front of me.' It was the woman from the pizza restaurant. 'You were asking about Friday, 4 May. I see that Agnar worked the shift from four until ten that evening.'

'Do they always go home on the dot of ten?'

'Usually,' the woman said. 'It can sometimes take a bit longer to clear up if the place is busy, but Agnar doesn't work in the kitchen; he's on deliveries.'

'Deliveries?'

'Yes, you know. He delivers the takeaway pizzas.'

'Oh, of course. Do the delivery guys help to clean up the kitchen after their shifts?'

'Sometimes. When there's a lot on, everyone helps out.'

Elma thanked her and ended the call. She knew perfectly well what pizza delivery people did, but she was wondering how sure they could be that Agnar had come straight back after every job. Could he conceivably have slipped off between deliveries? Though even if he had, she reflected, he was unlikely to have had enough time to drive to Grábrók and back; a round-trip of nearly 140 kilometres from Akranes. Then again, he could have gone there after work, under cover of night; although in May it didn't get dark until late. What about before work, then? Maríanna had probably died sometime after 3.00 p.m., if the time her phone had been turned off was anything to go by. And, Elma reflected, Agnar's alibi for that time was far from satisfactory.

The meeting room was empty when she went in and took a seat. A few minutes later Sævar entered, looking unusually smart. Instead of his habitual T-shirt, he was wearing a white shirt, his hair was combed to one side and he reeked of aftershave.

'What's all this in aid of?'

'What?' He sat down.

'The outfit. Have you got a date after work?' she teased, and was surprised when Sævar looked shifty. He avoided her eye and gave a rueful half-smile, muttering something about these being his only clean clothes.

Elma refrained from interrogating him further but gave him a speculative look. Were her eyes deceiving her or was that a faint blush? Perhaps he really did have a date after work. But who with? Perhaps the new female officer who had joined them in the spring. Her name was Birna; she was in her mid-twenties and had just graduated from police training college. Elma sometimes heard them chatting together in the coffee room. Birna was as open and unaffected as Sævar. She turned up to work bright-eyed and bushy tailed every day, and was always smiling.

Elma's thoughts flew to Jakob. He and Sævar could hardly be more different: Sævar with his dark hair and craggy face; Jakob blond and boyish. He had such fine, delicate features that he would probably never stop looking boyish. They were polar opposites when it came to their personalities too. Elma could never be sure when Sævar was being serious, and his teasing drove her up the wall at times. Jakob, in contrast, was so sincere that it would never occur to him to take the mickey out of her. That wasn't to imply that he was totally humourless, though. He was a big *South Park* fan and sometimes showed her cartoons in the paper that made him laugh.

Elma couldn't envisage him and Sævar getting on. In her mind they belonged to two different worlds, but she had to face it: if she went on a date with Jakob and their relationship developed into something more serious, the two worlds would have to collide sooner or later. For some reason, the thought made her uncomfortable.

She snapped back to the present when Hörður came in and sat down. 'OK, what's the latest?' he asked, stirring his tea.

Elma gave him a summary of the previous day's interviews. 'In other words, we're focusing our attention on Hekla. I spoke to Agnar's employer, who confirmed that he was at work. But it turns out Agnar's a pizza delivery boy, which means he could potentially slip off for a while without anyone noticing; between four and six, for example, before things got busy.'

'Really?' Hörður asked, his eyebrows raised sceptically. 'For long enough to murder someone?'

'It needn't have taken long — the time-consuming part would have been hiding the body. Agnar and Hekla could have taken care of that later in the evening. We don't know what he was up to between three and four p.m. either.'

Sævar nodded thoughtfully. 'That would explain the date of Maríanna's note. Hekla could have put out an old message from her mother to confuse us.'

Elma propped her elbows on the table and went over the sequence of events as she understood it. 'So, Maríanna goes to Akranes in search of Hekla, finds her with Agnar and something happens … there's a struggle that ends in Maríanna's death. Agnar goes to work; Hekla waits in the flat or goes to see her friends, and after he's finished work they drive to Grábrók together. They hide the body in the lava field, then return home.'

Hörður took a sip of tea. 'Until we have any proof, that's pure speculation. We have to find some proper evidence; something to link her directly to the murder.'

'But Hekla's the only person with a real motive,' Sævar pointed out. 'And she lied to us. Why lie if she has nothing bad on her conscience?'

'I got a phone call yesterday,' Elma said, 'from a woman called Bryndís. You remember, Sævar — the mother of Elín, Marianna's neighbour in Borgarnes?' Sævar nodded and Elma continued: 'I asked her about her son-in-law, Unnar, who lived upstairs from Marianna, and whether they might have been … more than just friends.'

'And?'

Elma shrugged. 'She didn't know. Though she did say he'd cheated on his wife before. Not with Marianna but with another woman.'

'So he could have done it again. Is that something we should look into?'

'We could talk to him,' Elma suggested. 'Though Bryndís wasn't actually ringing about him.'

'Oh?' Hörður put his teaspoon down on the table.

'No. She mentioned Anton, Marianna's brother. Said something about accusations against him that Marianna had dismissed as rubbish. Bryndís didn't know any more than that, so it's not much to go on.'

'He killed himself, didn't he?' Sævar asked.

'Yes,' Elma said. 'If I understood her right, the accusations may have been the reason for his suicide.'

'It doesn't always require a reason,' Sævar pointed out.

Elma knew that better than anyone but determinedly pushed the thought away. 'Anyway, the subject made Maríanna incredibly angry. I don't know, maybe Bryndís was just trying to be helpful and the incident didn't have any bearing, but it wouldn't hurt to talk to Maríanna's father again. We haven't spoken to him in person since the spring.'

Neither Sævar nor Hörður commented on this suggestion, and Elma could tell they found her idea far-fetched.

'It's not such a bad idea to speak to Maríanna's father again,' Hörður said eventually. 'They hadn't had any contact in recent years, but he may be able to tell us something anyway. And, for all we know, Hekla may be in touch with her grandfather.'

'What do we do now, then?' Sævar asked.

Hörður drew a deep breath. 'The only thing we've got of any substance is the fact that Hekla lied, and, as you point out, Agnar's alibi is hardly watertight. He could have acted as an accomplice. So the next step is to bring Hekla in to give a statement.'

'Great. Let's do it. But don't forget to call the Child Protection Agency and ask them to send a chaperone.' Sævar started gathering his belongings together.

Hörður glanced at his watch. 'See if she can come in after lunch today. Give her foster-parents a call.'

Nine Years Old

Funny how quickly everything can change. All these years it's just been the two of us. We've been living in our own little soap bubble, in a neighbourhood where nobody knows who I was or what I did. It was all so long ago that when I look back, I can barely recognise the person I was before she was born. That girl who was so full of anger, but also of shame. I rarely think about the past or the fact that I haven't seen my parents for years. They ring from time to time, and they've offered to pay our airfares to go out and see them, but I declined immediately. As far as I'm concerned, they might as well be dead.

Of course, there have been times when I've unexpectedly run into someone from my former life. It's always unsettling, like a kick in the gut. Part of me longs to scream at those people; to tell them I've changed and that they're wrong, but luckily I'm mostly indifferent these days. I've even amused myself by looking straight through them, when I've felt them staring and can tell that they've recognised me.

For the last nine years the world has revolved around the two of us, but now, all of a sudden, we've been joined by a third. And a fourth. The family I always used to imagine — the two children, a boy and a girl, and the loving partner — has become a reality. At weekends we wake with our limbs entangled under the duvet, and make love before the kids get up. Our days consist of trips to the swimming pool, walks, visits to the ice-cream van and laughter. We cook supper together, watch films chosen by the kids, and everything is … easy. So incredibly easy.

As the summer wears on, we talk about putting my flat on the market since we hardly ever use it. The only problem is that Hafliði's place is too small, and I can't see my daughter being willing to share a room with Stefán. So we scroll through property websites in the evenings, allowing ourselves to dream.

Hafliði has captured her heart as well as mine. Her eyes light up when she smiles at him, and she constantly wants to be near him. Sometimes he turns up the music in the sitting room and dances, as unselfconsciously as his son danced the evening we first met. It makes her laugh. I had no idea she could dance like a mad thing or laugh until she was out of breath. Of course, she's odd — there's no change there — but Hafliði treats her as if she's great. He takes an interest in everything she does and will spend entire evenings watching documentaries with her. She talks nonstop when Hafliði asks her about one of her interests, and would rather sit with us than go to her room. Sometimes I feel as if she and Hafliði belong to a secret club from which I'm excluded. They take hold of their necklaces with the H pendants, as if these form an unbreakable bond between them, and exchange knowing grins across the dinner table. It's sweet really, and of course I'm grateful to Hafliði for everything he's done, but there are times when I feel I should be the one exchanging secretive glances with my lover, not my daughter.

While I'm delighted that they get on so well together, it's possible to take things too far. She asks him to read to her every evening, wants to sit beside him while we watch TV and talks about him constantly when he's not there. It's like she has a crush on him in her innocent, childlike way, and Hafliði indulges her. Encourages her, even.

He has a talent for making people feel special. He never tires of telling me how beautiful I am, dashes out to the shop if I so much as mention that I have a craving for sugar, and asks me endless questions about myself. I tell him about my parents, what it was like growing up in a small town, and how difficult it was to have a child on my own when I was so young. I even shed a few tears when I talk about it, like a pathetic woman who longs for nothing more than to be rescued. He seems eager to take on this role. It feels as if he wants to know every inch of my body and soul. I find myself thinking I could reveal all my secrets, but that's dangerous, and I have to remind myself to be careful. It's too early to tell him everything, and it may never be the right time. But, until then, I'm happy to let him into our little soap bubble and just hope that nothing will happen to burst it.

'Come in.' Elma held the door open for Hekla. She smiled at Bergrún, who had taken a seat outside in the corridor, then closed the door. Bergrún looked uneasy as she sat there with her bag on her lap, watching Hekla disappear into the interview room. Elma could understand how she felt and had explained everything in great detail, introduced her to the representative of the Child Protection Agency, who would be sitting at Hekla's side during the interview, and assured her that everything would be fine. Fifteen-year-olds didn't need a parent present while they were giving a statement, but the law did require parents or guardians to be notified. A lawyer had been asked to join them, though Hekla wasn't officially a suspect, since that might change during the course of the interview.

Sævar recited the formalities into the recording device on the table in front of them before saying: 'The reason we wanted you to come in today is that there are some points we need to get clear. So, could you repeat for us everything that happened on the Friday your mother disappeared?'

Hekla's eyes flickered towards the door as if she was afraid Bergrún could hear. 'I went home after swimming,' she muttered, so quietly they had to crane towards her to hear.

'And what did you do at home?'

'Nothing special.'

'Didn't you order a pizza in the evening?' Elma smiled.

Hekla nodded.

'Because your mother left you some money and this envelope?' Elma placed the envelope with Maríanna's message on the table.

'Mmm,' Hekla confirmed.

'All right,' Elma said. 'And the next day, what did you do then?'

'I…' Hekla cleared her throat. 'I woke up and … and I don't remember exactly what I did. Maríanna wasn't back, so I tried to call her. Her phone … it was turned off, so I rang Bergrún.'

'What time was this?'

'Maybe five.'

'Great.' Elma glanced down at her notebook. 'So you rang Bergrún, and she came and collected you. Did it take her long to get there?'

'No, only half an hour or something.' When no one said anything, Hekla carried on: 'She wanted to call the police because …'

'Because it wasn't the first time Maríanna had disappeared,' Elma finished.

Hekla nodded.

Elma took a deep breath, then said: 'The thing is, Hekla, we had a chat with a boy called Agnar yesterday. Do you know him?'

Hekla lowered her eyes. 'Yes.'

'Could you speak up a bit?' Elma made an effort to keep her voice friendly.

'Yes,' Hekla repeated. 'Yes, I know him.'

'He said you were his girlfriend. That you'd been together for a year. Is that right?'

'Maybe.'

'You aren't sure?'

'Yes, but it wasn't, like, a whole year. And we're not

together anymore.'

'No, he told us you'd broken up,' Elma said. 'But a year is quite a long time when you're fifteen. At least, I remember it used to seem like forever when I was that age.' Her smile drew no response from Hekla. 'The thing is, he told us something else too. He said you'd asked him to come and pick you up from Borgarnes on the Friday your mother went missing. But that when he said he couldn't come straight away, you decided to manage on your own and caught a bus to Akranes instead. That's not what you told us.'

The black nail varnish looked new, but Hekla immediately started cropping at it. Elma wondered if the only reason she put it on was so she could pick it all off again.

'I ... er, I ...' Hekla raised her eyes to the representative from children's services, who had been silently observing. The woman gave her an encouraging smile, and Hekla continued, a little breathlessly: 'I was going to tell you but then ... then I didn't. And it didn't matter anyway, and then such a long time passed and ...' She bit her lip. 'I just didn't want you to think I was making it up because ... you know, because ...'

'It's all right, dear, it's OK.' The woman from children's services laid a reassuring hand on her shoulder.

'Hekla, it's extremely important that you tell us the truth. We have to get the facts straight so we can work out what happened to your mother,' Elma said. 'You want that, don't you?'

'Yes,' Hekla replied in a small voice.

'Right, then let's try again. When did you go to Akranes on Friday, the fourth of May?'

'I took the bus at two.'

'So you never went to your swimming lesson?'

'Yes, but I just ... I went to the toilet and then I left. He never notices.' Presumably she meant the swimming instructor.

'So you didn't go home,' Elma said. 'Do you think your mother could have spotted you waiting at the bus stop?'

'I don't know.' Hekla sniffed. 'She kept ringing and ringing, but I was so angry. I didn't want to talk to her because she was being so unfair, not letting me go to the tournament. I just couldn't stand her.' At this point, her voice wobbled and she burst into tears. It took her a moment or two to compose herself.

'We all have fights with our parents, Hekla,' Elma said. 'It's perfectly normal. OK, you went over to Akranes. What did you do there?'

'I went to see a friend,' Hekla said in a low voice. 'I was round at hers for a bit. I wanted to go and see Bergrún and Fannar but I knew that was the first place Maríanna would look. I didn't really know what to do. I just didn't want to be at home.'

'Can anyone confirm that you were at your friend's house?'

'Yes, Tinna,' Hekla said. 'And Tinna's mum; she was there too.'

'What time did you get home?'

'I didn't stay that long. I promise I'm telling the truth now. I was feeling bad and decided to go home because there was nothing I could do and I knew ... I just knew Maríanna would ring Bergrún and come looking for me.'

'So you took the bus home?'

'Yes, at around, like, six. I was home before seven and I really did order a pizza.'

'And you didn't see your mother at any point?'

Hekla shook her head.

'OK.' Elma glanced at Sævar and saw from his expression that he wasn't entirely convinced.

'I didn't think it would matter,' Hekla continued. 'Maríanna was going out to meet that man, and I thought she wouldn't notice I'd gone. Then I got home, but she never came back, so I called Bergrún. I was just scared that if I said I'd gone to Akranes, Maríanna would be cross and maybe Bergrún too. I didn't mean to lie. Or, you know, I didn't plan to. I just ... it just came out, and then I couldn't take it back. Because if I did, everyone would think I was lying.'

'All right, Hekla,' Elma said, closing her notebook. She studied the girl for a while. Her reactions seemed genuine, and Elma could understand how a lie like that could escalate, especially if Hekla believed her mother would be angry.

'I think we're done for the moment,' she said. 'Maybe one more thing.' She pointed at the envelope on the table with the message from Maríanna. 'The bill in the envelope is from last year. Did your mother really leave that note for you?'

'Yes,' Hekla said. 'It was on the table, I promise.'

'What do you think she was apologising for?'

Hekla leant back in her chair. 'I think she was feeling guilty about the football tournament. We had a fight the evening before, and she'd gone to work by the time I woke up. I didn't see the envelope until I got home, so I don't know if she left it there in the morning or later. If I'd seen it that morning, I might not have been so angry and gone to Akranes, and then ... then she'd be alive.' Hekla's head drooped.

She looked so small sitting there that Elma felt an impulse to give her a hug. She wanted to tell Hekla that it wasn't her fault and it would have made no difference if she hadn't sneaked off to Akranes. But the truth was that it had probably made all the difference.

'Why do you think she always refers to her mother as Maríanna?' Sævar asked, after Hekla and Bergrún had left. 'She never says 'Mum', just 'Maríanna'.'

'I don't suppose she felt Maríanna was much of a mother,' Elma replied. 'I don't know. But I've heard other examples of children deciding to call their parents by their proper names. For a number of different reasons.'

'Do you think she calls Bergrún 'Mum'?'

'Well, I … I don't know. Maybe.'

Sævar shrugged. 'I can believe she'd see her as more of a mother than Maríanna ever was. Given everything that happened.'

'Yes, it would be perfectly understandable.'

'Do you think she's telling the truth?'

'Yes,' Elma said, after a moment's reflection. 'Yes, I do.' She stood up and stretched, then went over to the window and looked out. The street outside was busy; a group of girls, who had clearly finished school for the day, were standing around in front of the boxy blocks of flats. They looked as if they were discussing something important. Eventually, three of them went into the same apartment block, while the other two walked off in different directions. She turned back to Sævar.

'Would you mind ringing Maríanna's neighbour? He was called Unnar, wasn't he? Judging by what Bryndís told us, it might not be such a bad idea to check if he knew Maríanna better than he ought to have done.'

Sævar nodded. 'Sure, will do. But I very much doubt he'd admit to anything like that over the phone.'

'No, I suppose not.'

'And we didn't find any messages between them.'

'No, but they lived in the same house. They probably wouldn't have needed to send each other texts or emails.'

'Handy,' Sævar commented.

Elma immediately felt herself blushing, though she had no idea if he meant to insinuate anything. But she had to admit that this perfectly described the arrangement she had with Jakob: handy.

Dagný greeted Elma with a beaming smile. The terraced house where she and Viðar lived was compact but cosy, with oak parquet on the floor and oak fittings. The Buddha statues Dagný collected were tastefully lined up on shelves all over the house, and one wall in the sitting room was painted royal blue, matching the velvet cushions on the pale-coloured sofa.

'Where is everyone?' Elma asked as she sat down on the sofa.

'Viðar took the boys to the playground,' Dagný said. 'Can I offer you something?'

'Maybe just some fizzy water, if you've got any.'

Dagný vanished into the kitchen and returned with two glasses of soda water and a bowl of Nóa Kropp, which made Elma smile. The chocolate-coated corn puffs used to be their favourite sweet — one of the few things the sisters ever had in common. An old memory popped up of her and Dagný sitting on the sofa, watching a cartoon, and hurling themselves backwards in such violent gales of laughter that they overturned a bowl of Nóa Kropp all over the cushions. Their expressions when they looked at each other had sent them into further helpless fits of giggling. Afterwards they had hurriedly picked them all up and put them back in the bowl before their mother could discover what had happened. Several days later, Dagný had nudged Elma when their mother got up from the sofa, and pointed with an exaggerated gesture to the large, brown smudge on her bottom. This had set them off again, much to their mother's puzzlement.

'I've got in touch with most of Dad's friends, and of course all the relatives I could think of,' Dagný said, handing Elma an exercise book in which she had written the guest list.

If only she could be as organised as Dagný, Elma thought.

'Could you check if I've left anyone out?'

Elma ran down the names. Of course her sister hadn't forgotten anyone.

'I've also ordered the food and drink, and put together a play list. A few people want to give short speeches — old school friends of Dad's and so on. And I thought that after supper we could have music and get Mum and Dad to dance. You remember the salsa classes they took the year they went to South America?'

Elma laughed. It was a great idea. After their parents got back from their trip, their father had kept pulling their mother into his arms at unexpected moments and executing a few salsa moves in the sitting room, until their mother had gone on strike. She had been more surprised than anyone by the way he'd taken to salsa, as the classes had been entirely her idea.

'He'd enjoy that,' Elma said, looking through the play list. Her sister had obviously put a huge amount of time and effort into planning the party, and Elma suddenly felt guilty for groaning and sighing over all Dagný's ideas and generally behaving as if their dad's seventieth birthday wasn't a big deal. Elma realised she hadn't actually lifted a finger beyond grudgingly agreeing to Dagný's suggestions.

'Now I feel bad. I haven't done anything.'

'It doesn't matter,' Dagný said. 'You know how much I enjoy it.' She popped a chocolate into her mouth and smiled at Elma. 'I can't wait to see his face. He has absolutely no idea this is happening.'

Elma smiled back. 'It's going to be great. And thank you. Thanks for taking care of everything. I know I've been totally—'

'Don't say that,' Dagný cut in. 'You've got more than enough on your plate.'

'So have you. I mean, you've got a job and a husband and two kids. I don't understand how you can achieve all this and be a great mum and do everything so perfectly.'

Dagný didn't answer. Her lip trembled. Elma stopped in the act of taking a sip of soda water and frowned at her sister. 'Is … is everything all right?'

This had the effect of making Dagný clamp a hand over her mouth while her eyes filled with tears. 'Jesus, I didn't mean to start crying.'

'What's wrong?'

Dagný got up and fetched a paper towel from the kitchen, then sniffed and heaved a breath. 'It's just … it's Alexander. Clearly, I'm not such a good mother. There's been trouble at school — some of the other boys are bullying him. Boys who used to be his friends. Now they've started hiding his clothes, and they tipped the contents of his school bag into a puddle and … oh, I know it's not that huge a problem but I just don't know what to do. Honestly, I feel like…'

'Going down to the school and giving those boys a good shaking?' Elma finished.

Dagný looked at her and laughed. 'Yes, seriously, I do. I want to shake them so hard their teeth rattle. I know they're only kids, but it's Alexander we're talking about — Alexander, the sweetest kid in the world, who'd never hurt a fly. How can they do it? What's wrong with them? What's wrong with their parents?' Dagný blew her nose. 'That's why Viðar's been so good about taking them out and doing all kinds of activities with them. To distract Alexander and help him forget about it for a while. I can't do anything, I just start crying every time I think about it, and that's the last thing Alexander needs — a bawling mother.'

'They're still so young,' Elma said. 'Only six. Surely, things'll get better soon. Like you said, they used to be his friends, so perhaps something's come up — something they'll soon forget. It's not until they're teenagers that you really have to worry, and that's years off.'

Dagný raised her eyes to Elma again. 'Oh God, Elma … Sorry, I know I wasn't … you know. I should have…'

Elma smiled and ignored the knot that was forming in her stomach. 'It doesn't matter. It was such a long time ago and, anyway, I wasn't talking about me. I got over it years ago.' This wasn't quite true. She had recently come to realise that the bullying and gossip she had endured as a teenager had left behind scars that wouldn't heal so easily. 'I just meant that Alexander will be OK. He's such a great kid, and the others will soon see that. I wouldn't worry about him.'

Dagný was silent, her gaze lowered to her hands. 'Well, in spite of that, I always wanted to say sorry. After what happened with Davíð too. I just never knew what to say and you always seemed like you didn't need anyone. Always so independent.' Dagný glanced up fleetingly and smiled.

Elma smiled back, too choked to speak. She was afraid that if she tried, her voice would betray her.

'Right, shall we carry on?' Dagný said after a pause and Elma nodded.

Dagný opened her laptop and shortly afterwards her shopping basket was full of all kinds of decorations that were probably a bit over the top but were bound to make the occasion go with a bang.

* * *

Hekla got permission to go out that evening on condition that she was home by midnight. Her interview at the police station hadn't been as bad as she'd expected. She had pictured an inhospitable, grey room, like in films or TV crime dramas, with a good-cop, bad-cop scenario, and that they would yell at her and berate her for lying. In fact, both cops had been friendly and neither had raised their voice or told her off.

Bergrún had gone on and on at her after the interview, until Hekla had caved and told her about Agnar. She didn't admit they'd been going out, though, just claimed they were friends. Mates. It sounded better, but she wasn't sure Bergrún had believed her.

Bergrún and Fannar were like her parents and had been for as long as she could remember. When she was younger, everything had been easier, and she hadn't even had to think about how to behave. She'd just been this little girl, and they gave her their unconditional love. Now she was afraid it wouldn't be enough anymore.

She and Maríanna had often quarrelled like sisters rather than mother and daughter. Their relationship had never been like that. Hekla had believed she could forget, but now it was as if all the things she had said and thought were growing inside her like weeds that she couldn't root out — all the lies, the ugly thoughts, words and deeds, all tangled up in one big, painful knot in her stomach.

Bergrún must never be allowed to see this side of her. Sometimes Hekla found herself telling her things that weren't quite true. Like about the time Maríanna had sent her to her room after she'd discovered that Hekla had sneaked off to Akranes. It wasn't true that Maríanna had locked her in, nor was it true that she'd hit her. But Hekla had told Bergrún this, and Bergrún had believed her and felt sorry for her, which had given Hekla the warm feeling that she and Bergrún were on the same side.

Now Hekla smiled at Bergrún, who was standing behind her, studying her in the large bathroom mirror, so close that she could smell the coconut scent of Bergrún's shampoo.

'You've got such beautiful hair,' Bergrún said, running her hands through Hekla's thick, dark locks. 'Do you want me to put some styling product in it for this evening?'

Hekla nodded.

'We could put it up in a bun, like this.' Bergrún gathered up her hair and twisted it into a thick knot.

'We just need to fix it with a few clips and take it back a bit to show off that pretty face,' she added, letting go of Hekla's hair and lightly pinching her cheeks.

Hekla grimaced. 'It's not pretty. I've got spots and a big nose.'

'Nonsense,' Bergrún said. 'There's nothing wrong with your nose.' She put her arms round Hekla's shoulders and studied her reflection. 'You're perfect just as you are.'

Hekla got a lump in her throat and saw that Bergrún's eyes were a little wet too. Hekla would probably never really understand why Bergrún loved her so much. She had nothing to offer, no special talents; she wasn't pretty or outgoing or ... In fact, she could see nothing positive about herself. But Bergrún loved her in spite of all her flaws, and she was desperate not to lose that.

The birthday girl's parents had bought the girls sweets and given them permission to enjoy themselves in the sitting room. The father had actually baked an ambitious cake filled with butter cream, with big, glitter-covered cardboard numbers saying '15' on top. The girls played music on someone's phone and connected it up to the speakers. Then they sat and gorged themselves on the sweets, while chatting and laughing.

Hekla felt as if she had been transported to another world. No one gave her a hostile glare as if she wasn't welcome. No one made a face when she talked or turned up their nose when she sat down beside them. She met Tinna's eye, finding it hard to hold back a smile.

'What do you think?' asked Freyja, whose birthday

it was, after they'd been chatting for a while. She got up and opened a cupboard to reveal a collection of bottles. 'Shall we top up our glasses?'

The girls laughed as she brought out a succession of highly decorative bottles.

'Won't your parents notice?' one girl asked.

Dísa looked at her and snorted.

'No, we'll just refill them with water. I've often done that before, and they never notice,' Freyja said, pouring a generous splash into each glass.

The girls took sips, grimacing at the taste; some hesitantly, others as if they were old hands. Although Hekla was used to the burning feeling in her throat, she only took a small mouthful. Bergrún had hugged her when she left, saying, 'I'll wait up for you,' and dropped a kiss on the top of her head.

Maríanna had never waited up for her. Instead, she had made spiteful comments, like saying that all the other girls in her class had been out together. 'Why weren't you with them, Hekla?' she would ask. 'You're always moping alone at home. Why don't you ring them?' Maríanna had known perfectly well that Hekla couldn't just pick up the phone and call those girls. She knew what Hekla had to endure, yet she insisted on playing it down. 'It's only a bit of teasing. Just try and make friends with them.' As if she couldn't understand that this wasn't an option for Hekla. She wasn't wanted and Maríanna must know that. Yet there was never any sympathy in her expression, only disappointment, as if she couldn't understand how she had come to give birth to such a weird kid.

At this thought, Hekla took a bigger slug of her drink than intended and made a face. Tinna got up, beckoning her to come with her to the bathroom. Hekla still hadn't got used to always going to the loo with other people, but in this group of friends it seemed to be perfectly acceptable to sit and pee while the others chatted or touched up their make-up.

'Are you enjoying yourself?' Tinna asked, once she'd flushed the toilet. She watched Hekla in the mirror as she was washing her hands. The bathroom was small with light-brown tiles and an open shower full of shampoo bottles and toys.

'Mmm.' Hekla nodded. The phone rang in her pocket and she glanced at it. Agnar's name flashed up on the screen. 'He won't stop calling me. Did I mention that he told tales on me to the police?'

'What did he say?'

'That I came over to Akranes the day that…' She dropped her eyes and drew a deep breath, suddenly afraid that everything was going wrong.

Tinna came closer. 'And what did you say?'

'Just the truth,' Hekla said. 'That I went round to your house.'

Tinna smiled. 'Close your eyes.'

Hekla obeyed. Her heart started beating faster and suddenly she was nervous. 'What are you doing?'

'Shh,' Tinna said. 'Stick out your tongue.'

Hekla obeyed again and felt a gentle touch on her tongue. Then a strange taste filled her mouth but she closed it anyway. 'What is it?' she asked, opening her eyes.

Tinna stuck out her own tongue. There was a small white pill on the quivering red tip; the same kind of pill as the one dissolving in Hekla's mouth. She grimaced. It tasted vile.

Tinna laughed. 'Have a drink of water if you don't like it.'

Hekla turned on the tap and took a big gulp. 'Tinna, seriously. What is it?'

'Just something I got from a mate.' Tinna smiled and took Hekla's hand. 'Don't be scared, it's nothing serious. Just a little something to make the evening more fun. I promise it's nothing that'll mess with your head. Trust me.'

Hekla nodded, and she and Tinna walked hand in hand back into the sitting room, where the other girls were still sipping their drinks. She trusted Tinna. Of course she did.

The evening passed in a haze. More kids arrived; boys Hekla had seen before and others she hadn't. Agnar kept ringing but she didn't answer. Dísa had clearly taken the same stuff as her and Tinna because her pupils were huge.

When Freyja's parents came back and saw what was going on, they threw everyone out. Tinna called some boys to come and pick them up, and luckily they agreed to give Hekla a lift home. Tinna and Dísa tried to persuade her to stay out longer, but Hekla refused. She couldn't stop thinking about Bergrún waiting up for her.

Once she was safely in bed, the evening merged into a blur. She stared up at the ceiling of her room, unable to wipe the smile off her face, not feeling remotely sleepy. Luckily, it had been dark, so Bergrún hadn't been able to see the state she was in. Hekla smiled, pulled the duvet up higher under her chin and closed her eyes. There was a warm feeling in her stomach. Perhaps she should have gone with the girls after all. She sat up in bed and turned to face the window, gazing out at the white snow illuminated by the street lights, thinking about all that the night had to offer. Suddenly she heard a creaking in the snow outside and instinctively jerked back in an attempt to hide in the shadows.

There was somebody outside her window.

Ten Years Old

My eyes flutter for a while, caught in the grey area between sleeping and waking, before finally opening. The phone is ringing. Somewhere in the flat I can hear my mobile. It must be night still, as it's dark in the bedroom. Hafliði is sound asleep at my side, emitting quiet snores. The phone falls silent, much to my relief. Closing my eyes, I try to get back to sleep. But only a few seconds pass before the ringing starts up again. I make up my mind to get up, and hurry out into the hall, following the noise to the sitting room, where the phone's lying on the coffee table. The illumination from the screen is the only light in the room.

Breathlessly I answer: 'Hello.'

I wait, but there's no response.

'Who is it?' My voice isn't as calm as I'd like it to be. Because there is someone at the other end. I can hear breathing and a sound that could be rain or the hissing of a radio. I wait a bit longer, then hang up and stare at the screen. Then I switch it off to be on the safe side before going back to bed.

It's three in the morning and I'm wide awake. That's the third phone call in two weeks. They always come at weekends, always at night, and I'm met by this silence every time. As if someone's deliberately harassing me. After the first call, I started to get the feeling that I was being watched. It's probably just my imagination but I can't shake it off. The other day I thought a car had been following me for a while, so I drove all round the houses until I shook it off. I couldn't make out the figure behind the wheel because of the dark, but I'm sure the car was following me. Wherever I went. However fast I drove. Could it be the same person as the one who sent me that letter all those years ago? Surely not: I moved and took care not to register my new address or phone number anywhere. But of course it wouldn't be hard to find me if someone really wanted to.

I turn over onto my side and stare at the Venetian blinds, which are moving gently against the open window.

Feeling suddenly boiling hot, I poke one leg out from under the duvet. Hafliði's snoring is getting louder. I wriggle to the edge of the bed, as far away from him as I can. After all those years alone it's difficult to get used to having another person sleeping beside me. To listen to unfamiliar breathing and feel another body turning over in its sleep. Sometimes, when I can't sleep, I lie there, watching him. Watch how he stops breathing for several seconds before starting up again. One night I dreamt I'd smothered him; pressed a pillow over his face and watched his hands scrabbling at the air until they gave up and fell limply back onto the bed. The strange thing is that it wasn't a bad dream. Not a particularly good one either, but not bad.

When I finally drop off it's past five o'clock, and two hours later I wake up to find Hafliði nibbling my ear lobes. I lie there passively, letting him pull down my knickers, and I'm relieved when he's finished. He doesn't notice anything, just kisses me on the cheek before stretching and getting out of bed. When I look in the mirror I'm met by greenish circles under my eyes. The ice-cold water I splash on my face doesn't get rid of them.

We're on our way to a lunch party at Hafliði's mother's place, with his siblings and their spouses and kids. Two older sisters and one younger brother. Hafliði is close to his mother. He talks to her on the phone every day, always stepping outside the flat as if he doesn't want me to hear what he's saying. I've watched her come round to visit him. Watched from the window at a safe distance. From my vantage point she looks perfectly harmless: a plump figure, with curly grey hair, always dressed in a cream-coloured jacket and a shawl.

We park in front of a small block of flats in Hafnarfjörður, not far from the town centre and the harbour. I take my daughter's hand. She hardly dares breathe. Although she doesn't say anything, I can tell she's nervous. I saw her standing in front of the mirror this morning, repeatedly combing her hair, although it was already smooth. Stefán, in contrast, races ahead to ring the bell.

'You're late,' says Hafliði's sister, who opens the door. She hugs Stefán and Hafliði, then gives me and my daughter a brief smile. I open my mouth to introduce myself, but she turns away and goes back inside, leaving us to follow.

The sitting room is full of people. Hafliði immediately offers to help lay the table, leaving me standing there. My daughter presses herself against me, and we wait awkwardly, ignored by the other guests. They're all too deep in conversation to say hello. I bend down and tell her to go and play with the other children, but she doesn't even answer, just shakes her head and goes on fingering her necklace, as is her habit when she's nervous. Only when Hafliði takes us round to meet everyone do they deign to notice us.

They're an arrogant bunch. Like Hafliði in their brash self-confidence, but lacking his warmth and charm. Last of all he introduces us to his mother. Her name's Guðrún and she's a chubby little woman with a perm, dressed in a rose-patterned blouse. Her smile is friendly and her voice velvety-soft, but her eyes give her away. They're an icy grey-

blue and directed uncompromisingly at the floor. When she does fleetingly meet my eye, she looks right through me. Her gaze lingers briefly on my daughter, then returns to Hafliði, and her whole face softens.

We take our seats at a long table that's already laden with food. Bread, toppings, iced buns and chocolate-coated Danish pastries.

'And what do you do?' asks the oldest sister, whose name I've already forgotten.

'I work in a legal practice,' I answer, as I spread tuna salad on my bread.

'Oh, so you're a lawyer?' I see how the eyes around the table open wider and study me with slightly more interest. I want to say yes. If Hafliði hadn't been there, I would have gone ahead and lied.

'No, I work in reception,' I say. 'But I'm planning to go back to college one day and study law.'

They murmur something polite, but it's clear that I'm no longer of interest. The conversation moves on, and my daughter and I sit there in silence.

'I didn't know you were from Sandgerði,' someone says after a while, and I glance up to find them all looking at me. Sandgerði's the last thing I want to talk about.

'Yes, I grew up there.'

'What was that like?' Hafliði's brother asks. 'It must be quite cosy growing up in a small community where everybody knows each other.'

'Well...' I hesitate. 'It was OK.'

'As it happens, I've got a friend from there,' the brother continues. He turns to Hafliði. 'You know, Ívar, who I work with.'

'Oh, yes, right. He's from Sandgerði,' Hafliði says.

'He must be about your age,' the brother persists. 'Do you know him at all? Ívar Páll?'

I can feel the blood draining from my face. I do know him. Well, maybe 'know' is an exaggeration — I know who he is. Or was. We were classmates. He was one of those terribly nerdy boys who lived more in computer games and fantasy novels than in the real world. All skin and bone, with glasses and rabbit teeth. We called him 'the squirrel' because, when he ate, he used to nibble at the bread with his big front teeth, scattering crumbs all over the table. We once filled his school bag with nuts, and when he went to take out his books, the nuts went tumbling and bouncing all over the floor.

'No, I don't recognise the name,' I say, poking with my fork at the unappetising pasta on my plate.

'Oh, right,' he says. 'But maybe he remembers you.'

I smile, though his words sound like a threat. Feeling a tug at my jumper, I look round. She hasn't touched her food and is looking rather pale.

'What is it?' I ask.

She pulls me down to her so she can whisper in my ear. 'I want to go home.'

Me too, I long to say. I want to go home too.

'Not just yet,' I say. 'Eat your lunch.'

She stares at me without speaking. A few minutes later there's another tug at my jumper. 'What?' I snap.

'I feel sick, Mummy.'

Only then do I notice that she's turned as white as a sheet. She closes her eyes slowly, then opens them wide and clamps both hands over her mouth. It's not enough. The vomit gushes out with such force that it splatters all over the table. I grab her and rush her away but it's too late: lunch is ruined. Everyone rises in a hurry and moves back from the table. Hafliði leaps to his feet and takes us to the bathroom, where we wash her face and give her a drink of water. After a little while he goes back in to clean up the sitting room, while we stay sitting in the bathroom. She rests her head on my chest, her whole body shaking.

'Can we go home now?' she whispers.

I gently stroke her sweaty forehead. 'Yes. Now we can go home,' I whisper back. At this moment there's nowhere I'd rather be than at home with my daughter.

Saturday

Elma had faked illness the previous evening when Jakob knocked on the door. She'd even gone as far as to wrap a blanket round her shoulders and cough unconvincingly. Remembering this now and cringing at her bad acting, she doubted he had believed her. She knew Jakob would connect it with their date and take it as a rejection, but it wasn't like that. It had absolutely nothing to do with their date.

It would simply have felt wrong to wake up with Jakob that Saturday morning, because it was Davíð's birthday. In the old days, they would have gone out for dinner at the Indian restaurant by the harbour, ordered a good bottle of red and chocolate mousse for dessert. Sat by the window, watching the boats rocking gently in the gloom, then walked home, a little tipsy from the wine.

Elma closed her eyes and concentrated on her breathing. The day shouldn't be a sad one, she told herself. She wasn't going to dwell on thoughts of what might have been. Yet she suspected that it would be hard to avoid doing so this evening. Was it too late to ring Davíð's family and cancel?

She looked out at the snow that had fallen during the night. Tiny flakes were dancing outside the window before softly settling on the ground. Davíð used to love snow. It was probably a coincidence that it had decided to snow on his birthday, but she doubted it.

Some things couldn't be a coincidence.

She sighed and slumped forwards on her desk. After a long day at work yesterday, she wasn't exactly in the mood to be back in the office on a Saturday morning. But she and Sævar had both agreed to take the weekend shift. Elma wandered into the coffee room. Kári, one of the uniformed officers, was sitting at the table, immersed in the paper.

'What's new, Kári?' Elma asked, sitting down opposite him with her mug.

'Nothing much.' He was poring over the paper, his black hair falling forwards over his small, dark eyes.

Elma grimaced when she tasted the coffee. It was so strong and bitter it was almost undrinkable. Usually people went out of their way to stop Kári going anywhere near the coffee machine, as it more or less guaranteed a big increase in the frequency of the staff's trips to the toilets.

'Quiet evening?'

'Well ... there was a girl who hasn't come home.'

'Oh?'

'Mmm. A fifteen-year-old. Daughter of that newsreader.'

'I, er...' Elma put down her cup, unable to stomach any more of the bitter brew. When checking various aspects of Hekla's statement, Elma had realised she needed to find out whether Tinna and her mother could confirm that Hekla had visited them on Friday, 4 May. Tinna's mother's name was Margrét, and after a brief search Elma discovered that her face was familiar: Margrét was a presenter on the evening news.

'You mean Margrét?' Elma asked Kári.

'That's the one.'

'What happened?'

'Oh, I expect she was at some party.' Kári didn't seem too concerned, but then it was common for kids not to be home by their appointed time at weekends. 'Her mother got in touch. I'll take a drive round later and see if I can spot her.'

'I'll talk to the mother. I need to speak to her anyway about another matter.'

Jörundarholt, which was lined mostly with detached houses and terraces, formed a rough U-shape around a large playing field. Elma had lived in the area until she was seven and had continued playing there for much longer, since her parents hadn't moved far away. The houses came in a variety of colours and designs, in contrast to Akranes's more uniform newer estates. Elma parked in front of Margrét's house. There was a woman standing at an upstairs window, looking out. She vanished as soon as Elma got out of the car and, before she had reached the front door, it opened.

'Margrét.' The woman who answered the door was tall and strikingly glamorous, despite the marks of tiredness and strain under her eyes. Her face was bare of make-up, she was wearing a dressing gown, tied tightly around her waist, and her blonde hair was pulled back in a gold clip, yet the way she coolly looked Elma up and down before inviting her in made Elma feel self-consciously scruffy, uncomfortably aware of her untidy hair, worn jeans and scuffed shoes.

Margrét had clearly taken pains over every inch of the house. Everything was so tasteful and welcoming that Elma wished she could hire her to decorate her own flat. The walls were greyish-brown, the furniture made of walnut, and the sitting-room windows were hung with white voile curtains. She took a seat on one of the large, beige sofas, her feet sinking into a soft, deep-pile rug. The room smelt deliciously of vanilla and fresh laundry.

'She's only fifteen,' Margrét said, once they were both sitting down. 'She's never failed to come home before. Never.'

'Do you know where she was yesterday evening?'

'A girl in her class had a birthday party,' Margrét said. 'I've called her parents, but it turns out the kids all left before midnight. Even her friends, Dísa and Hekla, are home, and the three of them always stick together.'

'Didn't they have any idea where Tinna might have gone?'

'No, they said … they said she was going to another party. I haven't a clue where.' Margrét's mouth puckered and she dropped her gaze to the pale-coloured floor tiles.

'I can get someone to drive around town and look for her,' Elma said. 'But I'd advise you to keep calling her mobile. It's not that late. Maybe she just fell asleep somewhere and she'll turn up soon.'

Margrét went on staring at the floor without answering.

'Actually, I was going to get in touch with you today about something else,' Elma went on.

'Oh?' Margrét raised her eyes.

'It's about Tinna's friend Hekla,' Elma said. 'We're looking into the death of Maríanna Þórsdóttir.'

'Maríanna?' Margrét frowned. 'Sorry, I'm not quite with you. Are you talking about Hekla's birth mother?'

Elma nodded. 'The day Maríanna vanished, Hekla came over to Akranes. She says she came round to see Tinna and that you were home too, so we were wondering if you could confirm that.'

'I...' Margrét paused. 'When was this?'

'Maríanna vanished on the fourth of May this year.'

'Yes. Yes, of course.' Margrét leant back on the sofa. 'Yes, of course I remember but I just ... I can't remember if Hekla was here. The fourth of May, you say? She's round here so often that I can't possibly remember specific dates, as I'm sure you'll understand. You'll have to ask Tinna when ... when she comes home.'

'What time do you usually go to work?'

'I have to set off between three and four to be in Reykjavík in time.'

'In that case you should have seen Hekla, if she came round,' Elma said. 'It would have been at about half past two.'

Margrét sighed. 'You know, I just can't remember. Sometimes I go in earlier, so it's possible I did on that day too. And sometimes I'm not even aware that she's here: they'll be in Tinna's room, up to goodness knows what.'

'Hekla said she met you,' Elma pointed out.

Margrét was obviously growing tired of her questions. 'Then she must have done,' she said impatiently. 'But I can't confirm something I don't remember. Look, I haven't slept all night, so I'm not in any state to answer your questions right now.' She gave Elma a quick on-off smile to show that the matter was closed.

'I see. If you do remember, this is my number.'

Margrét took her card and got up. In the hall, she suddenly grabbed Elma's arm so hard that it pinched.

'This ... I'd rather news of this didn't get out. I don't want any appeals for Tinna in the papers or anything like that. People talk, and they're bound to start imagining all kinds of things. Drawing the wrong conclusions, you know.'

'No, of course we won't put out any appeals at this stage. With any luck she'll be home before there's any need.'

'It would be best,' Margrét said.

After Elma had said goodbye, she reflected that Margrét came across as much more likeable on television. But perhaps that was unfair in the circumstances. The woman hadn't slept and she was frightened about her daughter, but the fact remained that Elma hadn't warmed to her at all.

* * *

Elma's brain was like a broken record, playing the same refrain over and over again until it became meaningless. Sævar, who was facing her across the table in the meeting room, looked equally baffled.

'Unnar flatly denied it,' he said.

'Of course he did.'

Sævar shrugged. 'Unnar's a vet. Apparently there was an emergency case the day we were supposed to meet him: a horse with colic.'

'I see,' Elma said. 'But did he have an alibi for when Maríanna went missing?'

'Yes, he was at home with his wife,' Sævar replied. 'They both confirmed it. I don't think we have any evidence to suggest there was something going on between him and Maríanna. We should focus on Sölvi instead. They were supposed to be going on a date, after all, and he doesn't have a solid alibi because we haven't got a clue what time Maríanna went missing.'

'But we don't have any evidence that Sölvi's guilty either,' Elma protested. 'Maybe we can't eliminate him completely, but there are other more likely candidates. Hekla and Agnar, for example. Or Bergrún. Though, to be fair, Bergrún's colleagues have confirmed that she was at work until almost five.' All their potential suspects seemed to be looking less and less likely as perpetrators. It was as if the more urgent their search became, the further the solution slipped from their grasp. They were drawing blanks everywhere. 'What about Fannar? Has his alibi been corroborated?'

'Yes, he flew to Egilsstaðir on the Friday morning and came home on the Sunday.' Sævar dropped his pen on the table and stretched his arms overhead. 'How was Margrét?'

'She was…' Elma paused thoughtfully. 'I don't think she was quite herself. She was worried about her daughter.'

'Understandably,' Sævar said. 'But the girl's bound to turn up.'

'I expect so. Margrét couldn't remember anything that happened on the fourth of May. Not whether Hekla had come round, nor whether she'd seen her.' Elma propped her cheek on one hand and looked at Sævar. 'Isn't that a bit strange? Usually, when something major happens, the things you do before and afterwards become imprinted more clearly on your memory.'

'True. Perhaps Maríanna's disappearance didn't seem that big a deal to Margrét at the time. After all, she didn't know her, and we thought Maríanna had probably done one of her usual vanishing acts.'

'So what do we do next?' Elma asked.

'We haven't exactly exhausted all avenues…'

'We've been in touch with the bus drivers and shown them pictures of everyone who could possibly have driven Maríanna's car to Grábrók and caught a bus back. We've checked all the available CCTV footage from Akranes and Borgarnes that day, without finding anything of interest. We've got no evidence and no leads.'

'Hekla lied about coming to Akranes,' Sævar pointed out, yet again.

'Yes, but she had an explanation for that.' Elma rubbed her eyes and yawned. 'And I believe it's valid. Hekla thought her mother would be coming back and didn't want to admit to her that she'd sneaked off to Akranes. Then, when the case began to look more serious, she felt it was too late to come clean, which I can well understand.'

'We should have a chat with her friend Tinna when she turns up.'

'Yes,' Elma said. 'Yes, I suppose so.' She rapped her knuckles on the table several times, then said: 'I'm going to Reykjavík later.'

Sævar had started collecting the glasses and coffee cups that were cluttering up the table. 'Oh?'

'Davíð's parents have invited me round as it's his birthday today. Or, you know, it would have been his birthday.'

Sævar stopped and looked at her. 'Ah.'

Elma smiled. She was used to people not knowing how to react when she mentioned Davíð. 'Anyway, I thought of visiting Maríanna's father on the way, since I'll be passing. I know they didn't have much contact, but given that we don't seem to be getting anywhere—'

Sævar interrupted: 'I could come with you.'

'No, it's OK. I mean, I have no idea how long my visit to Davíð's parents will last and you wouldn't want to hang around in town all that time.'

Sævar sighed. 'Elma ... I'm thirty-six years old. The only family I have is my brother, and all my friends spend their Saturday evenings with their wives and children. Believe me, I have nothing better to do.'

Elma laughed. 'You make it sound so tragic.'

'I'll do some Christmas shopping while you're having dinner. You can let me out at Kringlan, and I'll finish buying my presents and maybe go to a film. It actually sounds better than the Saturday night I had planned.'

'What about Birta? Will she be OK by herself?' Elma asked.

'Actually, my neighbour's offered to look after her on the days when I can't bring her into work,' Sævar said. 'He's recently retired, and I think he sees dog-sitting as a good way of getting himself out of the house every day to take some exercise.'

'OK, if you're sure.' Elma stood up.

'I'm sure.'

Ten Years Old

A week later Hafliði comes round to supper. It's a Friday evening, and Stefán's at his mother's, so it's just the three of us. The atmosphere at the table feels different. Hafliði is distracted, and I can't stop talking. In the end, my attempts to make conversation falter, and we eat our spaghetti silently in front of the TV. We didn't meet yesterday evening because he had to work. He often works late when Stefán's with his mother, but up to now he's always slept with me, however late he's got back. I lay there for a long time, waiting for his knock on the door. It didn't come but the phone rang at three in the morning and instead of hearing Hafliði's voice I was met by silence. I switched off the phone but found it impossible to get back to sleep.

Later in the evening we're halfway down a bottle of red when I turn to him and ask what's wrong. He scratches his head and opens and shuts his mouth before saying: 'Nothing. Nothing in particular.'

'Tell me,' I insist. 'Something's up.'

'It's just ... I spoke to my brother yesterday. That guy, Ívar, he remembered you all right and he...' His voice trails off but then he doesn't need to say any more.

I put down my wineglass. 'And he didn't have anything good to say about me, I suppose?'

We end up having a row. I must have had a bit too much to drink because I bring up the subject of his family. Since we left I've kept replaying the scene; seeing their faces, the disdainful way they looked at my daughter and wrinkled their noses when she was sick. Instead of helping or asking if she was OK, they just retreated out of range and stood there, exchanging contemptuous glances. Clearly, my daughter and I weren't good enough for them. Which was pretty ironic considering that the party was taking place in a block of flats in Hafnarfjörður, of all places. I say all this and more, and the row ends with Hafliði storming out.

Two days later we make up again, but in spite of that it feels as if something indefinable has changed between us. I can't put my finger on it. All I know is that I'd give anything to be able to rewind. I want us to go back to being the same happy family that we've been for the last few months. But Hafliði has become distant. Distracted. He no longer comes round every evening, but works late and invents excuses that didn't exist before. I behave as if it doesn't matter but inside I'm terrified.

Then one Saturday he doesn't answer the phone. I wait all day for him to return my call, but when suppertime has come and gone without any message from him, I grow worried. A feeling of misgiving creeps over me that I can't shake off. I try calling him again. And again. And a third time. I pace around the flat, unable to sit still, feeling as if I'm going crazier by the minute. He had some work event this evening; important clients to take out to dinner. So perhaps his day's been taken up with preparations and there's a perfectly natural explanation for his silence. I fall asleep in front of the TV, an empty wine bottle on the table and my phone in my hand.

I wake up early next morning with a headache and a bad taste in my mouth to find her sitting beside me. She's turned on the TV with the volume so low it's barely audible. All week she's been asking where Hafliði is. If he's gone. She's wandered restlessly around the flat, unable to concentrate on anything. It's the same now: the TV is babbling away, but her eyes keep flickering to me. I wonder what's going on in that little head of hers. What's she thinking? What does she want from me?

Leaving her sitting there, I go into the kitchen. I make coffee, then sit at my post by the window, from which I gaze down on a limited segment of the world outside. This window has framed my view of the world in recent years. From here I watch all the people who live around me but don't know I exist. I watch my neighbours, know when they wake up and when they get home. I see the lights going on in their windows in the mornings, what they watch on TV and when they go to bed. They're like little ants that go through life never varying their routine. I imagine squashing them with a finger. What would that change? Would anyone care? Maybe a few friends and relatives. Maybe some stranger would cry for a few minutes, only to have forgotten them by the next day. People always think they're so important when really they don't matter. Nothing matters.

She comes into the kitchen and smiles at me. Her smile is hesitant. Wary. When I smile back, she comes over to join me. She doesn't say anything, just lays a hand on mine. She stands beside me for a while, then goes away again. It's not much, but I get a lump in my throat because I know that this is her way of showing affection. She's not big on hugs or physical contact. Even the hand that always used to slip into mine when she was younger is a stranger to me now.

After thinking about it for a while, I decide to go downstairs to Hafliði's flat. I take the stairs instead of the lift because I don't know exactly what I'm going to say, and I need time to think. My hands are cold and clammy with sweat when I knock on the door. After a moment or two I hear voices inside. Footsteps. Someone fiddles with the lock, then the door opens.

The person standing in front of me isn't Hafliði or Stefán. It's a dark-haired woman, wearing nothing but one of Hafliði's T-shirts. Actually, she's not even a woman, just a girl. Years younger than me. Her legs are thin and white with prominent blue veins. Her hair is tied back in a ponytail that is leaking down, just like the mascara under her eyes.

'Hi,' she says and there's something malicious about her smile. I have a feeling I've seen her somewhere before. My heart's beating so fast I think I'm going to faint. There's a humming in my ears and the floor is moving in waves.

I take a step backwards. 'Who are you? Where's Hafliði?'

'I'm Maríanna,' she says and closes the door.

Elma's clothes only filled half the wardrobe these days. She had gone through them pretty ruthlessly when she moved and now regretted having given away various garments. Presumably they were kicking around at the Red Cross or wherever they had ended up. Hopefully they would come in more useful there than in her cupboard.

Elma looked in the mirror and tried in vain to untangle her hair, which was far too long. She rarely took the time to go to the hairdresser's, and it now reached down below her shoulder blades. With the onset of the winter darkness following a dreary summer, her complexion was pale with hardly a freckle to be seen. When she was younger, she used to break out in freckles at the first hint of sun and she had hated it. She sucked in her cheeks as her sister had once taught her and dabbed on some bronzing powder to try and add a bit of healthy colour.

Her phone vibrated in her pocket and Sævar's name flashed up on screen. Looking out of the sitting-room window, she saw his car and waved instead of answering. She grabbed her bag and was just locking her door when the one opposite hers opened.

'Feeling better?' Jakob asked. He was carrying a large backpack and wearing a woolly hat with a big red pom-pom.

Elma smiled in embarrassment. She was in her smart coat, wearing lipstick and didn't look ill at all. 'Yes, I am. I expect I managed to sleep it off.'

Jakob returned her smile. Although only a few seconds passed before he replied, Elma could almost hear them ticking by. 'That's good.'

'Where are you going?' she asked. 'Surely not outside in this cold?'

'Yes, actually. I'm going snowboarding with a mate. Now that we've finally had a decent snowfall.'

'Yes, finally,' Elma said, her expression apparently so unconvincing that Jakob started to laugh. He knew she didn't like snow. The tension between them dissipated a little. 'I'm going on a work trip to Reykjavík. I might try and buy some Christmas presents while I'm there.'

'For me?'

'Maybe.'

Jakob was joking, but in truth it hadn't occurred to Elma to buy him a present. Was he expecting one? She didn't even have to think that through to the end — of course Jakob would give her a present. That's exactly the kind of guy he was; the kind who never forgot birthdays and would turn up bearing gifts even when there was no special occasion.

Jakob slung the backpack over his shoulder. 'Anyway, best get a move on.'

'Yes, of course.' Her phone started ringing again. Sævar must be wondering what was keeping her. 'Me too, clearly.'

'Right.' Jakob paused. 'Maybe I'll see you later.'

'Yes,' said Elma. 'I'm bound to be late but … yes. Maybe.'

She watched him go, not quite sure why she was standing there like an idiot instead of walking out of the building with him.

* * *

It was past midday, but there was still no sign of Hekla. Bergrún had decided to let her sleep in after her party, but this was overdoing it a bit. The general rule was that everyone in the family had to be up by ten at the latest. Not that this had often been put to the test, because Bergur usually woke them before eight and Hekla wasn't one of those teenagers who overslept in the mornings. But the girl had had a difficult week, and as she'd been home by the agreed time last night, Bergrún had decided not to disturb her.

'It's great weather,' Fannar said, stamping his feet in the hall. His cheeks were red from the effort of shovelling snow off the drive, and strands of hair were sticking to his sweaty forehead. 'We should get out our skis.'

During their years studying in Norway they had learnt to cross-country ski, but sadly conditions in Iceland were rarely suitable. They sometimes dreamt of moving back to Norway. Had visions of the forests and high mountains, the superior climate and more laid-back lifestyle. If it weren't for Hekla, they might have gone through with it.

'Good idea.' Bergrún leant against the door frame, cradling a mug of coffee in her hands. The snow from Fannar's boots quickly melted, forming a puddle on the floor tiles.

'Maybe Hekla would like a go,' Fannar said. 'It's ages since she last got a chance to go skiing.'

Bergrún smiled reminiscently at the thought of Hekla's first time on skis at five years old. The little girl had clung to Bergrún's hand for dear life, shrieking with pleasure as they glided forwards at a snail's pace.

'Yes, we should ask her.' Bergrún glanced towards Hekla's room again.

'Is she awake?'

'No, she's sound asleep. It must have been a heck of a party.'

Fannar wrinkled his brow. 'I saw footprints in the snow outside,' he said. 'Are you sure she's in there?'

'I ... yes. She came home last night. I heard her. Spoke to her.' Suddenly Bergrún was assailed by doubts. The last few days had taught her that Hekla didn't always tell the truth, not even to the police. She had lied about her boyfriend and the trip to Akranes. Bergrún was hurt that Hekla hadn't trusted her with the truth. She'd thought their relationship was strong enough that Hekla wouldn't feel the need to keep any secrets from her.

Perhaps Hekla had just fallen in with a bad crowd. Bergrún liked Dísa and Tinna, but they were showing signs of becoming problem teenagers. The rebellious type. She felt so sorry for Margrét, who had rung that morning in search of Tinna. Bergrún hoped she'd never find herself in that situation.

'Have you checked on her?' Fannar looked at her enquiringly.

Instead of answering, Bergrún put her coffee cup down on the kitchen island and went over to the door of Hekla's room.

'Hekla,' she said quite loudly and knocked. No reply. She knocked harder. 'Hekla.'

When it became apparent that no one was going to open the door, she tried the handle. It was unlocked. Bergrún threw an uncertain glance at Fannar. When he nodded, she opened the door.

The first thing Bergrún noticed was the stench of alcohol. The room was dark, the curtains drawn and the floor covered in clothes. A pair of ankle boots lay on the parquet in a large pool of water.

'Who … what?' Bergrún stammered, but before she could say another word, she realised that Hekla wasn't alone in bed.

⋆ ⋆ ⋆

Returning to Reykjavík was a slightly disorientating experience for Elma these days. Familiar though the city was, with its heavy traffic, endless suburbs and high-rise buildings, she noticed that she no longer felt the same fondness for it she once had. The tables had been turned and nowadays it was always a relief to get back to Akranes and feel her tension easing as life reverted to a slower, more natural pace.

This afternoon, though, she was too distracted by arguing with Sævar to register the fact that they had entered the city. It hardly mattered what Elma said, Sævar could never agree with her. She suspected him of deliberately playing devil's advocate just to get on her nerves. By the time they parked outside the block of flats in the suburb of Árbær, Elma was red in the face with irritation. Sævar, meanwhile, sat in the passenger seat with a suspicion of a smile on his lips that Elma would have gladly wiped off with a wet cloth. She was so preoccupied that it took her a moment to remember why they were there.

They were hoping that Maríanna's father would be able to fill in some of the blanks about her past. Elma was especially keen to ask about Maríanna's brother, Anton, and the accusations that had supposedly led to his suicide. She was also curious to find out if anything more was known about Hekla's father.

On the way, they had received the news that Tinna had turned up safe and sound at Hekla's house. So tomorrow they would hopefully be able to get confirmation from her of Hekla's movements on Friday, 4 May.

'Bell number 502,' Sævar said, after peering at the panel on the wall.

Þór was a big man, tall, with broad shoulders. Maríanna must have inherited her tiny build from her mother, while their son had clearly taken after his father. Elma had seen a photo of Anton when she read his obituary online, and the likeness was striking. Both father and son had broad faces, big noses and a habit of screwing up their eyes as if shielding them from the sun. The only difference was that where Anton had been dark, Þór's beard was silver-grey and so were the few remaining hairs on his head.

Þór showed them into the kitchen and gestured to them to take a seat in the cramped corner. Then he reached up into a cupboard for two cups, one of which fell over with a crash.

'My eyesight's almost gone,' he explained, putting the cups on the table along with a light-brown thermos. He didn't offer them any milk. 'Age-related macular degeneration, according to the medics. Dad had it too; he was totally blind by the time he was sixty. I'll be seventy in three years, so I suppose I should count myself lucky. I've still got some peripheral vision and can see outlines, and distinguish light from dark.'

Elma wondered if that was why the flat was so brightly illuminated. Every single ceiling light was on and there were lamps in every corner. There was even one on the kitchen table, shining in their faces.

'From what I remember, there's a good view from the windows here.'

Elma looked out. There was Reykjavík, lit up in the darkness that had already begun to fall over the city. 'It's a beautiful view,' she agreed.

'I still feel like a visitor here,' Þór continued. 'I never intended to end up living in Reykjavík.' He sipped his coffee, then added: 'Mind you, by the time I left, Sandgerði had stopped feeling like home.'

'Um, that's actually one of the things we wanted to talk to you about,' Elma said.

Þór grunted, then extended an arm and opened the window. He pulled a cigarette out of his pocket and lit it. 'I hope you don't mind.'

Elma nodded, since she had no choice. It was his home and she couldn't say anything, though it would mean having to turn up to Davíð's parents' house reeking like a chimney.

'Aren't you having any luck in finding the person who did this to her?' Þór asked, blowing out smoke.

'Hopefully, we're beginning to get a clearer picture,' Sævar said.

Þór emitted a low rumbling laugh that quickly turned into a cough.

'You didn't see much of each other, did you?' Elma asked.

'No. That was Maríanna's choice. She was so angry. I could never understand how so much rage could fit inside such a small girl.' His mouth twitched down at the corner.

'Why was she so angry?'

'Yes, why?' Þór sighed and stubbed out his cigarette. 'I expect she was angry with me because she felt I didn't do enough. Angry with life for taking so much away from her. I suppose it all began when she was fifteen and only got worse over the years.'

They waited in silence for him to carry on. Elma tried the coffee. It was good.

'She got pregnant with Hekla at fifteen,' Sævar prompted, when Þór showed no sign of continuing.

Þór made a face. 'I haven't thought about that period of our lives for years. I try to avoid dwelling on it.'

He swung his head from one of them to the other, then sighed and carried on. 'We're from a small town. You'll know what that's like, being from Akranes yourselves. It has its pros and cons. We were very happy there for a long time. It was a good place to bring up the children; not too far from the city if we needed anything. We had our two kids, our jobs and so on. Things were going well for us.'

He lowered his gaze to the table and dried up again. Elma was on the point of breaking the silence when he resumed: 'It was like Maríanna changed overnight. She became moody and bad-tempered, and started answering back. She was five months gone before she let on what was wrong. You can probably imagine our shock.'

'Was it Hekla?' Elma bit her lip. What a stupid question; of course it was Hekla. But Þór didn't seem offended.

'Yes, it was Hekla. My granddaughter,' he said. 'She refused to tell us who the father was, and we decided not to put pressure on her. We thought the truth would come out eventually.'

'And did it ever?'

'Later, she told us it had been a boy her age. She

didn't want to mix him up in it, and I can understand that, sort of.'

'So you never found out his name?'

'Well ... I had my suspicions. She'd had a best friend since she was a little girl. His name was Hjálmar. After Maríanna got pregnant, he vanished. I always assumed he was the dad, especially after Hekla was born. She has a look of him.'

'Do you know where he is now?'

'No, no idea. His name was Hjálmar and his father was called Brjánn. You can look him up, if you like. Do one of those tests.' Þór waved a dismissive hand. 'Anyway, the whole thing was overshadowed by what happened next.'

'When Anton ...'

'Yes, when Anton died,' Þór finished. 'It was just such a terrible, terrible waste. So unnecessary. All because of ... because of a lie.'

'A lie?'

'Yes, and one bitch of a girl.'

Elma was taken aback by the hatred in his voice. 'What girl?'

Þór carried on as if she hadn't spoken. 'Anton wasn't like Maríanna. He was quiet and a bit of a loner, like his mother. Although he took after me in looks, we were very different types. He wasn't outgoing at all but spent a lot of time on his own and was terribly shy. He wasn't depressed or unhappy, though. It's like society wants everyone to be made in the same mould these days. Everyone has to be sociable and have all these friends and enjoy the great outdoors and eat healthily.' Þór snorted. 'If someone prefers their own company, it's considered abnormal; a sign there's something wrong. But it wasn't like that in Anton's case. He was happy. I tried to tell people that.'

'What happened to him?'

Þór looked at Elma in surprise, resting his unseeing eyes on her for a while as if sunk in his thoughts, needing time to ponder her question. As if he'd been talking to himself rather than to them.

'Anton went to a party.'

'A party?'

'Yes. He fancied a girl. A girl who was out of his league, though I heard rumours that she wasn't actually that picky when it came down to it. She was your typical dumb blonde who thought she could get away with anything she liked. Anyway ... this girl was at the party and somehow they ended up together and...'

Elma nodded.

'I expect she probably regretted it and felt Anton wasn't good enough for her. Though if you ask me, it was the other way round.' He lit another cigarette without bothering to ask if they minded this time. 'She claimed he'd forced her. That he was ... was a rapist.'

Sævar and Elma were silent.

'Anton wasn't capable of anything like that. He was a good boy. Shy and gentle. It was all lies. Lies because she wanted ... wanted to save her own skin.'

'Was he charged?'

'No, because there was no truth to her accusation. The girl only said it because she was ashamed. She never went to the hospital, and the police never pressed charges. There was no proof, just one person's word against another's. But that didn't matter. That didn't bloody matter because Anton had already been tried and convicted by the court of public opinion.'

Þór wiped the sleeve of his jumper across his damp forehead. Raking up the story was obviously painful for him. Elma had seen photos of the family on her way in. Nothing recent, only pictures from the good old days. A family portrait in which Maríanna could barely have been five years old. A picture of a young couple on a trip; Þór's thick, dark hair giving an idea of how much time had passed. In the kitchen there was a picture of Hekla fixed to the fridge with a magnet. It looked like something Þór had printed off Facebook.

'The whole town turned against us,' he said. 'It was unbelievable. We'd lived there all those years, had friends we'd known all our lives, but overnight it was all gone. It just … vanished into thin air.'

'Is that why you moved?'

Again, Þór ploughed on with his tale without answering Elma's question. 'Anton was so sensitive. For all his size, he had a tender heart. He could never bear to see anything suffer. I think that's why he did what he did. He couldn't stand seeing what we were going through. Couldn't bear to watch us suffer.' Þór was staring into space. His cigarette had burnt down between his fingers, and the ash fell on the table. 'I found him when I got home from work. He'd used a rope he found in the garage and he was just hanging there.'

Nobody spoke. Elma was picturing the young man's body hanging in the dark garage. And Þór opening the door, unsuspecting. It would be impossible ever to get over a shock like that. There would be no way of wiping the image from your mind.

Þór stubbed out his cigarette in the ashtray and drew a deep breath. 'Anyway, I don't think about it much these days. It's too painful. We moved away and started again in Reykjavík, but it was never any sort of life. We were grieving and hit rock bottom around the time Maríanna had her child. We couldn't be there for her, couldn't provide any support, because we'd chosen the worst possible method of dealing with it all: we tried to drown our sorrows. Maríanna was furious with us and cut herself off. I think she blamed us for the whole thing. At any rate, we've had very little contact since then, and hardly any at all since her mum died.'

'How long was it since you'd last heard from Maríanna?'

'Months. When she was younger she often used to ring if she'd been drinking, wanting to talk about what had happened. I tried to tell her that living with anger didn't do anyone any good, but it's easier said than done when it's become such a big part of you. It's years since I got a phone call like that from her, though, and I was glad. Grateful that she'd managed to let go of the past, even if it meant I wasn't part of her life anymore.'

'So you didn't hear from her at all in the weeks before she disappeared?'

'No, not a word. I … maybe it's a terrible thing to say but I'm glad she didn't disappear of her own accord. Because it means maybe she was OK and happy until … until some bastard did that to her.' Þór's mouth twitched and he grabbed the cigarette packet, but fiddled with it instead of taking one out.

'Do you remember the girl's name?' Elma asked.

Þór's voice was hoarse as he asked: 'What girl?'

'The one who brought the accusations against Anton.'

'Viktoría. The little bitch's name was Viktoría,' Þór said. 'I sometimes think about her and wonder if she remembers us and what she did to us. Has she any idea how many lives she destroyed? I hope so. I hope karma has paid her back. But life's not fair, and that girl had no conscience. I saw her once, years after Anton died, and I know she recognised me, but there was no sign of repentance there. Not a hint. She just looked straight through me, like I wasn't there. She's the one who should have been lying rotting in the lava field for months on end. Girls who lie deserve no better.'

'It must have been terrible — living with so much rage all this time.' Elma accelerated along Miklabraut. 'Especially for Maríanna. Bad enough being pregnant at fifteen years old, but then this has to go and happen as well.'

Neither of them said anything for a while. The weekend traffic was heavy. There wasn't much time left until Christmas, and everyone was frantically trying to finish their preparations.

'What if Anton hanged himself because he was guilty?' Sævar asked after a pause. 'It's difficult for families to believe something like that of a loved one — understandably. But that doesn't necessarily mean he didn't do it.'

'Of course not. Just because no charges were brought, that doesn't mean there wasn't a rape.'

Although there were cases from time to time, Elma didn't want to believe that anyone would lie about being raped. The prosecution process wasn't one that anyone in their right mind would choose to go through unless they had to, and so she had adopted the rule of letting the victim enjoy the benefit of the doubt. But the justice system didn't work like that. Cases weren't black or white. It was possible to argue over the perpetrator's intention to commit a crime, the circumstances, and a number of other factors. The justice system relied on specific types of evidence, and these were often in short supply in rape cases.

'No, you see quite a few cases like that,' Sævar said. 'It's a pity he couldn't remember the girl's full name.'

Elma indicated to turn off to the Kringlan shopping centre, only to find herself in a long line of cars that was barely moving.

'Viktoría isn't that common a name, and Sandgerði's a small town. We should be able to find out who she was,' Elma said, checking the rear-view mirror. Several cars had joined the queue behind them.

'We could give our colleagues there a bell and see what they say,' Sævar suggested. 'Even if no charges were brought, in a community that small an incident like that is bound to have been talked about.'

'Yes, maybe that would be best.' It was more than fifteen years since Anton had died, but someone must remember the affair. The traffic slowly started moving again, and a few minutes later they reached Kringlan.

'I'll jump out here,' Sævar said.

Elma stopped the car. Sævar opened the door and waved goodbye. Elma watched him run across the road and vanish into the covered car park before she drove on.

* * *

Davíð's parents lived in an attractive old house in Kópavogur, the town immediately to the south of Reykjavík. The front garden was overshadowed by tall trees, which provided shelter from the wind. When Elma was young, she used to dream about having a garden like that, full of big trees and places to hide.

She had always been a bit of an odd child, forever hiding in dark corners around the house. She would make tents out of blankets and never felt happier than when she was curled up in one of these dens with a book, a torch and a good supply of snacks. She had loved rain too; loved seeing the sky grow dark and smelling the odour of wet earth. As a little girl, Elma would have loved a garden like her former in-laws' one, but now, looking at the neatly pruned bushes and tidy flower beds, all she could think was what a hell of a lot of work it must be. Sadly, she had no interest in gardening.

The trees formed a sort of tunnel that she passed through to reach the front door. She remembered walking through it many years ago when she met Davíð's parents for the first time. If she had been nervous, Davíð was even worse. He had held her hand until they reached the front door but dropped it the moment they went inside, as if embarrassed to be caught holding it by his parents.

Elma knocked on the door. Davíð's father opened it and instead of shaking her hand he held out his arms and hugged her with such affection that Elma found it hard not to burst into tears. She forced herself to smile. The smell inside the house reminded her of the days when she and Davíð were first getting to know each other. His clothes always used to smell the same.

'It's so good to see you, love. Come in,' Sigurður said and closed the door behind her.

'You didn't buy much,' Elma commented, when she stopped in front of the entrance to the Kringlan shopping centre. Sævar was waiting outside, his cardigan zipped up to the neck, holding one small shopping bag and a can of soft drink.

He burped as he got into the car. 'Pardon me,' he said formally. 'No, I gave up straight away. All those people and all that noise.' He gave an affected shudder.

'So what did you do?'

'Went to the cinema.'

'But a film only lasts two hours.' Elma had been much longer than intended; five hours, at least. Dinner with Davíð's parents had been far more enjoyable than she had expected; full of happiness and laughter rather than grief, as she had feared. Admittedly, it had been a mixture of both at times, especially when his mother brought out the photo albums. Davíð in a nappy, taking his first steps. Davíð at the Family Zoo, patting a lamb. Davíð on the beach with an ice-cream. Elma had found herself studying the eyes of the smiling little boy for any hint of what was to come. Any inkling that many years later he would be overwhelmed by such despair that he would be unable to see a way out. But there was no sign of it. Not even in the photos in which he was older; a bolshie teenager refusing to put on a smile for the camera. Yet in spite of these moments of poignancy, the evening had left her flooded with warmth and gratitude.

'I went to two films,' Sævar said.

'Two?' Elma gaped.

'Yep. A perfect evening, if you ask me.'

Monday

Hekla wasn't imagining the glances she got from the other kids at school. She could hear the whispering and felt as if all the laughter was directed at her. Tinna didn't seem bothered by it, although she must have seen the gossip on the school's Instagram page. A photo of the two of them with a crude comment underneath about what they were supposed to have got up to together after the party. Of course it wasn't true. Nothing had happened. Tinna had come round to Hekla's place that night and asked if she could stay over because she didn't dare go home and risk bumping into her mother. Not with her pupils dilated like that and being so out of it that she could hardly get through a whole sentence without losing the thread. Tinna had undressed, got into bed and conked out in a matter of seconds. But Hekla hadn't been able to sleep.

She had lain there, watching Tinna. Watching her breathe, feeling the warmth of her body, and touching her very gently. She was so beautiful. So unbelievably beautiful, though she didn't realise it. Hekla wanted to tell her but couldn't. There was so much she couldn't say.

When she met Tinna that morning, Tinna hadn't even looked up, just carried on her conversation with Dísa. The glances of their classmates didn't seem to get to her. But that was the thing about Tinna: she never wasted time wondering what the other kids were thinking, and that was exactly what Hekla liked about her. Maybe that was why the kids left her alone, though she didn't fit into the same mould as them. Tinna was tall and not exactly thin, which made her seem rather grown-up. Her gaze was unwavering and ruthless, as if she didn't know the meaning of fear; and she was very clever — so clever that Hekla felt like an idiot around her.

The one person Tinna cared about making happy was her mother. Around Margrét, Tinna seemed to change. She worshipped her, that was obvious. Once, Hekla had asked Tinna why she died her hair blonde and she had answered: Because my mum wants me to be blonde. As if this was perfectly natural. When Hekla had dyed her own hair using a cheap packet, Maríanna had gone apeshit. But Hekla hadn't cared if Maríanna got angry, whereas Tinna would never do anything to displease her mother. She obeyed her in everything — when Margrét was present, at least. Hekla had often envied their relationship, though at times it struck her as a bit weird. Sometimes it was like Margrét only had to look at Tinna for her to nod and say or do whatever her mother wanted, as if they could read each other's minds.

Tinna whispered something to Dísa, who put a hand over her mouth to smother her giggles. Hekla pretended to be busy with her phone while her world collapsed around her.

⋆ ⋆ ⋆

The police officer from Sandgerði, who Elma had spoken to the day before, hadn't heard of Anton, Viktoría or Maríanna but had promised to ask around and call her back. Elma considered what steps to take next if nothing came of this line of inquiry. Up to now, every avenue they explored had turned out to be a dead end, and it looked as if Maríanna's tragic family history was going to prove similarly unhelpful in providing leads. Still, at least the story seemed to have ended well for Hekla, who was obviously happy living with her foster family. Bergrún and Fannar gave every impression of being good parents who took better care of her than Maríanna ever could have.

Elma closed her eyes and pictured the Hekla she had met seven months ago. The girl had changed. Not much, but perceptibly. She carried herself better, seemed a little more confident. Elma sincerely hoped they were wrong and that Hekla was innocent. After all, they hadn't actually found any compromising evidence, apart from her lie about going to Akranes.

A loud ringing shattered the peace. Elma hurriedly answered her phone.

'Hello Elma. My name's Gestur, from Sandgerði Police,' said the man at the other end. 'You called yesterday to ask about an old case.'

'Yes, it was about a young man called Anton Þórsson.' Elma turned her chair so she could stare out of the window as she talked. 'He took his own life fifteen years ago, and we were looking for the name of the girl who accused him of rape. She was called Viktoría something.'

'Yes, Palli asked me about it this morning, and I couldn't remember the incident, but I rang my wife as she always remembers that sort of thing. Anyway, as soon as she started talking, it all came back to me. It was a terrible business. The young man, Anton, hanged himself in the garage at home after becoming the victim of gossip in the town. I don't know how much truth there was in the stories, but the community was split down the middle, according to which side they believed.'

'About whether it was rape?'

'Yes, exactly. Anyway,' the man continued, 'whether or not the girl was lying, the family's life was ruined and a young man died. It was devastating.'

Elma couldn't hold back. 'Why were there so many people who didn't believe her?'

'Well, when it came to the point, she didn't want to press charges. And on top of that the girl had a bit of a ... what shall I say? A bit of a reputation.'

'Reputation?'

'Yes, she was quite the party girl. Not that I remember anything about it, but apparently she was known for being a bit free and easy with the truth.'

'I see,' Elma said, although she didn't see at all.

'Her family moved away as well after Anton died. I don't think her parents could look people in the eye after ... after what their daughter had done. Mind you, she seems to have come out of it all just fine.'

'Oh?' Elma swung her chair back to her desk. 'Did she move back to Sandgerði?'

'No, I don't imagine she'll ever do that,' the man said, with confidence. 'No, she appears regularly on our TV screens nowadays. Her name's Viktoría Margrét Hansen, though she always used to be known as Vigga. Today she just calls herself Margrét. She doesn't use Viktoría anymore, so perhaps she'd rather forget everything connected to that name.'

Ten Years Old

After the door has closed, I stand deathly still for a moment. My hands are still shaking. Rage is seething inside me, just waiting to explode. But the strange thing is that my first thought is not sadness at what Hafliði has done but at who he's done it with: a plain, dirty little slut like that. With a white face, blotched with red, and thin, straggly hair that looks as if it's about to fall out. If the circumstances had been different, I might have felt jealous, but instead I'm filled with disgust and humiliation. No one gets to treat me like this.

As I turn to go back up to my flat, Hafliði comes after me. He's ashamed and immediately starts making excuses. He employs his mellow voice and his eyebrows, like he does when he's trying to be charming. As I look at him now, I realise I have no feelings for him. I don't care if our relationship is over. Don't care if I never see him again. Hafliði has bad breath and several days' worth of stubble, and the wrinkles that have begun to form around his eyes don't suit him. The eczema on his neck and hands is particularly bad too, red and inflamed as if he's been scratching it. But even though I don't care for him, I'm still churning with rage over his betrayal and the humiliation of it all. After he's finished his piece, I leave him standing there in the stairwell and take the lift up to my floor. If I'd taken the stairs, my temper might have had time to calm down a bit before I opened the door to our flat. Perhaps the time would have been enough for me to recover my composure.

But no, I take the lift. The doors open and I'm as angry when I step out as I was when I got in.

'Turn off the TV!' My voice comes out much sharper than intended.

She looks alarmed. Jumping up from the sofa, she heads straight to her room without question or argument. I lie down on the sofa and close my eyes, picturing that girl in Hafliði's T-shirt. I can't stop thinking about the look in her eyes, both jubilant and provocative. There was something vaguely familiar about her. Of course, the most obvious explanation is that she's from Sandgerði and that we know each other from there, but I can't place her, however hard I try.

I pull the blanket over me. My thoughts are all over the place, images from past and future flashing around me. I reach out for the framed photo on the windowsill behind the television, which shows me as a pretty little girl with pigtails, in a white dress and black, patent-leather shoes, smiling to reveal straight, white teeth, as small as grains of rice. My parents are standing behind me, their hands resting on my shoulders. It meant so much to them that I should be their pretty little princess that they even christened me after two princesses: Viktoría Margrét. I never could stand my name. I found it so pretentious that I made my friends call me Vigga. My parents couldn't bear it. Couldn't bear me, come to think of it, after I stopped being their perfect, pretty little daughter.

I suppose we were quite comfortably off. Some might even have said we were rich. Dad was a ship's captain and mum a doctor. We lived in a large house on the edge of the town. I was my parents' only child and used to getting a lot of attention, by which I don't mean the sort of attention that all little children get. No, I was the centre of attention everywhere I went. I was praised for my hair, my eyes, my clothes and even my figure. She's so tall and slim, people used to say. She'll be a model one day.

I was six years old.

I didn't even know what a model was but I understood that people thought it a desirable thing to be. Then, when I started school, I looked at all those podgy little kids with their grubby faces, wearing their older siblings' hand-me-downs, and knew that I was better than them.

Yet I don't remember my parents showing me much affection when I was young. I was bounced between institutions and relatives; put in day-care for most of the day, then given a succession of babysitters in the evenings. Girls who rummaged around in Mum's stuff and let me stay up late as long as I didn't bother them. There was only one person in my childhood that I really loved, and that was my father's mother. Granny lived nearby, and I used to go round to hers for half the day, while the other half was spent at nursery school. She was nothing like my parents, who had no interest in me. Yet she wasn't particularly grandmotherly either, at least not like the grannies in stories. She was slim and strong, with hair that she refused to allow to turn grey and used to dye black with a sachet every third Friday. When I think about Granny I always picture her with her wet black hair swept back, a towel round her shoulders and a cigarette between two fingers, puffing smoke out of the window.

She claimed to have the second sight and owned a large collection of stones. According to her, they gave off different kinds of energy. One reduced anxiety, another inflammation and a third calmed the emotions. There was one stone that I found more beautiful than all the rest. It was big, black and shiny, with sharp edges. The sides were both jagged and mirror-smooth. Its scientific name was obsidian, but in Iceland it was known more poetically as hrafntinna or 'raven flint'.

Granny said it gave off an energy that protected and purified us. Sometimes the energy was so strong she had to keep it out on the balcony. Shortly before she died, Granny told me to take the stone. 'To protect you,' she said, pinching me on the cheek. That was another thing about Granny; she only ever showed affection by pinching you or tweaking your hair. She wasn't much of a cuddler. But that didn't matter to me: I wanted to be treated as an equal, not as a child. And she had done that ever since I could remember. She told me stories that some people would probably have considered too dark for little girls, but Granny said I was strong. Later, when my daughter was born with her black hair and grey eyes, I could only think of one name: Hrafntinna, after Granny's most beautiful stone.

Granny always said I was like that stone, a bit sharp around the edges, but smooth and pretty in between. My energy was so strong that sometimes it would be hard to contain it. Later, I wondered what the real reason was for her comparing me to a black stone. Was it because she saw who I was? Was it the colour of my soul? She was well aware that there were problems at school and that I wasn't always a little angel. I was mean and spiteful, and everyone knew that. But Granny saw something good in me that no one else could. There was no chance for the goodness to grow and blossom, though; not among all the lies that came pouring out of me.

I pull the blanket up to my chin, aware that I'm about to spiral into a bad place; a place that I've done well to avoid all these years. But now I can sense it again, the shame. That vile sense of shame that sucks all the blood out of my body. I picture their faces: the anger and contempt; the dis-

appointment in my parents' eyes. And I picture him. His fleshy face and red eyes. Hear his panting in my ear. Smell the sour stench of alcohol.

After she had hung up, Elma sat quite still. It just didn't fit. Or perhaps all the pieces fitted now. Margrét had lied — she had known Maríanna only too well. They'd lived in the same small town, and Margrét had accused Maríanna's brother of rape. Surely she must have recognised his sister fifteen years later? Then again, there was quite an age gap between them. Elma looked Margrét up and worked out that she would be thirty-seven this year. Maríanna, who had been six years her junior, would have been thirty-one now, had she lived. Two years younger than Elma, yet she'd had a fifteen-year-old daughter. It was a strange thought. When Elma was fifteen, having a baby had been the last thing on her mind, as indeed it was today.

She stretched, then finished the last drop in her mug. She would have to break the news to Sævar and Hörður. She got up, only to stop short as a thought struck her: the connection between the two women was even stronger than she'd realised.

'...Which makes Tinna Maríanna's niece,' Elma finished. 'They're related: Tinna and Hekla; Tinna and Maríanna. The policeman I talked to from Sandgerði said that Margrét and her entire family had moved away from the village. What if it wasn't because they were ashamed, as he thought, but because they wanted to hide the fact that Margrét was pregnant by Anton?'

'Well, there's a question,' Hörður said.

It was past midday. Hörður had been eating at his

desk when she and Sævar came in, and had put down his half-finished flatcake.

'Admittedly, there's always a chance that Margrét didn't realise Maríanna was Anton's sister,' Elma added. 'She didn't have any contact with Hekla's mother, only with Bergrún, so perhaps it never occurred to her to wonder where Hekla came from.'

'And Margrét claimed not to have seen Hekla the day Maríanna went missing?'

'She couldn't remember,' Elma said. 'But Hekla claimed that Margrét was at home when she went round to see Tinna.'

They were silent as they pondered this latest twist. A sequence of events was taking shape in Elma's mind that could be no more than conjecture at present. Supposing Maríanna had suddenly worked out who Tinna's mother was and gone to Akranes to confront her. She might also have realised that Tinna was her niece and been angry with Margrét for hiding the child. Blamed her for everything that had gone wrong with her family. Could there have been a confrontation, during which one of them had reacted violently, with disastrous consequences?

'I doubt Maríanna's family ever knew about the child,' Sævar said. 'Otherwise, I think Þór would have mentioned it when we talked to him.' He frowned, then added: 'Having said that, how come he didn't realise who Margrét was? He must have seen her on TV.'

'He's almost blind,' Elma reminded him. She had wondered the same thing when she first learnt Viktoría's identity. She drew a deep breath, then continued: 'Margrét moved away from Sandgerði and had Anton's baby. She never told anyone except her parents, who also kept quiet about it, so nothing got out. The news never spread to Sandgerði. But what if it all came out the day Maríanna died? What if Maríanna went round to Margrét's and they recognised each other? According to Þór and Bryndís — that's the old woman who used to have coffee with her — Maríanna was bitterly angry about what had happened. What if she'd wanted revenge?'

Sævar scratched his head. 'But it doesn't make sense. Why would Margrét keep the child a secret if she'd already told people that Anton had raped her? And why didn't she have an abortion?'

'Perhaps it was too late by the time she realised she was pregnant,' Elma suggested.

'Well, then why not have it adopted?'

'Not everyone can bring themselves to give their baby away,' Elma said. 'But it's a good question why she was so determined to keep the child a secret. Maybe it was to avoid the risk of interference from Anton's family. I can't imagine she'd have wanted any contact with his parents if he'd raped her.'

'Do you think there's any chance Maríanna knew who Tinna's mother was before she went over to Akranes that day?' Sævar asked.

'It's possible she'd only just found out,' Elma said. 'Perhaps she was on Facebook and saw Tinna's profile. That's all it would have taken for her to realise who the girl's mother was.' She thought about Tinna's profile photo of herself and her mother. She had looked it up after the phone call.

'Surely she'd have recognised her from seeing her on TV?' Hörður said.

'Yes, of course,' Elma agreed. 'But she wouldn't necessarily have known who her daughter was. Maríanna may have been eaten up with anger about the past, but she'd got her act together in the last few years, so perhaps she didn't freak out just because Margrét was on her TV screen.'

Hörður took a sip from his glass of water. 'Surely the only thing to do in the circumstances is talk to Margrét.'

⋆ ⋆ ⋆

No one answered when they tried the doorbell at Margrét's house, and her phone just kept ringing. When they finally got hold of her husband, he told them she'd gone to Reykjavík early. So there was nothing to be done but wait until she got back.

Elma used the time to gather more information about her. Margrét had moved to Akranes four years previously when she started living with a man called Leifur. He already had a son of around twenty, who lived with them when it suited him. They had married the same year. A big fancy wedding: white dress, red roses, the whole works. As Margrét and Leifur posed on the church steps, Tinna had stood beside her mother, her arms hanging down by her sides and her expression a little solemn for the occasion, as if she had her doubts. Eleven years old and her life with her mother was about to be transformed.

Before that, as far as Elma could discover, Margrét and her daughter had lived alone in Reykjavík since Tinna was born. Margrét had got her TV job a year before she moved to Akranes. She came across well, always spoke clearly and gazed into the camera with that typical TV-presenter intensity. Her professional manner and soothing voice had soon got her noticed.

Elma remembered seeing a full-page interview with her in the paper a while ago and tracked it down in the online archives. The interview was two years old; in it Margrét didn't mention Sandgerði once. On the contrary, she said she'd lived most of her life in Reykjavík. She talked a lot about her daughter and how rewarding she had found being a single mother. The piece was accompanied by two photos of Tinna: an old one of her blowing out ten candles on her birthday cake, and a more recent one of mother and daughter with their arms around each other, smiling into the camera, a glimpse of green grass behind them and sunshine in their hair.

I caught up with Margrét one lunchtime at a café in the city centre. Her face is well known after appearing on our TV screens, reading the evening news for the last two years. As she comes in, you can see heads turning and eyes widening, and you would expect no less, because Margrét cuts a glamorous figure, with her statuesque height and that signature mane of blonde hair. But that's not the only reason she attracts attention; she literally exudes charisma as she orders a big latte and bestows a friendly smile on the woman behind the counter…

Elma sniffed. Her own experience of Margrét had been quite different. Sure, she was beautiful and wasn't short on confidence, but the friendly smile had got lost somewhere along the way. Maybe she saved it for the TV cameras, rather than wasting it on police officers who asked her awkward questions. Elma clicked to turn the page of the digital newspaper and carried on reading. She skimmed over the bits that dealt with Margrét's job but paused when she spotted Tinna's name.

'There are two people in my life who have been more

important to me than anyone else: my daughter, Tinna, and my paternal grandmother, Svanhvít.' When the conversation turns to Margrét's grandmother, her face takes on a dreamy expression. 'Granny was probably the most important influence on my life. She wasn't like other grandmothers, always ready with the cakes and cuddles. No, Granny didn't have much of a sweet tooth. Instead, she taught me to drink tea and read auras. When I was five, she terrified me with stories about the black elves. She told me they lived in dark rocks, with the result that I didn't dare go near a lava field for years.' Margrét laughs, then continues: 'She had a big collection of stones that she claimed gave off different kinds of energy. The most beautiful of all was a big black chunk of obsidian or 'hrafntinna'. It gave off an energy that was supposed to have protective powers, and the day before she died she gave the stone to me.' Margrét is silent for a moment, gazing pensively out of the window. 'That's why I christened my daughter Hrafntinna. For Granny,' she says, smiling again. 'So it was a lucky coincidence when she was born with all this black hair.'

Elma closed the page. There wasn't much of interest there, though it gave her pause when she read the part about black elves and lava. The little boys who found the body had thought they'd seen a black elf. Yet she herself couldn't remember having heard anything about black elves being associated with lava fields. Elma yawned and rotated her chair towards the window. Perhaps she hadn't been quite fair to Margrét. Although the woman had come across as a bit arrogant when they met, there could be a perfectly reasonable explanation for that. Elma wasn't going to judge somebody she'd only met once. After all, anyone could have a bad day.

She switched off her computer and stood up. It was almost inconceivable that Margrét could have killed Maríanna, hidden her body in the lava field, then turned up and read the news reports for the TV cameras every evening, cool as a cucumber, with a smile on her face. Not unless she'd been completely unaffected by the murder. Of course, there were people like that — individuals who lacked any kind of empathy. Psychologists referred to them as psychopaths, and the condition was often associated with serial killers. But in Elma's experience few people who committed murder were psychopaths. They were usually under the influence of drink or drugs, mentally ill or blinded by passion. Thinking about Margrét's smiling face, though, Elma couldn't help wondering if she might be the exception.

⋆ ⋆ ⋆

When Elma arrived at her parents' house that evening, the dining table was littered with wax crayons. Alexander was kneeling on a chair with a sheet of paper in front of him, his tongue sticking out of the corner of his mouth as he drew a large fir tree decorated with colourful baubles and a star on top.

'Great picture,' Elma said, sitting down beside him. 'Is it a Christmas tree?'

'It's for Stekkjastaur.' Alexander straightened up and viewed his drawing critically. Stekkjastaur was one of Iceland's thirteen Yule Lads, who traditionally brought presents to put in children's shoes in the thirteen days leading up to Christmas.

'Is he coming this evening?'

'No, tomorrow.'

'I bet you'll get something really good in your shoe as a thank-you for this picture.' Elma stroked his blond head. 'The best toy he's got in his sack.'

Alexander looked at her, open-mouthed. 'Do you really think so?'

'Of course,' Elma said. 'It's a great picture.'

Alexander didn't seem convinced. He stared at his drawing doubtfully. 'Maybe if I write my name and … and his name too.'

Elma nodded. 'Yes. Yes, you know, I think that might work even better.'

'Can you help me?'

Elma smiled and wrote Stekkjastaur's name on another sheet of paper for Alexander to copy. His longing for a present in his shoe was almost palpable, and Elma suddenly envied him the innocence of youth. Believing in the Yule Lads and all the magic associated with Christmas lent the festive season an aura of wonder and excitement. If only she could go back in time, be transported to childhood again, just for a few days.

'No news on the case?' Her mother sat down opposite them with two mugs and handed one to Elma.

Elma put her hands round the hot china and lifted out the teabag. 'With any luck, it's close to being solved.'

'Let's hope so. I just feel so sorry for the woman's daughter.'

'Yes, though Hekla seems happy where she is.'

'I can believe it. Bergrún's a lovely person,' Aðalheiður said. 'I started going to her after Sveinn retired.'

'You go to her?' Elma looked up.

'She's a dentist. She works at the surgery just down the road, with Kalli. I started going to her before she got her son, the younger child,' Aðalheiður went on. 'I know they tried to have children for years, but nothing worked, and in the end they ran out of time.'

'Just as well I'm not getting any older,' Elma joked.

Aðalheiður's smile was wry. 'There's a time for everything, Elma love. At your age I'd already had you and your sister.'

'A lot has changed.' Although Elma wanted a child, she'd always felt she had plenty of time for that. Yet she was thirty-three and would probably have to make a decision soon. Her phone rang, sparing her any further talk of babies.

'Hi, Sævar,' she said, getting to her feet.

'Shall I pick you up at eight?'

Elma glanced at the clock. It was nearly seven. 'Yes, that would be good,' she said. 'Hang on a sec. What was that, Mum?' She turned to her mother who was speaking.

'I asked if he'd already eaten.'

Elma hesitated, then gave in to her mother's raised eyebrows. 'Mum's asking if you've already eaten.'

'We ordered plenty of pizza,' Aðalheiður said. She had come over to stand beside Elma.

'We've got plenty—' Elma began, but Sævar interrupted her.

'Yes, I heard her,' he said, laughing. 'I wouldn't say no to pizza. I'll be there in five.'

Elma ended the call and looked at her mother, who had already started getting plates out of the cupboard. She had a feeling Aðalheiður was smiling to herself as she laid the table.

Usually meals at Elma's parents' house were rather rushed affairs, but this evening it seemed no one was in any hurry to get up. All the plates had long been emptied by the time they finally left the table. Sævar and her mother had become absorbed in a conversation about English football. Her mother was a diehard Liverpool fan, just like Sævar. He couldn't hide his wonder as Aðalheiður recited the names of various players, knew exactly which clubs they'd transferred from and had strong opinions on what needed to be done for the team.

In the end, the conversation had moved on to fishing, at which point Elma switched off completely. She knew her dad loved angling. He had tried in vain to get his daughters interested when they were younger, bought them fishing rods and dragged them on trips with him. Elma had found it exciting at first, sitting on the bank, focusing hard on the orange float bobbing on the water. But when it began to rain and hours passed in uneventful waiting, she got bored and lost her concentration. When a fish finally swallowed her hook, the line had jerked so violently that she'd dropped her rod in the lake. Her father had tried to run after it in his waders but it was too late. The rod had sunk to the bottom and Elma had never gone fishing again. Her dad, on the other hand, still seized every opportunity to cast a line and liked to drive around the local lakes at weekends. It was news to Elma that Sævar shared his passion.

It was well past eight when they drove to Margrét's house and saw a car in the drive. When they rang the bell, a boy of about twenty opened the door, wearing a baseball cap and jeans that were too tight around the thighs.

'Is your mother in?' Elma asked.

'My mother?' The boy looked momentarily puzzled, and Elma realised he probably wasn't used to referring to Margrét as his mother. But finally a light-bulb seemed to go on behind his eyes. 'If you mean Margrét, she's in. Magga!' He shouted out her name without taking his eyes off them, making Elma jump.

From inside the house they heard an answering voice. The boy left them at the door without saying goodbye, and for a few seconds they stood there waiting, an icy wind gusting at their backs. Then Margrét appeared in the hall.

'Evening.' She looked much better than the last time Elma had seen her, but then she was still wearing her professional make-up from reading the news. She had obviously changed into home clothes, though, as she was now in tracksuit bottoms and had a pair of reading glasses on her head.

'Could we come in a minute?' Sævar asked, stepping inside before Margrét could say a word. 'Let's just close the front door before we all freeze,' he added, shutting it firmly. Elma, whose teeth were chattering, silently thanked him for his audacity.

'Yes, right,' Margrét said. She hesitated, then smiled. 'Do come in. Would you like some coffee? I've just made some.'

Elma declined the offer but Sævar said yes. Always accept a coffee, he had told her once. *It helps people relax. Just two mates having a cuppa together. Never fails.*

'I always drink coffee this late,' Margrét said, passing Sævar a cup. 'But then I suppose my hours are rather different from most people's.' She sat down. 'My husband tells me you were trying to get hold of me earlier. What can I do for you?'

'Last time we talked, you said you'd never met Hekla's mother, Maríanna,' Elma said.

'No, I don't think I ever did.'

'Here's a picture of her.' Elma put her phone on the table with a photo of Maríanna on the screen. 'This is the picture we circulated in the media when the search for her was taking place back in the spring. Are you sure you've never seen her before?'

Margrét's eyes darted to the photo, then back again. 'As I said: no, I've never seen her before.'

'But you must have seen this photo,' Sævar said. 'It was all over the media for weeks.'

'Of course I saw it but I never met her in the flesh.'

'Hekla and Tinna are good friends, aren't they?'

'Yes, very good friends. But their friendship was limited to the weekends when Hekla was staying with Bergrún and Fannar. I know them quite well through our daughters, but Hekla's real mother just … well, she wasn't in the picture. To be honest, I didn't give much thought to the fact she had another mother apart from Bergrún.'

'You're quite sure?' Elma persisted.

Margrét sighed and looked at the picture again. This time she studied it a little longer before replying: 'Yes. Yes, I'm sure.'

'Actually, you were both from the same town. From Sandgerði,' Elma said. 'It's not a big place so you're bound to have crossed paths.'

'I had no idea,' Margrét said. 'Honestly. I don't ever recall having seen that woman. But if we're both from Sandgerði, I suppose I must have done, though I have no memory of her. How old was she?'

'She'd have been thirty-one this year.'

'Ah, well, that explains it. She's several years younger than me, so I probably didn't notice her. We moved away when I was twenty-one, so she'd have been, what ... fifteen, sixteen?'

Elma simply couldn't work out from Margrét's expression whether she was telling the truth. Maríanna had only been fifteen when Margrét could have last seen her, and no doubt she had changed a fair amount in the intervening years. And even though they had lived in a small community, that didn't guarantee that they'd have known each other. Elma often failed to recognise people she'd been at school with, particularly those who were younger than her. It wasn't just their faces; their names often didn't ring a bell either.

'By coincidence, Maríanna and her parents also moved away fifteen years ago,' Sævar intervened, when Elma didn't say anything. 'The same year both your daughters were born. The same year her brother died. His name was Anton.'

'Anton...' Margrét looked at them both in turn, then put a hand over her mouth. 'Was ... was Maríanna his sister?'

Either Margrét was a very good actor or she'd genuinely had no idea who Maríanna was. 'So you knew him?' Elma asked.

'Knew ... no, I wouldn't say that.' Margrét stood up and pushed the kitchen door carefully shut, then sat down and cleared her throat. 'He came to a party at my friend's house years ago. I'd drunk too much and passed out in one of the bedrooms. I don't know how long I lay there, but I woke up to find him on top of me. It was ... horrible. Just horrible. I try not to think about it. Had I known it was his sister...'

'Would that have changed anything? Regarding Hekla, I mean?'

Margrét thought for a moment. 'No, I don't suppose it would.'

'Anton's family never believed the accusation,' Elma said cautiously. 'They were very angry when the story came out and blame the scandal for the fact that Anton killed himself.'

Margrét smiled contemptuously. 'Yes, that's the kind of society we live in, isn't it? Just because I couldn't face going through the whole gruelling process of pressing charges, I was branded a liar. I killed him, that's what they said. It didn't occur to anyone that he hanged himself because he was guilty. Because he couldn't bear the shame. Of course I understand his family. It's hard to believe your own child would be capable of something like that, but he did it all right.' Her lips tightened, and she turned her face away and looked out of the window. 'I suppose it was her who sent the letters, then?'

'What letters?'

'Years ago I started getting threatening letters. I assumed they were from someone connected to Anton.'

'Did you report them to the police?'

'Yes, I did — and the time I was pushed down the stairs at a night club in Reykjavík. They didn't take that seriously because I was drunk. It's unbelievable how, if you've had a drink, it negates everything you say. You're nothing but ... a girl who lies.' She smiled bitterly. 'Sorry, I just ... I haven't thought about it for a long time. Is there anything else you want to know?'

Elma glanced at Sævar, then back at Margrét. 'No. No, not at present.'

Ten Years Old

The morning afterwards I wake up on the sofa, still fully dressed, clutching the photo in my arms. My eyelashes are glued together with mascara, making it hard to open my eyes. I vaguely remember howling with my mouth open, crouching in a ball like a small child. It wasn't for Hafliði. No, I was crying for everything I've lost and for how my life could have been. I was crying for Granny, for the little girl in the photo and for what she's become.

When I raise my head from the cushion I see that there's a black streak across it. No doubt I look like a train wreck, my eyes all red and swollen. My daughter's expression when she comes in speaks volumes. But she doesn't ask what's wrong, just looks at me a little uncertainly before fetching her cereal. I sit down at the table with her and wonder how to explain what's happened. Because she's bound to ask. She already asks where Hafliði is, every day that he doesn't come over. At last I decide to tell her the truth. Little girls must prepare themselves for the future, for being betrayed. Because that's what will happen.

She watches me the whole time I am speaking. Eats her cereal, chewing with her mouth closed. When I finish, she is silent.

'Do you understand what I'm saying?' I ask, when I get no response.

She nods slowly.

'Good. Because he's not coming back here. Ever again.' I open the window and light a cigarette. I haven't smoked

for years, but yesterday I went out and bought a packet.

'Do you hate him?'

'What do you mean?' I blow the smoke out of the window, watching her.

'Do you hate Hafliði?'

'Yes,' I say, after pausing to think. 'Yes, I suppose I do.'

I can almost see my answer ricocheting around in her head before she gets up, puts her plate in the dishwasher, then goes to her room. Yet again, I'm reminded of how strange she is. In her world, everything is black or white. There are no grey areas, only good or bad. Beautiful or ugly.

Next morning, I hear that she is up and about before me. When I come out of my room she's sitting in the kitchen, eating her cereal. Fully dressed, with her hair in a pony-tail. It's quite neat, and I see that my endless criticisms have finally had an effect. She's managed to smooth it so that there are no hairs sticking up in the air. And she's also put on a top that she knows I like.

'You look nice,' I say.

'Thanks.' I see a hint of a smile on her lips.

I watch her from the window as she leaves, her pony-tail swinging as she walks. She's so small somehow among all the concrete apartment blocks; a tiny point moving through the streets. There aren't many people she has allowed to come close to her in her short life, but she'd become pretty attached to Hafliði, so it's just as well it's over sooner rather than later. Before I walked off and left him yesterday, he said she could come and visit him. As if I had any interest in sending my daughter downstairs to see him after what he's done.

I have no desire to talk to him again, so it's with reluctance that I open the door that evening when Hafliði knocks. Excuses come pouring out of him. He says he can't remember the evening, that he was in town but didn't drink much. Someone must have put something in his beer. As he stands there at the door, I almost feel sorry for him. But to tell the truth, I don't care about losing him. When I look at him, I feel empty. It's only the future he promised us that I mourn. I shake my head at everything he says and push him away when he tries to come close. I watch him leave without any regrets.

There are plenty of men to take his place, now that I know what I want. I also know that I want to work as something other than a receptionist at a law firm. So I skim the job adverts in the paper the following morning. I devote my lunch break to producing polished applications for the companies that I like the look of.

When I get home after work, there's an ambulance outside the building. Access to the car park has been closed off and a police officer directs me to park somewhere else. It's not that unusual for ambulances to stop here. The block of flats is full of pensioners, and I've seen the paramedics carrying them out on stretchers before now. But I've never seen the police here before, and it gives me a sinking feeling. Once I've found somewhere to leave the car, I walk over to the men standing outside.

'What's going on?' I ask.

'An accident,' one replies, his face grave.

'Who…? I live in the building and my daughter's alone at home. I need to go in to her. Please tell me it's not her who…?'

The man shakes his head. 'There were no children involved,' he says reassuringly. 'It was a man who lives on the ground floor who was injured.'

'Hafliði?' I looked at the men in confusion and they exchange glances. 'Is it Hafliði?' I repeat.

'Do you know him?'

'Well...' I cough. 'No. We were just neighbours.'

When I get up to the flat I find my daughter in front of the television with her headphones on. She smiles when she notices me. I sit down beside her and take her in my arms. The TV programme is about meerkats, and there's something soothing about sitting beside her, watching these little creatures on the screen. I feel the warmth of her body as she leans her head against my shoulder. For the first time for ages I'm sure that everything's going to be all right.

Hafliði had been sitting outside in the small garden that belonged to his flat. The weather was good so he was probably lying with closed eyes, letting the sun warm his face. Perhaps he was asleep when it happened. Perhaps he never saw the flowerpot fall, never felt the pain. I hope so.

The strange thing is that no one recognised the flowerpot. It was a heavy terracotta container. The detectives investigating the accident say it must have fallen from a considerable height, which means there are a number of flats it could have come from. Including mine. But the accident happened before I got home from work, so I have an alibi. A neighbour tells the police they heard us quarrelling at the weekend, and the police ring my employers to confirm that I was at work. A week later, I watch Hafliði's family carrying the furniture out of his flat to a large removal van. Since I have no interest in talking to them again, the only news I get of him is from the neighbours. Hafliði is kept in an artificial coma for several weeks, and when he wakes up, apparently he's changed. There's brain damage, but the doctors don't know if it's temporary or permanent. He needs round-the-clock care, the neighbours on our staircase whisper, their eyes agog. The poor man.

Two weeks after the accident I get a phone call. Most of the companies I applied to sent back formal rejection letters, thanking me for my interest but, unfortunately, blah, blah, blah. I destroyed the letters immediately and felt worthless. I had only gone to two interviews, one for a job as a dental assistant, the other for a position with a large media company. Neither of them had got back to me, but now there's a man from the media company on the phone.

'We wanted to know if you'd be interested in coming for an interview,' he says and I put down the jumper I've been folding.

'An interview?'

'Yes. You applied for the position of journalist but we've already filled the post. Now we're looking for someone for a different position.'

'What kind of job?' I expect him to say cleaning or answering the phone, so I can hardly speak when he explains that he's looking for someone to read the news.

'Read the news?' I repeat, dazed.

'A newsreader. You know, on television,' he says. 'We were struck by you when you came in to interview for the journalist post, so we'd like to get you back in for a screen test, if possible. Would you be able to come to the studio tomorrow?'

'I'll be there.'

'Great, then I'll put you in for two o'clock, Viktoría Margrét.'

'Margrét,' I say. 'Just Margrét.'

Tuesday

Elma wrapped the thick cardigan around herself and moved her chair closer to the radiator in the meeting room. The cardigan was like a big blanket that came down to below the knee. In this cold she wouldn't have minded turning up in woollen socks and tracksuit bottoms as well, but apparently that wasn't an option. Though now that she came to think about it, there were no rules for how detectives were supposed to dress, so perhaps she should see what she could get away with. Mainly for the look on Sævar's face. Not that he exactly made an effort to dress up in the mornings. He habitually wore a T-shirt and jeans. And sometimes a hoodie, as a concession to the temperature.

'Cold?' Sævar asked when he came in.

'Freezing,' Elma replied. 'I even feel cold just looking at you in that T-shirt.'

'Could be a vitamin deficiency.' Sævar sat down, stretched out his legs and crossed them.

'What?'

'You being cold. It could be a lack of some vitamin.' He adopted a knowledgeable expression. 'What would you say your diet was like? Do you eat enough cauliflower?'

Elma shook her head. 'Perhaps if my arms were as hairy as yours, I'd wear T-shirts more often.'

'That's why I'm growing it,' Sævar said, proudly

stroking his furry forearms.

'Jumpers work well too,' Elma said, hurriedly changing the subject before Sævar had a chance to boast any more about his pelt. 'I find it unbelievable that Margrét didn't realise sooner who Maríanna was. Tinna's almost certainly Anton's daughter, so she's bound to have kept an eye on his family.'

The previous day they had stopped short of asking if Tinna was Anton's daughter. The question had seemed inappropriate when Margrét was visibly suffering from raking up the past. But the timing fitted, and Tinna had not been given a patronymic, according to Icelandic custom, but took her second name, Hansen, from her mother.

'Not necessarily,' Sævar objected. 'Tinna's father could have been some other bloke she slept with.'

Elma put down the photo of Anton. 'Tinna has a certain look of her mother, but she takes much more obviously after her father.'

Sævar leant forwards. 'You think? But then you know how bad I am at faces.'

Elma looked up the article on her phone and handed it to Sævar, zooming in on the picture of Tinna, aged ten.

He gave a low whistle. 'OK, I take it back. They're very alike.'

'Maybe it's harder to see it now because Tinna dyes her hair blonde, but in that photo it's very striking.'

'She's changed as she's grown up.' Sævar passed the phone back to Elma. 'But if what Margrét told us was true, I can understand why she wouldn't have wanted anything to do with his family.'

'Absolutely. I can't imagine going through an ordeal like that and then not being believed.'

'It's not unheard of.'

'What?'

'For girls to lie.'

'I know,' Elma conceded reluctantly. She couldn't deny that it was true. 'But it happens very, very rarely. I mean, it's hell having to go through the whole legal process, and I don't think anyone in their right mind would—' She broke off when Sævar raised his hand.

'In their right mind. Exactly. But what if Margrét isn't in her right mind? I can't quite put my finger on it, but there's something about her that...'

'What do you mean?'

'There's just something about her that doesn't quite ring true...'

'Maybe her aura?'

'Her aura?' Sævar frowned.

Elma laughed. 'Oh, apparently Margrét's grandmother used to read people's auras. I saw it in some newspaper interview.'

'No, definitely not her aura. It's more like a sort of in-built sensor that I've got.' Sævar grinned. 'But I bet you Maríanna knew who Margrét was. It's not like she hides herself away. She's beamed into our sitting rooms every evening. What can it have been like for Maríanna to realise that Hekla and Tinna were friends?'

'And cousins. She must have suspected that if she saw pictures of Tinna,' Elma said. 'OK, so, if Margrét murdered Maríanna, she would have had to use Maríanna's car to drive up to Grábrók, then taken a bus back to Akranes. Do you think the bus drivers might be able to recognise her? Seven months later?'

'Ordinarily that would be a bit of a long shot,' Sævar said. 'But with Margrét's face being so well known, there's a chance someone might have recognised her.'

'It was a Friday, though. Shouldn't Margrét have been at work at that time?'

'We could ring her employers and check.' Sævar got to his feet.

The December sun, which suddenly lit up the office, was no more than a cruel illusion. It was still snowy and freezing cold outside. But Elma closed her eyes and warmed her face briefly in its rays, able to forget for a few seconds the long, dark winter months that still lay ahead.

When Sævar rang the TV company Margrét worked for, they told him they would need to see a warrant before they released any information about her absences. Meanwhile, Elma had sent photos of Margrét to the firm responsible for transport between Borgarnes, Bifröst and Akranes, and asked the managers to get in touch with the drivers who had been working the day Maríanna vanished.

It was lunchtime by then and she ate a flatcake topped with smoked lamb, ignoring the beseeching looks from Birta, who was keeping her feet warm under the desk. As she ate, she clicked idly through websites advertising hotels in warmer climes. She imagined basking on a sunlounger by a pool with a colourful cocktail in her hand. No, a beer; an ice-cold beer. With her head full of these images, she was in an unusually good mood when a knock came at the door.

'Come in,' she called and smiled as Sævar put his head round. For an instant she pictured him in the turquoise waters of the pool on the screen in front of her, grabbing her round the waist and pulling her towards him…

'Any news?'

She snapped back to the present. 'They're going to call me if anyone remembers seeing Margrét. But I was thinking, maybe we should look her up on the system. If Margrét really did go to the police about those threatening letters, it should show up there.'

'I'll ask Hörður to check LÖKE,' Sævar said, referring to the police information system. He lingered in the doorway. 'You looking at holidays abroad?'

'Yes, I…' Elma glanced back at the swimming pool and palm trees. 'A girl can dream.'

'Of course.' Sævar smiled. 'You should go for it. Let me know and I'll come with you.'

Elma blushed and closed the page. 'Maybe I will.'

They sat down side by side at the conference table. Hörður had printed out the results from LÖKE.

'Margrét's name came up in connection with two separate cases,' he said. 'The first dates from twelve years ago. She fell down the stairs at a nightclub in Reykjavík and claimed she'd been pushed. Since she suffered from concussion and a broken shoulder, there was a brief inquiry. But she couldn't identify the person who pushed her and there were no security cameras covering the area where she fell, so nothing more came of it.'

'Isn't it more likely that she just tripped over?' Sævar said. 'Because she'd had too much to drink?'

'Of course,' Hörður said. 'But she also presented the police with letters she'd received in the days before her accident. There were copies of them attached to the report. These here.'

He indicated a printout with copies of the letters.

They all appeared perfectly innocent. One was a christening card, though admittedly that was a little strange as Tinna had been three years old at the time. It had a picture of a pink cradle on the front and a message inside that would have seemed harmless had the sender been someone Margrét knew: *Congratulations on your little girl. Now I know where you live, I might pay you a visit.* But Elma could see why it would seem menacing if the sender was unknown. Especially after what Margrét had been through.

'The second incident her name crops up in connection with dates from five years ago and was a lot more serious.' Hörður laid the printout of a police report on the table. 'A man by the name of Hafliði Björnsson was seriously injured when a flowerpot fell on his head. He lived on the ground floor of an eight-storey block, and the flowerpot was believed to have fallen from one of the balconies near the top. As Margrét lived on the seventh floor, she was among the suspects. A neighbour also reported that Margrét and Hafliði had quarrelled the previous weekend, and that they'd been having a relationship. However, Margrét's employer confirmed that she'd been at work when the accident happened. They never managed to establish exactly where the flowerpot had fallen from. A ninety-year-old woman lived on the sixth floor, and one theory was that she could have accidentally knocked it over, though she swore she hadn't.'

'Is he still alive?'

'Hafliði? Yes, I expect so,' Hörður said. 'But who knows what kind of a state he's in.'

The incident didn't sound as if it could have any connection to Maríanna's case. It appeared to have been nothing more than a terrible accident. Margrét had been cleared of all suspicion, but the timing was odd, all the same. They'd quarrelled, then a few days later he'd had an accident.

'Probably no need to look into it any further, then,' Sævar said, disappointed.

'There's something about the timing of both incidents that rings a bell,' Elma said.

'What timing?' Sævar asked.

'The first incident was when Hekla was three years old, wasn't it?' Elma pulled over the file and did some mental arithmetic. 'And the second happened when she was ten.'

Sævar looked puzzled.

'I've got it,' Elma exclaimed. 'Both coincide with Maríanna going AWOL. Hekla was taken away from her when she was three, then again when she was ten. It can hardly be a coincidence, can it?'

'But Maríanna's name doesn't come up in either case,' Sævar protested. 'We've already checked if her ID number brings up any results on LÖKE, and it doesn't.'

'Yes, but … Maríanna was in a mess at the time, probably on drugs. Maybe she looked Margrét up and threatened her — in revenge for her brother.'

'It's possible,' Sævar conceded.

'That would certainly give Margrét a reason to be afraid of Maríanna. Maybe even to kill her.' Elma paused for a drink of water.

'They must have got quite a shock when they encountered each other after all that had happened,' Hörður said thoughtfully.

'Yes, I bet. Maríanna would have recognised Margrét again, no question,' Elma said. 'If it was Maríanna who sent the threatening letters, she must have known where Margrét lived. Kept tabs on her all these years. But it may have taken Margrét a while to work out who Maríanna was.'

Sævar moved a little closer as he pored over the copy of the letter. Elma was so used to his smell that she had almost ceased to notice it, but now that his body was so near, it filled her senses. She had a close-up view of his five-o'clock shadow, his dark hair and thick eyebrows. When Hörður cleared his throat, Sævar moved away again and Elma sat there, fighting the betraying flush that mottled her cheeks, and concentrated on staring down at the table.

What was she thinking? Elma opened one desk drawer after another and went through them mindlessly, unable to remember what she was looking for. She had decided months ago to regard Sævar as a friend and nothing more. What if it didn't work out and they were forced to continue working together? She inadvertently slammed the last drawer shut, making herself and Birta jump. Seeing the dog's anxious eyes, she scratched her ears apologetically.

As they were sitting having supper at her parents' house the evening before, it had occurred to her that Sævar had no one to spend Christmas with. There was only him and his brother, and Maggi usually preferred to spend his time in the community home. Apparently he had a girlfriend there. Sævar had plenty of mates, but from what he said it sounded as if they were like her friends, preoccupied with their families most of the time. Unlike her, he didn't have any parents to invite him round to supper in the evening or to make sure he had enough to occupy him at the weekend. She knew he was lonely, but it wasn't her job to see that he had company over Christmas, or indeed on any other day. Besides, he probably wouldn't want her interfering in his life.

Elma rotated her chair to face the window and picked up her phone. *Want to come round this evening*? she texted Jakob. *If you like*, came the instant reply. Elma thought she detected a hint of hurt behind his words, if it was possible to read anything into such a short message. She hadn't been in touch much over the last few days. In fact, she hadn't contacted him since he'd suggested going on a date. She rubbed her temple and was grateful when the phone started vibrating on her desk, signalling an incoming call. She snatched it up.

It was a man who worked for the bus company. 'I spoke to a driver who was working that day,' he told her. 'He's here with me now. Would you prefer to talk to him directly?'

There was a rustling, then another voice spoke.

'Of course I remember her,' the driver said. 'It's not every day I get a famous face on my bus. There's no denying she's a good-looking woman.'

Elma felt the adrenaline pumping through her veins and all her thoughts were instantly focused on the case again. 'Are you absolutely sure it was her and that this was on Friday, the fourth of May?'

'Positive. It was my last shift before my summer holiday, and I clearly remember her getting on the bus.'

'What time was this?'

He was quick to answer. 'I set off at 20.56. On the dot.'

'Thank you,' Elma said. 'Is it OK to call you back if it turns out we need more information?'

'No problem,' the driver said. 'It must have been her daughter with her. At least I think so, though they didn't look very like each other.'

'Margrét wasn't alone then?'

'No, she got on with a teenage girl. I just assumed they were mother and daughter.'

* * *

Hekla leapt into action the moment the ball landed at her feet. Before her opponents had a chance to react, she was past them. She heard shouts and cries all around her, saw out of the corner of her eye that the defenders were heading her way, but she was too quick. In front of her there was only the goalkeeper, who had come forwards to stand with arms and legs spread, ready to defend the goal. When there were only a few metres left between them, she put her toe under the ball and flipped it up, then watched as it sailed into the goal, hearing the cheers behind her.

After the training session ended, Hekla was still out of breath, her face split by a broad grin that she couldn't wipe off. Catching sight of her reflection in the changing-room mirror, she hardly recognised herself. Her cheeks were red, her hair wild and her eyes glittering. The yellow shirt suited her, and she wished that training sessions went on longer and happened more often. She didn't want to stop. Just wanted to play until she dropped and couldn't get up again.

'Hekla, aren't you going to have a shower?' Tinna had already changed out of her kit and was standing in front of her in her underwear.

'Yes,' Hekla replied. She sat down on the bench, quickly pulled off her yellow-and-black football strip, wrapped herself in her towel and went to have a wash. Showers were the worst thing about training.

When she was ready, she waited for Tinna while her friend put on her mascara and combed her hair. Tinna had suddenly become very distant and seemed to want to spend more time with Dísa than her. Could she read Hekla's mind? Hekla had suffered in silence, aware that her feelings probably weren't returned. She knew what she was now. Knew why she had always felt as if what she did with Agnar was wrong. She'd tried to persuade her body, to force a response from it when he kissed her, but it had been useless. Tinna might not be the same, though. Hekla simply couldn't tell from her expression what she was thinking.

'Shall we get going?' Tinna said abruptly, and Hekla looked up. She had been so sunk in thought that she hadn't even noticed that Tinna was standing fully dressed in front of her, waiting. Hekla got up and followed her. It was a relief to breathe in the cold, fresh air outside. Tinna's phone rang.

'Who was that?' Hekla asked, after Tinna had hung up.

'Mum,' Tinna replied, pulling up her hood. She met Hekla's eye for a moment, then smiled. 'She's coming to pick us up.'

'Why?' Hekla asked. They usually walked home as it wasn't far, and the weather was dry and windless.

Tinna shrugged without answering. A few minutes later, a white Volvo drove into the car park in front of the sports hall. Tinna got in the front, Hekla in the back. Margrét turned and said hello, her perfect face wearing a smile. Tinna had inherited her mother's smile and adopted many of her gestures, but apart from that they looked quite different. Sometimes, though, it seemed as if Tinna was trying to be exactly like Margrét. She wore her hair up in the same style, and pinched her mother's clothes. Margrét even did her make-up for her some mornings before school, and once she had made up all three of the friends before a school dance.

Hekla leant back against the seat. She could hear mother and daughter talking quietly in the front but didn't even try to listen in. The car picked up speed, and Hekla opened her phone. Next time she raised her eyes, the surroundings had changed. Out of the window she saw snowy fields and a bunch of horses standing in a huddle.

'Where are we going?'

Tinna twisted round. 'Just on a little outing.'

'But ... but what about Bergrún and Fannar?'

'I've spoken to Bergrún,' Margrét said. Hekla met her eye in the rear-view mirror. 'She said you could come with us.'

Hekla looked out of the window again. They were driving past the lower slopes of Mount Hafnarfjall now. On the other side she could make out birch scrub standing out black against the bluish-white snow, and beyond that the sea and the distant lights of Borgarnes, her old home. Hekla's thoughts suddenly went to Maríanna, and she was hit by a sense of loss that took her by surprise. The longer ago it was, the more she found herself remembering the good times and forgetting the bad. Strange, because all she had been able to remember immediately after Maríanna's disappearance were the bad times. When she lied to the police and told them she hadn't gone over to Akranes, it was because she'd thought Maríanna would turn up and she hadn't wanted to get into trouble. The last time she'd sneaked over to Akranes without permission, Maríanna had refused to let her go to Bergrún and Fannar's for the weekend, which meant she hadn't seen them for three whole weeks.

She gazed at the back of Tinna's head. Her friend had started braiding her blonde hair. Her fingers moved nimbly as the plait formed. Tinna seemed to sense her watching because she turned quickly and smiled. Hekla hurriedly dropped her eyes, feeling her cheeks grow hot.

* * *

'I'd say we have sufficient grounds to justify a house search.' Elma drew her hair back from her face and tied it in a pony-tail. She was hot and out of breath, as if she'd been running, and could feel sweat breaking out under her arms.

'Yes. I'll get a warrant,' Hörður said.

'We could go straight over there,' Sævar suggested.

Elma glanced at the clock. It was getting on for five. 'She'll have set off for work by now.'

'Wouldn't it be better to wait for her to get home, then?' Hörður asked. 'We don't want to risk her trying to make a run for it.'

'Lucky we live on an island,' Sævar commented. 'People can't run far, unless they take a plane, and then it should all be recorded.'

'Plenty of people have got round that,' Elma pointed out.

'It's still unbelievable how often people have disappeared on this little island of ours,' Hörður said, leaning back. 'You only have to look at this case. How many people must have walked through the Grábrók lava field without spotting Maríanna? There were locals staying in summer houses all around the area and tourists everywhere. No, I reckon there are quite a few hiding places in this country.'

'You're right, of course,' Sævar admitted.

'Yes, indeed, there are countless examples,' Hörður said, smothering a yawn.

Elma studied him speculatively. He'd been unusually hands-off for the past few days, leaving them to take care of the investigation more or less on their own, only dealing with the formalities. Gígja's illness had obviously taken its toll.

'Anyway,' he said. 'I'm going to get hold of that warrant and call out forensics.' He got to his feet and went out, closing the door behind him.

'Did she really drag her daughter into it?' Elma asked, once he had gone. She was finding it hard to get her head round the bus driver's claim. 'Or could it have been Hekla?'

'No, surely not. Isn't it more likely that Hekla was telling the truth? That she'd set off for home before her mother went round to Margrét's place?'

'Yes, maybe.'

'Not that I can picture it,' Sævar added, after a pause.

'Why not?'

'Margrét's just so…'

'I know.' When Elma pictured Margrét as she appeared on the TV screen, it seemed absurd to imagine her being capable of murdering anyone. She looked at Sævar, adding teasingly: 'Is your sensor on the blink?'

'What?' Sævar raised his eyebrows.

'Your sensor. You know, the one you claimed you

had.'

'Oh, that. It tends to malfunction when it comes to attractive girls.' He smiled wryly. 'That's why I can never read you.'

Elma blushed, though she knew Sævar wasn't being serious. Ignoring his remark, she said: 'Perhaps it was self-defence. Perhaps Maríanna started it.'

'Then why dispose of the body instead of calling the police?'

Before Elma could answer, her phone rang. She picked it up and saw Jakob's number. Muting it, she put it back in her pocket. Once again she would have to disappoint him and cancel this evening. And bad though it was, she couldn't bring herself to tell him.

* * *

The car stopped at last. It was getting on for six and already pitch dark outside. When Hekla looked out of the window, she could barely see a thing.

'Where are we?' she asked, rubbing her eyes.

'You'll see,' Tinna replied, opening the door.

Hekla followed her example. The snow crunched underfoot when she stepped out of the car, but apart from that the silence was complete. The sky was bright with stars and there was a half moon. She looked around. Now that her eyes had grown accustomed to the darkness she could see the lava on the other side of the road. The jagged rocks looked ominous in the moonlight, and she had a sense of being watched, as if she had caught a movement out there in the gloom.

'Right, follow me,' Margrét said, and set off along a path that led up a slope.

The snow squeaked underfoot. Ahead, Tinna was

walking beside her mother, humming a tune. After they had gone a little way, their breath rising in clouds, Hekla saw a summer house with a sloping roof and a large sundeck. She wondered if the plan was to spend the night there. She hadn't brought any luggage with her, only her backpack containing her sweaty sports kit. It struck her as odd that Bergrún had agreed to let her go with them to the summer house, since tomorrow was a school day. It wasn't like her.

Margrét had a bit of a struggle to get the door open, but once they were inside, Hekla forgot all about Bergrún. She'd never seen such a luxurious summer house. She had sometimes stayed in rented places with Bergrún and Fannar, but they had been nothing like this. The floor was tiled with grey stone slabs and there were large wooden beams running across the ceiling. In the sitting room, a dark-brown corner sofa and an armchair with a white fleece over it were arranged in front of a concrete hearth, and there was a reindeer's head on the wall. The dining table was large enough to seat ten with ease, and over it hung a magnificent chandelier that would have been perfectly at home in a Scottish castle.

'Wow,' she breathed.

'Nice?' Tinna grinned.

Lost for words, Hekla just nodded.

'It's freezing in here,' Margrét said. She turned on the lights and checked the contents of the kitchen cupboards. 'I'm going to light the hearth. Would you girls like to sort out your beds upstairs?'

Hekla looked up and saw that there was a sleeping loft with a handrail that opened into the living space.

Margrét stopped them as they were about to climb the ladder.

'Your phones, girls.' She gave a half-smile and held out her hand. 'We have different rules here. We're going to have a rest from electronic distractions for once.'

Hekla glanced at Tinna, who rolled her eyes but held out her phone.

'You too, Hekla.'

'OK.' Hekla pulled her phone from her pocket.

Margrét smiled. 'Don't look so horrified — you'll get it back.'

Hekla watched her disappear into the kitchen, then climbed up the ladder behind Tinna.

* * *

'We can't find Hekla anywhere,' Bergrún said in a rush when Elma answered the phone. 'She went to football practice but she didn't come home afterwards, which is most unlike her. She usually lets us know where she's going and she always, always comes home for supper. She knows it's important to me. I've been calling her and calling her, but I get her voicemail every time.'

Elma put down the pizza someone had ordered and wiped her hands on a kitchen towel. Then she left the kitchen and went into her office, pulling the door to. 'When did you last hear from her?'

'At around three. Before she went to football practice.'

'I see. And have you checked with her friends?'

'Yes, I've rung round all of them,' Bergrún said. 'Tinna's not answering either; her phone's off too. What if something's happened? I spoke to Tinna's stepfather, but he didn't know where she was, and

Margrét can't be reached either, but she's at work, so...'

'OK, I'll see what we can do,' Elma said, checking her watch. It was nearly nine o'clock and they were all on standby at the police station. Forensics were on their way up from Reykjavík and an unmarked police car was parked outside Margrét's house. The plan was to arrest her as soon as she got back from work.

'I've just got the feeling that...' Elma heard Bergrún heave a deep breath. 'That something's happened.'

'There's no reason to think that,' Elma said. 'We'll find her.'

She said goodbye to Bergrún, then sat down and thought for a moment before picking up the phone to Kári, who was on guard outside Margrét's house. 'Any sign of her yet?'

'Nope, not a thing.'

'Have you seen her daughter?'

'Apart from her husband, no one's come in or gone out,' Kári said.

Elma ended the call. Margrét should have been home by now. Could she have been held up at work or gone out somewhere afterwards?

After thinking a bit more, she tapped in the number of the TV company. While she was waiting, she was forced to listen to a tinny version of a song that had been popular thirty years ago. Finally, a woman answered, saying that most people had gone home and she should try again in the morning. Elma explained why she was calling and after a bit of insistence on her part, she managed to extract the mobile number of Margrét's boss. He picked up after the first ring and, unlike the woman Elma had spoken to first, he didn't waste time asking for a warrant or invoking the privacy law.

'Margrét didn't turn up to work today,' he said. 'We tried to call her but she didn't answer.'

Elma thanked him and hung up. Then she grabbed her jacket and practically ran down the corridor to Hörður's office.

Tinna and Hekla had last been seen after their football practice, at five o'clock that afternoon. Elma and Sævar parked in front of Margrét's house and peered up at the windows. There was a light on indoors and Margrét's husband's car was in the drive. Was it possible that Margrét had taken the girls somewhere, or had the two of them gone one way and Margrét another? If they were all together, was there any cause for concern?

Elma tried to tell herself that Margrét wouldn't hurt the girls. Even if she had murdered Maríanna, that was different; Maríanna had provoked her, accused her of lying. No, the girls probably weren't in any danger. Or, at least, not Tinna. Elma wasn't as confident about Hekla. What if Margrét and Tinna had both been responsible for Maríanna's death? The bus driver had seen them get on his bus together. But Hekla hadn't been born when the rape took place, so Margrét could hardly blame her for it.

Elma and Sævar got out of the car and walked up to the house. She listened as he knocked, three heavy raps. When Leifur opened the door, he looked first at them, then at the police car behind them. Elma saw a shadow pass across his face.

'Has something happened?' he asked in alarm.

'No,' she answered quickly, realising how it must look to him: a police car and two officers knocking on the door. All that was lacking was a priest. 'There hasn't been an accident. We're just looking for Margrét. We've been trying to get hold of her, but she's not answering her phone and she didn't turn up to work today.'

'What? That's news to me. She was supposed to be at the studio. Are you sure she's not there?'

'She didn't go in,' Sævar said.

'Then I haven't a clue where she is. As far as I knew, she was at work...'

Elma sighed under her breath. She would have liked to put more pressure on him but suspected it wouldn't achieve anything. It seemed pretty obvious that Leifur had no idea where his wife was.

'What about Tinna?' Elma asked.

'Tinna? No, she was at football practice.'

'That finished ages ago.'

'Well, I...' Leifur ran a hand through his thin hair. 'Tinna's often out and about. She's mainly Margrét's responsibility. I just ... Why do you want to talk to them? What's all this about?'

'We'll explain later,' Sævar said. 'Right now we need you to come with us.'

Leifur opened his mouth, then closed it again when he saw men emerging from a car outside. Several of them were already dressed in white overalls.

'What ... why ...?' Leifur stood there as if momentarily paralysed. Then he raised his voice. 'What's going on here? Who are they?' He waved a hand towards the men.

One of them arrived at the front door before they had time to reply. 'We want everyone out as soon as possible so we can examine the house,' he said.

'Of course,' Sævar said. He turned to Leifur. 'We

have a search warrant. You can come down to the station, and we'll explain there what's happening. Is there anyone else inside? Where's your son?'

'No, no one. He's not at home. But what do you mean … a search warrant? What's this all about?'

Sævar sighed and beckoned Leifur to go with him.

Elma watched the forensic technicians carrying their equipment into the house. Maríanna had lost a lot of blood, which meant that if she had died here, they ought to find traces. She glanced over her shoulder to where Sævar was waiting by the car with Leifur, who made a dejected figure, his face wearing an expression of utter helplessness. His forehead glistened with sweat, despite the cold, and dark, wet patches were visible under his arms. He probably didn't have a clue what Margrét was guilty of. The priority now was to find the girls as fast as humanly possible.

'Can you think where Margrét might be?' Elma asked, going over to them. 'Is there anywhere that springs to mind?'

Leifur stared at her for a while before answering, as if he was having trouble understanding the question.

'It … no.' His head swung round as a car entered the street, then swung back to them. 'Not unless … We've got a summer house. But she didn't say anything about visiting it, so I doubt she's there. Are you sure she didn't just have an accident on the way to work? That must be it. She'd never—'

'Where's the summer house?' Sævar interrupted.

'Not far from Bifröst. Right by Grábrók.'

* * *

Hekla was woken by the creaking of the floor as Tinna sat up. Feeling too hot, she pushed off the woollen blanket she had spread over herself. They were both on mattresses in the sleeping loft. The only light came from a small lamp under the sloping ceiling. When Hekla looked out of the window, she could see nothing but her own reflection. Downstairs, the wall was illuminated by an orange glow, and she could hear the crackling of a fire.

Tinna yawned and turned to Hekla. 'Did you sleep well?'

'Mm,' Hekla said. She hadn't meant to fall asleep, but the moment she lay down on the mattress her eyelids had grown heavy. What time was it? she wondered. It must be past suppertime, because her stomach emitted such a loud rumble that Tinna opened her eyes wide.

'I agree.' She laughed and called out: 'Mum!'

There was a creaking of leather downstairs. 'Yes, Tinna?'

'We're dying of hunger.'

'Come down, then.'

Tinna started climbing down the ladder, and Hekla followed close behind. She didn't want to be left alone up there, though if it hadn't been for the hunger pangs she could easily have slept until morning. Her legs were stiff from football practice and she had pins and needles in her arm after sleeping with it under her head.

Margrét was sitting on the sofa with a blanket over her feet. She pushed her glasses up onto her forehead when they came downstairs and laid down her open book.

'Did you have a nice rest?' she asked with a smile.

Her face and hair gleamed in the glow from the fire. Hekla thought she looked like an actress. She had always felt a little intimidated by Margrét when she went round to see Tinna. There was something about her that made Hekla feel self-conscious. She would find herself worrying about whether her hair was tidy enough or her clothes were crumpled. Hekla didn't know if it was because she wanted to impress Margrét or if there was something else behind it.

'Isn't there anything to eat?' Tinna asked.

'I brought along some bread and salad.' Margrét stood up and put on the slippers that were on the floor by the sofa. 'Sorry there's nothing more exciting. This trip was a bit of a spontaneous decision. Sit down and I'll get supper ready.'

She opened the cupboards in the dimly lit kitchen and took out some dark-grey plates that looked as if they were made of stone. Then she turned on the tap and filled a jug with water, then poured wine into a long-stemmed glass for herself. Hekla noticed that there wasn't much left in the bottle on the table. When everything was ready, Margrét joined them at the table and told them to help themselves.

'Hekla,' Margrét said, after a few minutes. Hekla raised her head and looked at her enquiringly. There was an odd light in Margrét's eyes, as if she was seeing her for the first time. Usually, Hekla felt as if Margrét was looking through her without really noticing her. But now her eyes seemed to see right inside her.

Yes, she meant to reply, but her voice got lost somewhere along the way. She coughed and took a sip of water.

'Have I ever told you that you and Tinna are related?'

Hekla almost choked on her water. She glanced at

Tinna, who merely grinned as if it wasn't news to her.

'It's true,' Margrét smiled faintly. 'You're cousins. Tinna's father was your mother's brother, so you're very ... very closely related. You're first cousins.'

'But...' Hekla didn't know how to react to this information. It must be a mistake. 'He's dead. My mother's brother died ages ago.'

'Yes.' Margrét nodded. 'He died before Tinna was born. He never knew about her, and I don't think your mother realised either.'

Almost all Hekla knew about her Uncle Anton was that he had killed himself when Maríanna was pregnant with her. Maríanna had hardly ever talked about him, but once or twice she had reminisced about things that had happened when they were young, like when he convinced her to open her Advent calendar in November and helped her eat all the chocolates. But whenever Hekla had asked any questions about her family, her mother had refused to answer. Hekla never let on that she had tracked down her grandfather on Facebook and sent him a message. Since then she had talked to him from time to time. But there had never been any mention of Anton having a child. It simply wasn't possible, let alone that the child could be Tinna. No, there must be some mistake.

'Tinna knows the whole story already,' Margrét said. 'But I wanted to bring you here to tell you about it. It's only right that you should know too.'

'Know what?'

'Well...' Margrét dropped her eyes to her glass and rotated it slowly, swirling the wine right up to the brim. 'Know what really happened. And why we need to stick together; keep quiet about our secret.' She looked up, straight into Hekla's eyes. 'Do you think you can do that?'

* * *

The drive to Bifröst felt as if it would never end. They were hurtling along the icy roads, way over the speed limit, their blue lights flashing, but even so Elma felt as if they were crawling past the slopes of Mount Hafnarfjall.

'What if Hekla saw something?' Sævar said, as they reached the bridge over the fjord to Borgarnes. Up to now, silence had reigned in the car.

'Saw something?'

'Yes, I mean, what if she witnessed her mother's murder, and that's why Margrét's abducted her?'

'It's possible,' Elma said. 'She could have been in the house when her mother came round. But, in that case, why stay silent about it all this time? Why protect Margrét? Surely Hekla must have cared more about her mother?'

'Really? Maybe she wasn't particularly fond of Maríanna. And what if it wasn't Margrét she was protecting?'

'Who…?' Elma hesitated. 'You mean she might have been protecting Tinna?'

Sævar shrugged. 'Or both of them. From what we've seen, Hekla has problems fitting in socially. I wouldn't put it past her to do something drastic to avoid losing her friend.'

'Her cousin.'

'What?'

'If it's right that Anton was Tinna's father, they're first cousins,' Elma said. 'Their parents were brother and sister.'

'Yes, of course.' Sævar slowed his frantic pace as they drove through Borgarnes. 'Then all the more reason for Hekla not to want to lose her. But we still can't be sure if she knows they're cousins.'

Sævar put his foot down again once they were back on the Ring Road, and soon there was nothing to relieve the darkness but the distant lights of the odd farmhouse in an otherwise empty landscape.

The phone rang in Sævar's pocket, and he passed it to Elma.

'We've found blood,' the man from forensics told her. 'The whole kitchen floor lit up.'

The summer house looked new. It was painted black and had a slanting roof and French windows that opened onto a large sundeck, complete with a hot tub. The whole place oozed affluence. But all the lights were off, and if it hadn't been for the car parked nearby, the house would have appeared empty. Elma strained her eyes to see inside but couldn't make out any movement. Curtains were drawn across all the windows downstairs.

'Do you think they're in there?' Sævar whispered, though there wasn't really any need.

'We saw a movement earlier,' said one of the police officers from Borgarnes, who had been first on the scene. Their car was parked further down the road from where they had been able to watch the house.

'So they're in there?'

'Yes, I think so,' the officer said. 'At least, there were footprints leading to the front door and there's somebody inside. It's possible they're in the room at the back of the house, with the windows facing away from the road.'

'Is there any reason to wait?' Elma asked Hörður, who had followed them in his SUV and was now standing beside her. 'Shouldn't we just go in?'

'Yes,' Hörður said. 'You and Sævar go and knock. The rest of us will take up position around the house to make sure no one gets out another way. I don't believe it's actually necessary, but it's better to be sure.'

Elma and Sævar walked over to the summer house and knocked on the door. As Elma strained her ears, she thought she could hear a murmuring of voices that could be coming from a television. Shielding her eyes with her hands, she pressed her face to the pane of glass in the front door. Inside she saw a cupboard for coats and some shoes. There were two pairs of trainers on the floor. She glanced at Sævar.

'Margrét!' he said loudly and banged again, harder.

As he did so, they heard footsteps, then the door opened.

Margrét stood in the doorway, seeming unsurprised to see them. 'Good evening,' she said.

'Where are the girls, Margrét?' Sævar asked.

Margrét didn't answer, just smiled and looked them up and down. Elma found it hard to interpret her manner. She looked exactly like she did on television: friendly, sincere.

'Where are they?' Elma said, stepping inside.

'They're in there.' Margrét gestured towards a closed door.

Elma walked past her, with Sævar on her heels. She went straight to the room at the back, from which the sound of the television was coming. She didn't know what to expect but gasped when she saw the girls lying on the sofa. Their arms were dangling limply and in the darkness she couldn't see if they were breathing. For a split second the world seemed to stand still, then Sævar switched on the lights and they stirred. Tinna raised a hand to shield her eyes, and Hekla rolled over onto her other side. When Tinna made them out, she didn't appear remotely alarmed nor surprised. She just sat up and pulled off the throw that had been covering her.

'What's going on?' Hekla asked in a low voice.

'You need to come with us, girls,' Elma said. 'We'll explain on the way.'

'Where's Mum?' Tinna asked.

'She's...' Elma hesitated. 'She's going with my colleague.'

'Why?' Tinna asked. 'Can't she come in the same car as us?'

'I'm afraid that's not possible,' Elma said calmly. 'We'll explain—'

'No.' The girl's voice was so determined that Elma was silenced. Tinna rose to her feet. She was much taller than Elma, and suddenly it felt uncomfortable standing there facing her. There was a look in Tinna's eyes that made Elma take an involuntary step backwards.

'Tinna, we—'

'I did it,' Tinna said. 'Mum didn't do anything. It was me who killed Maríanna.'

Wednesday

The forensics team was busy until late. When Elma went into work the following morning, she looked through the photos they had taken. There were clear signs of where the blood had splashed the walls and formed a large pool on the floor. A bloodstain-pattern analyst, who had examined the scene, concluded that Maríanna had been lying on the floor when she was beaten. In fact, it was still to be confirmed that the blood belonged to her, but they were working on the assumption that it did. All the indications were that she had been murdered in the house. The only remaining question was who had been responsible.

Elma strolled into the kitchen and filled her mug, then sat down at the table instead of returning to her office. She didn't believe Tinna was guilty of murdering Maríanna, as the girl had claimed the night before. Her confession had almost certainly been an attempt to protect her mother, but the police couldn't be sure. The bus driver had seen Margrét with a young girl whose description fitted Tinna: taller and more strongly built than Margrét. Elma guessed that Tinna would be admitted to a children's mental-health unit for a few days, just while the reports were being completed. As she had only been fourteen when the murder was committed, she was too young to be charged. There was no question of custody either, as too much time had passed, which meant the police had no justification for keeping mother and daughter apart. If Margrét and Tinna wanted to synchronise their stories about Maríanna's death, they'd already had ample opportunity to do so.

But where did Hekla fit in? Had she witnessed her mother's murder? Elma had been in the car with Hekla the previous evening. The girl hadn't spoken much, just sat in the back seat, staring out of the window. When she saw Bergrún and Fannar waiting to meet her at the police station, she had run into their arms.

Elma put down her coffee mug, having lost her appetite for the black swill. Margrét's interview was due to begin soon. She had asked if she could have her lawyer present, and he was on his way up from Reykjavík. It was past midday, and Elma felt as if she hadn't slept at all, although she had in fact had quite a few hours. Her head had been whirling with the events of the evening when she laid it on the pillow last night and closed her eyes, but to her surprise it had been morning when she next opened them. She was in mid-yawn when Sævar walked into the kitchen.

'The lawyer's here,' he said. 'Shall we get started?'

As Elma studied Margrét, she just couldn't picture the sequence of events that had ended in Maríanna's death. Had Margrét really stood over her body, beating and kicking her long after she had lost consciousness?

Sævar switched on the recording device and read out the formalities. Margrét watched him, her face grave, though her eyes were alive with curiosity. The only sign of nerves was the way she kept taking sips of water, and when she gripped the glass, Elma noticed that her knuckles were white.

'Right,' Elma said. 'Let's go over the events of Friday, the fourth of May. Can you tell us what happened?'

'Yes.' Margrét cleared her throat. 'I was about to leave for work when there was a knock at the door.'

'Was anyone else home?'

'Tinna and Hekla were in the bedroom.'

'All right,' Elma said. 'Go on.'

'Anyway, as I said, there was a knock, and I went to the door. I saw at once by the way she looked at me that the woman recognised me. I just assumed she knew me from TV. But she didn't say a word, just … stared.' Margrét dropped her gaze to her glass. 'Then she asked if I knew who she was and, when I said no, she said she wanted to talk to me. We went into the kitchen, and she told me who her brother had been. Naturally, I was startled. In fact, that's putting it mildly; I was shocked.'

'Could you explain who her brother was?' Sævar asked. 'For the recording.'

'Anton lived in Sandgerði like me. We met at a party, not that I remember much about it. All I remember is that I fell asleep alone in a bedroom but when I woke up, he was on top of me. He'd pulled off all my clothes.' She closed her eyes for a moment. 'Sorry, I … All my life I've tried to escape what happened. I've hidden from the people who didn't believe me and judged me for something I had no control over, so seeing his sister standing there in my kitchen was … I can't describe it.' Margrét paused, staring unseeingly at the table. 'I suppose I didn't react the way I should have done. I told her to go away and take … take Hekla with her. Of course it wasn't fair, but then what happened to me wasn't fair either. None of it was fair.'

'How did she react?' Sævar asked, when Margrét showed no sign of continuing.

'She called me a liar. Said she'd been watching me and had seen what kind of person I was. It suddenly dawned on me that it must have been her who sent the letters.'

'Tell us about the letters.'

'I started getting threatening letters three years after Hrafntinna was born. Anonymous letters congratulating me on my little girl. One mentioned the name of Tinna's nursery school, which made me afraid for her safety. Then one evening I was pushed down the stairs at a nightclub in Reykjavík. I didn't see who it was, but I assumed it was the same person who sent me the letters. My daughter and I moved after that.'

Elma nodded. She had read the letters and knew that Margrét was telling the truth. 'Did Maríanna admit to having sent them?'

Margrét looked up, smiling wryly. 'Yes, she did. She laughed and asked if I'd been scared. That's when I … when I completely lost control. I screamed at her and shoved her away because I wanted her to leave.'

'So there was a struggle?'

Margrét glanced at her lawyer, then back at Elma and nodded. 'She was only trying to save me.'

Elma leant closer. 'Who? Who was trying to save you?'

'Tinna,' Margrét said in a choked voice. 'She didn't mean to kill her. She just came out of her room and saw us. She must have thought I needed help or … or I don't know what she thought. All I know is that next minute Maríanna was on the floor and there was blood everywhere and … oh, God.' Margrét clamped a hand over her mouth, and tears started running down her cheeks. 'What will happen now? What will happen to Tinna?'

The lawyer intervened. 'Hrafntinna was fourteen years old at the time of the incident, which means she was below the age of criminal responsibility.'

Elma caught Sævar's eye. They hadn't been expecting Margrét to put the blame on Tinna.

'Can we take a short break?' Margrét pleaded through her sobs.

Sævar nodded and switched off the recording device. Elma rose to her feet, fetched some kitchen towels and handed them to Margrét. Shortly afterwards, Margrét had recovered her composure and was ready to continue.

'As you can see, my client is not guilty of murder,' Margrét's lawyer said. 'Her daughter has confirmed her story. She thought her mother was in danger and reacted accordingly.'

'Please don't interrupt the interview,' Elma said. A lawyer's role was merely to observe and protect the client's interests. He would have his chance to put Margrét's case when it came to the trial.

'What happened after that?' Sævar addressed his question to Margrét.

'I just didn't know what to do. Poor Hekla was there and saw everything. I told her to go home and begged her not to tell anyone what had happened.'

'Why did you hide the body?' Elma asked. 'If it was an accident, self-defence, why didn't you just ring the police?'

'Like I said, I was scared and didn't know what to do. I wasn't thinking straight. I rang work and told them I was ill. All I could think of at that moment was to make Maríanna disappear. To behave as if nothing had happened. I mean, I knew how she'd treated Hekla. I'd often talked to Bergrún, and she told me how that woman had just walked out and left Hekla alone at three years old. Three years old. Can you imagine? I didn't think anyone would miss her. Even Hekla didn't seem too upset by it. I told her that now she'd be able to move in with Bergrún and Fannar, as she'd always wanted. But my main priority was not to ruin Tinna's life. Even though she wouldn't be convicted like an adult would, she'd always have been branded a murderer. I know to my cost that the public don't need judges — they're perfectly capable of condemning people on their own. And the court of public opinion is far more merciless than the justice system.'

Margrét finished the water in her glass. She was wearing a thick, light-brown jumper with a V-neck. Her hair fell loose over her shoulders, and her face was bare of make-up, yet she could just as well have been on location. There was something about her posture as she sat there, very upright, looking straight in front of her as she spoke. And then there was that voice. Those familiar, mellifluous tones. As if she were reading a script. If Elma hadn't met Margrét in different circumstances, she probably wouldn't have noticed anything. But she had seen another side of her and this made her wonder if Margrét was telling the truth.

'We have a bus driver who remembers seeing you and Tinna catching the bus from Bifröst to Akranes on the fourth of May,' Sævar said.

'I couldn't go alone,' Margrét said. 'You must understand that. I tried to lift the body but I couldn't do it. I wasn't strong enough.' She slumped back in her chair and gave a loud sigh, as if exasperated by their inability to understand. For a moment the mask seemed to slip, and Elma caught a flash of anger behind her eyes. Then Margrét straightened her back again and said: 'Hekla and Tinna can both confirm everything I've said.'

* * *

She hadn't been expecting hugs. Reproaches, yes, but not hugs. She breathed in the coconut scent of Bergrún's hair. And then Fannar was there, his embrace a little clumsier and briefer, but still so warm and lovely. Like being wrapped in a soft blanket. After her witness statement had been taken, they'd gone straight home, where Bergrún had run Hekla a bath, and they hadn't even mentioned what had happened. She was grateful for that. Once she was in bed, though, she couldn't stop thinking about whether she could have done anything differently. Whether she would have even *wanted* to change anything.

On 4 May, Hekla had slipped away in the middle of her swimming lesson without anyone noticing. Ignoring Maríanna's attempts to get hold of her, she had contacted Agnar, but he hadn't had time to pick her up. As a result, she had taken the bus to Akranes with no clear idea about what she was going to do once she got there. She was so angry that all she could think of was getting away from Maríanna, who didn't understand anything and couldn't care less if Hekla missed her football tournament. But she couldn't go to Bergrún and Fannar's house because that was the first place Maríanna would look for her.

Tinna had answered the moment she rang. And Tinna's mother hadn't commented when she turned up at their house, since there was nothing unusual about it; Hekla dropped in to see Tinna most weekends when she was in Akranes. But Maríanna had gone on ringing, and in the end Hekla had come to her senses and decided to go home. She was so afraid of being grounded that on the way back she had racked her brains for excuses: she'd lost her phone, she'd been doing homework with some other kids from school (like Maríanna would believe that), she'd got permission to stay longer at the pool, she'd lost her house keys, she'd gone to the library where she'd been reading and had forgotten the time…

By the time the bus reached Borgarnes she had the story fully formed in her head, but when she got home there was no sign of Maríanna. Just that note: *Sorry. I love you. Mum*. Of course, she'd thought the message was about the football tournament and felt even more guilty about having sneaked off to Akranes.

When it became clear that Maríanna wasn't coming back, she'd seen the note in a whole new light. It wasn't because of the tournament at all, but because Maríanna Hekla decided to vanish forever. Or so she'd believed.

After that, everything had happened both quickly and slowly. The move, the change of school, new bedroom, new life. Supper at seven o'clock, wake up at half past seven, football practice five times a week. And Hekla was happy; too happy to think about Maríanna. If anything, she was grateful because it was as if Maríanna had finally set her free. That's how Hekla had felt after she disappeared: free.

But now Hekla knew the whole story. She knew

what kind of brother Maríanna had had and what he had done. She couldn't imagine how Margrét must have felt. The thought of Margrét, so beautiful, so kind, made her smile. Why had she ever been afraid of her? At the summer house she had felt so easy in her company. As if she was finally part of a real family; her blood relatives. She and Tinna were first cousins. That was something she had never thought she would have. Yet she felt a pang in her heart when she thought about Tinna and what could never now happen between them. Maybe it was just as well. Maybe it had never been a real possibility, and she had just imagined that Tinna had feelings for her. Maybe.

It didn't matter. What they had now was so much bigger and more important, and all she had to do was tweak the truth a little. Claim she had witnessed something that she hadn't, to save Margrét and Tinna from getting into trouble. Then life could continue just as it was. No, not quite as it was — better than before.

Now everything would be so much better.

Monday

They had discussed the case back and forth over the last few days, but in reality it was out of their hands. Margrét would be charged, though Elma doubted she would be looking at a long prison sentence. Both Tinna and Hekla had confirmed Margrét's story, and there was no evidence to disprove their version of events. Not only was Margrét convincing but people wanted to believe her.

Her story was all over the media; the tale of how the small town had turned against her after the alleged rape. Someone had got wind of the fact that Maríanna, the rapist's sister, had stalked her afterwards. There was a clamour of voices demanding Margrét's release. It was as if the case had been turned upside down, and instead of being guilty of murder, or at least of having covered up a murder, Margrét was now a victim. A hero. Admittedly, most people agreed that hiding the body had been a mistake, but an excusable one in the circumstances. She had only been protecting her daughter. Maríanna received much worse treatment at the hands of the press, who described her as a bad mother and criticised the Child Protection Agency for having allowed her to keep Hekla. Especially after somebody leaked the fact that Hekla had been left alone for three days when she was three years old. The very few voices who believed that Margrét deserved a heavy sentence were drowned out by the tidal wave of those who were active in the comments sections. Elma wouldn't be surprised if the persuasive power of social media ended up influencing the court.

Resting her chin on her hand, she looked at Sævar. 'There's something not quite right about this. Something about her that just … that just doesn't fit.'

'How do you mean?'

'There's some quality that doesn't come across on television or in newspaper interviews — or even necessarily when you meet her. It's like she puts on this face for the cameras. Like it's all just theatre. She's kept quiet about Maríanna's death for seven months, coolly pretending nothing happened. If the body hadn't turned up, she'd have got away with it too.'

Sævar sighed. 'Margrét has quite a strong story, and there's a variety of evidence to support it. We should be able to compare the handwriting in the threatening letters with Maríanna's writing, which would settle the question of whether she sent them. And if Tinna's guilty, it's quite possible that a mother would react like that. If she was protecting her daughter.'

Elma nodded. She couldn't provide any real reasons to justify her dislike of the woman. Perhaps it was just personal prejudice, influenced by the way Margrét had looked at her as if she wanted to laugh. It didn't matter how often Elma reminded herself that Margrét had been treated abominably over the rape, she just couldn't summon up any sympathy for her.

Maybe too it was the discrepancy she perceived between Margrét's public persona and how she behaved when she was talking to Elma. She wasn't the same person. Elma could understand how people fell for the friendly, warm, open, sincere woman they saw on their TV screens. But that wasn't the Margrét

Elma had encountered behind closed doors.

The phone rang, and Elma went into her office and shut the door. It was Gulla from reception.

'I've got a woman on the line. Can I put her through?'

Elma glanced at the clock: she'd been on her way out. 'Yes, OK. Put her through.'

The woman introduced herself as Guðrún. Elma found it impossible to guess her age. Her voice sounded youthful, but her diction was very clear and her language formal.

'She's lying,' the woman said. 'Margrét is lying about the whole business.'

'I'm sorry, who did you say you were?'

Sævar put his head round the door, and Elma gave him a sign to hang on. A few of them were going out to lunch together.

'I have a son called Hafliði who was in a relationship with Margrét,' the woman said. 'He was head over heels in love with her and very attached to her daughter, Hrafntinna. I only met them the once, but that was quite enough. There was something downright malevolent about her, and you didn't have to be around her long to see it. It was useless even trying to discuss it with Hafliði, though. Love is blind.'

Elma remembered Hafliði's name from when she'd looked Margrét up on LÖKE, the police information system. He was the neighbour who had been seriously injured in an accident. But Margrét couldn't have been involved as she'd had an alibi, so Elma couldn't think why Hafliði's mother was calling. 'I don't quite follow…'

'No, I don't suppose you would,' the woman said. 'My son and I were very close. I say were because although he's still alive, he's not the same person anymore. He's unrecognisable as the old Hafliði. Anyway, he rang me the evening before the accident, distraught because he'd wrecked his relationship with Margrét. He'd … been unfaithful to her.'

'I see,' Elma said. She recalled that a neighbour had heard Hafliði and Margrét having a row a few days before the accident. Presumably their bust-up had been about his cheating.

'I just know she was involved in his accident. I'm as sure of that as I am of my own name.'

'What makes you so sure?'

'It's obvious, isn't it? A flowerpot wouldn't just randomly fall off the seventh floor, directly onto Hafliði's head. It's too convenient a coincidence. No, if you ask me, it was deliberately dropped on him.'

Elma glanced at the clock again. Naturally, she pitied the woman. It had been a terrible accident. But she pitied her even more for her inability to accept what had happened and move on, instead of feeling she had to blame someone; find a scapegoat.

'Then there was the necklace,' the woman added.

'The necklace?'

'I gave Hafliði a necklace for his thirtieth birthday. A chain with an H pendant that he never took off. When he was found, there was no sign of the necklace. We searched his entire flat without finding it.'

'Couldn't he have lost it?'

'No,' Guðrún said flatly. 'No, somebody stole it. The same person who dropped the flowerpot.'

The claim struck Elma as absurd. 'I see,' she said.

Sævar put his head round the door again and tapped at his watch. Elma gave him a sign that she was almost done.

'Could I send you a photograph?' the woman asked.

‘A photograph?’ Elma got to her feet and took her jacket off the back of her chair.

‘Of the necklace.’

‘I don’t know how that will help.’

‘Please,’ Guðrún begged. ‘In case you come across it in the course of your—’

‘OK, send it over,’ Elma interrupted quickly. She was starving. Begga now looked into the office as well, her expression impatient. Elma gave Guðrún her email address and hurriedly ended the call.

After lunch, Elma returned to her desk. She sat there for a while, staring at the wall and stroking Birta’s ears, feeling strangely empty inside. She had been enjoying her lunch until Sævar had broken some news to her and Begga that had made her completely lose her appetite for her club sandwich. Apparently, Gígja’s cancer had spread to her bones, and Hörður was going to take indefinite leave as a result. Elma didn’t know much about cancer and was grateful for that, but she did know that once it had spread to the bones, the outlook wasn’t good.

Gígja and Hörður had been together since they were kids. They had children and grandchildren, and everything that Elma would like to have herself one day. However different they were, no one could fail to see how much they loved each other, and there was no mistaking either how badly Gígja’s illness had affected Hörður. He had been distracted for months now, and his worries seemed to be overwhelming him these days. If only there were some way she could help.

Elma’s thoughts went to her own parents. They’d had a rocky patch when the sisters were younger, but over the years their relationship appeared to have grown stronger. Perhaps it was all the holidays abroad or the hobbies they now shared. Last year, her dad had given her mum waders for Christmas, and in the summer they had gone on a fishing tour together. Now her mum was going to repay him in kind by taking him with her to a Liverpool game.

Elma sighed, took out her phone and selected Jakob's number. It was time to tell him the truth. She couldn't go on avoiding him like this. It wasn't fair.

After the phone call, she sat down again, feeling as if a heavy burden had been lifted from her shoulders. She then noticed that Hafliði's mother had sent her a message. When she opened it, a large jpeg began to download, bit by bit.

The man in the picture was strikingly handsome. He had dark, slightly wavy hair, warm eyes and a big smile, revealing perfect white teeth. Last of all, his neck appeared with the chain and pendant, and Elma remembered exactly where she had seen the same kind of necklace.

Thirteen Years Old

My little girl has become a teenager. A thirteen-year-old who loves rappers I've never heard of, spends an hour in the shower and takes another hour to get ready. I let her dye her hair blonde. It suits her, drawing out the grey in her eyes. There's not much left of the frightened little girl she once was. No one would suspect that she hadn't had any friends for the first ten years of her life or that she hardly spoke a word until she was three years old. No one, looking at her now, would see a girl who had hardly raised her eyes from the floor as a child and played obsessively with those green toy soldiers. They've long gone. We put them in a bin bag and threw them out, the day we moved to Akranes. Only I can see the odd glimpse of the child she once was. The hesitation when she finds herself in a situation where she doesn't know how to behave. Most people just see a girl who carefully weighs up her words before speaking. They don't know that what she's really doing is working out what people expect her to say. That normal communication doesn't come naturally to her.

After I started my job on TV, so much changed. I changed. I lost all the kilos I had gained and looked more like the girl I used to be. I didn't care who saw me now or who might recognise me, because I had no need to be ashamed of anything. I met Leifur at work. He was the TV company's finance manager. Hrafntinna and I moved to Akranes, because he lived there and commuted to Reykjavík every day. I enjoyed living in a small town again, and the change of scene did my daughter good too. Being at a new school gave her a chance to recreate herself, and she did it better than I would have dared dream. She's been so successful that I hardly recognise her anymore.

But her room isn't quite like other teenagers' rooms. I listen to mothers complaining about what pigsties their daughters' bedrooms are and how they spend hours on the phone and won't do their homework. My daughter's room is always immaculately clean and tidy. Everything has its place, and every piece of clothing is neatly folded and put back in the cupboard after use, while her shoes are lined up on a rack at the end of her bed.

I pause by the photo on her desk: Tinna at six years old, on her first day at school. At least I did one thing right: I took the conventional picture that all parents should take. Beside the photo is Granny's black stone, the hrafntinna.

I open the drawer in her desk. It's full of papers and books. Felt pens in all the colours of the rainbow and rubbers designed to look like food. A hamburger, a pineapple, a chicken. Once she used to arrange them on a shelf, but now they've found a new home. I automatically straighten the pile of papers and move the rubbers aside.

It's then that I notice the chain. It's hidden at the back of the drawer. When I take it out, I see the pendant with the H on it dangling in front of me. Suddenly the floor seems to be moving in waves, and I sink into the chair at the desk. I drop the necklace back into the drawer and sit there dumbly staring at it. Then I close my eyes and see Hafliði, the evening before the accident. I clearly remember the chain around his neck as he stood at the door, begging my forgiveness. And I see Hrafntinna, the day they first met, pointing at it and saying, 'Hey, that's my initial'. See the two of them holding their H pendants as though they were proof of their relationship. 'Do you hate

Hafliði, Mum?' she had asked. A black-and-white world. Either good or bad, nothing in between.

My hands shake as I stand up and carefully close the drawer. As I carry on cleaning the house, the questions keep running through my head: who is she really? Who is this girl I brought into the world?

Tuesday

Tinna watched the blender pulp the frozen berries until they were reduced to a pink mush. Now it was just her, Leifur and her stupid stepbrother in the house. She had come home yesterday after spending several days with a doctor who thought he could analyse her. It was rather lonely in the house without Mum. She wished her mother hadn't had to go away but knew she'd had no choice. With any luck, she wouldn't be away too long. Because there was no way Tinna was staying here for any length of time without her. She would have given anything to be allowed to go with her. It had always been the two of them together, her and her mum, and Tinna found it hard to imagine a different life.

In all these years Tinna had only once asked who her father was, and her mother's reaction then had ensured that she had never asked again. But now she knew. Since Maríanna had come round that day back in the spring, she had known that his name was Anton and he was dead. He'd died before she was born. When she looked him up online, all she found was an article from when he had represented Iceland in a maths competition as a teenager. She had inherited her interest in maths from him, then, along with her dark hair and large build. Tinna wished she was more like her mother: smaller, with finer features. That her nose wasn't as big and her hair wasn't as dark.

She had done what she could to make herself more like her mother. Dyed her hair blonde, wore clothes her mother had bought for herself, and imitated her manner. Studied her expressions and smile, practising in front of the mirror until her cheeks ached. It had pleased her mother so much, and she would do anything to please her. Everything was so much easier when her mother was happy.

Glancing out of the kitchen window, she noticed a car pulling up outside their house and a woman getting out. She recognised her. It was the policewoman who had come and fetched them from the summer house. Tinna reached for her strawberry lip gloss and put it on. Then she stuck a straw in the pink smoothie and went to the door.

Tinna could tell that the policewoman sitting in the kitchen chair facing her was nervous, in spite of her smile. The red blotches on her neck gave her away.

'I just wanted to talk to you,' the woman said. 'It's nothing serious, I promise.'

Tinna didn't return her smile. Now that her mother wasn't here, there was no need to put on an act. She was tired of trying so hard every day, terribly tired. She would have liked to tell this woman where to go, but she knew this would be unwise and managed to restrain the urge. Over the years she had learnt to control her impetuosity, which used to make her do things without thinking.

'That's a pretty necklace you're wearing,' the woman said.

Tinna automatically reached up and stroked the H, as she always did when she was feeling insecure.

'Where did you get it?' the woman asked.

'It was a present,' Tinna said, which was almost true. At least, he hadn't protested when she removed the chain from his neck. At first, she had hidden it in her desk, only taking it out occasionally to look at it. Her own necklace also had an H pendant, but hers was silver, while Hafliði's was gold. Then, about a year ago, she had started wearing it instead of the one her maternal grandparents had given her as a baby, which was now too small. Anyway, why should she wear something given to her by people who couldn't care less about her and her mother? Her mum had noticed the necklace one evening when they were sitting eating supper with Leifur. She had shot Tinna an odd look but hadn't said anything. Since then, Tinna hadn't taken it off.

'Who gave it to you?'

'My friend.' Hafliði was her friend. Or so she had believed. When Hafliði betrayed her mother, he had betrayed Tinna, and all his promises as well.

The policewoman suddenly held out her phone and Tinna looked down to see Hafliði's face smiling up at her. Always so happy and kind, willing to play with her and watch wildlife documentaries or sci-fi series with her. Explaining to her how physics worked and helping her with her maths homework — something her mother had never bothered to do.

'Do you recognise this man?'

'It's Hafliði,' Tinna said. She knew there was no point denying it. And she knew that it didn't really matter what this policewoman said because she couldn't do anything to her.

'Did he give you the necklace?'

Tinna nodded. Yes, the story could just have well have gone like that. Hafliði had given her the chain as a parting gift on the day of his accident.

'Do you remember his son, Stefán?'

'Yes.' Tinna remembered him well. She had never been able to stand the smug little prick who had wanted to keep his dad all to himself. If her mother and Hafliði hadn't split up, she would have had to find some way of getting rid of Stefán. She smiled, remembering her ten-year-old self dreaming up all kinds of plots to get him out of the way.

'He swears his father was wearing the necklace the morning of the day of his accident.'

'He gave it to me at lunchtime. When I got home.'

'So you were at home when the accident happened?'

'Yes, I was.'

'Did you see what happened?'

'No.'

The policewoman stared at her for a while and Tinna stared back. She saw that the woman had beautiful eyes: grey, brown and green. She wondered if she should say this to her but, after considering for a moment, decided it would be better to keep the thought to herself. Her mother had taught her never to trust people. She'd said that most people who were friendly were only pretending because they wanted to persuade you to do something for them. People were always trying to deceive you or fool you. Like Hafliði did.

'I talked to Hafliði's mother,' the policewoman went on. 'Maybe you don't remember her, but she met you once.'

Tinna had a clear memory of the plump, grey-haired little woman who had looked at her and her mother with such loathing.

The policewoman continued: 'She rang me and

told me about that necklace. About how they had searched for it everywhere. I think she'd be very grateful to have it back.'

Tinna clutched the pendant tighter, slowly shaking her head. 'Hafliði gave it to me. It's mine now.'

She watched as the policewoman drove away from the house, repeatedly running her finger over the H. If only Hafliði hadn't cheated on her mother and wrecked all her plans; the whole future she had imagined, with the three of them living happily ever after. She had been so excited about finally having a proper family, about having a dad of her own. He'd been so kind and such fun, not like Leifur, who did nothing but work, and turned bright red every time he tried to have a conversation with her. If Hafliði hadn't abandoned her and her mother, life would have been so much better. Never mind. Now at least she had Hekla, and soon her mother would be back with her again. Then everything would be perfect.

Epilogue

I

I feel as if I've been transported fifteen years back in time. I'm lying in bed, the papery white sheets sticking to my skin. Outside the door, the staff are keeping an eye on me. The only difference is that no one puts a child on my breast. No crying wakes me in the night. I'm alone.

I wonder what they're saying about me now. What the stories in the media are like; the word on the street. I get the impression they're on my side this time. I think I see it in the eyes of the prison officers. There's no hint of condemnation there, only pity and sympathy. I have to admit that I'm quite good at playing the role of victim. I know how to appear small and vulnerable. How to lower my eyes as if I'm ashamed; how to play the caring mother. After all, I've had many years' experience in that role.

I close my eyes and travel back in time to when I was living in Sandgerði without a care in the world, free from kids and the responsibility they bring. In those days Sandgerði was a small fishing community, a few minutes' drive from Keflavík Airport and the neighbouring town of Reykjanesbær. Apart from a pretty church, it had little to distinguish it. There was no landscape to speak of, just a big sky and the flat, treeless, volcanic plain at the western tip of the Reykjanes Peninsula. But you could see for miles across Faxaflói Bay when the weather was good.

In my early twenties I used to go out partying every weekend. Often both Friday and Saturday night, and sometimes during the week as well. It wasn't just me, but most of the other kids my age and plenty of older people who hadn't settled down yet. The type who didn't have families and still did the same jobs as when they were eighteen. People who'd been stuck in a rut for decades. It's all part of living in a small town where there's not much else on offer.

There was one bar in the town. It was popular at weekends, and it had become something of a custom for us to meet up there. Most evenings at the bar were so similar that they merge together in my memory. The same people, weekend after weekend. Drinks, dancing, drunken talk and stolen kisses. Sometimes we met at one of the other kids' houses first, when their parents were away, and occasionally at the homes of the older drinkers.

One evening at the end of August, my friend's parents were abroad and we invited everyone round to her place. It was summer, and the day had been unusually hot. All the doors were open, and there were people inside, outside and in the hot tub. It never seemed to get dark that night. The sun briefly dipped below the horizon but continued to light up the sky, as if the evening was endless. Someone gave us pills, and we took them without asking any questions. More and more people kept arriving, and in the end the house was packed. There were party guests everywhere — people we barely knew, who were much older than us. But once the pills had kicked in, we no longer cared.

I don't remember exactly what happened or how we ended up together. I just remember that there were several of us in a room. We touched, talked and smoked. Told each other things we would never otherwise have admitted. Then suddenly he was there too, this guy who was a few years older than us. He wasn't part of the in-crowd — quite the opposite. He was obese and acne-scarred, his hair shiny with grease. He always wore thin cotton T-shirts that stuck to his sweaty back. I'd forgotten his name but remembered his B.O. from when we were at school — the odour of sweat and unwashed hair. Normally we wouldn't have invited him to join us but that night no one commented on it.

It didn't seem at all odd either when the two of us suddenly found ourselves alone together and he started stroking my hand. When we kissed, his lips were soft, and I didn't object when he began to undress me. I can still remember what it felt like to touch his body and feel his weight on top of me. Remember how I stroked his sweaty back and pressed him against me. As if I couldn't get enough. As if all I wanted was to be closer to him.

I must have fallen asleep, because all of a sudden sunlight was streaming into the room, onto my naked body. Yet I was cold. I felt as bad that morning as I had felt good the night before. This didn't improve when I looked at the grossly fat, repulsive lump beside me. The cruel light of day revealed the white, scarred skin, the boils on his back, the shiny forehead. He didn't stir as I pulled on my clothes. As I did so, flashbacks to the night before kept running through my mind, filling me with such revulsion that I ran to the loo and threw up. I couldn't stop picturing what we'd done that night. It was disgusting. Revolting. I'd let him touch me, and I'd touched him back. What if somebody had seen us? What if someone knew we were in the room together?

Two weeks passed before the rumours got out. It was another weekend at the bar. A boy I hardly knew came over and asked me straight out. Of course I denied it, but I saw that he knew and then I realised that everyone did. I could tell from the way they were all looking at me with such mockery and contempt. The balance of power between us had shifted, so I did the only thing I could have done in the circumstances: I lied.

I nudged my friends and got them to go to the toilets

with me, where I started crying. I threw up, then described how he had held me down and I had tried to scream, but no sound would come out. It was like telling someone else's story, and I got a little carried away by the sympathy I received. At some point I started to believe it myself. To be honest, I didn't remember much about the evening. Perhaps he really did rape me, I told myself. He must have done. Because normally I wouldn't have touched someone like him with a barge pole, and everyone knew that. No one knew that better than me. One of my friends must have left the toilets and told the others, because suddenly the whole bar was talking about it.

Then everything went crazy. A group of boys we used to hang out with apparently went round to his house and beat the crap out of him. After that, all I had to do was sit back and watch.

I suppose it must have been pretty terrible for his family. I mean, they already had a pregnant fifteen-year-old daughter to contend with. After the story of the rape spread, rumours started going round the village that the baby was her brother's. It seemed logical enough, since no one knew who the father was. One weekend, I remember someone throwing paint at their house. When a bunch of us cruised past in the morning, the white garage door was covered in splashes of red. We saw the young man's father standing there with a sponge, desperately trying to clean it off. I'll never forget his face when he looked in our direction. It was so blank and empty. I was sitting in the back seat of a car with tinted windows, so he couldn't possibly have seen me, but still I felt his eyes boring into me.

I think the parents both lost their jobs. They probably weren't actually sacked, but something must have happened that meant they couldn't face working in those places any longer. I can't really remember. I don't recall seeing Anton around either. He just vanished. Before, you always used to see him at the fast-food joint, ordering a big portion of chips. Several weeks passed but he was never officially charged, due to lack of evidence, and of course he denied everything. It didn't matter, though. The town had already judged him and found him guilty.

Anton's father came across him in the garage sometime later, hanging from a noose.

Soon after that they left town. Before they could even sell the house. One day they just upped and went. I drove past their house every morning on my way to work, and for months I was confronted by the white garage door and the traces of red paint. If everything had gone according to plan, that would have been the end of the story. Of course, I would have had to live with my guilt, but it hadn't exactly been weighing on me up to then.

But after Anton's suicide, people started whispering. Some of the other kids who'd been at the party reckoned I was lying. It must have been my friends who betrayed me; the girls who were in the room with us before we found ourselves alone together. Perhaps we had started making out before everyone left. No one said a word to me at first, but I sensed that their manner towards me had changed. I was no longer invited along in the evenings and people gave me accusing looks. Like it was my fault he was dead.

In a way his suicide exonerated him, and I wondered if he'd been aware of that when he did it. Whether he understood that the only way to make people believe him would be to kill himself. Whatever, it worked. All of a sudden, everyone was sure I was lying. The people I had treated badly over the years made the most noise. They were like vultures. I heard them laughing, saw in their eyes how sweet they found this revenge. Of course I stuck to my story, but no one seemed to believe it anymore, and even my parents started having doubts. In the end, they asked me straight out, and I must have reacted oddly — dropped my eyes or said the wrong thing — because they stopped believing me. I could tell.

So there I was, their little princess, a despised outcast. People whispered that I was a murderer, that it was my fault Anton was dead. I wanted to point out that it wasn't me who put the noose round his neck. God, how I hated him for that. I wished I had put it round his neck myself and watched him jerking convulsively as it tightened round his throat. In the end, my parents couldn't take it anymore. They had always been one of those couples who care about their position in society. You only had to look at our house, which was redecorated every year, and the garden they paid to have looked after, to realise that. Appearance was everything in their opinion. So of course they moved away. In fact, it had long been their dream to move back to Sweden, where they had both studied when they were younger. They pretended it wasn't because of me. As if it was simply a coincidence that they had started viewing properties in Stockholm. They invited me to come with them, but I was over twenty and they were no longer legally responsible for me. I sensed that they didn't want me, and that became even more obvious when they offered to buy me a flat in Reykjavík.

It was around about then that I began to suspect I was pregnant. I let them buy me a flat, and in a week my childhood home had been packed up, my parents were gone and I was living alone in a rented flat on the outskirts of Reykjavík while waiting for the keys to my new home. That very day I booked an appointment with a doctor. I was already beginning to show, and the doctor only had to smear some gooey stuff on my belly and run the ultrasound over it to reveal the tiny, indistinct creature on the screen above me. Its heartbeat filled the small room, and I stared at the thing, hoping it was a dream. But it wasn't. There it was, the child that was half me, half a man I hated. I watched it moving on the black screen and hoped its little heart would stop beating so I wouldn't be confronted with the past every day for the rest of my life.

During the pregnancy I thought everything would change when she arrived, but it turned out that I was still the same person. More miserable and bad-tempered, but still me. All that changed was that now there was this child. A little girl who neither laughed nor smiled. Who sat there silently observing the world.

Hrafntinna was my karma, my punishment.

I turn over in bed and push off the thin duvet. The air in the room is cool, but I'm still too hot. During the last few weeks I've thought more about my life in Sandgerði than I have for the past fifteen years. My attempts to forget have failed. The memories were buried, not destroyed, and they reappear now as vividly as just after they had occurred.

I can replay the events of 4 May in my mind's eye like a film.

Maríanna had aged in the five years since I had last seen her. Then, she had been standing in Hafliði's doorway. But that spring day in May, Maríanna didn't say anything. Instead of grinning maliciously, she asked about Hekla, and I saw the fear in her eyes. After I told her that Hekla had just left, she stood there in the doorway as if she wanted to say something else. I wish she'd left it at that. We'd have said a polite goodbye to each other and behaved as if we'd never met before. But she had to go and rake it all up.

'Actually, I was hoping for a word with you,' she said.

I invited her in, let her take a seat in my kitchen and gave her coffee. She sat there at the table, nursing her cup, and I could see her little brain working, wondering how to begin. At last, she looked at me.

'Do you recognise me?' she asked.

I thought about lying. I could say I didn't remember her, and perhaps it would have ended there. Perhaps she would have been relieved and gone away, never to come back. But I didn't.

'We met five years ago, didn't we?' I said, then added, jokingly: 'I have to say, that jumper suits you much better than my ex's T-shirt did.'

She smiled briefly, then put her phone down on the table.

'Actually, we'd met before that,' she said and took a mouthful of coffee. When I didn't reply, she went on: 'I used to live in Sandgerði, just like you. I've always remembered you because you used to be so smartly dressed. So pretty. I longed to be like you. I even asked my mum to buy me a purple, one-shoulder jumper just like yours. I used to try and copy the way you smiled and flicked your hair. So did all the other girls, probably.'

I smiled and studied her, wary as always when someone said they were from Sandgerði. There was always a risk that people would remember the rumours, and I never knew what they would believe. Maríanna was several years younger than me and, however hard I tried, I couldn't remember her there. But obviously I wouldn't have paid her any attention when I lived in the town, as there was nothing remarkable about her.

'You don't remember me, do you?' She glanced around. There was no one in the house except the two of us, and Tinna in her room. 'No, I didn't think so.'

'Sorry, I just ... It's so long since I lived there.'

'I loved living there. We were so happy in Sandgerði until ... until my brother died. His name was Anton. Maybe you remember him.'

When she said her brother's name, I realised immediately who she was. The pregnant little sister. No wonder I didn't cotton on that she was the person sitting in front of me. Marianna had changed since she was fifteen. She always used to be overweight, like her brother, but now she was all skin and bone; so thin that her cheeks were hollow and her bony elbows poked through her thin cotton top.

I stood up and got a glass down from the cupboard while I was thinking. I ran the tap, feeling her eyes on me while I was filling the glass. When I turned back to her, I was braced to encounter anger, but instead I saw nothing but sadness. Although I didn't blame myself for what had happened to Anton's family, I knew my lies had had repercussions.

'Sorry,' she said unexpectedly. Her voice sounded sincere. I sat down facing her. 'I didn't come here to blame you or to be angry. I just wanted to say sorry for the whole thing. For how we treated you and for not believing you. I've wasted years being angry. Anton was everything to me. He was my best friend, and when I heard what he'd done ... I just didn't want to believe it. But it was true, wasn't it? He really did it. He raped you.'

I emptied the glass down my throat before looking at her. It was nearly four o'clock, and I would have to go to work soon. Maríanna's eyes filled with tears as she stared at me, waiting for my reply.

It had been harder than I thought to bear the burden of the lie all these years. Anton's face had appeared to me in my dreams, cold and accusatory, shocking me awake, soaked with sweat. But worst were the nights when I dreamt that I was caressing and kissing his body, and letting him do the same to me. I thought it might be a release to tell the truth at last and receive forgiveness. Perhaps I would be free of the dreams. So I made up my mind and told her. The moment I'd said the words aloud, I felt the relief. Everything that had happened in my life since the moment I first lied about it had been like a punishment. The birth, the child and all the years I had struggled, alone and humiliated. Now I would finally be free — free from the curse that had followed me ever since Anton died.

But then Maríanna looked up, her eyes no longer humble and submissive but burning with fury and hatred. 'I knew it,' she said. 'I knew you'd lied.'

'But…'

She laughed mockingly. 'I've been watching you all these years. Seen how you've hidden away like a little rat.'

'What do you mean you've been watching me?' I found myself thinking about all the times when I'd felt as if I was being followed. About the anonymous letters I'd been sent. 'Was that you?' I asked, staring at her, shocked.

She grinned derisively. The same spiteful grin as she had worn when I met her in Hafliði's doorway. 'Of course it was me,' she said, her voice rising. 'Do you think I'm going to let you get away with it? You destroyed my family. Because of you everything was ruined. For me, for my mum and dad. And for Anton. Just because you couldn't admit you'd screwed him.' Maríanna's face was dark red and her hands were shaking. She was shouting so loudly now that Tinna was bound to hear her. 'You don't deserve to be happy. I sent you the letters to frighten you, and when I saw you with that man just after my mum died…' She broke off, her jaws working strangely. 'It wasn't that difficult to go home with him. Not after…'

'After what?'

Maríanna didn't answer, but something else had dawned on me.

'The bar. The stairs. It was you I met in the toilets.' I had a clear image of the girl who had stood, staring at me in

the mirror. 'It was you who pushed me.'

Maríanna got to her feet and snatched up her phone.

'Where are you going?'

She shoved the phone in my face. 'Now everyone will know who you are,' she hissed.

Her phone was recording. She had recorded every single word.

As I listened to the playback, I saw my life crashing down around my ears. My job on TV, the fame I had earned and the family I had finally acquired.

My only alternative was to stop her.

It was lucky that Tinna wasn't fifteen yet when I killed Maríanna. She came out of her room when she heard the noise. Stared speechless at the scene as I made sure Maríanna would never say another word. Of course I explained everything to Hrafntinna, and she understood why I had been forced to do what I did. Maríanna was bad. She'd been planning to hurt us. That was enough for Hrafntinna, because for her the world was still black and white.

After all those true-crime documentaries, Hrafntinna knew exactly how to dispose of a body and get away with it. It was she who handed me the gloves and hat before we got in the car, and she who suggested Grábrók. After all our trips to the summer house, she knew every crack and fissure in the lava field. She told me to remove the plastic sack once we'd dragged Maríanna into the cave. That way her body would decompose faster and nature would eventually destroy all the evidence.

Hrafntinna also understood why she would have to take the blame. Fourteen-year-olds are not sent to prison. No, they're sent to a therapy centre for treatment, and even their names are concealed from the public. And Hekla was more than willing to testify in my favour after our talk at the summer house. I knew I would need another witness in addition to Tinna, as she was too closely related to me for her statement to be enough on its own. The cousins weren't that dissimilar: Hekla was as desperate for a family and friends as my Tinna used to be. When I realised that this was something we could give her, the situation could hardly have been more perfect.

As for Marianna, she never worked out the whole story; never realised that Tinna was Anton's daughter. The fool. I wondered if it would have changed anything. Would she have agreed to hand over the recording? Would she have been prepared to give up her vulgar plans for revenge?

It doesn't matter now. If Tinna and Hekla are good girls and stick to the story we agreed on, everything should be OK. Of course, I could be charged with concealing the body, but, according to my lawyer, the resulting sentence is unlikely to be long. When it comes down to it, my action was simply that of a good mother, concerned with protecting her daughter.

Which is exactly what I've tried to be all these years — a good mother.

II
24 December

This sun couldn't possibly be the same as the one that cast its feeble rays on Iceland all year round. These sunbeams were warm and soft on the skin. Elma allowed them to wrap her in a sense of well-being as she lay on the sunlounger by the pool. She reached for her ice-cold beer and took a long swig.

Coming to Tenerife for Christmas had been a brainwave. More than that: a stroke of genius. Elma wasn't sure she'd ever had a better idea. She drained her glass and turned over onto her stomach, letting the sun soothe away the stiffness in her neck muscles that had plagued her for the last year. Closing her eyes, she felt a pleasant numbness from the beer spreading through her body, while the shrieks of the children in the swimming pool faded to a background murmur that gradually died away.

Next minute she was shocked awake by an icy touch on her back.

'What are you doing?!' She twisted round.

Sævar blocked out the light as he stood over her, a bottle of sun lotion in his hand.

'Your back's on fire,' he remarked. He was grinning evilly. 'I was just going to save you from burning to a crisp.'

Elma groaned. It was true, though. Her back was an angry scarlet. Her pale skin had gone without seeing the sun for so long that she had barely stepped off the plane before she began to turn red. And the freckles sprang out too; all those freckles on her nose and cheeks and forehead that now made a triumphant reappearance after spending years in hiding. She let Sævar anoint her shoulders with sun lotion, then turned over onto her back.

'Do you miss being at home?'

She couldn't stop herself asking. It was Christmas Eve and they were far away from their families, from the snow and Christmas lights in Iceland. She still couldn't fathom how it had happened. There had hardly been any notice. Only twenty-four hours following that moment of madness as they sat in the office, listening to the wind screaming outside the window. Elma had been hungover from her father's seventieth birthday, and Sævar's brother had rung earlier that day to ask if he could stay with his girlfriend over Christmas. Like a miracle, a special offer on flights to Tenerife had flashed up on screen and five minutes later they had booked the trip. For the two of them. Without even thinking. Without really knowing what they were doing.

'Elma...' Sævar lay down on the sunlounger beside her and closed his eyes. His skin had turned the colour of coffee after only a couple of days. 'Do I really need to answer that?'

Elma smiled and laid her head back. The garden around the pool was crowded with families, pensioners and couples. From there, it was possible to walk straight down to the beach. They had wandered down there the first evening after drinking rather too many cocktails over dinner. Had sat down, gazing out to sea and digging their toes into the sand in the balmy darkness. Elma had never before experienced such a strong sensation of being in the middle of a waking dream.

Sævar propped himself up on his elbow and shielded his eyes with his hand. 'What about you? Feeling homesick?'

Elma smiled. 'Do I need to answer that?'

After a few minutes she got up and went over to the pool. She was so hot that the sweat was pouring off her. She dipped one exploratory toe into the water, which felt shockingly cold after the heat, then sat down on the edge and prepared to lower her feet in by slow degrees. Next moment, she felt a hand on her back and gasped as she plunged headlong into the icy pool.

Acknowledgements

When I was a little girl I loved reading above everything else. As I got older I started to write my own stories, but to get published was a distant dream. Thanks to many wonderful people, this dream has come true.

Thank you to my husband for being my number-one fan and for regularly taking on a job as my psychologist.

Thank you to Pétur and Bjarni at Veröld Publishing for believing in a young writer that nervously came in with an unpolished manuscript.

Many thanks to my agent, David Headley, and everyone at DHH Literary Agency.

Thanks a million to Karen Sullivan and Orenda Books for taking me in, making me feel welcome and being the biggest cheerleaders there are. You are amazing!

Thank you to Victoria Cribb for your seamless translation and a great eye for spotting every detail.

Finally, I am so thankful to those who read and enjoyed my debut novel, *The Creak on the Stairs*. To all the wonderful people who have messaged me about the book — your words truly brighten my day. Thank you!